Ebbtide at Coppins Bridge

EBBTIDE
AT COPPINS
BRIDGE

Elizabeth Daish

CENTURY
LONDON SYDNEY AUCKLAND JOHANNESBURG

Century Hutchinson South Africa (Pty) Ltd
PO Box 337, Bergvlei, 2012 South Africa

Century Hutchinson Australia Pty Ltd
89–91 Albion Street, Surry Hills,
NSW 2010, Australia

Century Hutchinson New Zealand Ltd
PO Box 40-086, Glenfield, Auckland 10
New Zealand

ISBN 0 7126 2228 4
Printed in Great Britain by
Mackays of Chatham

To Derek

Chapter 1

Jane Darwen pushed back the black veil and took the pins from her black hat. Her hair felt flat and hot under the close-fitting cloche and she wished that there was time to brush it out and remake the knot at the nape of her neck, but Janey looked cold and the others had lost all desire to do anything but get in from the chill and have a hot drink.

'There's hot potato pies and enough cake to sink a battleship,' she said. 'And ale for the men if they want it.'

'And ham and tongue,' said Lizzie with satisfaction. 'You sit down, Mother. I'll serve the ham and Harry can cut up the tongue.' She nearly pushed her mother into a chair. 'There's no need for you to stir,' she added, as if afraid that Jane might want to know what she was doing in the scullery.

Jane gave a slight smile. Even today, with Lizzie's father, Walter Darwen, just laid to rest in the plot shared by the baby Caroline, her daughter was all out for number one. Jane suspected that the best of the ham and tongue would be put aside for Lizzie and Harry to take home to Cowes after the funeral meal.

'I'm chilled to the bone.' Annie Cooper pushed past her husband and sat by the fire, rubbing her hands together before the bright flames leaping up from the good coal in the black-leaded range. She shifted her chair to get even more warmth and Jane saw that the knots of rheumatism on Annie's hands were tense and painful.

'You haven't taken cold, Annie?' Jane sounded anxious but Bert Cooper gave a laugh.

'There was no call for you to stand about in wet graveyards, Annie. I said I'd tell you all about it but you would come.' He grinned. 'Afraid of missing something?'

Annie looked furious and ignored her husband.

'It was good of you to come,' said Jane. Annie looked

1

such a shrivelled-up thing today and old habits died hard, so she reached over to the cupboard by the range and found a pot of medicinal cream and herbs that she had made up for Annie such a short while ago. Had she done that only the day before Walter died so suddenly, and the world went mad as the Great War came to an end? She opened the damper a little more and flames roared up the chimney. She recalled pounding the herbs just before putting the fish to bake. Emily was making cakes at the other end of the table and wanted to be free for the celebration the next day.

November the eleventh, 1918, she thought. At the eleventh hour of the eleventh day of the eleventh month, the war was over and Peace was declared. A few hours afterwards, on the very same day, Walter had collapsed over a heavy bucket of water and died in the stables.

'Are you all right, Jane?' asked Bert Cooper awkwardly.

'Fine, just fine,' said Jane softly. 'It's as if he went away as he did to the Boer War and I expect him to walk in through that doorway with his hat on one side, demanding attention.'

'But this time he's gone for good,' Annie broke in bluntly, 'and you'll have to get used to that, Jane. I expect you'll have a very busy time clearing everything out.'

'He's not been in his grave for more than an hour or so, Annie. Show a little respect,' said Bert.

'I did show respect. I saw him buried and even if my rheumatics are bad tomorrow, I'll not regret it.'

Jane looked at her, surprised and touched. 'It was very good of you, Annie, and I know it would have pleased him.'

Annie's sallow cheeks brightened. 'We've known each other a long time, Jane. Walter was good to us in the past and I don't know what I'd do without you.' Bert patted his wife's shoulder with unaccustomed affection and cleared his throat. 'I don't often say much, Jane, but I am fond of you,' said Annie with genuine sincerity.

'Put this ointment in your bag, Annie. I know you mean well and we understand each other,' said Jane. She felt at a

2

loss and wondered a trifle guiltily if Annie had some other favour to ask. It was seldom that Annie Cooper had a good word for anyone, even the dead.

Bert moved away to help himself to a pie and some ale, and Annie pulled at Jane's sleeve to make her come closer. 'I was wondering what you'll do with all his clothes,' she whispered. 'Bert's brother Dan could do with first pick if they're going begging.'

The bile rose in Jane's throat but she made an effort to be calm. 'Let it be, Annie. I haven't got my breath yet,' she said in a low voice.

'You'll have to think of it,' Annie declared. The familiar whine was back in her voice. 'You don't want to leave it to get on your nerves.'

'That wouldn't get on my nerves half as much as people trying to rush me,' retorted Jane, unable now to hide her annoyance. She felt the pressure of Janey's hand on her shoulder and glanced up at her eldest daughter. 'I'll see, Annie,' she said more naturally. 'Just give me time.'

Annie looked pleased. If Jane Darwen said that, she would keep her word. 'You look poorly,' she said to Janey. 'You are more and more like your mother each time I see you.'

'I'm not poorly and I'm not expecting!' said Jane.

'But you had that same look about you each time,' said Annie, with a gleam in her eyes. 'I knew long before you ever told me and you never lost that look. It was there every time, even after seven babies.'

'Nine,' murmured Jane, so softly that only Janey heard.

'I've made fresh tea, Mother. Would you like another cup?'

'Aren't you having one?' Jane took the fresh tea and Annie held out her hand for hers. Janey shook her head and made a face. Her mother smiled. 'Tastes funny? It did with me for weeks, and you know how I like my cup of tea. Walter used to bring me fresh lemons, even when they were dear.' She stared into the fire. That was another man, surely. That was the good husband and father of her children, who cared for her, not the heavy-handed man he had become. She sighed. 'We haven't had lemons in the shop for so long, I've almost forgotten them. I hope they come from abroad again soon now the war is over.'

'I think I'd like that too, Mother. What else can I drink? I'm tired of water and milk.'

'You do look peaky,' said Annie. 'You need all the milk you can drink.'

'I have a bottle of Camp Coffee. I used to like that sometimes,' said Jane. 'It takes away the bland taste of milk.'

Annie put down her cup. 'We'll have a good chat on our own tomorrow, Jane,' she said as if Janey intruded. 'I'm coming down to get some cabbage as Bert says he has to go over to the West Wight about some property. I'll be all alone, so I might as well come down here.'

'I'd stay in by a good fire,' said Jane. 'Stoke up and get rid of that ache.'

'Hardly seems worth lighting a fire for one,' began Annie. She glanced over at Bert who was helping himself to more ham under the watchful eye of Lizzie.

'I never let this fire go out,' said Jane. 'If you'd been warmer over the years, you might suffer less now.' The thought of Annie and her grumbling by the fire for a whole day was more than she could bear. 'Tomorrow, I'm looking after two of Vikki's friends and the noise would worry you, Annie, so make up a good fire and stay by it. Emily will give you what you want from the shop as you go home.'

'You don't want to take on other people's children! It's bad enough having to take in a grandchild, though heaven alone knows what would have happened to her after she was left by her parents.'

'That's enough, Annie! Vikki is my own flesh and blood and her father is dead.'

'But you are in mourning! You shouldn't let people take advantage of you. Who is coming to play with Vikki?' she asked, ready to disapprove further.

'Just two little friends,' said Janey drily. 'I think that Uncle Bert wants to leave now. Shall I get your cabbage?'

Bert wiped his moustache with a large silk handkerchief

4

and came towards them. 'Annie, get your coat and basket. I'll be out in a minute.'

Annie moved away reluctantly, helped along by Janey's firm grip on her arm. She shivered as she passed from the warm living room to the shop on the other side of the door.

'I'm sorry,' said Bert. He shifted from one foot to the other.

'No need for that, Bert. Thank you for all you've done over the past few days . . . since it happened. I'm glad it was you who found him. I'll never forget it.' She pressed his hand between both of hers. 'We Irish have long memories for good and bad and my memory is longer than most.' She smiled. 'But I've come to a time when I only want to recall the good about people and there's plenty enough of that.'

It was an unspoken truce and a forgiving, and Bert went bright red. He stammered, 'I only wanted to say that all the books are in order and there'll be plenty for you from the brickyard and the properties and other bits of business that we did. Walter signed a paper a few days before he died, making over some more cottages to you and a house he bought empty on the Mall. I'll explain about the shares when you have a minute and if there's anything else, just ask.'

He looked down into the brown eyes and saw the young Jane again, lovely in her dark Irish way, and still handsome now, and warm, so warm and womanly.

'You made him put a lot in my name, Bert. Don't think I never knew what you were doing. It was kind when he began to lose his grip on things and neglected his business, and now, I know I shall be fine, just fine, and the girls will lack for nothing.'

Bert took out his handkerchief again and blew his nose hard. 'At least the children are off your hands now, all but Emily. I never had that worry, or that blessing.' He tried to smile. 'I've missed a family, Jane, and a man has to take what he can to make up for that lack of warmth.'

Jane looked sympathetic. Annie wasn't affectionate, and

5

with no children, their marriage couldn't have been close.

Bert went on quietly, 'Walter : . . going, makes me think I'm not getting any younger and I have a lot of life left in me for a while at least.'

'You aren't old, Bert. In your prime, I'd say.'

'Walter died,' he said.

'But he was ill,' said Jane, and bit her lip. How much did Bert know? How many other people knew that the disease her husband had picked up from a loose woman in Pretoria had killed him all these years later?

'Well, I'm hale enough,' he said, and laughed. 'And I'll make the best of my time.'

Jane gave him a smile that was almost mischievous. 'I know about men, Bert. Don't try to confess anything to me.'

He relaxed and winked. 'Don't worry, I'll not burden you, Jane, but whatever you hear about me, I hope we can still be real friends.'

'We can be friends,' she agreed. 'Good friends and business partners. Business always did interest me and we had to be partners when Walter was away in Africa fighting the Boers for two years, so why not now when we are older, wiser and more tolerant?' She squeezed his hand. It was true. We're both older, she thought. I'm not the girl you fancied all that time ago and I can do business with you Bert Cooper, knowing that now, you'll never try to cheat me.

'I'll be back from the West Wight in a day or so and I'll pop in with the books to save you coming up to the office,' he said.

'Bring Annie and have a bite to eat,' said Jane, with a twinkle in her eyes. 'We can't have you losing your reputation with a widow, Bert.'

He went an even deeper red and turned away. Now what's making him uncomfortable, she wondered? Was he planning to go back to his visits to the woman in Portsmouth now that the ferries would be running for pleasure as well as business? Poor Bert. He'd been Island-bound for so long that he might feel that he was past it.

'I'd best be off. Annie will be cold, waiting in the motor,' he said.

Jane watched him go and saw that many of the others had left too, with a wave from the door, not liking to interrupt them. Bert looked well-dressed and had kept his figure even if it had thickened a little. He needed a woman who could give him more than Annie would want to give. Did women like the one in Portsmouth manage to make a living? She shrugged. Why think of a dockside tart now? But she knew that in the back of her mind was the fact that Walter had been with such women ever since he could no longer share her bed and comfort.

Lately, however, he had stayed on the Island and taken only one woman, Maudie Dove. Poor Maudie, Jane thought. She would miss Walter, and all the little extras he used to bring her. She found she could think of Maudie without rancour and even with a feeling of gratitude. She may have saved my life, as another baby would have killed me, she decided. In a way, I owe her something. I'm glad I took her Lucy under my wing and got her work with Janey at the Lodge . . . The talk in the room flowed over her and she said goodbye almost automatically when the others left.

As if reading her mother's thoughts, Janey bent over her and said, 'Lucy is here. She asked Emily if she could help in the shop for a while to relieve her.'

'That was kind,' said Jane warmly. 'But don't let me take her away if you need her.'

'I'm glad she can help, Mother. I don't need her tomorrow as I've two girls from the workhouse to do the rough. Lucy can come and look after Vikki and her friends while you have a rest.'

'Are you sure? That would be grand,' said Jane, beaming. She smiled as Lucy came into the room with Emily and they helped themselves to pasties. 'Come early tomorrow, Lucy, and have dinner here,' she said. 'Janey tells me how well you look after both her and Clive and I'm glad you are here while he is away at sea.'

Lucy blushed with pleasure. 'I love living at the Lodge,

7

Mrs Darwen, and Janey has taught me to cook some really nice dishes.' Her blue eyes shone as she looked at Janey, and the expression of complete innocence was refreshing. At least Maudie hasn't corrupted the girl, Jane decided. Leaving the house in Sea Street before Lucy guessed that her mother wasn't exactly the best moral guide had come just in time.

Jane watched the girl. She was fair-haired and pretty, and if rumour had it right, she might have been the result of a meeting between Maudie and a Scandinavian sailor on Newport quay when Maudie's husband Ben was away at war. Whatever her antecedents, she was sweet and bore no taint of depravity. Thanks to Walter, of late, Maudie had seemed respectable.

Lucy stood half on tiptoe to look at the big photograph of Sidney, Jane's youngest son. Jane shook her head, wishing that Lucy wasn't so besotted with each new picture he sent from America. 'He's so handsome, Mrs Darwen,' Lucy breathed.

'I had another letter,' said Jane. 'I doubt if he's had my last one and he can't know about his father.' She looked up at the good-looking face and was sad. 'He's on tour with a travelling show and will not be back in New York for several weeks.'

Lizzie stood in the doorway with her husband. She clutched a bag bulging with food and backed towards the door. 'I think we'll be on our way, Mother. We've done all we can for you,' she said kindly. 'It gave you time to have a nice rest.'

Janey stifled a laugh. She looked meaningfully at the shopping bag but said nothing, and Lizzie coloured up and handed the bag to Harry to hold. She saw Lucy gazing at the picture and hid her own embarrassment by saying maliciously, 'Still sweet on Sidney? He'll never come back here if he's any sense. He's doing far too well and we'd all be too ordinary for him now.' She saw the confusion she caused and enjoyed Lucy's reaction. 'I haven't heard that he has a sweetheart yet, but I expect all the girls are after him. You'd better be quick if you want him.'

8

Jane's lips tightened. 'I think it's time you went, Lizzie. Good night, Harry. I hope you have everything you need.'

'Yes, Harry has to be up early for work tomorrow,' said Lizzie. 'I'll just take a cabbage as I go.' She backed away hastily before anyone could suggest washing-up.

The draught from the open shop door found the edge of the thick tablecloth and the fire glowed red. Janey went to shut it and came back slowly. 'I didn't talk to everyone,' said Jane. 'I hope they understood.'

'They know, Mother. Everyone who came offered help if you need it and grumbled that you hadn't called on them earlier.'

'There wasn't much for me to do with you girls to help,' said Jane.

Janey gave a rueful smile. 'Too independent as usual. You have everything done before most people even think of it.'

'You can't talk!' said Jane lightly.

'Well, you aren't doing anything more tonight,' said Janey firmly. 'I feel energetic, so Lucy can help me wash up before we walk home while you and the girls go up to the Town Hall to see what news there is.'

'Is Vikki in bed?' asked Jane. Somehow, everything but the funeral and some of her oldest friends had faded into the background, but she knew that everything that needed to be done was done.

'Clare read to her and Emily made sure that she washed,' replied Janey. 'I think Clare wanted to avoid talking to Annie Cooper who is always so nosy about her house up north.'

'They can go and tell me the news,' said Jane. 'I can't go out walking in the town on the day of the funeral. What would people think?'

'When have you worried about people, Mother? You know you hate going to bed after being in a stuffy room all day. It's a fine night and no wind now.'

'Why don't you go with them?' asked Jane.

'I shall have a walk when I go back with Lucy and I'd rather clear up here.' Janey laughed. 'Besides, I get so cold across my front. Did you feel cold there, Mother?' She bit into a pasty as if she had eaten nothing all day.

Jane's heart warmed to her. Of all my children, you are most like me, she thought. It gave her a deep and satisfying sense of kinship that Janey could talk to her as an equal, confide in her and understand so many things.

'I do remember that,' she agreed. 'It used to catch me when I was walking along the quay or when I went to Sam Walmsley's fruit warehouse. You'll need some thick vests and you must eat plenty of hot food when the weather turns really cold, and the sickness is gone.'

'You must do as you like,' said Janey firmly. 'If you want to stay in, then stay, but if you want a walk, go out. It's dark and nobody will see you. As for me, I feel fine and shall do the washing-up.'

'There's no need to coddle me, my girl,' said Jane. She touched Janey on the cheek. 'You are a blessing, but I feel all right, too. I should do, I've been waited on, hand, foot and finger all day. Even the cemetery didn't make me as tired as I thought it would. It just didn't seem to have anything to do with me . . . or your father. You and Emily prepared the food and I noticed that our Lizzie didn't leave anything to go bad!'

It's true, she realised with a sense of guilt. I do feel all right. I suppose it will come later.

Clare came downstairs wearing her hat and coat. 'Are you ready, Emily?' she asked.

'Mother is going with you, so wait, Clare, and look after her,' said Janey. 'Don't let her get tired out. I'll have some cocoa ready for when you all get back.'

'Hurry up then,' said Clare. 'I heard shouting up by the *County Press*, or in that direction. There may be news about the election.'

Jane put on her hat and was glad that it hid her face. She twined a scarf round her neck and found her gloves. The coat she had worn to the funeral lay over the back of a chair in her room but she left it there and wore a loose, warm coat of worn velvet that was an old friend.

The night was mild and the air soft and she breathed

10

deeply. Janey was right. She'd never get to sleep without some fresh air. Clare put a hand under her elbow in a friendly manner and they walked up the main street with Emily to the offices of the local newspaper, opposite the Town Hall. A small crowd had collected as it did in every crisis or time of public thanksgiving. War had been announced there when Victoria was on the throne, and again when Kaiser Bill got up to his tricks and started the Great War in 1914. Now, the buzz was of the coming election.

'The war hasn't been over for more than a week,' said Clare. 'Alan said that he thought they'd have an election soon before we all found out what an old fraud Lloyd George is, but he didn't think it would be before Christmas. The papers say it will be in December, only a month away, so no wonder they have all these posters out.'

'You mustn't talk about the Prime Minister like that,' said Jane. She drew her arm away. 'At least he brought our boys home and ended the war.' She pointed to the poster that was soggy from the afternoon rain but still readable. THE MAN WHO ENDED THE WAR. 'I know it was a coalition government, but he led them and we have him to thank,' went on Jane. 'Walter says . . . well, everyone knows what a good man he is.'

Emily bought a paper and her eyes were misty. The headline quoted once again, 'VOTE FOR ME AND MAKE A COUNTRY FIT FOR HEROES TO LIVE IN.' Heroes, like Arnold, who never fired a shot in anger but died of influenza on the battlefield. She gave a shuddering sigh. 'Some of the heroes never came back,' she murmured.

'What do you know about it, Em?' said Clare in a harsh voice. 'You were never in love as I was.' She glanced at the headlines. 'But you are right. Some never came back.'

'We must all look to the future,' said Jane. The air had cleared her brain and she felt a strange kind of contentment. She also felt slightly irritated by her two daughters, for surely hers had been the greatest loss? The future was hers alone and as far as she could see, predictable. No war and she was her own master. It would be as it had been when

11

Walter was away fighting and she had been left with seven children, the shop on Coppins Bridge and other bits of business to run.

I can decide what to do now. I can do what I like with the rest of my life and I'll have more help and fewer mouths to feed, she realised with awe.

'What about the horses?' The future could look after itself but there were immediate matters to consider. 'Has anyone given them a thought?' she asked.

They walked down Quay Street and over the quay. The high arches of the railway loomed above them in the dark and a soft murmur came from the pen where the ducks had a run by the water of the river Medina. The stable door, set in one of the other arches, gave to a touch and a slipping of the bolt, and inside the warm smell of a clean stable and fresh dung was pleasant enough for the women to hurry in and close the door again away from the night.

Clare lit the lantern and hung it high on the hook by the tack shelf and Jane saw that the racks were full of hay and there was fresh water in the trough. Even the muck had been raked from the stalls.

'Bert Cooper said he'd look in at the stable, Mother,' said Emily, 'but it looks as if he's done it all. Dan will take over tomorrow, he promised, until you get someone for good.' She hesitated. 'He told me to keep you away for a while, but I knew you'd want to see that everything was all right.'

'You were right, Emily. This is the first time I've been here since it happened, but I wanted to come, with someone.' This is where it happened, she thought. This is where my husband died after drinking heavily and lifting a bucket of water. She looked round the stable and at the shapes of the two horses bending their necks for the specky fruit that Emily found in a basket. They know more than I do, thought Jane. Dr Barnes said that it could happen at any time, that Walter could die of what he called an aneurysm which might burst a blood vessel, so that is what must have happened.

12

'So be it,' she said softly. 'Goodbye, Walter, I shall never know what really went on in here.'

The river was sullen grey and cold as they hurried back along Sea Street and over the Bridge to the shop. 'Vikki is sound asleep,' said Janey in greeting. 'I'll be on my way now with Lucy. If you've finished with the *County Press*, I'll take it and see what ships are in the offing. Clive might be home next week but if the war is over it could be any time.' She yawned. 'I'm really tired now, and I think I shall sleep. I enjoyed the Camp Coffee, Mother.'

'Take the rest of the bottle, Janey, and make sure you take some fish from the shop. It's body-building and good for you.'

'If Lizzie has left any,' said Janey, laughing. 'Did you ever see such scrounging? Harry encourages her and they make a good pair. I hope she has a baby and is off her food for a month. It would kill Lizzie if she couldn't eat.'

'I'll make up the fire,' said Emily. She emptied the tea leaves into the grate and listened to the hiss the wet leaves made on the hot coals.

'Bank it up well as we may be later getting up,' said Jane. 'We'll clear up now and have nothing to do in the morning.' She looked in the scullery and then back at the neat living room. It was all done and Janey had left even the tea-towels rinsed and hung on the airer to dry. A big pot of hot cocoa sat on the hob and cups were ready on a tray. For the first time since the funeral, Jane wanted to weep. Not for sorrow and not for loss, but in gratitude for such daughters.

Emily poured the cocoa and even Clare who had looked so sharpfaced when she came home for the funeral sat relaxed and more as she had been before she married Alan Dewar and was taken to the grey stone house by the canal in the northern midlands.

The girls were laughing softly as if the day was well over and all the grief had been exorcised. The tall case clock that had replaced the old cuckoo when he finally choked on the passing of time, gave a mellow reminder that it was late and Clare switched on the light above the stairs

13

after making sure that the door to Vikki's room was closed.

Jane looked out of her bedroom window into the darkness. She wondered what Sidney would think when he heard of his father's death and if he would come home. He had met so many people and travelled so far that he might forget his roots, but she couldn't blame him. Walter had never been fair to the boy . . . The night seemed long but not lonely. If I'd shared Walter's bed for the last few years, it would have been different, she thought. The room smelled of sweet soap and powder and clean clothes. She turned in bed, luxuriating in the soft feather mattress and the width of the double bed.

'Tomorrow, I'll turn out Walter's room and perhaps dwell a little on the past, but not tonight,' she murmured to herself.

She dreamed and tossed and turned, with many people in her dreams all telling her what to do. She was being pulled in every direction but the one in which she wanted to go. There was Annie Cooper telling her to sell the shop and go into one of the cottages, Archie from the farm at Wootton wanting her to marry him and Clare nagging about almost everything.

She woke at six and stirred the kitchen fire into life to make the first pot of tea of the day. 'I'll please myself,' she told the ghosts. 'I've made up my mind what I want to do.'

Chapter 2

'Take down that black shutter or you'll get no trade,' said Bert Cooper. 'It's a month now since Walter went and people don't put as much thought or importance to mourning these days. Everyone has lost someone in the war and one black shutter on a shop window makes no odds.'

'Do you think I could?' Jane felt only relief. The sight of the slim black board down across the window made her depressed each time she returned to the shop and she had noticed people hesitating before coming in to buy fruit and fish. She missed the easy gossip of the women who came regularly and stood about the shop while she served them, lingering after their baskets were full and enjoying her company and advice.

'Get me a chair to stand on and a screwdriver and I'll take it down now,' Bert offered. She eyed his smart grey suit with amusement. 'I'll take off my jacket and it won't take a minute.'

'You look all dressed up and nowhere to go, Bert.'

'I've business out the back of Wight and I wanted you to see these deeds before I go there.' He avoided looking at her directly.

'Perhaps I'd better come out with you to see what Walter bought,' she said, and turned away to fetch the tools he would need, hiding her wicked smile.

'Er, no call for you to do that just now,' he said hastily. 'I'll take you later when all this has settled down.'

'I'm not going into a decline, Bert,' said Jane drily. 'I've had far too many shocks in my life for that, and I need something to fill my mind. Vikki is a great comfort but I think sometimes that young children are not like they used to be when mine were growing up.'

'You make yourself out to sound old, Jane.' He waited

for her to bring the tools and regarded her seriously. 'You still keep your looks, Jane. Any man would be proud to have you for a wife and now you've got over the shock, you wear your widow's weeds like most women wear fashion.'

She smiled, genuinely amused that Bert Cooper should have mellowed into some kind of big brother figure as far as she was concerned. She no longer dreaded his company, and felt that under his brash manner and devious ways, there now lurked a man who was fond of her in a protective way. I wonder why, she thought. 'How's Annie?' she asked aloud.

'Middling. Grumbling as usual and carping about the expense of everything with all the shortages.' He shrugged. 'No need to stint herself or me for that matter, but I'll be glad when the Bugle serves good dinners again.' He climbed uncertainly on to the chair and began to remove the screws holding the plank in place. Jane held the chair steady and caught the board as he dropped it.

'Thank you, Bert. That was a real good deed. Your good deed for the day.' She laughed. 'Now you can go and enjoy yourself.'

'What do you mean?' he asked sharply.

'You enjoy driving that great car of yours, don't you?'

'I see what you mean.' His face cleared. 'Yes, it's a wonderful feeling driving along the Military Road and back along the spine of the Island.'

'What does Annie think of it?'

'I don't take her,' he said shortly. 'There's a lot to do and I have a couple of lads to do up the last batch of cottages and a woman to see to the curtains.' He glanced at her. It might be as well to spread that fact. If Maudie Dove was seen so far from home, at least she had a good excuse for being there.

'Annie isn't much of a seamstress and since her hands got bad, she can hardly hold a needle,' said Jane. 'It's a good idea to have a woman on the spot. Measurements never seem right if they come secondhand, and the curtains are either too short or too long.'

'That's right,' he agreed solemnly, as if the length of

16

curtains in rented holiday accommodation was of supreme importance. 'Is your Clare staying on for Christmas?'

'Yes. Alan sent a wire that he was home but she sent one back to say she was needed here.' Jane shrugged. 'I think she needs a change. From what I hear, it's even foggier up there than it is in Hampshire just now, and Clare never did get on well in winter.'

'Foggy across the water, but clear on the Island. It's mild for December and dry, so I go over to the cottages as often as possible to see to things before the weather worsens.' He handed her the addresses of the four cottages that now belonged to her.

'Are these near yours, Bert?'

'No, mine are on the other side,' he said vaguely. 'Yours are nearer Colwell.' When he had gone, she wondered where he was going. He never said where his properties are, she thought.

Jane brushed away the dust from the pavement in front of the shop and waved as Janey came down the hill from Staplers. 'You've taken down the shutter! I am glad. It would have been awful to see that at Christmas.' Janey looked at her mother approvingly. 'You look so much better.' She laughed. 'Like me, full of energy and nothing to do. Lucy is cleaning the Lodge with the help of a girl we took on from the workhouse and I have done my shopping.'

'I didn't see you walk by,' said Jane.

'I drove up through the town,' said Janey. 'I'm quite good now and want to go further but I need someone with me.' She looked at the empty shop. 'Is Clare about?'

'Emily is making puddings and Clare is ironing her blouses.'

'So there is no need for you to be here?' Jane shook her head. 'Can I come here for dinner and then take you out in the car?'

'I don't know,' began Jane. 'Is it safe? What would Clive think?'

'Clive is away and like you Mother, when Father was fighting, I have to make my own decisions. Anyway, Clive is anxious that I should be able to drive well before the baby comes.'

'We could go a little way,' said Jane, and she smiled. 'It's a fine day and it might rain tomorrow,' she said as if that settled it.

'I'll walk back and bring the car here,' said Janey and turned back to face the hill.

Jane walked up the road to the small shop that sold newspapers and magazines. She bought *Jungle Jinks* and *Tiger Tim* comics for Vikki to look at, and a gaudy-covered journal about American film stars for Clare. Emily had her *Weldon's Journal* and when Jane added a quarter pound of Sharp's Creamy Toffees to her gifts, she knew that the girls in the shop on Coppins Bridge would be content to read, between serving customers.

Clare made very little fuss about being left behind and as soon as the meal was over, cleared the table and settled down to her magazine.

Jane dressed warmly although the new Singer motor car was covered-in and had no draughts. She put a basket of cakes and a bottle of cold tea in the small luggage compartment and a bottle of lemonade for Janey.

'We're not going for a week!' said Janey when she saw the basket.

'You never know,' said Jane darkly. 'These contraptions break down and if that happens, I'm coming back by train.'

'Why, where did you want to go?' I thought you were afraid to go further than the top of the High Street,' teased Janey.

'I've been as far as Cowes and back and to Wootton several times with Dr Barnes and once with Monty Morris. Could you go Carisbrooke way?'

'I think so. This car has one of the new self-starters but we can use the handle if it doesn't work,' said Janey cheerfully.

'You mustn't wrench yourself with that!' exclaimed her mother.

'Don't worry. There's always a very helpful man about,

18

just dying to get his hands on one of these cars, even if it's only to crank the engine. Not that I've needed help so far, and I'd only ask a respectable man,' said Janey when she saw that Jane was shocked.

'Don't go too fast,' ordered Jane and settled down in the front passenger seat with a delighted smile on her face.

Outside the Town Hall the newsboy sat with the latest papers and the placards hinted at what they contained without giving away anything. READ ALL ABOUT ELECTION RESULTS they announced. 'They can't have any yet,' said Jane. 'The polling booths are still open, and I'm not buying a paper until there is some real news.'

'Clive says that Lloyd George will get in on his own without having to have a coalition this time,' said Janey. She pressed the hooter to scare a dog from the middle of the High Street and several people turned to see who was in the car. 'Quick, think of something sad, Mother. Everyone will think we are far too happy to be in mourning.'

'Holy Mary! I'm a wicked creature to be sure, coming out with you for pleasure, but I can't pretend, Janey. I have my bad moments, remembering the good times, but now I feel well and independent and I can't help but smile, seeing you so blooming and the baby coming.' However Jane put on a suitably serious expression and when they passed the car driven by Dr Barnes, she was able to incline her head to him with solemn dignity.

'I feel the same, Mother. The war is over and Clive may be home for Christmas and then he will be safe after all those horrible mines have been swept from the seas.' The motor sounded efficient even to their ears and before Jane knew where they were, Carisbrooke Castle lay far to the left and the path led along the Clatterford Road.

'We've been no time at all! Do you feel tired?' asked Jane.

'When Clive was here, I drove all the way to Freshwater and back,' said Janey with pride. 'And that's when I was having sickness.'

With growing excitement, Jane saw the hedges flash by

19

and the bare branches of winter give way to scrub and open fields where the dark earth was rich and ready to yield up spring crops. Vestiges of golden gorse clung to the hillsides and cattle looked up as the motor engine was heard, but they no longer ran away when an internal combustion engine shattered the silence.

'The farm at Wootton will be finished with sowing and be getting root crops out of the clamps now,' said Janey, as if reading her mother's thoughts. She glanced sideways and then back at the road. 'Uncle Archie will be in soon with the carrots and swedes. Will you save me a big turnip?'

'Is that what you crave now? At least it's cheap,' said Jane. 'Yes, the dear man said he'd come in at the weekend.' She thought of Archie and his quiet devotion and was sad. If things had been different and it had been Archie who had married her, would life have been different? Not in the early years of love and family . . . not for her at any rate, but for him it would have been better than a marriage giving him one fragile daughter who had died like a faded rose, of tuberculosis and a wife who had followed suit.

'He's a good man, Mother.'

'A good friend,' conceded Jane. 'I know that the whole of Newport will be looking to see which way the wind blows, but don't you try to marry me off yet! I have an idea what I want to do but it can wait until after Christmas.'

'I'm glad you don't want to change anything,' said Janey.

'I didn't say that. There will be a lot of changes and a few shocks for some people.'

'You've got that look about you that you had when Father went to Africa,' said Janey.

'Keep your eyes on the road and you'll see nothing to make you think!' said Jane cryptically.

'I'll be in Freshwater soon,' said Janey. 'It seems no distance at all. Where shall we go?'

'Could we see the cottages? I brought the addresses and

20

a measure. If they are to be ready for letting next year, we must have some curtains and covers. Bert has a woman to see to all that, but even if I do the same, I'd want to run my eye over the houses first. Knowing him, he bought a job-lot and sold the worst to Walter.'

The train whistle came over the fields on the clear air. 'I've only been this far by train,' said Jane. 'Can you find your way to Colwell?'

After losing the way twice, Janey found the village green and the row of cottages that were empty and looked it. Jane stepped out of the car and checked the house numbers, then produced the first key. 'I feel as if we are breaking into someone's home,' whispered Janey. 'Others have the same idea. Did you see those curtains twitching?'

The cottages were soundly built and dry but chilly without furniture and a fire. The two women measured windows and noted what was required in the way of basic furniture and then locked up again, pleasantly surprised at the quality and the situation and excited at the prospect of seeing them put to use.

'Bert said his were on the other side,' said Jane. 'He didn't let on just where, but I think he once mentioned Yarmouth.'

'We'll stop and have some lemonade and drive back that way,' said Janey. 'Not that we shall see him if you don't know the addresses, but it will be a change to go back a different way.'

'He has some in Ventnor and Totland but the new ones are those he bought when Walter bought ours. He'll own half the West Wight before we know it.'

Janey slowed down by the railway station and had to avoid a motor car parked by the entrance. She glanced at the number and frowned. 'That's Bert's car,' she said. 'If he's driving, why be at the station?'

'Drive on and don't look back,' said Jane. She drew a deep breath as Janey steered round the next bend and stopped. 'He was meeting someone off the train,' Jane smiled wrily. 'Now I know who is doing the curtains for him, but not a word to anyone, Janey. Certainly not to Lucy Dove.'

She was quiet on the drive back to the shop. Walter and Bert had shared so many things; business, drinking and talking and almost surely, women, but Jane couldn't take in the fact that Maudie Dove had been left as a kind of legacy to Bert Cooper. No wonder he was upset at the idea of taking me there today, thought Jane.

'Where have you been?' demanded Clare. The magazine was not as interesting as she had first thought and the afternoon had dragged, with Vikki crying over a broken toy and the shop suddenly busy, with most people wanting potatoes which Clare hating weighing out.

'Just for a drive,' said Jane. 'We saw the cottages and there'll be a lot of work for Miss Joyner if she's up to it. You can choose the material for the curtains if you like, Clare,' she said to placate her.

She showed Clare the rough sketch of the rooms and the measurements. 'I wish I had one,' said Clare. 'They look quite big and I like the West Wight.'

'You have a home of your own,' said Emily. 'A home and a husband, Clare.' There was a note of reproach in her voice, but she bent over the growing band of delicate crochetwork and Clare was unaware of her real feelings.

'I know I have,' snapped Clare, and flounced out of the room.

'What's the matter with Madam?' asked Janey.

'A wire came after you left, Mother. It was from Alan. If Clare won't go home for Christmas, he's coming here.'

Jane raised her eyebrows. It had been in her mind to invite him, but he was never one for waiting to be asked. 'He has a right to be with Clare,' she said mildly.

'But Clare was very cross,' replied Emily. 'You'd think she'd be delighted, wouldn't you?'

'We'd better get the big front room ready,' said Jane. She sighed and put the kettle on the fire to bring the water to the boil. In a way it was good that now there was no excuse to leave Walter's room untouched. It was the only spare double room that would serve for Clare and her husband, and everything had to be turned out at some time or other. 'Run up and ask Dan to see me tomorrow. He can take some of the clothes.'

Jane tried not to think of the men she had seen in the town over the past year. Wounded, back from the war with a leg or arm missing, sometimes two limbs and badly scarred; their gaunt faces and thin clothes made her feel guilty when she went back to her warm living room and warm woollens. I must sort it all out and save nothing, she decided. It would be wicked to leave a stitch of anything in the cupboard when there was need of it out there. Vikki came in, pink-faced from her evening wash and her plump cheeks dimpled and healthy. Jane hugged her hard and sent up a silent prayer for all the young creatures in the workhouse on the hill.

'I'll start tonight,' she said suddenly. 'Janey, put your feet up for an hour before supper and Emily see to the shop. If it's her Alan who is coming here, then Clare can help make ready for him.'

Grim-faced, she opened the door to the room in which Walter had slept and had been laid out after he was brought home from the stable. It was cold and well-aired and she closed the wide-open window. Jane shivered, but when Clare complained that it was too cold to work there, she merely asked her to put a match to the fire laid in the grate.

They stripped the clothes from the big wardrobe and laid them on the bare mattress. Jane selected three suits for Dan and some warm shirts with ties and socks enough to satisfy even Annie Cooper and her avarice, then put sets of clothes, of trousers, shirt and socks with a jacket or extra knitted cardigan in bundles. Shoes she put in a big linen laundry bag and couldn't bear to see them as they, more than anything, bore the imprint of the man who had worn them.

Clare helped but was subdued. 'It will be done soon and best done now,' said Jane kindly. 'He didn't die here, Clare, and there'll be nothing to remind you when you sleep here with Alan.'

23

'Couldn't I have Sidney's old room?' asked Clare.

'Vikki is in there, and you can't have separate rooms! You haven't been married five minutes!'

'I know.' Clare turned away. 'I wish that Joseph had come back,' she said in a low voice.

'Wishing doesn't make marriages. You have to accept things of your own making, Clare.'

'We aren't right for each other.' Clare's eyes were bright with tears.

'He was sure that you were what he wanted and you took him for better or worse.' Clare made an impatient movement. 'You made your bed, Clare. Now you must lie on it.'

'We're not all like you, Mother. Not all of us want a houseful of babies.'

'Not all of us can have them,' Jane retorted. 'I loved each one of you and so did your father.' She bit back the lump in her throat. 'We were happy for most of the time and the bad times only showed how lucky we'd been. You haven't begun your marriage yet, Clare. Take a leaf out of Janey's book.'

'Janey! She's as bad as you, Mother. I'd have done better to have gone with Sidney and found something worth having in life.'

'Alan will be here tomorrow or the next day, Clare, and under this roof we'll have no argument between you, if that's what happens.'

'We don't quarrel,' said Clare. 'It might be better if we did.' Angrily, she tied string round the bundles and set them out on the landing. The room was soon cleared and as it grew warmer, it lost the feeling of loss and depression and even Clare cheered up when the bed was made and the bright patchwork quilt was spread over the blankets.

'I'll do the drawers in the bureau,' said Jane. 'Would you take Dan's things, and that bundle there up to the man by the Town Hall. He looks shrammed with cold under those arches.'

Clare looked as if she wanted to refuse, but thought better of it under her mother's calm gaze. 'Emily will

24

have to lay the table and do the potatoes, then,' she said.

Jane sorted out the papers that the solicitor had not needed and wept over letters that Walter had kept, ones that she had sent him in Africa. There was even a lock of her hair that she had cut off one bright summer day on an impulse, and it now lay as bright and raven-black as the day she sent it, a living thing on the palm of her hand. It was the first time that Jane had openly cried since the funeral and the last heavy load of bitterness and loss melted with the tears. She burned all the letters in the bedroom fire and the lock of hair curled in the flames as if in agony, making her regret tossing it in with the rest. The bare drawers she lined with fresh newspaper and set new writing paper and envelopes in the top ready for whoever might use the room.

Jane breathed deeply and looked back into the bright impersonal room where once she had conceived so many babies, some in joy, some in dread and once in hate. It was done and the tide could not be held back. Walter was gone.

'I met Dan up by the *Press*,' said Clare later. 'He'll be here first thing tomorrow, after doing the stable.' She seemed cheerful now, as if there had never been a hint of her former mood. 'The papers are full of the new fashions and the films coming over from America.'

'Did you give him the clothes?' asked Jane.

'Oh yes,' said Clare carelessly. 'He was very pleased. Did you know that there's going to be a pantomime up at the Drill Hall given by that travelling company that used to put on plays like *Murder at the Red Barn*?'

'That will cheer up a few people but it doesn't help those in real need,' replied Jane.

'The war is over and it's time that we had some fun,' Clare pouted. 'If I could stay here, I can have some new clothes made up. I can use some of that material that you put by when we thought it might be difficult to obtain.'

'I thought you lived next to a mill that makes cloth,' said Jane. 'Besides, that is Emily's. You had your share the last time you were here.'

25

'Emily never goes anywhere and the mill makes heavy woollens that don't drape well,' explained Clare as if she had the right to take anything she wanted.

'There's no time for all that before Christmas if we are to make it happy for Vikki. Dan will bring in a small fir tree and we can decorate it for her upstairs so that she doesn't see it before the day.'

'We didn't have trees when we were little,' said Clare.

'It was the Old Queen who made them popular, and poor little Vikki has no sisters and brothers to amuse her.'

'I think I'll move into Father's old room tonight now it's nice and warm,' said Clare. 'I'll get my things.'

'Have you seen Ethel? She said that Fred was still in Germany with the occupying forces. It doesn't look as if they will be together for Christmas, so you could ask her to come over.'

'Ethel said that the soldiers are having a lovely time there. They travel free on all the trams and buses and have nice food even though there is nothing in the shops. The food queues are worse than any we had here during the war.'

'Poor creatures,' said Jane. 'It's winter and the little ones must be hungry.'

'The Germans? Serves them right. We won the war and they should pay. You are always on about our wounded and the men who ended up in the workhouse because of the Germans, so why should we pity them now?'

'But the war *is* over, Clare. Mr Lloyd George has promised that this was the war to end all wars and that there will be jobs and food for everyone soon.'

Clare put on the expression that Jane had come to resent. 'They killed my Joseph, didn't they? They killed many of our friends and now they expect us to pity them.'

'Don't ever say that again, Clare! When Joseph was alive, you had no time for him and it was you who sent him off to the war when he had no need to go. It was you and Ethel who sent him a white feather and nearly drove him mad with shame and if anyone is to blame for his death, then look a little closer to home!'

Jane went down the stairs, slowly. The old healed ulcer in her leg throbbed and her head ached. Vikki came and sat on her lap and snuggled close, sleep heavy on her eyes. 'You should be in bed,' said Jane, but rocked her to sleep as much for her own comfort as the child's.

Chapter 3

'If you're going down to the Bridge, you could give Mrs Darwen this from me,' said George Foster. 'You can have some for your missus too, Bert, if you think she'd use it,' he added, hastily glancing towards the door to see that nobody had come in to overhear what he was saying.

'What is it?' Bert Cooper turned the package over.

'Dried fruit. The first I've had from Greece for more months than I care to say. There isn't enough to put on the counter so I'm letting it go to regular customers.'

'Give me Annie's share too, then,' said Bert, and George stooped to find a package like the first one, but with reluctance. He regretted mentioning the fruit to Bert now. It was one thing to work with the man on the council and to have the benefit of his advice about stocks and shares and a number of profitable bits of business, but Annie was a different cup of tea.

Bert grinned. 'Annie likes her fruit secondhand, made up ready in some of Jane's good cakes and so do I, so I'll pass this on without mentioning it to Annie. You needn't look like that, George. You've had enough of Jane's cooking in the past to know that most of this will be given away.'

The shop was empty and the women who had thronged in earlier had gone home to prepare the midday meal. Bert sat on the edge of the counter and picked at the cheese until George asked how much he wanted weighed out. Then the shopkeeper pulled out a newspaper. 'Seen the *Press*? There's more going on here than meets the eye, Bert. Quite a boom and what Lloyd George said is true. More jobs and it looks as if we've got the Peace Treaty ready for signing. They've removed the blockade from Germany so trade with them and rest of the continent will freshen up, and the Germans seem to be quiet.'

28

'Don't be too sure, George. With the end of fighting, they'll need less armaments and rolling stock. Who wants tanks and guns now, except to keep the peace? Ireland takes some with the Troubles there, and there are the other pockets of rebellion over the globe, but there's no trench warfare, no Verdun, no Somme – so no guns!' He smiled at the councillor's fraught expression. 'Did you hang on to your shares in munitions, George? Walt and me got out months before it all ended and made a packet.'

'I sold most of them but now I have it lying in the bank doing nothing much.' He pushed a bag of sweets over to the man perched on the counter, and smiled hopefully.

'You'd be better off in bricks and mortar, George. Or if you're brave, in one of the fashion houses. I hear, on good authority, that women with money are hungry for pretty clothes again.' Bert opened the bag and put a sugared almond into his mouth, and wished he had kept quiet.

'Oh, who do you know that knows a yard of ribbon from a bit of liquorice? I keep to what I know best, Bert, and you'll come a cropper if you start up in that market.' George laughed. 'Did you get your information from Annie? She's not exactly a fashion-plate herself and I can't see her knowing anything about drapery.'

'She wears the fox fur I bought her for the Armistice celebrations. Furs can make even a plain woman pretty and she said she could get a liking for furs.' Bert thought of the simple coney tippet he had bought at the same time and given to Maudie Dove the first time she went to the West Wight to meet him. He remembered the sight of it against her bare skin, and wondered what she would be like in full-length fox, or chinchilla.

'It's time all these politicians stopped talking,' said George. 'They promised enough but they seem to be taking their time over it. America holds up everything with Woodrow Wilson's "fourteen points". We all want disarmament and peace but there are ways of doing it. Freedom between nations to trade would be good, so long as they don't let foreigners dump goods on us, and I'm all for the formation of a League of Nations if it keeps the

29

peace, but we can't let go our hold on the seas. Britain still rules the waves. Freedom of the seas would be a disaster.'

'Well, they are signing the Peace Treaty at Versailles about now.' Bert loosened his collar slightly. 'I hope it's cooler in that place than it is here.' The June sunshine made the jars of rice and lentils shine on the high shelves and the dust showed in the sunbeams as the door opened and shut.

Bert stood up to see who had come into the shop. 'If you aren't busy I'll give you my order, Mr Foster,' said Jane Darwen. She smiled. Bert brushed off a patch of flour from his coat. 'Hello, Bert,' she said. 'Doing Annie's shopping or just putting the world to rights?' She was thinner than she had been before Christmas and Mr Foster pulled a chair forward for her to sit down. It crossed his mind that she no longer cooked for a man and so might not be eating well, but she had Emily and little Victoria to feed as well as Janey and Lizzie when they came to the shop, and he couldn't imagine Jane Darwen without a good larder. Dan Cooper never went home hungry after helping with the stables and the shop, and she had taken to going over to her son Edward's wife every two weeks laden with pies and fish, and cakes for Edward, as the diabetic Alice spent most of her time in bed or in a chair.

'How's Janey?' asked Bert.

'Fine, just fine,' said Jane and beamed. 'The baby is the image of Clive and they are both well. The monthly nurse is going on Tuesday and Janey is sitting out and feeding the baby well.'

'Well, mind you don't wear yourself out over them,' said Bert sternly.

'Babies are not hard work until they get on their feet,' said Jane. She had a misty, reminiscent smile on her lips. 'I love the smell and feel of a baby that's clean and bubbling with milk, and Janey has Lucy full-time and a girl to do the rough, so she's in clover. Vikki loves the baby and looks in to see him most days when she comes back from school.'

'Has Clive seen his son?' asked Bert. A twinge of envy

was sharper than he imagined possible. That was one way that Walter had scored over him. A big family, and Bert with none and nobody to put in his will as his progeny. It could be that Janey, so like her mother, would be as fruitful, as warm and as womanly.

'He was home two days after the birth,' said Jane. 'He was at Scapa Flow when those wicked men sank the German fleet and his ship was one of the escorts to take the generals and members of parliament to France before the signing. They make a lovely sight, those three, and Janey is so happy and active that I fear she might do herself harm.'

'You should have a picture of them, Jane. I haven't given anything for the baby, so I'll go up the High Street and get the photographer to go to the Lodge before Clive goes back.' He saw her hesitation. 'You want a picture, don't you? You can send one to Sidney and to Clare.'

Jane smiled. 'It will have to be today. Clive goes back tomorrow. Thank you, Bert. I'll hurry along and warn them and give Janey time to brush her hair. Sidney would be pleased and it might give Clare ideas about a family.'

She put her groceries in the basket and hurried out, refusing Bert's offer to carry it for her. On the way to the Lodge, she slowed down. Clare might be pleased to have lasting proof of a happy marriage, but then, she might not. At Christmas there had been an atmosphere between Clare and Alan that had worried Jane. He was polite and attentive but quiet and his eyes seemed to follow Clare as if he was disappointed.

Alan Dewar was so sure he was right and that Clare was the one for him, she thought, as she rested on the brow of the hill. Clare had tried to send him home alone after the holiday, but he had insisted on her returning to the stone house by the canal. At night, she had heard raised voices once or twice, and in the morning Clare had made herself useful in the scullery rather than be with him.

The bundle of magazines all about movie stars like Valentino and Clara Bow and the new jazz musicians had been left behind but only Lucy was eager to read them, hoping to see some reference to Sidney between the lurid covers.

Jane thought of the gifts that Alan had brought with him, the fine woollen dress material for Emily and the length of quality worsted for herself that Jane had accepted with surprised pleasure. Miss Joyner the dressmaker had seized on it eagerly as a pleasure to make up, and had transformed it into an elegant two-piece suit with a long, fitted jacket. Jane had sensed from Alan a plea for help, but no one could help him with Clare, and he had gone away with a tense and unwilling wife who watched the shore of the Island fade through tears, trying to live in a dream world that had failed her.

The sound of a baby crying made Jane hurry now and she walked in through the open door to the small sunny room that Janey had made into a nursery. Clive sat on the floor with the baby on his knees and Janey was buttoning up her blouse. 'You'll make him sick if you jog him up and down like that,' said Janey, but her eyes were laughing.

'If he's to be a sailor, he'll have to get used to it,' teased Clive.

Jane bent to pick up the baby. 'He's full of wind,' she said. 'Look at that blue round his little mouth!' She put the baby to her shoulder, loving the softness and the small movements and the satisfying belch that followed her gentle tapping. 'There, you can have him back now,' she said and handed him to Clive who had watched her with an amused smile.

'Do you always close your eyes when you wind a baby, Mama?' Jane blushed. 'Janey does when I kiss her,' he said, and glanced at his wife with such tenderness and humour that Jane wanted to cry.

'It's all part of the same,' replied Jane. 'Women are all like that.'

'Not all, only the good ones,' he said. He held the baby away from him. 'And the best ones never leave a smelly bundle like this to a helpless man.'

Jane told them about the photographer and Clive was

delighted. 'Can he have it ready by tomorrow for me to take with me?'

'If Bert can't make him do it, nobody can,' asserted Jane. She took the baby again, and told them to get tidy and ready, then changed the diaper and dressed the child in fresh crisp frills and a tiny bonnet.

'Clive wants me to wear my yellow dress,' said Janey, laughing. 'I told him the colour won't show but he said he wants my wedding dress in the picture and if it doesn't fit, we'll have to pin it on!'

'The back isn't important,' agreed Jane, and when the photographer came with a huge box on a tripod and a dark curtain under which he put his head before squeezing the bulb to take the pictures, Janey looked almost as she had done before the baby was conceived, and Clive was in the full-dress uniform of a sub-lieutenant in the Royal Navy.

It was all over within half an hour and the man rushed off to get the first prints developed, spurred on by the generous promised bonus that Bert had dangled before him.

'I'll go home now,' said Jane. She longed to stay, enjoying the laughter and the baby, but they had such a short time together and she tried to resist the temptation to stay.

'Stay to dinner,' suggested Clive.

'I'll come one day when you are back for your long leave,' she promised.

He kissed her cheek and held her close. 'Look after them for me, Mama . . . whatever happens?'

'I promise,' she whispered and wondered why she felt cold.

'When we have the day's holiday for the Day of Jubilation, Clive will be busy,' grumbled Janey. 'There will be warships and frigates dressed over-all in the Channel and he will have to be on board. I'd love to go to London to see the march through the streets. They say that Marshal Foch will take a salute and the Royal Family will be there.'

'There'll be plenty to see here,' consoled Jane. 'After

33

the last war, we lit beacons on every hill all over the Island and they plan to do the same on Jubilation Day, with fireworks and parties for the children. Vikki is excited even now as they told the children at school to bring a Union Jack with them as they are to parade and sing for the Mayor. She wants to have a red, white and blue ribbon in her hair and so she shall, the love.'

'I heard from Sidney at last, Mother,' said Janey. 'He was away for three months with the travelling circus and then went to a place called Hollywood to see some people who think he might do well in the movies, so he didn't get any of our letters for months.'

'What could he do there?' Jane was bewildered. 'Sidney isn't a film star like Valentino!'

'No, at first he will dance and act small parts but they say he will have bigger parts to play if the public like his face.' Janey looked impressed. 'He might be famous one day, Mother, and then we can all go and see him in America.'

'No wife of mine is going off across the Atlantic,' said Clive firmly. 'You are prettier than Mary Pickford and twice as intelligent.' He grinned. 'I'd lose you in a week if you went there. They could never resist you.'

Jane slipped away down the drive, her eyes shining. They were like children in love, with a spontaneity and sweetness that caught at her throat. She sighed. Clare couldn't look like that for any man.

Jane pulled her straw hat on as she walked and then blinked in the strong light. 'Alex!' she cried. 'I haven't seen you for such a long time.' He shook her hand and smiled, but the lines on his young face had deepened. 'How are you?' she said softly.

'Better, Mrs Darwen, but I'll be glad to be back at sea.' He glanced towards the Lodge. 'Anyone at home?' She nodded. 'Mother said she'll drive us to the ferry tomorrow as Janey isn't out yet. I'll tell Clive.'

'They've just had photographs taken,' said Jane. 'Clive is in uniform, so don't have a shock! He isn't ready to go yet.'

34

'Nor would I be in his shoes.' Alex Barnes smiled. 'Look in on Mother sometimes, Mrs Darwen. She enjoys your company.'

She watched him go into the house. How terrible for him to witness the bubbling happiness there when his own fiancée had died in the last influenza epidemic. Jane shrugged. One day he will find another girl, she told herself. He is like Clive and life without love would not be right for him. And what about Archie, a small accusing voice whispered inside her. It was about eight months since Walter's death and the usual year of mourning would soon be over. To be truthful, the year had been a defence against all the suggestions that had been showered on to her in an effort to arrange her future, but soon, she would be expected to make whatever changes she had in mind. She crossed the road to the shop. Archie would be coming to dinner on Sunday, bringing a truck load of vegetables, and that eager question in his eyes. He would hand her the cheeses and choice ripe fruit from his private garden and say nothing of the love he still held for her, but soon, he would ask and she didn't know how to tell him that she could never marry again nor could she live on the farm where his wife Amy had died.

The notice that Edward had made for her hung in the shop window. FISH SOLD ON FRIDAY ONLY, it said. With Aaron Sheath dead and his family giving up fishing, except for George who supplied one shop in Cowes, it was a good excuse to shut the side of the shop that sold fish and had done so ever since she married Walter all those years ago.

Tomorrow, she promised herself, she would put up the final notice announcing that the shop would henceforward sell only fruit, vegetables and flowers. The last load of fish had been taken up to the Officers' Mess at Albany Barracks and Dan would be free to help in other ways. Jane sighed with relief, knowing that she secretly dreaded another winter serving cold wet fish and cooking crabs and lobsters.

Lizzie had been appalled at the news. 'Where can I get

35

my fish now, Mother? Surely you'll oblige a few customers and friends?'

'You'll have to buy your fish like everyone else,' Emily had said with a sly smile, knowing just how much Lizzie took from the shop each week. 'There's Fred's friend in Cowes, quite near you. He'll give you good measure if you say who you are.'

'But you will have to buy it too!' Lizzie smiled hopefully. 'You can get mine at the same time, Mother.'

'No, in future I shall only buy what we want, when we want it. It might make a change to have more rabbit and a good round of beef. Emily is fond of lamb chops and if they are young and sweet so am I, although your father wouldn't have them as he said there was no meat on them.' So Lizzie had gone home, very disgruntled, and her visits grew fewer.

Meat was still in short supply, but with Archie on the farm, the family on Coppins Bridge never went short and nothing was wasted. Offal and calves' heads went into brawn and savoury ducks and the good soup went to the chapel to serve the growing numbers of poor who sang a hymn with one eye on the steaming cauldrons, and swallowed pride and soup in equal quantities. Jane had asked Archie to bring any marrowbones and pork spines he could find and each Monday the huge copper that once had boiled crabs, now seethed with broth containing onions, turnips, potatoes and pearl barley.

'Bert Cooper came in,' said Emily as her mother entered.

'What did he want? I saw him earlier in Mr Foster's.'

'He left some papers for you to look at but said he'll be back on Wednesday to talk about them.' Emily laughed. 'He gave me two tickets for the cinema and said it was good.'

'If it's one of those Lon Chaney frighteners, you can ask someone else to go with you,' said Jane. 'Even the music that man plays on the piano to go with it makes my blood turn cold.'

'This is Mary Pickford,' said Emily. 'It's a new one

called *Daddy Long Legs* and it's ever so sad, they say.'

'We'll get there early and take those sweets that Mr Foster gave me and have a lovely cry,' suggested Jane and felt more cheerful. She could forget for a few hours that Janey would be lonely tomorrow night and that Clive and Alex would once more be back at sea, with little idea when they would have leave again.

As they left for the cinema, the High Street was full of people, with men sporting new suits bought from gratuities; in the shops, tills rang merrily as trade was brisk and spare money was squandered in the sure hope that there would be plenty more when full employment came again. More consumer goods had appeared, and fruit that some children had never seen, like bananas, were in the windows again. However, Jane was aware of the real poverty under the new elation and the misery of ex-servicemen on small pensions and with no means of employment, due to wounds gained in the service of an ungrateful country. Meanwhile, men in reserved occupations like Harry, who worked in the engine division of Saunders Roe, prospered and looked down on those who had given everything but their lives.

'Thank Heaven Lizzie has a good provider,' Jane said when she saw women in shabby clothes trying to keep up appearances. 'And Clare doesn't know how lucky she is,' she said to Emily.

'I don't think she is,' said Emily quietly. 'I wouldn't like to be married to Alan. Clare was silly to marry on the re-bound but she must have liked him well enough at the time.' She sighed. 'Clare gets more bitter each time she comes home, Mother, and she hates the house where they live.'

'They'll sort it out between them,' said Jane hopefully, but she didn't take in the first half an hour of the moving picture as her thoughts were far away in a part of the country where she hoped she would never have to be.

The audience shuffled out in the warm night air, most of them wiping away tears and smiling. 'Lovely, wasn't it, Mrs Darwen,' one of the customers said. She matched her step to Jane's. 'If you're going home, I'd like some fish for their supper,' she said. 'I meant to look in earlier but my Nancy came and talked and I just had time to get here.'

'Haven't you heard?' said Emily. 'We aren't selling fish any more.'

'But you must! What will happen if there is no shop open when we want it? I was counting on you, and now, I don't know what to give them.'

'I have a box of bloaters and some smoked mackerel,' said Jane. 'But the fresh has all gone and we did put up a notice in the shop.'

'I'll come in for some bloaters, then.' She looked at Jane with open curiosity. 'Closing down altogether?'

'No.' Emily laughed. 'We can't manage the fish side with just Mother and me and Dan to help with the deliveries. I like the flowers and we can manage the fruit and vegetables, and we might have to make more posies and bouquets for weddings now that the war is over and a lot of men are coming home from Germany.'

Jane said nothing, but left Emily to serve in the shop while she went in to make tea and cut bread and cheese. Close down altogether? Someone had said the words that had been teasing her for months. She lifted the pot from the fire and tasted the broth she had left to simmer. Walter had been fond of her soup even in the hottest of weathers and she couldn't get out of the habit of preparing it even when there was only Emily and Vikki there. Tonight, however, Ethel had come in to mind the shop and see to Vikki and she would want something before she went home.

'Vikki is asleep,' said Ethel. She passed a hand over her face and shivered.

'What's wrong?' Jane stared at the face that was never pretty but now looked white and mottled. Ethel's eyes were rimmed with red and her voice sounded weak.

'I'm tired. Cold out?' Ethel sat by the fire and put her hands almost on the hot metal of the range.

'Here, have some hot broth,' said Jane, but Ethel took one sip and pushed it away.

'I think I'll get to bed,' she said, and tried to stand.

'I think you'd better,' agreed Jane. 'Now, where have

you been to catch cold this warm weather?' She spoke softly but her alarm grew. The young woman's skin was hot and dry and her pulse beat rapidly against Jane's hand.

'Our Amy is bad in bed,' said Ethel Sheath. 'I went to see her two days ago and was going again today but I was too weary.' She took a deep breath as if the effort was overwhelming. 'I think she has the 'flu.'

Emily stared as she came in from the shop. She exchanged anxious glances with her mother and reached over to touch the limp hand that rested on the back of a chair. Jane nodded. 'Mrs James came in when she saw me serving and told me that Ruby Sheath was taken poorly this evening,' she whispered. 'George is out in the boat with the new lad and Fred is still in Germany, so there's no one to look after them.'

'We must get her home,' said Jane. Together, they almost carried Ethel to the door of the shop and rested. She was a dead weight and had grown much heavier over the past six months, due to her first pregnancy. 'I can't carry her,' said Jane. She felt breathless and Ethel was slipping to the ground. It seemed terrible to let a sick women sit on a doorstep but the street was empty and no help in sight.

'Ethel! Wake up,' said Emily. 'Come on, Ethel, you can't stay there all night.' Ethel stirred but seemed to settle more firmly into a heap. 'We need two men and a trestle or a door,' said Emily, but the Bridge was deserted and the town was settling down for the night.

'We'll have to put her in the wheelbarrow,' said Jane. She went to the back of the store and appeared with the wide-based barrow.

'What if someone sees us?' asked Emily with a nervous giggle.

'If they see us, they can help,' said Jane drily. 'There'd be enough curtains moving if there was anything scandalous to see, but never a face at a window when you want one.'

With great difficulty, they half-pushed and half-bullied Ethel on to the cart and began to push her home. The wheels creaked and needed oiling and the slight rise on the

Bridge took all their strength, but at last, Ethel was inside her front door and Jane pulled her on to the couch as the nearest resting place.

'She'll have to stay there until morning,' she gasped. Emily held a cup of water to Ethel's parched lips and she drank greedily, then fell asleep.

Jane peeped in at Ruby but she too was sound asleep although her breathing was laboured and the room smelled of sweat.

'I'll leave a note in for the doctor and ask if he knows of a woman to come and see to them,' said Jane. 'We can't do more now.'

The air outside was good and clean and Jane breathed deeply. 'We must eat and get some rest now, Emily. They both have the influenza. I hoped it had gone but I did hear that another wave of it is coming over France and Germany and it has now reached our shores. Dear Mary, preserve us! Come on now, hot soup and a good wash and put your clothes out for airing.'

Anxiously, long after Emily was asleep, Jane stood over Vikki's bed and listened to the soft intake of air and the sigh as she breathed out. Ethel was very fond of Vikki and liked to play with her and to kiss her. They said that more people had died from the epidemic of influenza at the end of the war than had been killed in the trenches. It attacked young and old, and the rich had no way of making sure that it touched none of their families.

Was there no end to misery, she wondered. Was the nation and the world so wicked that they had to suffer so? Emily had gone to bed with hardly a goodnight and Jane ached for her. Arnold, the one man who had loved Emily had died of this terrible disease and now she might have to see her close friends smitten.

The early morning train from Cowes came over the railway bridge and Jane got up and washed and put on a cotton dress that she could launder easily. She put clean towels in a basket, with soap and disinfectant and a bottle of cool lemonade, and walked over the Bridge to see what was happening.

Chapter 4

The door between the shop and the passage leading to the living room at the back of the shop was firmly shut, in spite of the heat. Archie stepped forward to open it but Emily stopped him. 'Mother says that we must keep it closed and she'll come out to see you in ten minutes.'

'But she means the customers, Emily, not me!'

'Everyone. I ring this bell if there's someone to see her and she comes out.' Archie looked amused and then anxious. 'It's Vikki,' explained Emily. 'She has the 'flu really badly and Mother doesn't want to spread it.'

'Open that door, Emily. I've lived among illness for long enough and if Jane needs help, I must see her.'

'I'm here,' said Jane, closing the door again behind her. She looked pale and the lines round her eyes seemed deeper today.

He took her hand. 'You aren't ill, too?' he asked. Jane moved impatiently. 'You mustn't take on so much,' he chided her.

'She's my own flesh and blood, Archie, and she's very ill. I'll not get my death from her any more than I got it from your Amy when I nursed her.' Her mouth trembled. 'The poor mite has no flesh on her but Dr Barnes says she's over the crisis. It's a wicked thing, Archie and one that is sweeping the country and killing more each day.' Her head drooped and she found his strong hand comforting.

'You are eating enough?' he asked. She nodded. 'And sleeping?' She shrugged. 'Why don't you come to the farm, Jane?'

She looked up at him and her eyes were filled with tears. 'I would if I could, Archie. I sometimes lie awake and think of the cottage where Jack and Nellie lived and wish I could go in there and close the door.'

41

'I don't mean the cottage, Jane. I mean the farm. I've had improvements made since you saw it and surely you can't spend the rest of your life here?'

'I've got Vikki and Emily, and just a step up the hill is Janey and little George. I can't leave them, Archie.' She tried to hide the catch in her voice. 'I have Vikki and nearly lost her. She doesn't eat, Archie, and I wonder whether the doctor is telling me the truth.'

'Does Nellie know?'

'Nellie?' Jane's expression was uncomprehending.

'Yes, Nellie – the child's mother, Jane. She should be informed.'

'Jack gave Vikki to me to look after and Nellie swore she would never come here again to upset her.'

'What if she came too late?' Archie spoke quietly. 'You would never forgive yourself, Jane.'

'I don't know where she is.' Jane sat down heavily on a wooden stool on which customers usually set heavy baskets. 'I thought of her and asked Edward to try to find her when Vikki was first taken ill, but as she began to recover, the need grew less.'

Archie took a folded newspaper from his pocket. 'I had no idea about Vikki but I brought this to show the girls as they like to see advertisements for music hall.'

Jane stared at the picture of Nellie, dressed in furs and a silk dress with a wavy hemline just above her knees. Her hair was expertly waved and hugged her small well-shaped head in a way that added to the general elegant picture.

'She's appearing at Southampton for two weeks, Jane. I could write to her if you like.'

'She can stay at the Bugle and come here just once, to see Vikki, but tell her that Vikki has never asked about her mother and father and so Nellie must keep her promise not to unsettle her.'

Archie nodded. 'And you must rest, Jane. I'll unpack the lettuce and tomatoes and Emily can fetch the flowers and put them in buckets. After that, I'm coming in the back room for dinner with you. You need a good glass of stout with yours. I'll get some at the Jug and Bottle.'

Jane didn't protest. It was wonderful to lean on a man for a change and not to have to make all the decisions, telling others what to do and seeing that work was done.

'Emily? Is your mother really eating enough?' Archie demanded as the girl helped him to unload the back of the motor car.

'Yes, but she worries,' said Emily. 'We have far less to do now than at any time I can recall and this gives her time to think. The shop is clean and sweet-smelling as the fish is gone, and I love the flowers, but Mother has worked hard all her life and feels guilty if she isn't on the go all day.' She laughed. 'You'll see that we feed well, Uncle Archie. There's good Irish stew in the oven and stewed fruit and custard. You get the stout and I'll turn over the card and close the shop before I dish up.'

He took the jug she offered him and walked slowly down to the Jug and Bottle, then changed his mind, left the jug there to be filled and ran up to the Post Office. He sent a telegram to Nellie at the theatre where she would be working that night then went back to bring the stout to the shop.

'I'll write today,' said Jane as soon as they sat down.

'It's done,' said Archie. 'You'll be glad when she comes, Jane.'

'No! I shall hate every minute, Archie. If Vikki knows who she is, we'll have no peace after she's gone. Look at that picture! What child could resist a woman like that bending over her sickbed?'

'I told her to send a wire and that I would meet her boat. I'll make sure she knows what to say and do, Jane, but she has the right to see Vikki.' He looked reproachful.

'You don't understand. I love Vikki and I do care about Nellie. I am glad that Monty Morris has married her and I think they are made for each other, but Vikki has something of my Jack in her and she will live in the clouds if we don't keep her feet firmly fixed on the ground.'

'Lucy is in the shop, Mother,' said Emily. 'Janey sent her to see if she could come here tomorrow.'

'Not yet. Janey mustn't bring the baby here and nor

should she come near Vikki until the doctor says she's no longer infectious.'

'Lucy says the doctor is with the Sheaths again and two nurses went in with black bags.'

'Holy Mary, it's Ethel and the baby! It can't be! She's only seven months or less,' Jane reached for the big spoon and ignored Archie's refusal. She ladled more stew on to his plate as if that action would help Ethel. 'Tell Lucy to ask at the Sheaths' door but *not* to go in. Janey doesn't want any germs brought back to her house.'

'Is Ethel ill?' Archie began to eat again.

'She has the 'flu like her mother. They've both had the doctor there at all hours. I know he was worried about the unborn baby, but when Vikki fell sick I couldn't be in two places at once and Dr Barnes had found a nurse to live in for a week or so. Ruby is on the mend now but weak, and if you go there Lucy, you can leave some of this stew with them. The nurse isn't a good cook and they can't live on porridge and savoury ducks from the shop in Pyle Street.'

'You already give enough to the soup kitchen,' reproved Archie.

'And would you see me stand by and let my friends starve?' said Jane with a burst of temper. 'Ruby and Aaron were good friends and it would be a poor world if I forgot it!' She wouldn't admit it even to herself, but the fact that Archie had taken it on himself to interfere over Nellie had riled her. It put her in the wrong and made her seem unfeeling.

'You do too much,' he said appeasingly and smiled at Emily when she served him a plate of apple and custard, while Jane covered a dish of stew and put it in a shallow basket for Lucy to take. As always, the girl looked at the mantelpiece where Sidney's latest picture stood, next to the portrait of Janey, Clive and the baby.

'Have you heard anything?' she asked.

'Not for a week or so, Lucy.' Jane smiled. 'You should write, Lucy. He said he's glad when he gets letters from any of his old friends.'

'I couldn't do that.' Lucy blushed.

44

'He was always fond of you,' said Emily. She had finished eating and now sat with her crochet in her hands and didn't see the pain in the girl's eyes. 'I'm sure he'd like to hear from you,' she encouraged.

'I'll take this over to the Sheaths,' said Lucy and escaped.

'Poor Lucy. She is still sweet on him, isn't she?' Archie laughed. 'She should go there and find him.'

'He could do worse,' admitted Jane. 'Lucy is as pretty as her mother but her features are more refined and she sings very well. Janey is teaching her to play the piano and showing her what books to read. She still loves all that talk about films but I think it is because of Sidney.' She sighed, and wondered if she would ever see her handsome son again. Mrs Lee, the gypsy woman, had told her that one of her sons would never marry and Sidney was the only one of the boys left unmarried.

She concentrated on clearing away and her heart was heavy when Archie sat in Walter's old chair and filled a pipe of tobacco. So many of the old lady's prophecies had come true over the years, and as she did each time she was reminded, Jane shut out the rest and hoped that the gypsy was wrong in at least a little of it.

Emily called down the stairs to say that Victoria wanted a fried egg. Jane turned to Archie, her face aglow. 'That's the first thing she's fancied.' She reached into the cupboard under the range for the frying pan. 'I'll put it on snippets of toast with a morsel of bacon to give it a flavour,' she said and Archie knew that he was in the way.

'I'll fetch Nellie tomorrow then,' he said.

'We should have waited. Vikki's going to get better and there's no reason for Nellie to come here,' snapped Jane, and the fat in the pan hissed angrily as if to echo her mood.

Vikki ate nearly all of the egg and dipped the toast triangles in the yolk. Jane watched each mouthful and sent up a silent prayer of thanks. She washed the little girl all over after she had eaten and changed all the bed-linen and nightclothes. The room was fresh and smelled of lavender and she knew that the infection had gone.

45

Later on that afternoon, while Vikki was having a nap, the man who Bert Cooper employed to collect his rents and who also collected rents from Jane's property up by the school, came in smelling strongly of eucalyptus. Jane stood back but he explained that he wasn't ill, only careful as he had to visit so many houses where at least one of the family had influenza.

'I came by the Sheaths and saw the midwife. Ethel Sheath had her baby early and she's very poorly. It's a boy and weighs next to nothing.' The man shrugged. 'It'll mean another visit to the cemetery soon, if the baby dies.'

'Is Ruby any better?' asked Jane. If the infection was over, she could go there with no risk to her own family.

'They have a nurse there day and night now, and the doctor's ordered straw to be put down outside,' he said, shaking his head.

Jane stood in the road outside the shop and looked along at the house where her children had played so long ago. Wisps of straw from the thick layer put down on the road to deaden the sound of hooves and wheels came floating across to her. It was an old-fashioned idea but it did show that there was illness in the house and made passers-by careful and quiet.

'She must be ill,' said Emily, awed by the sight.

'It's not the 'flu they are worrying about,' said Jane. 'Even if that started it.' A loud scream shattered the silence and Jane turned pale.

'What was that?' gasped Emily.

'I hope it isn't what I think,' said Jane. 'There is a kind of madness that comes after a difficult birth and a high temperature.'

'No, Mother, stay here! We can't help her now!' and Jane soon saw that this was true. The ambulance came half an hour later to take Ethel to the hospital where mental illness was contained if not cured. The baby lay in a wicker basket and went with his mother and Ruby looked down helplessly from her bedroom window.

Jane turned away, her shoulders shaking with emotion and Emily turned out dead flowers and fruit as if her life

46

depended on it. They cleaned the house and made the living room gleam with polish and effort, both determined to show a good tidy house when Nellie came the next day.

The last post of the day came and with it, a parcel from America. Emily begged to open it and Jane sat reading the enclosed letter while the contents were spread over the tablecloth.

'*I travel a lot but soon I shall be in a show in New York and stay for at least three months in the city.*'

Jane tried to read between the lines and discover if he was happy or not, but he didn't write about intimate friends. There were references to famous stars he had met or seen, and the fact that as from now, there was a ban on the sale of alcohol in most of the United States. '*All liquor sales are prohibited and there are heavy penalties for anyone caught breaking the law,*' Sidney wrote, '*But already there are houses selling it to private parties, and clubs where people drink behind locked doors.*'

Jane frowned. Sidney had never been fond of drink and she hoped that the new life hadn't changed him. She smiled as he mentioned other things that he knew would please her. The colours and magnificence of flowers and trees he had seen on his travels and the places he wished she could visit.

'It sounds grand, just grand,' she sighed. 'Now – what has that rapscallion sent us?' His letter and gifts did a lot to soften the sorrow they felt over Ethel. At least she was in a place where they knew how to deal with puerperal insanity and she wasn't a burden to Ruby in her weak state.

Emily went into the shop to close the door and put up the sign. Friends could knock, but these days the two women tried to close during the evening as there was no fish that could go bad over night and should be sold.

Jane heard voices and then laughter. She peeped round the door, half-hoping it was Janey but anxious that she should stay away if there was the slightest possibility of taking the 'flu back to little George. She saw the silhouette of a woman against the light. 'Clare! What are you doing here?'

47

'Mother?' Clare sounded unsure of her welcome.

'Whatever it is, tell us later! Come in, you must be tired after that long journey.'

'Not such a long journey,' said Clare. 'Alan had to go to Winchester on business and suggested that I went with him. In return, he let me come here for a day or so. I shall meet him for the Victoria train the day after tomorrow.' Clare smiled. 'It was worth it,' she said, looking at the gleaming dishes on the dresser and the fresh flowers in the copper bowl. She eyed the small parcels on the table. 'Have I missed a birthday?'

'No, that came just now from Sidney,' said Jane.

Clare sniffed and picked up her small suitcase. 'Where do I sleep? In the room we used at Christmas?'

Jane nodded, and Clare went up the narrow stairs without a glance at the present with her name on it.

'She's jealous of Sidney, Mother. She wishes that she had gone away as he did, but I can't see how she would have made a living. She can't act or dance or sing and she knows nothing about the theatre or painting.'

'Clare must learn to be content with her life,' said Jane, but both knew that there was no way to happiness for Clare if she ran away from Alan at the slightest excuse. 'It's as if they struck a bargain,' Jane said softly. 'How can you bargain with love?'

'A few days and nights together in exchange for two or three days alone here,' agreed Emily with an understanding of the situation that seemed odd coming from her mild lips.

Clare came down to the living room and sat by the window. 'It's good to be back,' she breathed.

'Is Alan coming here to collect you?' asked Jane. 'Why don't you both stay here for a while, unless his work calls him, of course.'

'I'll meet him on Portsmouth station,' said Clare shortly. 'Now – what's all this rubbish?' she asked, to change the subject. She picked up the small parcel with her name on it and ripped it open. 'Well, whatever next?' she sneered. 'You'd think he was sending it to a woman he loved.'

'He loves us all, Clare,' said Emily. 'Look what I had – a lovely little pearl brooch. I shall wear it on the side of my cardigan like they do in the fashion magazines.' She picked up the necklace that Clare had dropped on to the table. The slender chain held a cluster of marcasites in the shape of a heart on a wide bow of small pearls.

'It's lovely!' exclaimed Jane. 'You will wear it and send a nice note to thank him, Clare?'

'I might,' she said, but left the necklace on the table.

'I'll put the others away until they come to see us, Mother,' said Emily and put the unopened packets in the big blue and white tureen on the dresser.

'Make the tea, Clare,' said Jane. She pinned the gold filigree brooch that was her gift, to her dress and gathered up the waste paper, leaving Clare's gift on the table. She then sat down and read the letter again, a smile gradually smoothing away her displeasure. Sidney wrote of the old days and reminded her of many things she had almost forgotten but which he had treasured all the time he was away. Little things like the smell of Christmas puddings and the scent of primroses.

She sighed. It was sad, as if he knew that nothing could bring back his childhood. He mentioned many of his old friends and even the time when Jack had fought Percy Cantor and had two black eyes. He enquired about the Coopers and Mr Foster and Lucy Dove, Dr Barnes and the girl on the Mall who had worked in the jewellers and been in the local dramatic society.

The shop-bell rang and Lucy came back with an empty basket. 'Ethel didn't know anyone,' she said, and the tears welled up in her eyes. 'They've taken her away to that place, Mrs Darwen, and some say if you go there, you never come out alive!'

'It's the infection and the baby,' said Jane. She hugged the girl close. 'Don't take on like that, Lucy. It will pass and she'll be home one day, but if she's violent, she could hurt the baby.'

Clare listened, wide-eyed, and Jane had to tell her what had been happening over the past few weeks. 'Will they let me see her?' asked Clare with something of her old concern for her friend.

'I'll ask Dr Barnes,' Jane promised. She went to the door. 'Take a few flowers back for Janey,' she said to Lucy. 'Clare's made tea, so have a cup before you go.'

She gathered up flowers and fern and wrapped them in tissue paper for Janey, but before she could go back for her own tea, customers came in and talked and it was half an hour before she was free. Lucy came through the shop while she was serving and took the flowers. Her face was glowing with something that had nothing to do with the beauty or scent of flowers. Her eyes shone and a happy smile that burst into breathless laughter made the women in the shop turn and stare at her.

'Lucy looked happy,' said Jane as she went back into the living room. Clare poured some tea and went back to sit by the window without speaking. Her face was pink and her eyes over-bright and Jane wondered if she was sickening for influenza.

Emily plied her crochet hook as if stabbing an enemy and she looked very annoyed.

'What's the matter?' Jane saw the necklace had gone from the table.

Clare twisted her cuff as if to pull it over the split nail that she hated to show. 'Nothing,' she said. 'I think I'll go to the surgery and ask if I can see Ethel tomorrow.' She ran up to her room and came down ready for her walk. Emily didn't speak until she heard the shop bell ping as the front door closed behind her sister, then she put aside her work and cleared the cups on to the tray.

'Sometimes I think that Clares loves to hurt people,' she said in a low savage voice.

'She's worried about Ethel. They've been friends for most of their lives and were best friends at school,' said Jane. 'Was she rude to you, Emily?'

'I don't take any notice, Mother, but I don't think I can forgive what she did to Lucy.'

'Lucy? She went off as if she had been given a hundred pounds and a handsome husband,' said Jane, smiling.

'I wish she had either of those things. All she has is a dream based on a lie, Mother.' Emily looked pale. 'I didn't know what to say. It all happened so quickly and at first I thought that Clare was joking. I should have spoken up, and now it's too late, it would only make matters worse.'

'What do you mean? I've never seen Lucy so happy.'

'Clare said that Sidney had written and sent his love to Lucy. We all know that Lucy is fond of him and she has been teased about him often enough for it to mean nothing, but when she blushed, Clare went on, and Lucy thinks he really did send his love.'

'So he did, to all his old friends,' said Jane quietly. 'He did mention Lucy and that shows he thinks of her, so it isn't too bad, is it?' She felt the muscles of her face tightening.

'But Clare picked up the necklace and gave it to Lucy. She said she had opened it in error and he'd sent it for her, with his love.' Emily bit her lip. 'Clare even pointed out that it was in the shape of a heart and Lucy took it and kissed it, then said she ought to go back with the flowers and ran into the shop. Clare laughed, but Lucy really believes that Sidney sent her a token of love.'

'Sweet Mary! What devil is in my daughter?' breathed Jane. 'Is she so unhappy that she has to do this?'

'Say nothing,' suggested Emily. 'It will only make it worse.'

'We'll see about that,' said Jane and tossed her head in a way that showed she was really angry. 'She's no right to fill the girl's head with such ideas. Janey needs her and if she's swayed by romantic nonsense, she'll be no use at all.'

'She loves little George and Vikki,' said Emily. 'And as it's unlikely that she'll ever see Sidney again, she can have her dreams. We all have dreams, Mother.' She bent over her crochet again, the smooth neat top of her unfashionable hair plait hiding her face.

'I suppose you are right, Em. We'll say nothing, but I'd like to take a hairbrush to Madam's bottom and make her yell!'

'Lucy needn't know the gift was for Clare. It's time she

51

had something private to call her own. She doesn't have much that we don't give her.' Emily smiled. 'In one way, it will do good, Mother. A keepsake from someone you love means a lot.' She could feel the pressure of the finger ring made of hair that Arnold had once given her before he went to the war. It hung between her breasts on a silk cord and she was never without it.

'I'll peep in at Vikki,' said Jane. 'If she's awake, she might like a piece of bread and butter and jam. And I'll look out a good dress to wear when Nellie comes,' she went on. 'I don't want to look like a poor relation. But how I wish that Archie hadn't sent that wire! I know that no good will come of it.'

'I'll fill the boiler and make up the fire,' said Emily. The nightly round of fires and hot water and the putting up of shutters over the shop windows was easy now there were few people living in the house above the shop. The shutters of heavy wood had given way to lighter ones, slatted and easy to fit and which Emily could manage alone, but Jane wouldn't hear of buying one of the newfangled gas stoves for cooking, and so the ritual went on each night of the year.

'Fires are living things,' said Jane when teased about having the range lit winter and summer. 'I couldn't rest in a house with no fire.'

A strong scent of roses met Clare as she came back inside the shop. The windows were closed and the air was warm and she leaned against the cool door and hesitated before going into the lighted room. She recalled her mother wearing the scent of roses when they were all children, and the warmth of love that surrounded them all.

She took a deep breath and went into the room. Emily looked up from her book and smiled and Jane stood up to put the kettle over the fire from the hob where it had been singing quietly for the past half an hour.

'I don't suppose they gave you anything?' said Jane.

Clare relaxed. Perhaps Emily had said nothing and it would all blow over and Lucy would forget what had been said. 'Dr Barnes wasn't there, Mother. I waited with Mrs Barnes and when he came back, the doctor suggested that I might go to the asylum and look at Ethel through the window. If she recognises me and smiles, I can go in to see her. She was given a strong sleeping draught and has been asleep for several hours.'

'Perhaps Janey can drive you there,' said Jane. She hesitated. 'Wait until the afternoon. I want you all here when Nellie comes, and she'll come in the morning if she has a show in the evening.' Even Clare was better than no one, Jane decided, and if she expected welcome when she arrived out of the blue, then she could stay and be helpful.

Clare made a face but agreed. 'I wonder what she'll wear?' she said. 'She's quite well-known now and I heard that Monty has given up being a bookie and now acts as her manager and arranges all those pictures in the magazines.'

'You are not to tell Vikki who she is unless I say,' said Jane firmly. 'No hinting – nothing, do you hear? I mean it, Clare!' It was the only indication she gave that she knew about Lucy and didn't trust Clare to be discreet, and Clare looked down and mumbled her promise.

Jane moved restlessly about the living room long after the others were in bed. She made a bowl of arrowroot for Vikki and flavoured it with sugar and lemon juice and watched the child eat it with more appetite than she had had for weeks. It was midnight, but what did it matter? If Vikki needed food all night, she would gladly prepare it. She wiped the child's mouth and settled her under a light coverlet, loving her and dreading any disruption that a visit from Nellie could bring.

My children are close tonight, she thought as she sank into bed at last. Sidney can put into words everything I need to hear, just as he did in letters to Walter on the veldt in Africa during the Boer War. And Jack was with her in spirit, drawn to the shop on Coppins Bridge by the family being together; and the others were not far away.

'But tonight and for the future, this is a house of

women,' she whispered. 'Just Emily and me soon, for good, and too much work for us both.'

She got up early and washed all over, putting on new underclothes as if she were going to the doctor. Her smart skirt and blouse could wait until later in case she spilled fat on them, but she brushed her hair well and powdered her nose with peach-coloured powder and touched her hairbrush with jasmine oil, before putting on an old dress that could be changed quickly.

The old bureau in the corner of the living room was locked. She opened it and took out the papers that referred to the now considerable properties she owned and the stocks and shares in her names. She had no need to be beholden to a living soul. She sat straightbacked in the chair and looked at the deeds of the large house on the Mall, just above the main street and leading to Carisbrooke. It had a small garden in the front, she recalled – privet hedges and grass with a hydrangea bush in the corner. At the back was another garden with flowerbeds and fruit trees. She dreamed of sitting in a garden instead of in a warm room when the sun shone, and knew that she must decide what to do with the house, soon. As Bert said, it was money lying idle and that was wasteful.

Jane locked the desk and put the kettle on to boil. Time enough for business. Vikki might be awake and ready for a drink or breakfast. Jane made porridge and cut bread and called the girls as if they had to go to school.

Chapter 5

'She's sound asleep.' Jane looked across the bed and smiled. 'Come down and have a cup of tea, Nellie. You look as if you need one.' The two women left the room quietly and Jane felt a deep sense of relief. Nellie had come soberly dressed in a grey costume with a neat white blouse and a hat that hid most of her face where the wide brim dipped low over her brow, and her manner had been quiet and anxious, but in no way pushing.

'You are so kind, Mother,' said Nellie. She made no attempt to hide her tears, and took the cup offered in both hands as if to warm them even though the day was sultry.

'She's happy with us, praise be,' said Jane. 'We all love her and she has your good looks and Jack's humour, Nellie.'

'I hope not too much of our temper,' said Nellie and wiped her eyes. She smiled. 'Seeing her asleep I can't believe that she is my child. I haven't seen her for so long that all this is unreal.' She glanced up, pleadingly. 'Am I wicked, Mother? Am I unnatural to want to leave her with you even if I go far away?' She shook her head. 'It's far too much to expect. You have brought up a large family and you've earned a rest. If you ever find you can't look after Vikki, you must let me know and even if Monty raises the roof I shall take her back and do my best for her.'

'If she can't have a loving father, she's better off staying with us,' said Jane firmly, and tried to hide her elation. Nellie was on her best behaviour and didn't want Vikki. For the first time, Jane wondered just how Nellie had felt when she received the wire telling her to come to the bedside of her sick child. There must have been a tug between her natural concern, and panic that she might have to take the child away and look after her.

'I shall never send for you again, Nellie, whatever

happens,' promised Jane. 'If that's what you want.'

'Yes, that's what I have to want if I am to stay with Monty.' Nellie sighed. 'Even now, he hates me to mention her or Jack, although he often mentions you with affection. He sends his best regards.' She fiddled with the smart crocodile handbag on her knee. 'In a way, it's good that you sent for me, Mother. Monty wants to go away, for good, to America.'

Emily took the empty cup and Nellie shook her head when she was offered more tea. Jane saw the sudden rush of colour to Nellie's cheeks and knew that it was an effort to speak.

'You must go where your husband takes you,' said Jane softly. 'I know that he is a much better husband to you than my son could ever have been and you must follow him.'

Nellie flung herself into Jane's arms and sobbed. 'If only you had been my real mother. If only you could come with us . . . if only we could begin again.'

'If only never got you anywhere,' said Jane as if telling Vikki that she was naughty. 'We all have our crosses to bear and regrets, but you must look to the future. Now tell us all about your plans.'

Clare listened with a half-smile on her face, and Emily took the tea tray into the scullery and came back to hear everything. The front doorbell told them that there was someone in the shop and Clare gave a sigh of exasperation when Jane indicated that it was her turn to serve, but she came back at once, followed by Lucy Dove.

'I know you!' said Lucy. 'I have all the pictures of you cut out from magazines and I remember you when you lived here.' She smiled at Nellie and her eyes sparkled. 'You look wonderful, Mrs Morris.'

'I'm here for only a few hours,' said Nellie. 'I came to say goodbye.' She glanced at Jane for approval and received a nod and a smile. 'Monty wants to go to America and he's arranged work for me there in some of the nightclubs.'

'How wonderful. Is that where all the gangsters go?'

56

asked Lucy, her eyes wide with wonder. 'Do you think you'll see any of the real gangsters like Al Capone?'

Nellie laughed. 'That all happens in Chicago which is a very long way from New York where we shall be. There is Prohibition everywhere and some illegal trafficking in whisky but Monty wouldn't book me in any place where there might be trouble.'

'Sidney wrote to us and told us about the speak-easies,' said Emily. 'I'd be afraid to go out with all those gunmen about.'

'It isn't like that,' Nellie assured her. She was gaining confidence. 'It's a different world. I can't wait to be a part of it. They want me and are paying well and even paying for a suite on the *Mauritania* for us. I shall sing in the cabaret on board and that will make people know me when I arrive in the States.'

'It sounds wonderful.' Lucy's voice was envious and sad. 'I wish I could go, too.' She touched the thin chain round her neck and even though it couldn't be seen under her high neckline, Jane knew that the chain carried the heart and pearls that Sidney had sent.

'Can you find a place for me, too, Nellie?' asked Clare. 'I could do with a change.'

'You know that's impossible.' Emily looked at her sternly. 'You are a married woman, Clare.'

'I do need someone, but I don't think you'd do, Clare.' Nellie tried to lighten the atmosphere. 'I need someone to do all the boring things, like mending my dresses and the costumes I wear for certain dances like the tango and the Black Bottom.'

'You don't dance that?' said Emily. 'One of the Bishops denounced it from the pulpit as immoral!'

'It's only a dance,' said Nellie, and laughed. 'All the men in the audience love it and when I ask for a volunteer to dance with me, there are more offers than we can cope with.'

'What else would she have to do?' Lucy came closer.

'Check luggage to see it all arrives safely when we are travelling, make sure the hotels know we are coming and dress my hair before performances.'

'Would she have to cook, too?'

'That would be heavenly!' Nellie laughed. 'That really would be wonderful. Late at night, usually when everywhere is shut except for nightclubs, and Monty feels hungry, I am far too tired to cook and I'm not good at it at the best of times. If we take an apartment instead of staying in hotels all the time, I do have to prepare meals, and where would I find such an angel?'

'I can cook. Ask Janey,' said Lucy. Her face was pale. 'I can sew and make things and I often do Janey's hair, and once or twice I've done Mrs Barnes' hair when she had a dinner party.'

Nellie regarded her with interest. 'You're Maudie's girl, aren't you?' She took in the slim dress and the shining hair and the air of gentility that Maudie herself lacked. The finely-chiselled features, more Nordic than English; and the innocent mouth showed the influence of Janey and her friends and not Maudie.

'Are you serious, Lucy?'

'Yes, Mrs Morris. If only you would take me with you, I'd work and work and you'd never be disappointed.' She spoke with passion and Jane put a hand to her own throat as if to take comfort from the cameo brooch that she had given away years ago but which she sometimes imagined was pinned to her neckband.

Clare was looking down at her hands and seemed embarrassed. Emily picked up her crochet and hid her face over it, and Jane willed Clare to look up and face what she had started.

'Sidney is in New York,' said Lucy. 'I'd like . . . if I could . . . I'd like to meet him again!'

'So you'd have a ready-made friend?' Nellie laughed. 'That would make a difference. I am so busy that you would be alone a lot, working and when you had time off, but if you had a friend you could trust, then you could enjoy New York very much.'

'Sidney might not live anywhere near you,' said Jane. 'New York is very big, isn't it?'

'What does he do?' Nellie began, then looked at the

58

photograph on the mantelpiece. 'Of course, why didn't I think! He's at the Broadway Theatre. I saw the programme.' She looked at Jane. 'Monty says he is an up and coming star, but I didn't think it was your Sidney. He has a juvenile lead in the next production and it's only a few blocks from where I shall be working.'

'You seem to have it all planned,' said Jane drily. 'Arrangements like this take more than five minutes.'

'Monty went over last month and brought me all the news and programmes of what is on in New York.' She blushed. 'I said I'd go with him but I would have said goodbye. If I didn't come here, I'd have written, Mother.'

Jane nodded. How alike they were, Nellie and her dead husband, Jack Darwen. Jack was a one for leaving notes when he was too embarrassed or afraid to meet a situation. 'I'd like to know where to find you, Nellie,' was all she said.

'You can write and tell us about Sidney,' said Emily. 'He writes often but you could tell us more.'

'No,' said Jane. 'Just keep in touch if you move on. Let's go on as we have done and then Vikki needn't be upset.'

Nellie wrote down the address of the nightclub where she would be working and promised to send details of where they would be living as soon as they were out of hotels. 'Do you really want to come?' she asked Lucy again. The girl nodded. 'Why not sleep on it? If you still decide that you can be out of England for a year, write to me at this address before next week and be ready to board the liner the week after.'

'So soon?' Emily looked shocked. 'What will Janey do without you, Lucy?'

'There's hardly enough work for me to do there now she's well again after the baby. The girl who does the rough is very good with little George, and her sister would like to come as nanny.' She looked tense. 'I shall miss them and I shall never forget any of you, but I must go, Mrs Darwen.' She hung her head and whispered. 'It's fate.'

'Monty can't wait to get there. He says that they need

men like him to manage the movie stars, but I know that what he really wants is to watch the next Dempsey fight and perhaps become a boxing promoter.'

She glanced at the clock and as if on cue, Archie came in. 'Ready to catch the ferry?' he asked. 'I'm not late, am I? The bank manager took a long time this morning and I thought he'd never finish. Then I had some oats to complain about and to leave them a sample, but we have plenty of time.'

'Vikki is awake,' said Emily. She saw Archie and then looked at Nellie who was pulling on her gloves.

'Do you want to go up?' asked Jane softly.

Nellie listened to the child calling for Gran and tears fell over her powdered cheeks. 'No, she's not my child, Mother. If I touch her now, I shall regret it and never have a moment of peace again.' Quickly and almost fiercely, she hugged Jane. 'Goodbye, and thank you for everything.' She ran into the shop and out on to the pavement. Archie held the motor car door open for her and she didn't look back.

'What are you doing out of bed?' asked Jane, when she'd climbed the stairs to her grand-daughter's room.

Vikki giggled. 'I was watching the lady get into the car. Who was she, Gran?'

Jane picked her up and put her back in bed, tucking the bedclothes round her closely. 'Just a lady,' she said. 'Now, what do you want for dinner?' The flow of laughter and words came to her in a mist. Jane wanted to hug Vikki hard and shout to the world that she was her child, hers alone, but she smoothed the tousled hair and told her to be quiet or she'd get hot again and never eat a thing.

Mealtimes for the sickroom were at any time they were needed, with Vikki demanding fried fish for breakfast or bread and butter pudding for supper, but she was eating again and losing the terrible translucent fragility of the past three weeks.

Clare was gone when Jane came back downstairs. 'She went to the hospital. Dr Barnes sent Alex to fetch her and he'll bring her back later,' said Emily.

'I thought Alex was back on his ship,' said Jane.

'He is being sent to the Mediterranean Fleet and will be away for six months, so they gave him extra leave now.'

'Oh, dear, does that mean he can't be with Clive? They are such dear friends,' said Jane. 'I like to think of them together. They are alike in many ways and I think that Alex needs someone he knows.'

'I think it's a good thing they are parted,' said Emily. 'It must hurt Alex each time Clive has letters from home and news of people they both know. It's time he made new friends if he is ever to forget Millie.'

Jane nodded. 'I think you're right, Em. I wish he could find another girl to love.'

'Other than Janey.' Emily bit off a loose thread. 'He could love Janey if he stays here, and that wouldn't do.'

'Rubbish. Janey is married and in love with Clive.' Jane turned away. Archie had loved her when she was married to Walter and he loved her still. 'Dear Mary, keep Alex away but safe, until he finds a girl,' she murmured.

The motor horn announced Archie's return. 'There was no need for you to come all this way back here,' said Jane. 'She caught the ferry?'

'I saw her on to it,' Archie said. 'At the last moment, I thought she'd come back here, but she got on just as they wanted to take up the gangway.' He put a hand on Jane's shoulder. 'She's gone for good, Jane.'

'Thank you, Archie. Until today, I have never been sure that Nellie would keep her word, but now, I am certain that she will go out of our lives. The Atlantic Ocean is very wide, and America can offer her more than she'd have here.' She patted his hand. 'You were right to send for her. Have you work that can't wait or shall I put out some tea and drop scones?'

'I can take an hour,' he said. Emily was feeding Vikki and reading to her. 'Where's Clare?' he asked.

'Gone to see Ethel.'

'I could have taken her. Did she have to go by bus?'

'Alex is home on leave and Dr Barnes sent him to collect her.'

Archie raised his eyebrows. 'Driving with a married woman. That's more than I dare suggest!' Jane blushed. 'You still refuse to drive anywhere with me alone, Jane.'

'People talk,' she said.

'Let them. No, we can leave the drop scones for five minutes. Come and sit down! It's time we arranged something. You know I want to marry you, Jane. God knows how long I've wanted you, and now you're free. You can begin to live your own life now, with me on the farm. You can come and go as you please, do as little or as much as you like there, but be with me, Jane. Warm my house and make it a home and warm my heart.'

'My dear,' she began. 'I shall love you until my dying day.' She checked his effort to kiss her. 'It's a special love, a dear and deep love that I don't deserve to feel for anyone after all this time, but it isn't married love. I could come to you and give you less than you deserve, and make the years of wanting turn bitter. I have borne seven live children and two dead. I have been a good and faithful wife to Walter, and although the Book says, "Till death us do part", I shall never be free. I married one man and he is here now, watching me.'

Archie made an impatient gesture. 'Walter is dead and gone, and for years didn't deserve you.'

'As long as I am in this house, he will be with me.'

'Then leave this place. Sell up and come to me, Jane.'

'What about Emily? And there's Janey so near who needs me at times.'

'Emily and Vikki are welcome and Janey can teach you to drive a motor or you can have a light trap.'

'And can you see me driving one of those monsters?' She laughed. 'No, Archie. Everyone has told me what I should do. You take it for granted that I shall come to the farm. Annie Cooper insists that I should sell the shop and live out in the wilds in one of my cottages. I think she hopes to get me out of the way.' She smiled. 'Poor Annie, she never could see an inch in front of her nose. I'm no threat to her. Bert and I can't stand each other except for business and he has other fish to fry. Clare suggested that I go to stay with her and Alan for three months to see if I like it there, and most people who come in the shop think that Emily will take over the shop and find a nice husband.' She smiled. 'Even Sidney asked me to go over to see him, but I'm sure he doesn't really mean it.'

'So what have you decided?'

'To do none of these things. I shall sell the shop and move into the house on the Mall. Emily can still make up bouquets and posies and if Janey has to join Clive at any time, there will be room for George and his nanny. I am not going to make hard work for myself and I shall enjoy the garden, with your help, Archie.'

'So I may come to visit you?' he said wrily.

'As often as you wish, Archie. We have shared far too much to lose each other altogether.' She stood close to him and reached up to kiss him on the lips. 'You're a dear man, so you are,' she said. 'Now hand me that basin of batter and we'll have some scones.'

Clare came back, followed by Alex Barnes, and Jane fussed over him and made him stay to tea. 'How was Ethel?' asked Archie.

'She was bad,' said Clare. 'They wouldn't let me see her. The nurse said she'd ripped the dress off one of the orderlies and they are keeping the baby away in another ward.'

'Holy saints,' breathed Jane. 'It isn't her fault.' She recalled the time when she herself was ill, deep in a trough of incomprehension and pain, with her heart beating sluggishly and hard enough to stifle her, and the battle she fought to claw her mind back to reality. But please God, never violent, she thought, but would never know, as none of the family would discuss that time with her. Surely I never raised a hand against my own, she prayed.

'They'll know more in a day or so. The afterbirth didn't come away whole and until it does, there will be a risk of fever,' said Alex. Clare looked away. How could an unmarried man and one as good-looking as Alex talk about these things as if he was a doctor and not an officer in the Navy?

63

Jane handed out scones and went back to the fire to make more. The past was suddenly with her, bound up in the present and with a grip of iron. She looked at Archie and wished that she could take him upstairs with her, to make him happy and to wipe away the pain. Not here, she told herself. Not in Walter's house where my children were started and born.

'Fred should come home,' said Archie.

'Dr Barnes said the same,' said Clare. 'He's writing to the authorities to see if Fred can have compassionate leave from Germany. Surely they'll let him, as the war has been over for ages now and there can't be anything much to do out there.'

'It's getting better since they raised the blockade,' said Alex. 'No country can take the humiliation of being treated so badly and nearly starving.'

'They would have done far worse to us,' said Archie. 'They robbed every country they overran during the war and even now, there is terrible news of mass murder.'

'You mean George Grossman, "the Butcher",' said Alex. 'He's mad and will be executed.'

'What did he do?' asked Emily.

Alex grinned. 'Better not walk out alone in Berlin, Emily. The Butcher might get you, cut you up and sell you for meat.' Emily gave a small scream and covered her mouth with her hand.

'Alex, you shouldn't!' said Jane. 'Did he really do that?'

'Dozens of females, and there's another man who killed men by biting through their windpipes! They haven't caught him although people say they know who he is. I think I'd be a vegetarian if I lived there.' He laughed in a ghoulish way to make Emily scream again and Jane smiled, even though the subject was so terrible. He looked younger, teasing the girls and forgetting for a while that he was heartbroken.

'It's sad that Europe is such a devastated, unhappy place when all we hear about America is how prosperous people are and how bright and glamorous the theatres are,' said Archie. 'Nellie will do well there. She always did have that extra something that made people stop to look at her.'

'Like Sidney,' mused Emily. 'I hope that Lucy is doing the right thing.' She told Alex about Lucy and Nellie and he glanced at Jane to see her reaction.'

'Sidney will be glad to see her,' she said. 'But we must all make sure that Lucy understands that she is only one of many friends he would welcome there.'

Clare cleared away the tea-things and didn't return from the scullery, but Jane said nothing more and gave no hint of Clare's part in Lucy's decision to leave everything she knew, to go across the ocean to a man who had never done more than give her a quick hug at Christmas or when he was pleased with something she had done for him.

'I'll be going,' said Archie, seeing that the others showed no sign of leaving him alone with Jane.

'Come to dinner on Sunday,' suggested Jane. 'By then, Fred might be back and I'll try to get Ruby here if she is stronger. Dr Barnes says there is no risk from her now and the nurse aired all the rooms before she left.'

'How long is Clare staying?' Archie wanted to know.

'She has to meet Alan and go home,' said Emily. 'Where she belongs,' she added quietly.

'I almost forgot!' Archie went out to his motor car, and came back carrying a heavy box. 'Nellie left this for you, Jane. She didn't bring it in but asked me to give it to you after she'd left.'

'What is it?' Everyone gathered round and when the lid was open, Alex said in a voice that was once more eager and excited, 'It's one of the new gramophones. Father wants one but it isn't easy to get a good one yet. This is American!'

'Monty must have brought it back with him. How does it work?'

'This horn goes on there,' said Alex. 'This handle slots in at the side and you wind it up – like this! Hey presto!' He took a clip from the lid and beneath the wooden partition found three records. He glanced at the titles, and grinned. 'I think Nellie used this for practice,' he said. The swivelled head of the arm came down and the needle gently touched the smooth edge of the record. It slid into the groove and the music came, loud and vibrant to the astonished ears of the girls.

Clare came out of the scullery and looked excited. 'That's one of the tunes they play at the Kit Kat Club where the Prince of Wales goes dancing,' she said. 'I read about it in one of the magazines. They call it the *Shimmy*.'

Jane looked disgusted. 'It sounds indecent, and I wonder our Prince lowers himself to go to such places. I've seen pictures of the kind of women who dance there. All legs and no bust, and made up to look like dolls. The Queen would never wear such short dresses, and she is a fine figure of a woman, with dignity and bearing.'

Clare looked superior. 'It isn't fashionable to be fat, Mother.' Jane eyed her daughter with interest, and Clare turned away so that her mother couldn't see the tight binding that was cutting into her breasts in a very uncomfortable way.

'Does Alan like you looking like a stick of rhubarb, Clare?' The pale silk stockings and cuban-heeled, one-bar shoes added to Clare's height and Jane wondered how long it would be before Clare emerged from illusions of glamour and settled down to making a true home and having babies.

'Now listen to this one,' Alex chuckled and exchanged looks with Emily.

'Yes, I think this was put in for you, Mother,' she said, and the strains of violins came over the theme of *In a Monastery Garden*.

Emotion caught Jane by the throat. Walter used to sing this tune at the harmonium. She looked at the sideboard that had replaced the harmonium after Walter's death, and knew that when alone, she would never play that record again.

'Try the other,' said Clare. 'What is it?' She turned the record and read the title. It was excerpts from *The Merry Widow* and soon they were all humming along. 'Nellie still sings that, she told me,' Clare informed them. 'Audiences love it, especially the men after they've had something to drink.'

'It's beautiful. I shall play that over and over,' said Jane. 'Show me how it all works, Alex.'

'Have you an old sock or something soft?' he asked. 'If it's too loud, you can stuff something in here to deaden the sound.'

'Whatever will they think of next?' said Jane as if this was the height of discovery.

'New needles are in this box and you have to change them after every ten or twenty records, I think. It will tell you on the label.' He showed her how to change the needle and then shut the lid. He laughed and opened it again. 'Now be sure to wind it as much as I did, or this happens.'

He put on the record of the *Shimmy* and they listened to the fast rhythm that gradually slowed down and grinded painfully to a halt, after making the most weird noises.

Emily was delighted. 'It sounds better like that,' she said. 'What do the others sound like?'

Jane left them huddled round the new toy like children. She went up to Vikki and dressed her to bring her down for half an hour. She found the child dancing round the room to the music that was clearly heard in the bedroom. 'It's too slow now, Gran. I want to dance quickly.'

'You'll see what we have when you're dressed, and you mustn't dance too much yet, dear.'

'But I like music, Gran. I want to dance when I hear it. One day, I'll dance a lot,' she said.

'Yes, I think you will,' said Jane. She thrust the child's arms into the sleeves of a dressing gown and tied up the cord at the waist. 'Put on your slippers and come down to see Uncle Archie before he goes,' she said.

Vikki ran downstairs, showing no sign of weakness and Archie hugged her. 'Look, Uncle Archie, I can dance,' she said. Alex put on the dance record and Jane watched with growing apprehension as the small energetic figure began to look more and more like Nellie Morris.

Chapter 6

'I've done all I can to stop her,' Jane Darwen moved about the room restlessly. 'I even got Archie to talk to her but he only made matters worse.'

'What did he say to her?' Janey sat on the bed and watched her mother folding the baby clothes. 'I didn't like to ask her as she was in tears when she came home, but she's busy shopping this morning, so we can talk in peace.'

'He said outright that men on their own and especially men on the stage, had lots of girl-friends and Sidney might have forgotten her, but Lucy turned on him and said he'd sent his love and a gift that showed he loved her.' Jane sighed and held a soft muslin diaper to her face to make sure it was aired. 'I wish I'd never mentioned it to him now. I was just trying to make her understand how far away America is and how lonely she would be if she didn't meet Sidney or make friends there.'

'Clare has a lot to answer for,' said Janey. 'I think she's persuaded herself now that the necklace really was for Lucy all along. You know Clare! She'll swear that black is white if it suits her and she hates to be in the wrong.'

'Lucy is determined to go and now we have tried to stop her, she seems even more set on it. It's as if she sees his face as it is in that picture, smiling, almost beckoning and showing nothing of what he felt when the camera stopped taking photographs. She had a long argument with her mother, too, from what I hear. Maudie Dove heard that Nellie was here and when she asked about her, Lucy said she wanted to go with her as her dresser. Maudie didn't like that idea one bit, not because she'll miss Lucy, as she hardly ever sets eyes on the girl any more, but because she hated Nellie when she sang in the Bugle and made all the men look at her and not Maudie.'

'That must have made Lucy even more stubborn,' said

Janey. 'Do you want me to talk to her?' She picked up a tiny sock and put her finger through a hole in the toe. She smiled. 'I'm not the one to convince her. I'd go to the ends of the earth after the man I love, Mother, and she knows it. In a way, she might think that she could have the same kind of life with Sidney as I have with Clive. She sees us in love and so very happy and thinks that marriage is like that. Poor Lucy. She's starved of love.'

'That's what worried me.' Jane opened the sewing box and threaded a needle with fine wool and began to darn the sock. 'If she doesn't meet Sidney, or if she finds that he has no need of her, she might fall into the hands of a man who will not be right for her, but who would offer her love of a kind, or safety.'

'Nellie will look after her.' Janey tried to sound reassuring. 'She is a woman of the world and will see danger before Lucy can be hurt. After all, she meets all kinds of men and some must try to make up to her when she sings and dances, and afterwards, when she sits by the stage smiling and being gracious.'

Jane pricked her finger and hastily sucked it so that the blood wouldn't stain the sock. 'Monty will look after her, too,' she said. 'He's never had a family and might welcome a daughter like Lucy.'

'Will she be safe with Monty Morris, Mother?' asked Janey bluntly.

'That is one thing I'm sure about,' her mother replied firmly. 'He has loved Nellie faithfully and thinks the sun shines out of her eyes, so he does. He's a good husband and this might make up for the family he never had, and make up for Nellie having to part with Vikki. I know he feels badly about that, but who can blame him? Yes, it would be more than any man could stand, to have Jack's eyes looking at him every time the child saw him.'

'So, will you see them off, Mother?'

'No. As far as I'm concerned, Nellie has gone even before the *Mauretania* sails.' Jane put down the mended sock. 'I thought that if Emily went over to Southampton with Lucy to see that she meets up safely with Nellie and

Monty and to help with the baggage, you could go too. I'd stay and look after George and Vikki.'

'But you'd enjoy it, too, Mother,' Janey smiled. 'Oh, it would be fun to see her safely on board. Are we allowed on board to have a peep?'

'Yes. They sound a bell to let visitors know when it's time to leave, and then the band plays while the ropes are cast off.' Jane beamed at her daughter. 'I'm glad you can go, Janey. Lucy will be frightened when the time comes and she'll need help with her things, not that she has much, poor girl. She's never seen one of the huge liners close to. They loom up and seem to overpower everything in the docks.' Her eyes had a faraway look and she broke the wool from the needle and rolled it into a ball.

It wasn't only that the children needed her to look after them; Jane knew she couldn't bear to see another ship leave harbour, carrying those she loved. Yet it might be different this time, she told herself. Lucy was a dear thing and this wasn't like the other times. Jane could say goodbye now with no anguish, and enjoy seeing how people lived on board a floating palace, but the bright paint would inevitably fade in her mind and once more she would see the rows of white faces above a wave of khaki and kitbags, and smell the fear from the iron decks.

'No, I'll not come,' she said. It had rained when the troopships had left and the band played stoically with the rain dripping off the end of the bandmaster's nose. She had never dared go near the docks when Walter left for the Boer War, but during the Great War, she had gone, and imagined how it must have been when Walter left.

'You'll need a warm coat,' she said. 'Look out anything you think Lucy might wear and I must write to Sidney and warn him that she is coming.'

'Letters go in the liners, Mother. You could give it to Lucy to post when she gets there.'

'No, I'll send one,' said Jane, and didn't think it necessary to confess that she had already sent a wire to him at the theatre where Nellie said he was rehearsing. 'He'd have the shock of his life if someone from the Island appeared out of the blue, without warning.'

'Warning? You make it sound as if he needed to brace himself for an invasion,' said Emily, who had called for her.

'And so he should,' said Jane quietly. 'Lucy is going to America with stars in her eyes and I can't see any future for her with Sidney.'

'He was fond of her,' suggested Emily. 'He hasn't said he has a sweetheart and Lucy is very pretty . . . .'

'Just look after yourself, Lucy,' said Jane, the following morning. 'Write to me when you have the time and when you come back, there will always be a place with me if you're short.'

'Thank you, Mrs Darwen.' The girl's face was bright with happy expectation. 'I might not see you for a long time, but we'll come back one day.'

We, Jane thought. The girl was bewitched. She meant Sidney and her. 'You may not meet Sidney for a while, Lucy. When you do, give him my love. Tell him . . . just give him my love.'

'Oh, I will, Mrs Darwen. I'll write and write once I'm settled and I shall work hard for Mrs Morris to repay her for all her kindness.'

'That may not leave you much time for seeing friends,' warned Jane.

'It will be enough to know I'm in the same city,' said Lucy simply.

Jane waved as the motor car gathered speed and the trunk strapped to the grid on the back obscured the view. Three young women looking happy was a sight for sore eyes, but as Jane sat and looked at the sleeping child Janey had left with her she wanted to cry.

She picked up the newspaper and read of the grand opening of the Cenotaph in Whitehall, London. The pictures of the Prince of Wales and of King George V were good; the two men were solemnly watching the gun carriage, on which the coffin carrying the Unknown Warrior lay, go slowly past and on to the Abbey, there to be laid to rest as a gesture to all who had died unidentified in the stench and ordure of the Somme and Ypres and all those other senseless battles that had laid a generation of young men to waste among the bright poppies.

Did it matter to the dead that one hundred men who formed the Guard of Honour all wore the ribbon and medal of the Victoria Cross? And that the King himself sprinkled the dust of Flanders over the coffin as it was lowered? Jane turned the page and scanned the item about the Assembly of the League of Nations, that still didn't bring America or Germany or Russia to Geneva.

'What's the use of it if they don't all join?' she asked Bert Cooper who came into the shop for flowers and fruit.

'It's a beginning,' he said. 'We need to get together for trade, and it's too early to set up trade with Germany. The politicians can talk until the cows come home, but it's the businessmen who will settle what's to happen.'

He picked an apple from the pile of polished fruit and bit into it. 'Did you want to buy some?' asked Jane sweetly. 'You can have a pound with one taken off, or a few specks if you can't afford to buy.'

She eyed his smart velvet-collared jacket and his silk necktie. Something or someone had made him even smarter than when he and Walter used to go out for the evening or on a jaunt over to Portsmouth.

'I'll have a bunch of flowers for Annie,' he said. 'Her rheumatics are playing up again and she can't get out today.'

'You can give her these from me, Bert. I'm sorry she's in pain again. How is the new maid managing?'

'You know Annie. Hates to pay anyone to clean the house and yet can't do it herself now. I don't know how long this girl will stay, but I pay her a bit over the odds to make her sweet.' He glanced at Jane. 'Annie doesn't know and she thinks I pay the least I can, but you don't get something for nothing and the girl is clean and bright.'

Jane weighed out the apples and selected a bunch of bananas. She saw that Bert had something on his mind. 'What is it, Bert?' she asked quietly. 'Flowers for Annie?

72

The pick of the grapes and you shifting from one foot to the other as if you had sat in a puddle?'

'I saw Dr Barnes and he says it's more than rheumatism. Annie is worse than she knows and will get even worse.'

'Oh, dear God!' Tears sprang to Jane's eyes and she put a hand on his arm. 'Oh, Bert, is she very bad?' She tried to imagine Annie as she had been when younger, but could only see the shrunken figure she had become. 'I think I've known for some time,' she said slowly. 'She has that look about her.'

'If you could just pop in sometimes?' Bert lowered his gaze and picked a grape from the bunch. 'She thinks more of you than anyone else and you do her good.'

Jane gave a faint smile. 'You do surprise me. I've suffered often enough from Annie's tongue and she's been the first to gossip.'

'It's her life's blood,' he admitted. 'If we'd been lucky and had children, both of us might have been better people, Jane. As it is, she's vented all her envy on you and me and my poor brother Dan. How he's stayed with us all these years amazes me, and now that you have sent the horses to Wootton to Archie, he is home more and has the edge of her sarcasm.' He paused. 'What about the stable, Jane? Are you sure you don't want to keep a pony and trap?'

'No, Get rid of it all, Bert. Take the arches for storage or get rid of them. I never want to go there again.' Her face felt stiff as she recalled the night when Walter was brought home dead from the stable under the arches of Coppins Bridge railway.

'Leave it to me, Jane. I'll see to it and never mention it again.' He grinned. 'You're a lady of property now, you know. What shall I do about the house on the Mall? I've said it before and I'll say it again; it's money lying idle.'

'I'm going to live there.' Jane laughed a trifle breathlessly. 'There! I've said it to you. I told Archie but even the girls don't know yet. Don't tell Annie for a week or so as I want to prepare the girls first before the whole of Newport hears.'

73

'You'll miss the shop,' he said. 'Still, you've been here through two wars and a lot of unhappiness, so I suppose you do want to go away.'

'A lot of happiness, too, Bert. A lot of warmth and good friends and good times, praise be.' She picked the stalk from an apple and dropped it on the table that had replaced the heavy old counter.

'You'll take warmth with you wherever you go, Jane. Walter was a lucky man.'

'We shared a lot, Bert,' she said, and in that instant he saw that he must never say more about her dead husband, however much he knew. 'I'll need your help, Bert.' He went red. 'Yes, I know I don't ask for it often, but since Walter died, you've been good to me and never once sold me short. If you'd see the lawyer first and get the papers ready, I want to give some of my cottages to Emily while I'm still alive. She will never marry and I know it's good for a woman to own something and to have something behind her.'

'Like pickle money?' he laughed.

'It added up and Walter never knew how much I made from jams and pickles and later, the flowers. It helped,' she said simply. 'A woman likes to be able to give away something without having to ask first.' He saw the proud tilt to her chin.

'You may marry again, Jane.'

'No, I've done with marriage. Archie wants me to go to the farm but I'll take myself off to the Mall and live like a lady.' She laughed. 'I may even have a drawing room and a maid in cap and apron.'

'And when anyone needs you, it will be you who helps, not a maid sent to see what needs to be done, even if it's scrubbing floors.'

'I don't scrub floors any more, Bert Cooper,' Jane said with dignity, but she looked pleased. 'I want Emily to be independent, even if she lives with me for the rest of my life.'

'She will marry. Em is quite pretty and with property, a nice little catch.'

74

'She'll not marry,' repeated Jane. 'She loves Vikki and baby George and is content with little outings like today. I'll have to make sure she does get out more once the shop is sold. There's a very big conservatory at the back of the house and she can still make up wedding posies and nice bunches of flowers . . . but not wreaths. She's been asked, but neither of us want that.'

Bert took the gold half-hunter watch from his waistcoat pocket. 'I have to go and take these back to Annie, then I have some business to do out West. The man who sees to the bookings needs an eye kept on him.'

Jane nodded gravely. 'Janey took me out to mine and we have ordered the curtains and covers.' Bert choked on a grape. 'We shall go out most Fridays until it is done. Janey can manage to take me then.'

Bert looked relieved. He took the fruit out to the motor car and Jane hid a smile. He had been so kind lately, and it was only fair to let him know when she would be at the cottages in case she ran into him with Maudie Dove.

'Now I'll have to tell everyone,' Jane said as the exhaust from Bert's motor drifted away. She looked out on to the empty street and felt a wave of excitement. Next year, she would have the house as she wanted it and the garden neat. Flowers in pots and a big asparagus fern would look nice along the path and someone else could weigh potatoes for a change!

George was crying and she picked him up and held him close. Vikki came in from the back yard to hold his bottle while he drank and Jane soaked his soiled nappies in Rinso.

'Why can't I go on a big ship across the sea like Lucy?' asked Vikki.

'Do you want to leave Gran?'

'No, you'd have to come with me. And Baby George and Aunt Emily and Aunt Janey and Uncle Archie and . . .'

'That's enough to fill a boat,' exclaimed Jane. 'But we are going away, to a house with a garden where you can play and have little friends to tea.'

'*And a rocking horse?*' Vikki spoke in a sibilant whisper. 'A real rocking horse, Gran?'

'A wooden horse, is it? I'd rather see you on a live pony.' Jane teased her and eventually agreed that wooden horses didn't bite or toss children from their backs. 'My children didn't have a rocking horse,' she said, and when Vikki was having a nap and George was snuffling happily in his cot, she wondered if her family had been deprived. She looked at the sleeping children. They were only little. Janey would have more, but Vikki would never have brothers and sisters. 'Poor little mite. You shall have your rocking horse,' she whispered, and went down to make tea.

The shop was busy for an hour and then she had nothing to do but wait for the girls to come back. She heard the sound of a motor horn and smiled. Janey made sure that her mother heard her before the car stopped. Emily rushed in and Janey followed more slowly after shutting the car door and making sure that the brake was on.

'Have they gone?' asked Jane, and laughed. 'Of course they have or Lucy would be with you.' She lifted the tea cosy and emptied the pot to make more tea. Fresh bread and butter and jam, with a plate of fancy cakes from the new shop in the High Street were ready, and Vikki came down in time to choose the first one. Jane gave the girls a warning glance. 'Just tell me about Lucy,' she said. 'Little jugs have big ears.'

'They were all there,' murmured Janey. 'Everything was fine,' she told her in a normal voice. 'Lucy was overwhelmed by the ship and so were we. It's a real palace, with wooden panelling like in a castle and lovely palm trees in the lounges.'

'We saw the cabins and the restaurant and where they play the band for . . . people who sing in the cabaret to work.' Janey bit her lip. 'We met some nice people who will look after Lucy,' she said, and relaxed. Vikki would never know that the 'nice people' were her mother and stepfather.

'Did the ship leave when you were there?' asked Jane.

Emily began to cry. 'It was beautiful, Mother, but so sad. We were in the cabin, or rather the suite of rooms where Lucy will be, and the hooter went to tell people to leave. "All ashore who's going ashore!" they called, and we all filed off the ship down the gangway to the docks. Lucy burst into tears and clung to Janey and said she didn't want to go. I think she was frightened, but . . . the lady I mentioned took her and held her hand and we left.'

'The band was there, dressed in very smart uniforms as one of the Royal family is travelling on the *Mauretania*,' said Janey. 'I think it was the band of the Guards. They played *Auld Lang Syne* and everyone cried a little. People on board threw down coloured streamers like they do at Cowes' fireworks and even the bandsmen had them over their capes and hats. It looked so pretty at first, but then they cast off the ropes and raised the gangway, and as the ship left the dock, the streamers broke and fell into the water.'

'I picked up a piece and brought it back for you, Mother,' said Emily. She handed Jane a strand of bright pink paper that snapped as Jane took it.

'Put it in the big blue tureen,' said Jane. 'I don't like to think of them going.'

'I want it,' said Vikki. She took the streamer and twisted it into a ball, then tried to smooth it out again but it was damp. She screwed it up tight and tossed it into the fire, laughing, but nobody said anything. Even Emily who had brought it, was glad to see it go.

'So, that's that,' said Janey. 'How was George?'

'Good as gold and Vikki fed him with his bottle. He's still asleep so stay until he wakes naturally or he'll be crotchety when you take him home.'

'I'm going to have a horse,' said Vikki. Janey raised her eyebrows, knowing that the horses had gone to the farm at Wootton.

'A rocking horse,' said Jane.

'I shall play with it in the garden,' said Vikki grandly.

Emily laughed. 'It will get muddy in the yard.'

77

'No, a real garden,' insisted Vikki.

'I want to move to the house on the Mall,' Jane announced quietly. 'The shop is too much for Emmy and me and we don't need it now.'

'I'm glad, Mother. I only wish that it was this side of the town,' said Janey.

'It's but a step,' said Jane. 'What do you say, Emily?'

'You hinted at it Mother, and I hoped you'd decide to go. I like the Mall and it doesn't look as if I shall travel far.' Emily took out her crochet and bent over it.

'You can still do the flowers and we can have little trips together to Portsmouth, sometimes. I shall visit Edward and Alice more and you can come, too. It means that we need never stay at home to mind the shop.'

'I can catch the bus out to Niton to see Nora. She comes in from the farm on market days and pops in to see me but now, I can visit her!' said Emily. She looked up and her eyes were bright. 'I think it will be lovely.'

'And do you want to live there with me?' asked Jane.

'Of course, Mother.' Emily looked startled.

'I'm glad, my dear, but if you ever needed to go away, or if you met a nice young man and wanted to be married, I'd like you to have something to call your own. Janey has Clive and a good living and you shall have two cottages up by Cross Lanes which have good tenants who pay their rent regularly.' She put up a hand to stop Emily speaking. 'I don't know what you'll do with them and I don't want to know. Have the income or sell them and invest the money, but they'll be yours to do with as you wish.'

Janey nodded her approval, and Emily was pink with pleasure. 'And with the flower money, I shall be able to buy nice presents for people,' she said.

'Keep it for a rainy day,' said Janey. 'Just as Mother did when she made pickle money.'

'Oh, Alex came to say goodbye,' remembered Emily. 'He said he'd called at the Lodge and you weren't there.'

'When was this?' asked Janey sharply.

'Yesterday,' said Emily. She looked at her sister. 'He's gone, Janey. We shan't see him for months.'

'Poor Alex,' said Janey. 'I shall miss him.'

'Clive will be here soon and then you'll have eyes for no other,' Emily teased.'

'Alex will miss us too, and now that Millie is dead, I think we help him,' said Janey defensively.

'I think you have helped him,' corrected Emily. 'It's time he made new friends now.' She went to the door to the stairs. 'I think George is awake,' she said. 'Clive will see a big difference in him.'

'I can hardly wait,' said Janey. 'I talk about Clive to the baby every day and show him his picture.'

'I'll fetch him,' said Emily. 'Come on, Vikki, tell me if he needs a clean nappy.'

'Do you mind Emily having the cottages and not you?' Jane asked her eldest daughter as Emily disappeared upstairs. 'I feel guilty but I haven't mentioned it to Lizzie or Clare. They have husbands in good jobs and Emily may never marry.'

Janey hugged her mother. 'Don't tell them, and I'll make sure that Emily doesn't, either. I think it's grand, just grand,' she added cheekily, imitating her mother's accent when excited.

Emily brought the baby down and changed him while Jane prepared the feed, and once more, Vikki held the bottle carefully so that he didn't suck air.

'Talking of good jobs, Mother, I heard on the ship that some people were leaving England because they feared a slump worse than the present unemployment.'

'Not in engineering,' said Jane. 'Not on the railways, and that's what concerns us most. Harry is firmly fixed at Cowes and Alan has a very good job in the midlands.' She laughed. 'I can't see Edward ever doing anything other than being assistant stationmaster and he might even be in charge one day!'

'It was the midlands they were discussing,' said Janey. 'And a place called Jarrow, in the north. They said that people were going hungry there and ex-servicemen were not getting work.'

'But Alan will be all right,' said Jane stoutly. 'You do

think that he will be?'

'He was talking to Harry the last time he was here and they said that marine engines were still needed. I think Harry was trying to impress him as usual and making his job sound more secure than most, but Alan was quiet after Lizzie and Harry left.'

Jane carried the baby to the car and put him in the basket on the floor. A motor cycle engine rent the air and made the baby cry as the young man raced it over the Bridge towards Ryde. 'Silly young things,' said Jane, bending to hush the baby. 'They all bought those machines with the money they had coming out of the army and now they do nothing but scare babies and old people. They should never have been invented.'

'There are a lot up for sale, secondhand,' remarked Janey. 'It isn't easy to pay the rent and to eat with so little money coming in.'

'And we thought that Peace would bring prosperity,' said Jane and went into the shop feeling restless and unhappy. She shrugged. They were all grown up and living their own lives and she had enough to feed them if need be, but she didn't like to think of any of her family losing their pride.

'What did Nellie say?' she asked when Vikki was asleep.

'She sent her love and thanks and said she'd look after Lucy. She gave us some programmes and some sheet music and asked if you liked the gramophone.'

'The gramophone is grand, but what can you do with sheet music now that the harmonium has gone?'

'Could we have a piano when we move house?' asked Emily. 'I loved to hear Father play and often wished I had lessons.'

'You could have lessons. There's a lady on the Mall a few doors away who teaches the piano and we can buy a piano to put in the drawing room.'

'Oh, Mother – thank you! Incidentally, Nellie was anxious to show how grateful she is and said she'd meet Sidney and tell him all about us.'

'I doubt if she'll know much,' said Jane drily. 'Still, she

80

means well, I suppose. How did she look?'

'Very pretty and dressed all in pale blue. Even her fur was dyed blue and her shoes to match. She had some scent that smelled of all the flowers you can imagine and everyone was looking at her.'

'I hope she does look after Lucy,' said Jane. 'With Janey she was safe, but we can't tell how much of Maudie will come out in the girl.'

'Lucy is different,' said Emily with conviction. 'She hated that house in Sea Street and she had very little to do with her mother this last year.'

'Blood tells,' said Jane cryptically. 'I just hope that Lucy isn't expecting too much of America and of Sidney.'

Chapter 7

The throbbing grew louder and Lucy felt the surge of power as the *Mauretania* turned by the Needles and thrust out to sea. The porthole framed the lighthouse for a moment and then there was green water and clouds and more green water. She tried to peer out to the land but she had seen the last of the Island and of England.

The scent of California Poppy made her turn, to see Nellie standing by the cabin trunk, weeping. Her cloche hat was discarded and her hair, flattened by the pressure, lay close to her head as if painted. One kiss-curl was intact but the other stood away from her cheek and the tears threatened to ruin her make-up.

'Oh, Mrs Morris!' cried Lucy and in another moment, they were locked in each other's arms, swaying and shuddering with emotion.

Monty Morris paused in the doorway and coughed. 'I'll pay the purser a visit and see about supper,' he said, retreating hastily. 'They want to see you in an hour,' he warned Nellie as he left.

'I was all right until the streamers broke,' sobbed Nellie. 'It was cruel, and I shall never be able to sing *Should Auld Acquaintance Be Forgot* without crying.'

Lucy patted her back as she would a child and began to recover. 'You'll be better in a minute, Mrs Morris.'

Nellie sat on the bed and wiped her eyes. 'It rubs off on you,' she said with a watery smile. 'You sound like Jane Darwen.' She sniffed and blew her nose into the small lace-edged handkerchief that she had waved when the boat sailed. 'I'm glad you came, Lucy. Monty is impossible when I cry and it's going to be wonderful to have another woman with me.'

'Your husband said you have to see someone in an hour,' reminded Lucy. She pointed to a mahogany table top. 'Is that a sink under there? I saw a picture of one in a magazine.' With more assurance than she had ever felt, Lucy lifted the lid to reveal the neat sink.

'This is your cabin, Lucy, It's small and you'll have to put up with some of my trunks too, but Monty and I will be next door. Come and see.'

Considering that they were on a ship with hundreds of people on board the suite was spacious and comprehensive. Lucy stared about her in a kind of dream and then remembered her responsibilities. 'I'd better do your hair, Mrs Morris,' she said.

'You must call me Nellie, and yes, I do look a mess.'

Lucy unpacked the dressing-case and when Nellie had washed her face and hands, brushed the lustre back into the closely-cut hair, then left Nellie to put fresh cream and powder on before sticking the curving kiss-curls on to each cheek.

'You look lovely,' Lucy said with genuine admiration. 'Tell me what you want to wear.'

'I'll stay as I am as I shall have to change later for the cabaret and this is just a business meeting.' She handed Lucy a map of the ship. 'You'll have to find your own way around for a while. Monty wants me in the lounges to show myself and make sure that people know I am singing tonight. If you want anything, like tea or coffee or a drink, just sign the bill with this cabin number.' She saw Lucy's face. 'Don't worry, it's all in the agreement. We aren't paying, except for things we might buy in the souvenir shops and if I buy clothes or need more face cream.' She looked in her beauty-case. 'Here, take this and see if you can buy some more Larola Rose Bloom and some more Larola Cream.' She gave Lucy five shillings. 'The rouge is a shilling but I'm not sure how much you'll need for the other. Get the biggest jar you can.'

'I didn't know there were shops on board!'

Nellie laughed. 'There's everything here. Beauty parlours, shops and cafés, bars and huge dining rooms. You'll forget that you are on the sea.'

'Shall I come back here?' asked Lucy. 'I don't know what you want yet but I do want to be useful.'

'Don't worry. I shall work you to death,' said Nellie airily. 'Meet us in the Veranda café at half past six and we'll have coffee there.'

Lucy found the Veranda on the map and the shops. She clutched her own purse and took a deep breath as she left the suite. It was frightening and yet wonderful to be alone in the long corridor, to climb the stairs and to linger by the marvellous flower arrangement by the main dining room and to see the glittering display in the small shops, waiting to coax money from the rich travellers.

A couple passed her and gave her a curious glance, and several people were standing on the deck watching the blue line that was all they could see of Home, but Lucy explored and her eyes sparkled. I'm going to see Sidney, and New York and I'm here, on the *Mauretania*!

She stopped at the barrier that separated the first class from the rest of the passengers and her cheeks grew pink. If I'd come on my own and had to pay, I'd have travelled on the other side of that gate, she thought. The people thronging the lower decks looked the same, they talked and laughed and wept according to their moods and their reasons for travelling across the world, but for the first time in her life, Lucy knew what it was like to be treated as if she was entitled to respect.

'Would you like a lounge chair, Miss?' A young steward paused with a couple of soft rugs over one arm.

'No, thank you,' she said with dignity. 'But could you tell me how I find the Veranda café as I am meeting my . . . friends there.'

He walked ahead of her until he could point along to a wide entrance through which she could see cane chairs and soft drapes. Lucy smiled and went in as if she had spent her entire life travelling. She felt self-conscious at first. Being alone was odd when all around her couples and families talked and ignored everyone else, but she pulled the thin gold chain and arranged the marcasite heart on the front of her pale beige dress and it gave her courage.

'You found it!' Monty looked pleased. The girl had class and it had added to Nellie's status to refer to her 'dresser'

84

as an essential member of the team. He rubbed his hands together and asked Lucy what she wanted to drink.

'Tea?' she ventured. He made a wry face and snapped his fingers for the steward. 'Tea for the young lady,' he ordered. 'And a whisky for me, with soda.' He looked at Nellie.

'I'll have tea, too,' she said. Monty looked surprised. 'I'll have wine later, and gin will only make me depressed,' she said, laughing. 'Lucy will be a good example and I shall keep my schoolgirl complexion longer if I stay off liquor.'

'I intend making the most of it,' said Monty. 'Remember, there's Prohibition in New York and this might be the last chance I'll have of a decent drink.'

'It will do you good to be dry,' said Nellie.

'Sufficient to the day!' he said piously, and winked at Lucy. 'They sell a good line in one of the shops here. Two, in fact. Good thing that walking sticks are fashionable or I'd have to pretend to an old war wound and limp.' He picked up the stout walking stick from behind his rattan chair and unscrewed the ebony handle. The hollow stick was empty. 'It holds more than you'd think and I'll fill it before we dock. I'll fill this flask, too. See, it fits snugly in this holder under one arm and nobody would know I had it.'

Lucy giggled. 'It's like a gun-holster that the gangsters wear. I saw pictures in one of the movie magazines.'

'Be careful, Monty. If they frisk you and find it, you could be in trouble,' warned Nellie.

Monty raised his eyebrows. 'Now who is talking American? Frisk? I didn't know that ladies knew such a word.' He was in great good humour and knew that America would love Nellie. 'Have a cake or something, Lucy,' he suggested. 'Dinner will be very late for us as Nellie has to sing first to the other diners, but in America, you'll find that people do eat later than we do at home, so get used to it.'

He called the waiter and asked for cream cakes and Nellie smiled as Lucy ate two with all the pleasure and hunger of a slim child.

Nellie lit a Sobranie cigarette and watched Lucy through the curling blue smoke. Maybe she would be useful in more ways than one. 'You are very nice to me,' said Lucy shyly.

'You don't know me,' Monty said and grinned. 'I can be a mean so-and-so when I like, but if you have any problem, any trouble, come straight back to Nellie or me at once.'

'What sort of problem?' Lucy looked wide-eyed. She was on a liner taking her to the man she had loved since she was a small child. What possible trouble could she meet?

Monty looked at the slim almost boyish figure with the gentle curves and the delicate, near-translucent skin of her cheeks. He picked up his glass. 'Just remember what I said Lucy, and you'd better call me Uncle Monty.' He glanced at Nellie who nodded. 'We don't want to meet trouble halfway so drink up or your tea will be cold.'

Lucy sighed with contentment. It was like having a family who cared about her. 'Everyone looks so smart,' she said, gazing about her in wonder. The cane chairs were now full, with people taking tea or coffee, and most of the men drinking as Monty did, and talking in loud voices as the whisky brightened their thoughts. One or two men eyed Lucy with interest but Monty's basilisk stare made them turn away uneasily.

Nellie saw the interchange, and as soon as she went off to dress for her first cabaret act, leaving Monty talking to a couple at the next table, she locked the cabin door and stripped off her dress. 'Did you leave a friend behind?' she asked.

Lucy folded the dress carefully and laid it on the bed. 'I'll press it before I hang it up,' she said. 'Friends? Oh, yes, I shall miss them very much. Janey has been so good to me and all the Darwens; and girls I went to school with gave me a nice scarf when I came away.'

'Lucy, you're a big girl! I mean men friends.'

'Men?' Lucy pushed the hat-box on to the top shelf above the bed near the porthole.

'A special friend, a sweetheart,' continued Nellie.

'Of course not.' Lucy fingered the crimson heart at her throat. 'I dance with boys and sometimes we have picnics with Janey and Clive and some of his friends. That's nice, but I'm going to find Sidney,' she said. 'He sent me this.'

Nellie turned on the taps and soaked her sponge in warm water, then washed under her arms and breasts, quite unselfconsciously. 'Hand me that towel,' she requested. 'Has he said he wants you?' she asked abruptly. 'Did he ask you to come?'

'No, but he sent his love and Clare gave me this pendant and said he sent it for me.' Lucy tossed her head and thrust away the doubts she had at times. 'In any case, I wanted to work for you, Nellie, and see the world.'

'My advice is to hold back a little, Lucy. Men hate women who throw themselves at them.' She laughed, seeing the growing distress. 'It pays. They like to make the running and they are more keen if they have to chase.'

'I see,' said Lucy. She brushed Nellie's hair with vigour. 'I've known Sidney all my life and he's always been fond of me. Now I'm grown up and I know he hasn't a sweetheart in America, so why not me? I shall see him and be with him and that is enough.'

'Even if he doesn't love you?'

'He does love me.' Lucy spoke calmly. 'If he doesn't, then I shall make him.' She sighed. 'I know he sees beautiful girls all the time now. He might have changed. Sometimes I wonder . . . but I have to see him. You do understand, don't you, Nellie?'

'I understand. Now hand me that slip or I'll be arrested if I don't wear it under that dress!' Nellie powdered her body with scented talcum powder and gave the long-handled swansdown powder puff to Lucy to do her back.

Lucy was glad when Monty led her to a table at the back of the dining room in a dark corner. All the women were smartly dressed and she felt like a schoolgirl in her plain frock, but when she remarked to Monty about the clothes on a woman nearer the band, he said, 'Tonight they aren't dressed up as it's the first night on board. You wait until tomorrow! Fashion plates and peacocks!' He regarded her with amusement. 'You needn't worry. Most of the women are old hags who need two coats of paint to make them presentable and they'd give their back teeth, if they've still got them, for your complexion.'

'But that lady is wearing a costume that must have cost a fortune!'

'Probably,' he said, and shrugged. His gaze followed Nellie as she went into her routine, warming the audience, singing and dancing and making her manner never vulgar, never too much directed to the men and always with humour and style. He chuckled. 'She's got them in the palm of her hand,' he said. 'America, here we come!'

Nellie slid between the tables and inclined her head to the prolonged applause, then sat in the shadows with Monty and Lucy, while the laughter and noise grew and she could relax for her own dinner.

Lucy was tired. The smoke from a hundred cigarettes made the air stifling and she was hungry.

'Food,' said Monty and took the large menu from the waiter. Lucy was handed one and she gasped. 'Choose what you want,' he said kindly.

'Do they have all this in the kitchen?' Lucy looked up anxiously. 'I don't know what it means. It isn't written in English.'

'It's sheer snobbery,' said Nellie. 'They do this to confuse us and I've had to learn some French to manage in restaurants. I'll lend you a phrase book, Lucy. You ought to be able to read a menu.'

'This is fish and this is meat,' said Monty. 'Do you like crab? Or would you rather have a steak? Or both?'

'What are you having, Nellie?' Lucy asked shyly.

'Melon and then grilled salmon,' decided Nellie. 'Salad and no potatoes.'

'That sounds lovely,' said Lucy. 'But you didn't read the menu.'

'There's always salmon and melon and salad and if not, I just look as if there should be,' confided Nellie. 'It takes the snooty waiters down a peg.'

88

'Could I have that and some potatoes?' asked Lucy.

'Lucky Lucy!' said Monty. 'And I suppose you'll eat more than we two put together!'

White wine appeared, wrapped in a spotless napkin and then placed in a silver ice-bucket and Lucy ate until she could eat no more. One or two people came to say how much they'd enjoyed Nellie's singing and Lucy drank in the atmosphere as if in a dream.

'If I'm to parade round the ship in the morning looking fresh, I need sleep,' Nellie yawned at last. 'You do, too, Lucy,' and as soon as Lucy sank into her narrow berth, she fell asleep. The motion of the ship was soothing and she was completely happy, but at dawn, the ship began to roll and toss and from the next room Lucy heard Monty swearing and moaning.

Lucy washed and dressed and tapped timidly on the door to the big cabin. Nellie called, 'Come in' and then bent over her husband once more. 'I've rung for the stewardess and he's feeling a bit better now he's been sick,' she said.

'What can I do to help?' asked Lucy.

'Keep his head cool with this sponge while I dress.' Nellie stepped out of her dressing-gown and swiftly washed and put on a warm skirt and smart blouse with a long thick cardigan over it. Lucy wiped the sweating forehead and clammy hands and wondered if she would be sea-sick, too, but there was no sign of it yet.

'Good. You'll know what to do,' said Nellie with a ravishing smile, as the dumpy little stewardess came in, carrying fresh towels and a tray of remedies. The girl smiled, and Nellie pressed a coin into her hand. 'I'm going to the dining room with my dresser,' she said. 'Look after him, won't you?'

'Are you sure we ought to leave him?' asked Lucy anxiously.

'Quite sure.' Nellie laughed. 'It's her job to cope with sea-sick passengers. I might be queasy later, but I doubt it. I was fine the last time I was on a big boat and it was rough.' She noted with satisfaction the bloom on Lucy's face. 'Sea-sickness sometimes runs in families. Were your parents safe on a boat?'

'I don't know,' said Lucy. 'My mother is, or so she says, but she never goes far. I never knew my father as he was killed in the Boer War.'

Nellie watched her as she ate. Ben Dove might have been Maudie's husband but rumour had it that even when they were married and long before Lucy was born, Maudie had been fascinated by the boats from Scandinavia that brought timber and blonde sailors to the River Medina. Nellie smiled. Vikings were sailors and Lucy showed no sign of discomfort. 'I'm glad you came,' said Nellie. 'Monty will be fine in a day or so, but I shall need company.'

The cabin smelled stale and sour and the stewardess seemed to prefer to have her patient to herself, so Nellie took Lucy on deck and to the shops. 'Wrap up warm,' she said. 'The wind is up and it might be cold, but if we can find a sheltered spot we can have some beef-tea up there later.' She yawned. 'We'll get a couple of chaises longues and rugs and be quite snug. I could do with a nap as Monty was groaning half the night.'

The chairs were mostly stacked as many of the passengers were sick, and it was easy to find a spot away from the wind and the smuts from the funnels. The four huge funnels seemed even taller and broader now that Lucy saw them at close quarters. The whole ship was immense, and snuggled down under the thick rug with a mug of hot bouillon by her side, she felt pampered and happy. A few people walked the decks and the air was fresh after being below.

'Go where you like and meet me for lunch, at one in the smaller restaurant,' murmured Nellie who was half-asleep.

Lucy luxuriated until the hot broth was gone and then felt stifled under the rug. She slipped away and buttoned up the thick jacket of blue melton cloth and pulled on a close-fitting hat. The deck took all kinds of odd angles as she walked, but it was exhilarating and fun. Two children slid from side to side and giggled, chased by their nanny who looked slightly green, and Lucy noticed a man watching her and smiling at her obvious pleasure.

She went down to the clothes shop she had noticed and gazed at the expensive and pretty garments. In her purse she had the ten pounds that Jane Darwen had given her but she had enough sense to know that these clothes were far too over-priced and that she could do better in New York. She dreamed of what she would buy, making mental notes of what was now fashionable. Janey could look at a new style, remember it and then make it up at home for a fraction of what it would have cost. I wish she was here, thought Lucy, and for the first time a pang of homesickness swept over her.

She groped for her handkerchief and wiped her eyes. The shops suddenly looked less bright. She turned away and walked along to the Veranda café, where she felt more at home and sat by the window.

'Coffee, Miss?' She looked up, startled, then nodded. Nellie had said, half-joking, that she must get used to drinking coffee in America. It arrived in a silver pot with a small jug of cream and a dish of brown sugar crystals. The cup was thin and elegant and bore the motif of the Cunard line on the saucer. She poured a cup, more for the novelty than because she was thirsty and sipped it, enjoying the new experience.

At the next table, she dimly saw a man who seemed familiar. She glanced up. Yes, she recognised his shoes. She smiled, faintly. Who could forget them? She had seen similar ones in newspapers and remembered that they were called 'correspondent's' shoes; they were white and black in shiny leather and laced with wide silk bows. The man's suit was well-cut and his silk tie was slightly brighter than any worn even by Monty, who favoured colour. The man smoothed back his brilliantined hair when he saw that Lucy had noticed him and smiled, showing white teeth under a neat moustache.

Lucy looked away and shifted slightly in her chair so that she could no longer see him. He had been on deck, strolling past Nellie and her and then again by the shops.

Men had tried to get into conversation with her on several occasions but her aloof manner usually discouraged them, and she had no time for lounge lizards, as Clare called men who dressed in this way.

She glanced at the clock on the wall. Nellie would be ready for lunch in a quarter of an hour. She left the table and had to pass the man who now openly stared at her.

With downcast eyes, she made her way out on to the windy deck and hurried to find Nellie, who looked relaxed and rested. 'I wondered if you would be awake,' said Lucy.

'I feel wonderful. Let's pop down to see how Monty is feeling and then have lunch. I'm starving.'

Nellie noticed the man who was now leaning on the railing. 'Monty doesn't like those shoes,' she whispered. 'They wear them a lot in America but they're too flashy. He probably owns a speakeasy or a pool-room.' She swept past him with Lucy in her wake, and he tossed his cigarette butt into the ocean and followed them.

Monty was still groaning but looked better. The cabin had been tidied up and the porthole opened to let in the fresh air. The idea of eating made him turn pale again, so Nellie hastily left him with the promise to come back to talk to him after he'd had another nap.

'He'll be fine tomorrow,' she told Lucy. The dining room was half-empty and they lingered over the meal, with Nellie talking about places she had visited and people she had met.

'I'd be frightened to speak to a film star,' confessed Lucy.

'They are human just like you and me,' said Nellie comfortably. 'All you want is a bit of nerve and a pretty face and that will get you anywhere.' She laughed. 'Sidney Darwen will be a star if this revue of his is a success. You'd better make sure of him before the Broadway vampires get at him!'

'Now that I'm here, I am a bit scared,' said Lucy. 'I shall come over all shy when I see him.'

'That's a novelty in his profession!' said Nellie. 'Stay as

you are and you'll have half the stage-door Johnnies grovelling at your feet.'

'I'm not in the theatre,' protested Lucy.'

'Oh, yes you are. As my dresser you will be there for hours each day, and be seen with me wherever I go. I may not look shy but I can be much more secure if I have company. I need you Lucy, and I hope you stay with me.'

'I agreed to stay for a year if you want me,' said Lucy.

'I may have to remind you of that,' said Nellie. She saw the man with the too-smooth hair watching them. 'Be careful in New York, Lucy. Men are beasts at times. Have fun and dance with them, talk to them but never be alone with men like that one over there who looks as if he wants you for dessert.'

'You are funny,' said Lucy, and her innocent laughter made Nellie feel far too experienced and world-weary.

'Go and do what all horribly young and healthy girls do on ships. Play shuffleboard or something and be back at the suite by five. We are having cocktails with the ship's doctor and first officer at six, before my turn. If Monty can't come, you'll have to be with me.' She saw that Lucy looked scared. 'I'll lend you something to wear. Don't worry. All men are alike under their clothes and some uglier than others.' She laughed. 'Clothes do make a difference but look beyond them every time, Lucy. Look at their eyes; and the mouth gives away a lot.'

'I'll pretend I'm acting a part,' said Lucy. 'In a way, I am. This can't be the same girl who looked after little George and mended socks and ironed. I am in a different world, Nellie.'

'You still have to iron and mend,' said Nellie drily.

'It's not the same,' answered Lucy.

'More difficult pressing crêpe-de-chine than cotton,' Nellie insisted.

Lucy went along to the library to find something to read and took Nellie's French phrase-book with her. She looked at the good selection of new books and saw that they were as good as the choice in the subscription library where Mrs Barnes got her reading matter.

There were books by authors whose names meant nothing to Lucy but she found a Nick Carter detective story and was soon deep in drama, suspense and the cosy conviction that Nick Carter never used swear words, respected all women and didn't smoke, drink or lie.

Sidney was like that, she thought. He didn't run after girls, but one day he had to find the right one. She turned to the last page, hoping that in this tale, Nick Carter would find real romance, but no, he was still pure and unsullied, and suddenly boring.

The heap of magazines on the glass-topped table was tempting, although she had every intention of studying French. *True Romance*, *Love Story Magazine* and others offered a choice of similar themes, where the heroine found love and romance, in the best of taste and with an incorruptible man. Lucy sighed. The stories were beautiful and just as she imagined love to be. Another stack contained issues of American magazines, like *Ladies' Home Journal* at ten cents a month. Lucy frowned. American money was different and she must learn about it. There would be so much to learn in a new country. Ten cents? How much was that in English money?

She put the book back on the shelf and looked at the notice-board which told of events on board. There were bridge parties and competitions, contests in the billiard rooms for men and shuffleboard on deck. A fancy-dress ball would be held on the last night before docking and each night a cocktail party entertained sections of the passengers.

Nellie had told her some of the names of the drinks offered there, but Lucy was still completely confused. Cider and ale and the occasional glass of sherry wine had been the extent of her alcoholic education. She walked out and found the sun shining. The wind had died and more people, looking slightly fragile, walked the decks. A girl of her own age came along and smiled. 'I'm Dulcie Weinberg,' she said with a pronounced American accent. 'You alone, too? My parents are sick and I'm bored. Come and play on deck.'

'I'm Lucy Dove,' said Lucy. She followed the girl who seemed to take it for granted that she would do so, and played shuffleboard with her and four other young men and women. Lucy concentrated and won and everyone laughed and insisted that they should go down to one of the bars to drink to her win. Lucy found herself swept along with them but refused to drink anything but lemonade and looked at the clock, anxiously.

'Got a date?' asked Dulcie.

'No, but I have to meet someone at five to get ready for the cocktail party,' she replied. 'I'm with Nellie Morris.'

One of the boys gave a long, low sigh. 'She's gorgeous.' He eyed Lucy with interest. 'Do you sing, too?'

'No they've . . . brought me along to visit a friend in New York. Uncle Monty said I could help Nellie on the voyage and be company for her.' Somehow, with these obviously rich young people, she couldn't bring herself to say she was Nellie's dresser.

'See you at the party,' said Dulcie. 'And, say . . . are you going as something dramatic to the ball?'

'I don't know,' said Lucy. She escaped. How could she go to a fancy-dress ball when she had no idea what to wear and how to find a costume? But she longed to join her new friends and envied their easy manners and effortless humour. She hurried back to Nellie and passed the man in the black and white shoes again. He seemed to appear wherever she was. When she was playing shuffleboard he had been there, smoking and leaning on the rail.

'Monty is better but not up to parties,' said Nellie firmly. 'You'll have to come with me and learn to make small talk.' She laughed. 'Don't look so frightened. Just be natural and let men talk about themselves. They love that, and even if you don't say much, they'll think you intelligent. It never fails.'

She opened the wardrobe and threw a gown on to the bed. 'Take this away and fit it on. It should be your size. It's tight on me and I was going to give it away so you might as well have it.'

The pale green silk was soft and flowing into a series of

points over a satin underslip. The low waist was trimmed with rosebuds and the neckline was modest but the thin material suggested a lot more. 'It's lovely. I'll take great care of it, Nellie.'

'It will be useful, but don't worry if someone spills wine on it. It's yours now and I've plenty more.' She asked for her face cream and rouge and Lucy watched as the delicate blush appeared under the fine bloom of peach powder, and Nellie outlined her lips with pink salve.

'You are clever,' said Lucy, as she fastened the many tiny buttons at the back of the lavender dress. 'I couldn't put on rouge and make it look natural.'

'You don't need it yet, but you should learn as there might be a time when you feel unwell and have to look blooming!' Nellie made a face at her perfect reflection and brushed a speck of face-powder from her shoulder.

'You really are sure you can't come, dear?' asked Nellie. Monty turned away. 'Have a sleep and I'll tell you all about it in the morning. Lucy will keep me company and watch the show and we'll stay on for dinner and not disturb you.' She turned round so that Lucy could drape the heavily-fringed shawl round her shoulders and then gave Lucy a pretty beaded jacket to wear over the dress.

'It's lovely,' breathed Lucy.

'You'll wear out those words.' Nellie laughed. 'It's refreshing to find someone who hasn't seen and done everything.' And it's a miracle that she is like she is, coming from Sea Street and that awful tenement, she thought privately. Vikki would be fortunate to have such a loving and good background and to grow up in innocence. The Darwens had gone all this for Lucy and would do even more for Vikki.

An alien sensation bordering on maternal tenderness made Nellie smooth a tress of hair that fell from the band round the girl's head. It was good to have her with them.

A burst of music from the Victrola in the corner of the salon and laughter and polite murmurs of introduction met them at the door. Nellie paused, waiting for someone to come forward to introduce her to the officers giving the party, and she was ushered in with courtesy, as word had spread that she was not an ordinary cabaret artiste but had a contract for the American stage and nightclubs. She was also very pretty and vivacious and heads turned as one after another, people spoke to her and told her how much they were looking forward to her next performance.

Lucy stood back but stayed near and watched the faces. Such different faces. She had never seen so much make-up on women before now and as for the men, they had hard expensive expressions as if money was everything and human kindness came last.

Dulcie and two of the young men from the morning edged near. 'Come and join us,' said Dulcie. 'My, you look pretty, Lucy. Where did you get that dress?'

'Uncle Monty is sick and I said I'd stay with Nellie,' said Lucy with a slightly nervous glance at Nellie. 'I'll try to see you later.'

They drifted away and she longed to be with them. A man with a silk cravat and elegant matching handkerchief in the top pocket of his suit took her hand and squeezed it. 'What a pretty little thing you are,' he said with a hint of condescension. 'With the cabaret, are you?'

'No, I'm travelling under the care of Uncle Monty, but I am not on the stage,' she said, and removed her hand.

She turned away and found herself staring into the face of the man she had seen so often on the ship. He smiled but made no attempt to touch her. 'May I fetch you a cocktail?' he asked.

Lucy gave an agonised glance towards Nellie who was lost in the centre of a group of men. Nellie was laughing softly in a muted, throaty, intimate way and the men were loving it.

'I don't know what to drink,' said Lucy. 'Something cold and lemony if they have it. Lemonade would be nice,' she added without much hope, as the tiny, funnel-shaped glasses she saw were filled with brightly-coloured liquids and had olives and other strange things floating in them.

'I'll do my best,' he said. His accent was American but softer than some she had heard. It was almost sibilant and she felt reassured. His hair looked as if it had been polished and his eyes were hooded with heavy lids, but she felt safer with him than with the man who had tried to hold her hand.

'Try this.' She took the glass and admired the pale colour and the trace of sugar on the rim under a curl of lemon.

'It's pretty,' she said and sipped. He watched her face as she sipped again and smiled. 'It's delicious.' She drained the glass.

'More?' he said.

'Please.' He smiled and took her glass. The first sensation of timidity left her and she was aware of a deep and growing warmth as the people around her lost their hard edges.

Nellie glanced back and saw her. She left the group and came towards Lucy just as the man brought the second drink. Nellie took it from him and sniffed. 'You worm,' she said softly. 'If you so much as look at this girl again, my husband will throw you to the fishes.'

'But it's delicious,' protested Lucy.

'So it is,' said Nellie. She poured the liquid into the base of a potted palm. 'Now, come with me and have some fresh orange juice that I asked the steward to prepare for us both.' Lucy looked round at the man, who now tapped a cigarette on the back of a gold case. His face was a mask that gave away nothing and he went to the far end of the room and disappeared.

'I can see that you need me,' said Nellie. 'Cocktails are poison. They make you drunk quickly and ruin your looks. You can never be sure what is in them and with men like that, it's usually something very strong to make you an easy prey. Who is he? Did he say? You haven't made any arrangements to meet him, have you?' Nellie sounded shrill.

'His name is Frank Garsey,' said Lucy. 'He asked me to look him up in New York.' She sounded sulky. The liquor was not so nice now and she wanted to belch but it wouldn't be polite.

'More likely Franco Garcia with a complexion like that,' Nellie sniffed. She looked anxious. 'You are going to bed, young lady. There was more in that drink than even I thought.' She led Lucy to the door and asked the steward to fetch the stewardess from the cabin.

'Take Miss Dove back to her room and make sure she locks the door,' she requested quietly. 'Keep an eye on her.' She gave the woman a generous tip and went back smiling, ready for more flattering conversation, and to forget Lucy, Monty and everything but her role as entertainer.

Chapter 8

'Clive is coming home!' Emily rushed into the shop to tell her mother. 'I met Janey in the High Street and she's so excited she couldn't drive the motor today, so she walked up and is coming here on her way back.'

'It's time he had leave,' said Jane. 'With Lucy gone to America and the house as she likes it, Janey has far too little to do. George is a good baby and there's no reason why they can't go away and leave him with us for a few days. They need time together.' She tidied her work-basket and went up to change her skirt.

Emily made tea and when Janey came in, pushing George in his perambulator, Jane was ready to hear the news. 'He says that he will have three weeks. Three whole weeks, Mother! It's the most we've ever had together. He wants to get to know his son and to relish being at home.'

Jane said nothing about taking George, but smiled. That could come later when the first rush of domesticity had faded. After a week, Clive might be glad to leave his lively little son for a while and rediscover his pretty wife. 'Has he heard from Alex?' she asked.

'Alex is still in the Mediterranean. He can't get back for short leaves, so he spends them in North Africa and Italy.' Janey frowned. 'I wish he could come here, too. Clive misses him and I think he's still unhappy.'

'He'll find himself again,' said Jane. 'Men do.'

Janey swallowed her hot tea and went to buy fruit in the shop. 'There's no need,' Jane told her. 'You never take anything, unlike Lizzie, and you know you're welcome to anything you see.'

'I like to keep things straight,' said Janey. 'What will poor Lizzie do now that you are giving up everything? First the fish and now fruit and vegetables! Clive will be able to help you move.'

'No! You are not to suggest it. If I want strong arms, there are plenty who will be glad to earn a little and Dan will see it all goes smoothly.' She thought of the men who lined up for dole money and eyed the more prosperous of the townsfolk with bitterness. 'It's only right that those who have enough should make work for the others.' The shabby clothes and thin bodies of people who had once held their heads high, tugged at her heart. The children who she knew had little to eat broke her heart, and she spent more and more on the good ingredients for the soup she took to the Chapel each day.

'It's not as bad here as it is in some of the big factory towns, they say.' Janey weighed up apples and added the amount to her list. 'I heard that another big engineering firm was laying off men in Wales and that men working in the mines were talking of going on strike.'

'Trouble, just when we thought it was all over!' Jane lamented. 'And poor old Ireland is in the news again.' She shook her head and her eyes were dark with painful memories. 'Ireland will give trouble for ever. We have memories that are too long for our own good and people will never forget the English bringing in the Black and Tans.' She sighed. 'There's blame on both sides and stupid arrogant pride, and it costs the lives of men who should be brothers, not flying at each other in war.'

'If they get independence, there will be peace,' suggested Emily.

'I hope so,' said her mother, 'but the Irish are a race apart. I should know.' She no longer felt the hurt of parting with her family when they had made it clear that she was not welcome if she married an English soldier, but she was sad to think that nothing had changed. 'Have you everything you need, Janey? Clive likes your cooking, but you mustn't spend all your time in the kitchen.'

Janey smiled, showing the dimples that still made her look very young. 'No, I'll not be in the kitchen for long, Mother. There are other places.' She hugged her mother. 'I can't wait to be with him. You of all people know how I feel.'

'I do. Be happy and if you need anything, send for me to take George. Bring Clive down later but we shall leave you alone until you want us.'

Janey walked back, pushing the baby carriage as if it weighed no more than a pound of feathers, even though George was heavy and the fruit and vegetables made the springs sag. She hummed to herself and put George into his cot then sorted out her groceries and chopped vegetables for soup. A bird made a warning cry outside the window and she started, then went back to her cooking as the bird flew away. She looked out of the front window, past the thick laurel hedge, wiping her hands on her apron and brushing back her untidy hair with a floury hand, but there was no familiar footstep on the gravel path.

The soup simmered gently and the lamb chops were ready, sprinkled with rosemary and pepper. The fruit bowl of cut-glass held an enticing arrangement and on the sideboard was a bottle of French wine and glasses. The soup could be warmed up and the rest could be cooked now or hours later and she now hoped that he had missed the boat and would give her time to make herself presentable.

'I could have met the boat with the motor,' she murmured, but Clive had insisted that she wait at home as it wasn't certain when he would arrive, and she was used to the vagaries of the Navy and the fact that Clive would have to do what was decreed, even if it meant his wife waiting for hours for news.

George was sound asleep and the front door unlocked in case Clive came while she was upstairs. Janey ran warm water into the bath that still gave her pleasure and made her feel luxurious. After the wash-stands at home, it was like living in a palace, she often said, and urged Jane to have a real bathroom installed before she went to live on the Mall. Just to turn on a tap and see the water gush without having to fill a bath brought in from the outhouse was heaven. She sank into the water and soaped her body. Her hair hung down and was wet, so she decided to wash that while she was lying in the water. I must smell sweet and hair gets all the odours of the kitchen, she decided, so she took her time and emerged, clean and smelling of lavender, with her head swathed in a towel.

She pulled the dressing gown from its hook and gave an annoyed tug at the cord. George was crying. It was early for his feed but he was becoming hungrier each day and once he opened his mouth to protest, nothing would stop it but food.

Janey changed his nappy and went to the kitchen to fetch his food. Her hair was still wet and she was just warm enough in the thick old dressing-gown that belonged to Clive but which made him seem close when she wore it. George smelled her warm body and tried to snuggle closer to take the breast but she held him away and soon he accepted the spoon. Even now, when feeding him like this, she could feel the urge to give him the breast. I want another baby, she thought. I'm like Mother. I love to have a baby at my breast.

She rocked the child and he burped loudly, then smiled. She hugged him close and made him sleepy, then heard a sound at the door of the nursery.

Clive stood leaning against the white painted wood. His smart naval uniform made him seem even more handsome than she remembered. Janey blushed deeply. 'How long have you been there?' she asked. 'I thought I'd be ready for you. Please don't look at me. My hair is still wet.'

He came and took his son in his arms, and laughed. 'Where is the baby I left? You have been deceiving me, woman! This is a monster.' A bubble of milk formed and and fell from George's mouth and dribbled over the navy serge but Clive didn't notice. 'Yes you have deceived me, Janey. You didn't tell me you were even more beautiful.'

He put the child back in the cot and tucked him in. Janey hung her head. The exquisite dread of her nakedness made her shy and when he took away the towel and ran his fingers through her thick wet hair, she gasped.

He kissed her as if he had needed her for a very long time. His hands were gentle but irresistible and he carried her to their bed and undresssed, shedding his rank and

103

becoming husband and lover, with a passion and reverence that made them complete.

'The soup!' cried Janey as they lay relaxed and spent.

'I turned it off,' he said calmly. 'I heard you talking up here and thought I'd surprise you with your lover before we ate.' He kissed the lobe of her ear. 'And what did I find? My rival locked in your arms.'

Janey looked up. He was half-serious. She sat up and dragged on the gown, then stopped. George was asleep and there was no real need to go to him now as she had intended. Suddenly she recalled the jealousy her own father had shown if Jane was absorbed in a new baby and had less time for him.

'It's been so long,' she whispered, and bent to kiss Clive on the lips. 'You see that your son is still breathing while I dress and prepare a meal for my lover.'

Clive laughed. 'I'll open the wine. It's time I came home and found out all your other vices.' He was singing softly when he came down to the kitchen and he had found old clothes in which he felt comfortable. 'It smells good and I'm ravenous.' He hugged her from behind, cupping her breasts with his hands.

'If you want soup that isn't burned, you'll open the wine,' said Janey sternly. Her hair was dry and curling and she felt limp with fulfilment. She gave a roguish smile when he was safely engaged with the corkscrew. 'We don't need wine,' she said.

'We have three weeks together and I want you all to myself,' he said. The cork came out with a plop. 'With the baby, too, of course,' he added.

'There's a lot to be done here,' said Janey as they finished the chops. 'I want your advice on so many things.' Clive looked pleased, and she realised more and more that he might have come home and thought he wasn't needed.

'We must take some time for ourselves, though.' She glanced at him from under her unruly newly-dried hair. 'Is it very wicked of me to want George out of the way for a few days?' Clive looked startled. 'Say if you think we should have him here all the time, but just for a few days, I want my husband to myself,' Janey smiled. 'Mother and Emily love him and would have him there if I asked them.'

'Not yet,' Clive protested, but the tense lines of his face softened. 'We have had a gruelling time at sea,' he confessed. 'I'll get to know my son and then you shall have me all to yourself and we'll walk across Tennyson Down and Afton and along the beaches and make love.'

'Not at the same time,' she teased him. 'Just let me know when you've had enough of one howling baby.'

'He's crying now,' said Clive, and left the table to fetch him.

'You'll spoil him if you go to him each time,' said Janey.

'At least he stopped and I think he likes me.'

'So he should. I hold up your picture every day for him to see and tell him it's Daddy.'

'He's smiling.' Clive sat with the child on his knee while Janey cleared away and left the dirty dishes for the girl to wash when she came in during the evening to clear up the kitchen. 'We'll take him for a walk,' said Clive. 'Up the Mall and you shall show me where your mother is going to live.'

'That's quite a long way.'

'We'll stop on the way back and see your mother. She'll give us a cup of tea.'

Janey smiled to herself. He was doing everything she wanted but thought that the ideas were his own. I'm learning, she thought. 'What happened at sea?' she asked later when they were walking with the perambulator and George was sitting up in his blue coat and hat, with a leather harness to stop him falling out.

'There are still hundreds of mines in the Channel that the mine-sweepers are trying to find and blow up. Two small fishing boats caught them in their nets and all hands were lost, only last month.'

'But the war has been over now for nearly three years!' exclaimed Janey.

'The recent storms have thrown up a lot of mines that were on the sea-bed and there are still a vast number floating out into the Atlantic and North Sea.'

'I'm glad that Lucy got to America safely,' she said. 'We had a letter when she arrived but nothing since and that was a long time ago. I hope she hasn't been disappointed.'

'In what way?' Clive bowed slightly to a friend of his family who smiled at the baby.

'She was set on meeting Sidney and she thinks she's in love with him.'

Clive gave a short laugh. 'Bad luck, little Lucy.'

'What do you mean? You haven't seen Sidney for years and even then you didn't know him well. He might be just the man for Lucy – an old friend and a pretty girl at that.'

'He never had lady friends here, did he?'

'He had lots of friends,' said Janey, slightly annoyed. 'Sidney was popular wherever he went and the girls hung on every word.'

'He'll make a good matinée idol,' said Clive. 'But I doubt if he's the marrying kind.' He saw that Janey was worried. 'They'll sort out their own lives, darling. Don't bother your pretty head with things you don't understand.'

'I understand about love and marriage,' said Janey.

'Yes, you are the answer to every dream a real man could have.'

'And you think that Sidney isn't a real man? Don't be silly, Clive.' She laughed and changed the subject, pointing out the shop where she bought the best and most expensive groceries. 'It will be handy for Mother, but I think Mr Foster would be very hurt if she patronised anyone but him.'

'He can deliver, can't he?'

'Yes, he does have a lad with a basket on a bicycle, but he won't have a van and that makes it difficult to cover a wide area. Annie Cooper wanted him to deliver but you know how mean she is. Her order isn't worth the trouble but Mr Foster does it because of Bert. They are hand-in-glove in lots of council affairs.'

'Is Bert helping your mother without cheating her?'

'Yes, and I'm really surprised how well they get on now. When my father died, Bert seemed to change as if he owed us something more than just his friendship with my father. He's suggested a lot of improvements to the shop in case Mother sells it and he says he will find the buyer. I know he makes an effort to help and I don't think it's just because Annie is ill and needs us more.'

They reached the house on the Mall and Janey produced a key. 'Mother gave us each a key in case we wanted to go in to measure something.' She smiled. 'When Lizzie saw the house, she soon said she didn't need a key as there was nothing for her in the garden at this time of the year.' He nodded. 'I come here sometimes with George just to give the house something of us. Houses do absorb something from the people who live there, and I want Mother to be happy.'

'If our happiness influences it, then come on and show me all the house,' said Clive. 'When I stepped into our Lodge today, I knew you were there. I knew I had come home and that I wanted to stay for ever.' They were in the hall. Clive closed the front door and put the brake on the baby carriage where it stood on the bare boards. He kissed Janey gently. 'When I am away, don't let my memory fade, Janey. Wherever I am I want to think of you there, whatever happens.'

She clung to him. 'I'll be waiting whenever you come home and someday you will have a job on shore and come home like normal working men.'

'I can't see that far ahead,' he replied soberly. 'Now – what's this room going to be?'

Janey wrinkled her nose. 'The new linoleum has come. Oh, it is pretty, and I suppose the smell will fade before the furniture arrives. This is the morning room where Mother will have breakfast and do sewing and mending. She chose a nice warm Turkish rug for the floor and they've made a good job of the wallpaper.' She ran a finger over the crimson flocked wallpaper and sighed. 'She'll spend all her time in here and forget that she has a lovely drawing room.'

'And where does my son sleep when I come on leave and take you away?'

'There'll be room. It wouldn't matter how many

children we had, Mother would make room for them and welcome them all. She loves babies.'

'Just as well.' Clive took her hand. 'When we go down to the Bridge, I shall ask your mother to take George for a day or so. Suddenly three weeks seems a very short time.' The lines that she had erased from his face now came back. 'So little time, Janey.' He hugged her almost roughly. 'Tomorrow, I want to feel free and we'll take a picnic to the Downs. I don't care if it rains or snows, I want to feel the downland under my feet and smell the scent of the gorse.'

'We ought to go now,' she said, drawing away from his arms. 'We may leave George but he still needs to be fed at very frequent intervals. I wrapped a full bottle in a napkin and I can warm it up at the shop, and he can have an egg, too.'

Janey locked the door behind them and they walked back down the High Street, making slow progress, as one after another, friends stopped them to say hello to Clive and to make very unwelcome advances to the baby who was wet and hungry and didn't care for faces thrust at him without warning, or fingers prodding his ribs.

'If we go down Quay Street we shall avoid Foster's shop,' said Janey. 'We can cut through the lane at the back of the stables and not have to stop again.'

Boats were being loaded on the quay and the smell of newly-milled timber came from the sheds as the men stacked the wooden planks that were being replaced by ballast in the hold of a Scandinavian boat. A girl sat on a bollard watching, and Janey was reminded of Maudie Dove who had done the same a long time ago. She chuckled and told Clive that Bert had a secret hideaway everyone in Newport except Annie Cooper knew about, and that Maudie had begun to put on airs and was hardly ever at home in the run-down apartment in Sea Street.

Jane greeted Clive warmly and took the baby upstairs to Emily and Vikki who loved to change and feed him. 'Now,' said Jane. 'Let me look at you!' She kissed her son-in-law's cheek and fussed round the couple with tea and bread and butter and jam. 'You'll want to eat a proper meal later when George is asleep,' she said, 'but this will fill a gap.' They talked about the house and once again, Jane firmly refused all offers of help. 'I've Dan and two men who need to earn their money and a girl to scrub out the cupboards before we put anything away. The floors have been laid and the curtains are up, thanks to Janey and Emily, and I've taken my time over it so that nothing will be done in a hurry.'

'But you will be very busy,' said Clive slowly.

'Not too busy to have the baby here. He's company for Vikki and you need a bit of time to yourselves.' Her dark brown eyes were tender. 'You'll need this time to take away with you, Clive, and Janey will have something precious to remember.'

'No wonder I love your daughter,' said Clive, hugging Jane and trying to lift her in the air. 'If I'd seen you first, she wouldn't have had a chance.'

'Put me down and stop that talk! I'll have you know I've refused better-looking men than you, Clive, and isn't it my own daughter you're married to?' She blushed and enjoyed the feeling of his young strong arms and the smell of his skin as he kissed her cheek.

'May I bring the baby here tomorrow?' asked Janey.

'You can bring him when you bring this dish back. No, you'll take it and no argument! There wasn't time to cook, I'll be bound, and it's only a rabbit pie. Now, Emily has finished giving him his supper, the dear mite, and you must get him to bed before he starts crying. I'll see you in the morning.'

'Do you think I'm selfish, Mother?' whispered Janey.

'Selfish? You selfish, Janey – that'll be the day! No, enjoy him while he's here. None of us know what lies ahead.'

Clive was talking to Emily and holding George in his arms. Whatever happens, she will have a part of him, Jane thought, and raised her hand as if to cross herself, but pulled at the button on her blouse instead, hating the vision of old Mrs Lee the gypsy who had died long ago.

'I see you've turned out the cupboard by the range,' Janey remarked.

'I'm going through everything before we leave here,' said Jane. 'If there's anything you want before I throw it away, then take it and be done.' She sniffed. 'Take what you want before Lizzie comes nosing again. She said that Harry would like the blue and white platter but I told her I wasn't dead yet!'

'I could use those old sheets for dust-sheets after you've moved in,' said Janey.

Emily picked up the old army hussif that her father had taken with him to the war before the Great War, and to camp when he instructed recruits in the 1914 war. 'I would like this and the tin box with Father's medals,' said Emily. 'Look, it still has some green webbing Blanco, a button stick and polish and some green thread for mending.'

Jane busied herself over the baby carriage, and wished that she had disposed of the hussif after Walter died. It made it difficult to forget what Mrs Lee had said, when she had proved her powers by saying that Jane had forgotten to put in the green thread when her husband left for the Boer War. There wasn't much left now of the gypsy matriarch's prophecy and Jane wanted to make Clive stay safely at home with Janey for ever, making babies and living . . . *living*.

'George has got the wind still but he'll last out until you're home,' she said brusquely. 'Be off with you and let that man rest, Janey.'

'The new furniture will be ready at the end of the week,' Emily said when the others had left.

'Now, I know I said you could have what you wanted, but don't try to make me sleep on anything but a feather-bed. I like to be comfortable, not sleep on a board,' teased Jane. 'But the chairs are nice with all those downy cushions and I think I shall get used to having the sideboard in the dining room. Not that I shall get rid of the old dresser. That goes in the kitchen, and this table. I want to feel I live there and I'm not just there on a visit!'

'I saw the piano today. They put it in the shop window to show it off before they deliver it. It has green silk behind the frets and two brass candlesticks if I want to play without bothering to put the other lights on.'

'I'm glad you chose a pretty one, Emily. Most of the latest are so plain, but that one would be at home in the drawing room of old Queen Victoria,' announced Jane, as if this was the highest praise she knew.

'I start lessons as soon as we are in,' said Emily. 'Tomorrow, I shall stop the order for flowers to be sent here, and I'll ask them to send a few to the Mall next week. The ones we have left after we shut the shop can go to Janey and Lizzie, if she shows up when she knows there is work to be done! The rest can go to Mrs Barnes and Ruby Sheath.'

'I never thought I'd leave here before they put me in a box,' said Jane. She sighed. 'There's a time for everything and this is the time to move away. I'm tired, Em, and tonight I think we'll open a bottle of sherry wine and ask Ruby to have some with us. Poor soul, she hasn't much of a life, with Ethel in that place still.'

'Did she know Fred when he came home this time?' asked Emily.

Jane shook her head. 'He went to see her but she tried to get at him and they had to lock her away again, and now that the baby is dead, too, it's no wonder that he doesn't write or ask about her apart from when he sends the money.' She stood up, wearily. 'There's a goose walking over my grave, Em. Go and fetch Ruby and ask her to have a bite with us. If I'm going to be miserable, I might as well share hers as well.'

Ruby shut her door behind her; she hadn't even bothered to comb her hair. 'Sometimes, I think I'm going mad, sitting there all alone,' she complained.

'You should come here more often,' said Jane gently. 'You know you're always welcome.'

'I know, but I'm not used to putting myself in other people's pockets any more than you are, Jane. I go up to the hospital twice a week, but it's a quite a pull walking up there, and when I get there Ethel doesn't know me – all she wants is Fred. And then when he does go to see her, she says he is the devil and begins to get violent.' Ruby sighed tearfully. 'I don't blame him for signing up for the Regulars. It's no life for a man, having that on his mind.'

'It takes two to make a baby,' said Jane drily. 'But if he upsets her, it's best to stay away. Is there no improvement?'

'None. Even when your Clare went to see her, Ethel was as bad and you know how friendly they have been since they first started school.'

Ruby sat with her body slumped and her eyes dull. Even the sweet sherry had done little to raise her spirits and after half an hour when Jane put the hot pie on the table and Emily served well-cooked vegetables, Ruby was still grumbling on about her lot. Jane felt a twinge of impatience.

'At least you have your health and strength, Ruby,' she said at last. 'There's many without food or proper beds, and you have a bit put by from when Aaron had the boats.' She sat down to her own meal. 'You need something more to do, Ruby. If I didn't have Vikki and now little George to fill my mind, I would have to do something.' She poured more wine, not because she really wanted it but because Ruby was getting on her nerves. Ruby pushed her own empty glass closer and watched it being filled.

'I'd go up to the church more, but they don't want me there. I know at one time they thought we all smelled of fish and maybe we did, but now the boats have gone except for the one that we rent out, the cellars are empty and the house smells sweet.'

'There's plenty to be done at the chapel,' said Jane. 'I'm worried that when I go to the Mall the soup won't be made properly. It's one thing to fill bellies with bread and something hot but when they water it down as I caught that Maisy Daws doing last week, it does no good at all.'

'That woman needs taking down,' said Ruby. 'She's another Annie Cooper and as mean as they come.'

'Then why not take over from me and see that it's done well,' suggested Jane. She smiled. It was well-known

112

that Ruby and Maisy had been sworn enemies for years.

'I can't carry heavy jugs of soup,' said Ruby.

'They have a handcart and a lad to help now. You make the soup and follow him and see it served. The vegetables and beef bones can come to you just as easily as here.' Her expression softened. 'It does one good to see how much it means to folk, Ruby, and it would be a real weight off my mind.'

'I thought they'd finish with all that,' said Ruby, 'but now they've laid off more men at the woodyard and it's said that even the boatyards are feeling the pinch.' She sat up straighter. 'If you'd get me started, Jane, I'll do the soup. I think I'll enjoy it.'

'You haven't heard anything about the factories at Cowes? The engineering is safe, isn't it?' asked Jane anxiously.

'Safer than most, they say, and there are new orders for engines from abroad. The Navy had to have a lot of repairs done and needed small boats and new mine-sweepers for the Merchant Navy.' Ruby took another helping of pie as if she had rediscoverd her appetite. 'They are still building those horrible submarines, but not here. I saw one in the Solent on trials when I went to Cowes and an uglier thing I've never seen. It was like a big grey slug on the water. I can't see how men can live down under the water, with no fresh air.'

'Clive was talking about mines,' said Jane. 'Please God he never meets one at sea, but they haven't found all of them yet, and some of them are ours and not German ones. I don't care who laid them in the sea, it was a wicked thing to do. Walter didn't like them,' she added as if that proved a point.

'Janey did well for herself,' said Ruby. 'And your Clare looks as if she knows where to find the next meal. Is she coming down to see the new house?'

'Alan doesn't like her being away when he is at home,' said Jane. 'Or that's what she says.'

'Is he close with money? If he won't give her the fare, then she can't get away,' said Ruby.

'She can get away if she needs to,' said Jane. There was no need to tell Ruby of the twenty gold sovereigns sewn into the lid of the velvet-lined trinket box that Jane had given her daughter when she married Alan Dewar. 'I think she's settling down to marriage at long last.'

Emily listened and said little, but finished one of the intricate sections of the crochet that was growing slowly and was now long enough to trim one side of a double bedspread. It was exciting to turn the corner and to see that the rose pattern came exactly where it should before she started on the next side.

'That's pretty,' said Ruby kindly. 'You'll have a good start when you get married, Emily. I know people who would pay a lot for lace like that.'

'It's not for me,' said Emily calmly. 'I'm not going to be married. I promised this to Clare a long time ago and I don't know when it will be finished.'

'I've suggested that she makes it to fit her own bed,' said Jane, 'but she insists it is for Clare.'

'I like crochet,' said Emily. 'I don't do this all the time and I've made some nice doileys for Mother for the new house.' She smiled. 'They grow faster and so does lace edging. I made some for Mrs Barnes as she likes her maid to have handcrocheted lace round her starched caps, or tatting, but I don't really enjoy doing that.'

'Hand-made doileys? The vicar's wife has them but never much on the plate,' said Ruby. She chuckled earthily. 'I'd rather have the plate with something good on it!'

'You'll have both when you come to tea with us,' Jane promised. Emily went up to peep in on Vikki, and Jane lowered her voice. 'I'm not fond of frills as you know, Ruby, but if Em wants to take all that trouble to make them, it's doileys on plates from now on!' They shared a conspiratorial giggle. 'She's a wonderful comfort to me, and I don't know what I'd do if she did find a nice young man, but I wish she would. She gets quieter all the time and if Vikki didn't make her laugh, I don't think anyone could. She's taking up piano lessons and keeping on with

114

the flowers, and I think she's as contented as she can be, but I do wonder about her at times.'

'She's a lucky girl to have you,' retorted Ruby. 'Most girls have to leave home and work now if they aren't married. She's better off with you than losing her eyesight over a typewriter all day, or working in a shop. The girls in the drapers in the High Street work all hours for next to nothing and feel lucky to get anything at all.' Ruby looked indignant. 'If they make a fuss, they are sacked on the spot and there are plenty who will take their places at a reduced wage.' She frowned. 'Mark my words, I think Mr Foster is right. If the government reduces wages even more and puts so many on the dole without any chance of paying rent and buying food and clothes for their families, there will be big trouble. The money that's being spent on that fancy Exhibition in London would build decent houses for thousands of ex-service families. Mr Foster was in London and he's seen what they are doing. They've built new roads just to lead up to his place at Wembley and they've invited every country in the colonies to take a pavilion and show what they do and make to sell in their own countries. A waste of money, I call it.'

'It will help trade,' said Jane. 'Bert Cooper has taken a few shares in it, but I refused. I like to see if a thing works before I put money into it, and I think it's too big.'

'It would be nice to see,' Ruby admitted. 'If they run excursions on the train, I might even go when it's opened.'

Jane laughed. 'I'll come too! That is, if we can get you further than Ryde Pier. You took a lot of persuading to come as far as that to see Clarkson Rose's show at the Pavilion in the summer, and then you saw *Twinkle* at least three times.'

'It was lovely.' Ruby sighed. 'I wish they did pier shows in the winter, too.'

'They are too busy with pantomime now,' said Jane. 'I shall take Vikki up to the one they have at the Drill Hall. That's done by local people and doesn't have smutty jokes.'

'Your Sidney would have done well here,' said Ruby.

'He's doing better where he is,' said Jane with pride. 'He is acting now and they write about him in the papers over there.' She showed some cuttings to Ruby. 'They have huge tents that they take all over America called that.' She pointed to the headline CHAUTAUQUA WEEK IN MAINE. 'I don't know how you say it, but that's what he's doing now. They travel all over the place and perform everything from Shakespeare to musical revues and even politicians like Edgar Hoover join them to give speeches. They have magic and cookery lessons and they say it takes education to people who have never seen an actor or heard good music. Clive brought me a record of a singer called Ruby Green. She sings jazz and although I haven't much time for such music, she is very good.'

'A black woman,' said Ruby.

'With a name like yours?' Jane laughed. 'And Green, too! I don't believe it.'

'It's true. Her picture is in one of the magazines,' said Emily who had settled down again over her work. 'Black people have lovely voices and a great sense of rhythm.'

'Well, I never!' said Ruby. 'Fancy you knowing about her and about jazz.'

'I read a lot about America now that Sidney is there.'

Jane looked at her daughter with curiosity. So much went on in that quiet head that seldom came to the surface. 'America is such a big country,' said Jane. 'I wonder when Lucy will meet Sidney? He's been travelling for months, away from New York, and must have left just before the *Mauretania* docked.'

'I'm glad they haven't met,' said Emily. 'Lucy needs time to get to know America.'

Chapter 9

'March is a treacherous month,' said Jane. She looked at
the thin blouse that Emily had been ironing. 'That's too
thin. I hope that Janey is well wrapped up. They have
been all over the Island this two weeks and the sun's been
warm but now, there's a nasty wind.'

'If George goes back home tomorrow with them Clive
will have only a few days left, so even if the weather breaks
they won't mind if they are at home.' Emily laughed. 'Did
you see George this morning? He was dragging himself
around the big chair and then falling down. He could walk
if he gave his mind to it, but with Vikki there ready to help
him, he likes the attention.'

'Yes, it's time that Clive saw what he can do.' Jane
looked towards the door, half-expecting Janey and her
husband to come in. They had been so happy, like
children let out of school, and when they had come to see
George being put to bed each evening, they had filled the
house with their happiness, but it wasn't the same as
having him with them and being a family on their own,
and Janey now showed signs of wanting her child with her.

'We'll have supper together and then they can take him
home,' said Jane. 'Only a drink now for George as he had
his supper when you were with Ruby.' She packed his
clean clothes in the basket and left it by the perambulator
in the shop. 'It's better that he goes home tonight and
wakes up in his own cot, and Clive sees him wake up. He's
such a pretty boy when he's asleep.'

'Are you tired of having him here, Mother?' questioned
Emily.

'No, but I have the feeling that I may have too much to
do and he is so active that he might hurt himself if we
aren't with him all the time. I must go up to the house in
the morning, early, to see Dan about the broken glass in

the conservatory where the wind took it, and I said I'd tell him where I want the rest of the furniture.'

I'm thinking about my own future, she thought with wonder. I'm looking forward to moving out and now that the rooms look bare, this is no longer my home.

'We'd best be moving soon or we'll have not a chair to sit on,' said Emily. The long dresser had gone and the wallpaper where it had stood was bright and unfaded, and the patches where pictures had hung showed the same pattern, hung long ago and almost forgotten as it dimmed into pastels and sank into the background of the room.

'The sooner the better, now,' said Jane. 'George . . . Daddy and Mother are coming to take you home.' She handed him his favourite toy which she knew he liked to show people and hoped that he would laugh as soon as he saw his parents. We might have spoiled him, she thought with a guilty smile. It's time he went home.

'Where's my boy?' Clive lifted him high and George banged him on the nose with the toy motor car of wood, and laughed as if it was very funny.

Janey saw the basket of clothes ready and smiled. 'Give him his drink and then put him in the baby carriage, Clive. He can stay there while we have supper and then we'll take him home.' She followed her mother out into the scullery to fetch plates. 'Mother, you've no idea what this time has meant to us. Everything has been . . . even better than I'd dreamed possible and Clive has been so very happy.'

'I know,' said Jane softly. 'I know.' She thrust the pile of plates into her daughter's arms. 'Take these in and we'll eat at once. I've put a bottle of gripe water into the basket as George has red patches on his cheeks and may be teething again, but he's very good and a quiet boy, so he shouldn't keep you awake.'

Clive teased her about being without house or home and offered to put a tent up in his garden if they were left with no furniture. 'The next time I come here, you'll be a lady of leisure and I shall have to wipe my feet on the mat.'

'You'll certainly have to do that,' said Jane. 'I'm pleased

118

with the runner in the hall, and we bought one of the latest carpet sweepers to keep down the dust.' She watched Emily talking with more vivacity than usual and at the contented faces round the table. Please God it stays like this, she prayed, and helped Clive to more potatoes. Emily was happy and that was important and Jane shrugged off any misgivings she had now that the move was so close.

She wrapped George in a shawl over his coat and put him low in the carriage. Clive kissed her and thanked her, and the young family vanished into the night.

'Did Janey tell you?' said Emily.

'Tell me what?' Jane looked startled.

'No, she isn't expecting, or I don't think so,' replied Emily. 'Clive may be leaving the big ships and going for training up North.'

'He's already an officer,' said Jane. 'Don't they consider that being trained?'

Emily picked up a fork and examined the tines for dirt. 'They didn't say but I think he's going to be promoted and will serve on one of those submarines.'

'Oh, no, not that,' whispered Jane. 'Holy Mary, not under the water.'

'I think Janey will tell us when he has gone back, so we must not show what we think, Mother. It's as safe as anything on the water, or so they say, and the new ones aren't the death traps of the old ones. We aren't at war,' she pointed out. 'What can they do but sail up and down and play at being sailors?' But she looked almost as unhappy as her mother when at last they settled down by the fire for almost the last time.

'Did you open the letter?' asked Emily.

'No! I forgot it completely. George took it and began to tear it so I put it under the scales in the shop for safety.' Emily fetched it for her and smoothed out the chewed edges. 'Clare doesn't often write a letter.' Jane opened it and at first she looked puzzled, then alarmed.

'Is something wrong?' asked Emily.

'I suppose not. Read it and tell me what you think.'

Emily scanned the closely-written sheet, then looked

up. 'Alan wants to work here, on the Island? I can't believe it. Is it that or is it that Clare wants to come home?'

'You saw the other?' Emily nodded. 'He's been writing to Harry and Lizzie and neither of them said a word.'

'Well, at least Alan has a job to come to, if we can believe this. Harry and he were as thick as thieves the last time they were together, and Lizzie doesn't tell us much now that we can't give her unlimited food from the shop. You'd think we were leaving here just to spite her.'

'Where will they live?' asked Emily. She thought of the pleasant and spacious house awaiting occupation and dreaded having Clare with her all the time.

'Not with us,' said Jane firmly. 'Christmas and Easter and any holidays they want are quite all right and they'd be welcome, but they are not going to live with us, and that is final.'

'Clare does ask in the letter if you have any ideas, Mother.' Emily looked anxious. 'I know what she means. She doesn't like living alone with Alan and she'd be back with us in a flash if we let her.'

'They haven't given us much time,' said Jane. She was annoyed. 'If they think we shall have to take them in because there isn't anywhere for them to go, they can think again! If he's working at Cowes, they'll need to live there or in Newport, that's certain, but not with us, Emily. I think we've earned a little peace and quiet and to choose what we do.' She went to the corner where the desk had been and then realised that it was with the rest of the furniture at the new home.

'Speak to Archie,' said Emily.

'He's away buying lambs,' said Jane. 'As soon as I've finished at the house tomorrow, I must find Bert. I think he bought up a small house with a few sticks of furniture last week. He might rent it to them until they find what they want, and until their own things arrive.'

Emily nodded. If Alan Dewar once got his feet under their table, there was no knowing when they could get rid of him again, so even if Clare hinted that they could stay 'for the time being,' it was better to be firm and to have an alternative that they couldn't refuse.

'They could have one of my cottages,' said Emily. Her face was red as if the effort to speak was painful.

'Don't you dare suggest it!' said Jane. 'Those are no more than you've earned over the years and they are your security. There are ways and means without that, Em, and I'll see to it. If necessary, I'll sell one of the holiday houses in the West Wight and buy something in Cowes for them to rent.'

Emily looked relieved. 'Lizzie mentioned your properties the last time I saw her and said she thought you ought to pass on something to her and me and Clare.'

'Oh, she did, did she? Or was that Harry putting ideas into her head? When my time comes, you'll all have what I think you need and deserve. It's all signed and sealed and I am not going to die yet, you can tell her from me!' Jane spoke with spirit, hurt that Lizzie should be picking away as usual, trying to get something for nothing. 'And keep your affairs to yourself, Em. You earn your keep and more and if I like to give you extras, that's our business.'

'When are they coming?'

'Alan starts work in two week's time and Clare says here that if she could stay with us, Alan could go to the Bugle or somewhere if we haven't room!'

'We shall be very busy for the next few weeks, Mother. They know that and even if we wanted them to come and stay, this isn't the right time.' Emily looked crosser than Jane had seen her for years.

'I'll see Bert tomorrow,' repeated Jane. 'I'll even put off moving to get their place settled first if we have to.'

'They could come here when we leave,' suggested Emily. 'We haven't agreed to sell yet, and if we rented the shop to someone, it could be Clare.'

'No, I couldn't bear to come back once we leave. That part of my life is over. I haven't sold yet because I don't want the shop to be as it was. I'd rather it was a draper who bought it, or a chandler, but not anything that people could think belonged to us, selling the same things,' Jane confessed. 'I think it will go to the ironmonger from Ventnor. I said I'd talk about it the day after tomorrow.'

'I've made out the list you wanted for Dan,' said Emily. 'I'll come up to the house with you tomorrow and then find Bert.'

'Tomorrow, they will take the new furniture into the house and soon this bed will follow and I shall lock the door behind me,' Jane said to herself that night as she folded back the counterpane and plumped up her pillows. She smiled when she thought of the empty rooms below. Clare couldn't come back to the shop. Even the double bed in which she and Alan had slept at Christmas and for one weekend since, had been taken to pieces and re-erected in a room on the Mall. Perhaps we should all stay at the Bugle until we are settled in the house, she thought as she fell asleep. That would be a shock to everyone!

Jane woke early and heard Emily moving about downstairs. They ate a hurried breakfast and Emily pulled on her coat. 'If I take Clare's old bicycle, I can catch Bert before he leaves for the day. If he has left, then I can cycle to his office in Pyle Street or wherever he might be, unless he's left for Totland in the motor car.'

Jane watched her go and then washed the dishes. She filled yet another tea-chest with china and books and put it ready in the shop to be collected. From under her bed, she dragged the boxes in which she had stored so many memories, like her wedding dress and veil and the first shoes that Edward had worn as a baby taking his first steps. Lace collars, so out of date that they were coming back in fashion again as designers tried to bring in longer skirts and fuller blouses, lay neatly folded in tissue paper. Clare might like them, she thought. There were embroidered samplers, still grubby from small fingers and unfinished, and some of Sidney's painted programmes from the days when he gave puppet shows.

Jane put them all away again and lugged the boxes down to the shop. I'll let Emily turn them out and do what she wants with them, she thought. Even the wedding dress raised no more than a sigh now and the smell of mothballs was unpleasant.

Jane thought of Edward with a pang of guilt. He lived on the mainland and he of all people needed help with his wife Alice when he was away. I'll go over next week, she promised herself. I'll be able to leave Emily busy sorting and I can take them something to cheer them up.

Dr Barnes had spoken of a possible cure for diabetes, but he doubted if it would happen yet. 'They are on the brink of something and yet it seems to be just out of reach. It might come in time to save your daughter-in-law, and I am keeping in touch with the doctors who are involved. They trained at my old hospital and when they have the result they want, I shall offer to try it on some of my patients.'

Jane hadn't paid a lot of attention to him at the time, but she had seen Alice since, and the sunken eyes and feeble breathing had made her sad. Edward, as devoted as ever to the invalid, had tried to convince himself as well as his mother that Alice was no worse.

'She ate something that didn't agree with her and that set her back,' he maintained. 'Now I'm home for a week, she will have the right food and the neighbours can't sweeten her stewed fruit and give her cakes.'

Jane had smelled the 'new-mown hay' scent as she bent to kiss Alice goodbye and remembered the time that the girl had lapsed into a deep sleep and they thought she would die. 'I'll be over as soon as I can,' she had promised, but time had gone on and now she must make the effort.

Bert came in an hour later and sat down to the cup of tea and fresh bread that Jane had ready. 'Ah, that's better. I knew you'd have the kettle on,' he said. 'I didn't stop for anything at home when Emily came and told me.'

Jane regarded him with misgivings. Bert was very much better than he had been in the days when Walter and he were powerful men in their own small environment, and he had grown kind to Jane and all the Darwen family, but behind him was Annie who still gossiped to everyone about everyone.

'I shan't tell Annie if that's what's worrying you,' he said bluntly. 'I learned that a while ago and I'll not have her doing you harm, Jane.'

'You're kind, Bert Cooper. I never knew how kind,' she replied and pushed the pot of home-made jam closer to his plate.

'You're a one to talk of other people being kind. I hear things you thought nobody knew and you know I respect you more than any woman in this town,' he said gruffly. 'Now, what's young Clare been up to?' Jane handed the letter to him to read. 'Gone sour has it? I never thought it would work. Clare isn't the type to sit by a canal doing knitting.'

'She has a nice home,' protested Jane. 'She boasted enough about it when she was first married and drove us all mad with it.'

'Is that what sent Ethel up the hill?' he said and then saw Jane's horrified expression. 'No, I didn't mean it.' He read the letter again. 'You'd best have that house I've just bought. It's clean and has enough furniture to be comfortable and they can rent it until they see what they want to do, and then there will be no need for you to be bothered with them on the Mall.'

'If you give me the keys, I'll go with Emily and make sure it's ready.' Jane smiled. 'You're a good man, so you are. I can move into the Mall with an easy mind. How is Annie?' she asked, and they both knew that this was a polite afterthought.

'Middling,' he said and shrugged. 'She's taken to the motorcar and I have to drive her to Ryde today.' Jane hid her amusement. 'I wanted to go out to see the cottages in the West Wight but she has this bee in her bonnet about visiting her cousin who she hasn't bothered about for years.'

'Family feeling can be strong,' said Jane demurely, and wondered what fragments of gossip had filtered back to Annie about her husband and Maudie Dove. 'I'll not have time to go out there for at least another two weeks,' said Jane. 'If you are out there on Friday, the day I usually go,

124

would you drive past and see that everything is all right?'

Bert grinned. 'It will be a pleasure,' he said. 'I can manage Friday. That's the day that Annie makes the girl wash the paintwork and she likes to stay and see it done properly.'

It seemed odd to be helping Bert Cooper to Maudie Dove and adultery, and yet simple, and Jane felt no guilt. They discussed business and Bert said he would ask people he knew in Cowes just what was likely to happen in the engineering industry. 'I worry about Lizzie and now about Clare,' Jane confessed. 'If Alan wants to move to the Island, I think it's more than his marriage that's not as it should be.'

'They need a family and then she'd have no time for day-dreaming. I saw Janey and she looks like one of those paintings of women with babies. She's like you, Jane. You know, I think you had a cuckoo in your nest when it came to some of the others. Lizzie and Clare are twins in more ways than one and it would do them both good to have babies, and to give and not take all the time.'

'They're not as bad as all that.' Jane flushed, ready to defend her own.

Bert laughed. 'I could always rile you when I put my mind to it. Here are the keys. If you need to make changes, I'll pay. It will add value when I do sell and they might even like to buy it themselves, as it's a nice little property near to Shide Mill.'

'I can walk out through Pan this afternoon. It's not too far,' said Jane.

'And not too close for comfort! You could call in on Annie sometimes on the way back if you come up Medina Avenue.'

'But it will be a bit far from the Mall when we move,' said Jane, and found it a comforting thought.

'You should have kept the trap and one of the horses,' said Bert. He hesitated. 'It's none of my business, but people do talk and everyone is wondering about you and Archie. I tell them to mind their own business and that you haven't been widowed long enough to decide, but I know he's always wanted you and you need a man about the place.'

'I managed when Walter was away and when I had all the children here. It's easy now with Emily to help and keep me company and the others with homes of their own. I shall live on the Mall and grow flowers and take Emily on trips sometimes. Alice is ill again and I ought to go over to see her. I shall never lack things to do and I enjoy being independent.'

'Poor old Archie.' Bert glanced at her sideways. 'Men need their comforts.'

'Women give them but they should be given with love and enjoyment or there's no virtue in it,' said Jane softly. 'I'm glad I'm not young. I enjoy life now and I don't need all that. Vikki and little George are all I want, and my friends.'

Bert turned at the door. Jane stood tall against the light of the window, her dark hair still raven and shining and her figure curving and supple. 'You are still a very goodlooking woman, Jane. You could make some man very happy.'

He left her abruptly. Damn it! he thought. Half an hour in her company and Maudie seemed like trash, but his steps quickened as he walked to the motor waiting by the kerb. Friday could do as well as today and Annie would never know. Perhaps people would talk less if Maudie left Newport for good and lived in the cottage. Out of sight, out of mind.

The cart belonging to Dan Cooper stopped outside the shop and Jane went out to explain why she hadn't been up to the house. 'I just heard from Clare and had to see Bert on business,' she said.

'I went to the station to collect some things for Bert and the stationmaster said he had a note that Lizzie gave to the guard of the Cowes train.' Jane smiled. Lizzie would walk a mile and put other people to endless trouble to save postage. 'He said it was an urgent message,' said Dan slowly, his stolid face anxious.

Jane tore open the envelope, and turned pale. 'Sweet Mary!' she whispered. 'Lizzie is very ill.'

She called urgently to Emily who had come back with the bicycle and was turning out the last of the cupboards. 'She wrote the note,' Emily pointed out calmly. 'In a nice firm hand, too. If she really was ill, Harry would have written or sent a wire. If I know Lizzie, she's playing up and wanting attention. If Clare comes to Newport, Lizzie will feel left out and think she's not getting something that Clare may have. That's what's making her ill!'

'I think I'll have to go down to Cowes,' said Jane.

'Yes, Mother,' said Emily patiently. 'You go and see for yourself and I'll cycle over to Shide and make a note of anything we need to do there. After doing the cottages, I shall know at a glance.'

'I'll be back as soon as I can,' said Jane. She stuck a hat-pin dangerously close to her scalp and knew that the hat was pulled too far down over her face, but looks seemed unimportant as she hurried along Sea Street and up the rise to the railway station in time to catch the Cowes train. Some of the fields were still full of cattle and the farms looked trim and peaceful but here and there new villas had sprung up and nests of new smaller houses were in places where she remembered orchards, in the days when a train journey to Cowes was a treat and a mixture of fresh air and smuts from the belching funnels.

The narrow road where Lizzie lived looked even more dismal than usual to Jane, and as she knocked on the front door she wondered how anyone could choose to live there with the view of the gasometer and the back of a building yard. It wasn't as if Harry was hard up, and there were some very pretty houses well within their range of expenditure. Well, if it suits them, that's all that matters thought Jane, and tried the door handle as there was no sound from within the house. The door opened and she stepped into the tiny hall. Through the living room she could see out into the back garden and heard laughter.

Jane stood back and watched her daughter hanging out clothes on the line to dry. She was talking to her neighbour and they were laughing as if neither had a care in the world. Lizzie put down the peg-bag and lifted the empty zinc bath in which she had carried the clothes and swung it on to one hip. She came back into the house and saw Jane.

'Oh, Mother! I'm so glad you came,' said Lizzie. Her face crumpled into despondency and tears and she set the bath down on the floor of the kitchen.

'What's the matter, Lizzie?' Jane spoke briskly. The hat-pin *had* pierced the skin and was now hurting. 'What's this about being very ill? You look all right to me and I heard you laughing out there.'

Lizzie brushed a hand across her eyes and sighed. 'I may look well, Mother, but I'm not.' She sank into a chair and put on her pathetic expression that Jane knew only too well. 'I get terrible stomach upsets and feel as limp as a rag at times.'

'You aren't limp now, so put the kettle on and we'll talk over a cup of tea,' said Jane without sympathy. 'I hurried over, thinking you were at death's door and I think I feel worse than you do. Emily has had to do all my errands and we are expecting Clare.'

'She isn't coming to live with you, is she, Mother?' Lizzie sounded sharp.

'You know more about her than I do, by the sound of her letter,' said Jane, and Lizzie went red and went to put on the kettle. 'She will live in one of Bert's houses and I can get on with moving,' said Jane.

'I don't know why you want to leave the shop. It was so convenient and it ought to be precious to you as it is to us.' Lizzie carefully measured out the tea and Jane reached over and added an extra teaspoonful.

'Convenient for you to take what you wanted, Lizzie.' Jane felt annoyed. Her head ached and she was hungry and Lizzie looked blooming. She eyed her daughter with speculation, and then laughed.

'It isn't funny, Mother. I am ill and this morning, I nearly made Harry send for the doctor.'

'You're expecting, Lizzie.' Jane laughed at the consternation on her daughter's face. 'You are going to have a baby, praise be! It's what I hoped for and it will be a blessing to you.'

'I can't! I don't want a baby yet and neither does Harry. He said we wouldn't and he's careful!'

'Not careful enough,' said Jane. She sipped her tea with satisfaction. 'I'm glad I came. It's put my mind at rest and you must go to the doctor as soon as you can. Think of little George and how happy he has made Janey. You'll love it when it comes and so shall I. All babies are sent from heaven and made to be loved.'

'I can't tell Harry,' wailed Lizzie. 'It isn't fair.'

'If he comes home from work and sees you like that, he'll be cross,' said Jane. 'Wash your face and comb your hair and tell him as soon as he sits down. I'll catch the next train back and I'll come down next week if I have the time.'

'If I'm pregnant, I shouldn't do housework,' said Lizzie petulantly.

'Housework is the best exercise, Dr Barnes says,' said Jane with complete lack of sympathy. She hugged Lizzie and picked up her purse. 'Enjoy it while you can, dear. Learn to love it even before the baby is born and you'll be a happy woman.'

She went back on the train and unpinned her hat. The trees seemed greener and the flowers in the hedgerows peeped out in pale yellow banks so that she could almost smell primroses, buttercups and celandines. New life was everywhere and as she walked home from the station, she noticed babies in deep perambulators as if seeing them afresh. 'I'll buy Lizzie a nice pram,' Jane told herself and cut bread and butter to eat alone as Emily was still away, and wished that she had a shop full of customers to tell them the news

I'll tell Annie first, she decided. It will be like a tonic to her to be the first to know and to spread it all over the town. It might even make her walk more just to meet people in the shops.

Emily took the news with a serious nod. 'Lizzie isn't a natural mother,' she said. 'She'll try to put upon you, Mother, and expect more than you ought to give her.'

'We're not short,' said Jane.

'I don't mean money. She'll sap anyone who helps her

and Lizzie is not as frail as she likes to imagine. That type never are,' Emily added.

'Is the house ready?' asked Jane.

'It's very pleasant and there's enough there for them to move in tomorrow. It's clean and tidy and the girl who scrubbed the floors did them well. I asked Mr Foster to deliver some groceries to start them off and he'll leave them in the back porch. If I cook some beef, it will do them for a day or so, cold, and there is a shop nearby where they sell potatoes and cabbage.'

'You can't cook the beef until they are coming,' said Jane.

'They are coming tomorrow,' Emily informed her. 'Another wire arrived just now.'

'They'll be so surprised and pleased that they have somewhere and can just walk into it.' Jane's face glowed. 'Everything is working out fine, just fine.'

'They'll be surprised,' said Emily. 'But not pleased. They think they can live with us.'

'They'll be pleased,' insisted Jane. 'And with Lizzie's good news, what a homecoming it will be!'

'You didn't read the wire, Mother.'

'Read it to me. I can't make out that print on the buff paper.'

'It says they are arriving tomorrow night and that Clare is in an interesting condition.' Emily tossed the flimsy paper on to the table. 'Only a man as insensitive as Alan would put that in a wire for everyone to see. I'm glad they aren't coming to us. I think I'd leave if they did.'

'Two babies! What a wonderful double blessing,' said Jane. 'We'll have to buy two prams. They'll be company for George, and Vikki will be pleased and be the real little nurse.'

Emily sighed. It was happening again. Just when she hoped her mother would relax, she would have more and more work piled on to her. 'I asked Mr Jenkins to meet their train and take them to Shide,' she said.

'If Clare is tired, they could sleep here for one night,' suggested Jane.

'Start them off in their own home, Mother. We'll have enough to do with moving. I'll make a pie and we'll be there to welcome them with a fire lit in the grate and the groceries put away, but we don't want them here.' She laughed, as if very relieved. 'You forget, Mother. They *can't* come here. We have only your bed and mine left and those go tomorrow.'

'Yes, we are leaving.' Jane fingered the brooch that Sidney had sent her. 'If we'd known that they were both going to have babies, perhaps we should have stayed on here.'

'No, not here. You need to get away from the shop, now there are just the two of us and Vikki.' Emily raked out the fire in the range and knew that it was for the last time. In the morning, she would leave it to die after they had made breakfast and cooked the pie for Clare. 'I need to leave the shop, too,' she said simply. 'I need to forget a lot of things.'

Chapter 10

'Dr Barnes says that Harry needn't be careful now,' said Lizzie and giggled. 'He didn't say it to me of course, but Harry went in after I'd been examined and came out all smiles. We have to wait another fortnight or so to make sure the baby is safe and then go on as we would normally, but taking no precautions.'

'I wonder you didn't go to a doctor in Cowes,' sniffed Clare. Her face was pale and she had a miserable pinched look about her. 'Dr Barnes doesn't know everything. Think what Mother went through when she had Caroline, and the last time.'

'It wasn't his fault. Mother couldn't help herself as we can, and besides, she still believes in her heart that preventing babies is a mortal sin.' Lizzie sighed. 'Harry is being very kind and now he's used to the idea he says he wants a son.'

Lizzie eyed her twin sister with curiosity. The proud lift to Clare's chin had gone and she appeared depressed. It was puzzling. The small house was really pretty and in a very nice area and it had been ready to step into without fuss or hard work. The tiny garden was full of spring and early summer flowers and the shop on the corner supplied vegetables and fruit and some groceries.

'Is Alan pleased?' she ventured.

Clare twisted her handkerchief round the split fingernail without knowing she did it. Her mouth set into a hard line. 'He did it on purpose,' she said bitterly. 'I didn't want a baby and to tell you the truth, I'd thought of taking a boat to America and leaving him but he knows now that I can't.'

'You know you don't mean that,' said Lizzie. 'You always did say you wanted what you couldn't have, Clare.

If you'd not been able to have a baby, then that would have been your dearest wish!'

'That's enough! You may feel well but I don't. I've never been so ill in my life and it isn't just in the mornings, as they told me.'

'You should go to Dr Barnes. He gave me some white mixture that helped the sickness and he does know us all.'

'He gives white mixture for anything from colds to backache and worse,' replied Clare. She turned away and fingered the edging to the floral curtains, staring out of the window. 'I wish I could lose it before it makes me really ill,' she said softly.

'You wouldn't *do* anything?'

'Why not?' Her eyes were hot and seemed even more dark than usual. 'Look at Ethel! She's in a madhouse because she had a baby.'

'Ethel had 'flu and that set if off,' Lizzie tried to say, but Clare moved impatiently and went into the kitchen to make tea.

Lizzie followed her, missing nothing as her sharp brown eyes picked out the table that Jane had given to Clare and the fresh linoleum on the kitchen floor that must have been laid the day that Clare moved in and therefore was likely to have been paid for by Jane.

'I always said *I'd* like that table,' she said resentfully, as she accepted the cup of tea from Clare.

'I don't want it. I don't want this house either if that's any consolation to you, Lizzie, and if he thinks that I'm going to let him touch me again, he's got another think coming!'

'I like it,' said Lizzie. She smirked. 'Even when I don't, I find it useful to get my own way. It's a very useful weapon when Harry gets angry or won't let me buy things.'

Clare smiled for the first time, and they looked more like twins as the two pairs of dark eyes sparkled with malice. 'Yes,' she said slowly. 'You are right, Liz. I shall use it when I want something. He doesn't make much of a fuss when I say no, but he still wants me very much, I can tell.' She opened the biscuit tin that had once held neat rows of Marie biscuits but now was full of fruit cake made by Emily. 'I think I fancy a bit of cake for the first time.'

'We have to eat for two,' said Lizzie piously, and took two slices.

'Did you walk from the station?' asked Clare. Lizzie looked surprised. 'I forget that I have a station just along the road at Shide,' Clare said. 'I was so used to the one at the back of the quay and we never used this one unless we came out for watercress.'

'The train was crowded with children going to Sandown for a Sunday School treat but I managed to get a seat,' said Lizzie.

'And you didn't have anything to carry.' Clare laughed. 'You still carry that bag everywhere. Habit, I suppose now that Mother doesn't give away fish, and it's no use looking in this garden as we have no fruit trees.'

'Now that I know it's easy to get here, I can come more often,' said Lizzie, taking more cake. 'I'm not trapesing up the Mall too often and it's quite a walk from the station to Janey.' She smiled. 'Besides, little George is quite a handful now and I think he's spoiled. When my baby comes, I shall see that it behaves,' she said.

'Since Mother moved, she's been here once.' Clare sounded resentful. 'Janey could bring her in the motor car more often and she could come and take me out in it, too.'

'It is a long way to walk,' Lizzie admitted. 'Harry took me to see the house last weekend in the sidecar but Emily was too busy to sit and talk. She would keep getting up and going to the kitchen. I never make cakes on a Sunday but she was quite short with me when she knew we expected to stay to tea.' Lizzie looked complacent. 'I like fresh seedy cake and Emily makes a nice one. Harry needed his tea after driving all that way to see them, but they didn't give us anything like the teas we had when Father was alive.'

'Nothing is the same,' Clare said. 'Nothing will ever be the same for me now that the man I really wanted was killed in the war.' She glanced behind her as if Jane might hear. Lizzie was the only one to whom she could say certain things now. 'I think I'd like a nice little shop of my own if I can persuade Mother to help out. Nothing dirty like fish.' She wrinkled her nose in distaste. 'Ribbons and artificial flowers and some materials for baby clothes, perhaps.'

'Mother can't be expected to set you up,' said Lizzie, quickly making a mental note to ask Harry how much money would be needed for such an enterprise. 'But you could try and ask her,' she added. If Clare was given something, then surely she would have the right to expect something, too? She recalled the visit to the house on the Mall. Even the name was more suitable for someone like Dr Barnes or the family of the local mayor: *Briony Lodge*. She sniffed. The front door was well-polished grained varnish and the new door-knocker was a curving fish in brass. Harry had been impressed, and had wiped his feet so many times on the coir mat in the hall that Lizzie wanted to scream. The sun, shining through the picture of sailing boats on a blue sea that rainbowed the hall through stained glass, showed up one of Emily's best arrangements of flowers and leaves and gave the entrance a welcoming aspect.

Jane had been surprised but pleased to see them and quickly took them round to show them every room and all the new furniture.

'They didn't buy this cheap,' whispered Harry, and said he'd seen a table like the one under Emily's flowers in the best furniture store in the Island. Most of the old chairs had been replaced with solid and handsome ones covered in crimson plush.

'We could have gone to stay with Mother,' Clare went on. 'There's plenty of room there and if I'm not well they could look after me. All Mother thinks about is Vikki and George and brooding over letters from Sidney.'

'Has he met Lucy yet?' asked Lizzie.

'No, he went back to New York for a few weeks but by that time, Lucy had to go with Nellie Morris to Baltimore where she is singing with a jazz band, like Helen Morgan does – you know, the girl they call a torch singer who sings all those sad songs. Perhaps they will never meet. I didn't know how big America was until Alan showed me on the map and explained the distances.'

'So you do talk to him sometimes,' said Lizzie.

'Of course. It's only the times we spend in bed that I hate. At other times, I'm surprised at what he knows. He reads more and more and studies history.'

'Yes, when he is with Harry, they talk about the war and even about the Boer War, although neither of them can have any idea what it was like except for what Father told them.' Lizzie laughed. 'Harry missed that and kept a very good job and they can't do without him now.' She regarded her sister with curiosity. 'I thought that Alan was well settled where you were. He didn't have to leave, did he?'

'No, they wanted him to stay but I said I was coming back to the Island even if he didn't follow me,' said Clare. She shrugged. 'He never says much now, but he hates to let me out of his sight.'

'You couldn't leave him, Clare. How would you have managed to get here without the fare? And if Mother wouldn't help you, there would have been rent to pay.'

'I have some money,' replied Clare and went to fetch more hot water for the teapot. Lizzie was far too nosy and if she thought that Jane had once given Clare twenty sovereigns for emergencies there would be tears and recriminations. 'You should do as Mother did and make pickles and jam to sell, Lizzie,' she added as the weaker tea was poured.

'I didn't know you did that!' Clare smiled and didn't deny it. 'I can't start that now with the baby coming. I shall need all my strength,' said Lizzie as if she really wanted to make pickles, and it was sad that she couldn't do so.

'I must ask Alan to fetch my bicycle. It would be useful here and I could get to see Mother more quickly if I wanted her,' said Clare.

'You can't ride now! It's bad for you, Clare.'

136

'It might help. I feel as if I have something I hate growing inside me. Don't look at me like that, Liz. I don't want this baby and when it comes, I'll give it away.'

'I want mine now,' said Lizzie. She picked up her purse and her empty shopping bag. 'I think I'll take the next train back.'

'Are you going to see Mother on Sunday?' asked Clare in a chastened voice. 'I'm sorry, Liz. I don't know what I'm saying half the time. I didn't mean what I said, and I do like you coming here.'

'Not this Sunday.' Lizzie looked annoyed. 'Janey said that Mother needs a change and she's taking her out to the cottages before the next lot of people move in. Emily is going too, and they may be out every Sunday if the weather is fine.' She sighed. 'Harry does like his high tea on a Sunday, but he can't expect me to do it all in my condition.'

'You can come here,' said Clare impulsively. 'It would help to pass the time when Alan is as home, and I like cooking when I'm in the mood.'

'And we needn't have George crawling all over us and Vikki shouting and making the boards creak with that rocking horse.' Lizzie beamed. 'The men get on well and we can chat in peace. We'll take the three o'clock train, Clare, and I'll bring my knitting. We can make baby clothes together.'

'Just look at the time!' Lizzie made for the door. 'If I don't catch this train, I'll not have Harry's tea ready. He's working overtime and he'll be tired.' She rushed out and Clare heard voices. She looked at the clock. Alan was home earlier than usual. From the window she saw Lizzie climb into the bullet-shaped sidecar of a motor-cycle combination and the engine spluttered and then roared, as Lizzie was borne off to the station.

Ten minutes later, when the potatoes were boiling and the cold lamb was on the plates, Alan came in, removing driving goggles and a new thick jacket. He smiled. 'Lizzie caught her train,' he said. 'Come and see what I bought.' Clare looked at the vehicle. 'It isn't new,' she said.

'Of course it isn't. I'm not made of money. I thought you'd be pleased. We can go for drives more and you can visit your mother on Sundays.'

Clare tossed her head. 'We can't go there for tea. Janey has taken it on herself to say that Mother has been doing too much and needs to be taken out more. They are going to the West Wight on Sunday and I've asked Lizzie and Harry to come here.'

'Well, that isn't so bad,' said Alan. 'We can go there on Saturday. Now that they have settled in, they'll be glad to see you. I used to enjoy Sundays when you lived in the shop on Coppins Bridge.'

'They're going to the farm at Wootton on Saturday,' said Clare shortly. 'They don't want us there or they would have let us stay with them on the Mall.'

'I like it better here. With the baby coming, we can get to know each other again, Clare. We need to be together more.' The pleading in his eyes made her turn away.

'I'll turn down the gas on the stove and you can show me how that thing works,' said Clare. 'In fact, I'll turn off the vegetables and you can take me up to the Mall to show the motor to Mother.'

'Let's have something to eat first. With the light evenings, we have plenty of time and I'll take your mother a bottle of sherry wine.'

'You seem to have plenty of money, all of a sudden.'

'I saw Bert today at dinner-time. He was in Cowes and we had a bite in the Osborne together. He's letting us have this house dirt cheap, Clare, and I got a good price for the old one up North.'

Clare turned up the gas under the potatoes until the water boiled over but she didn't seem to see it. 'You've bought this place without saying a word to me?'

'You wanted to come back here. If it isn't to your liking, then you'll have to lump it!' he said harshly. 'Now – where's my tea? I've done a hard day's work and I'm hungry!'

He reached across the table for bread and spread it thickly with butter. Clare served the food and sat down

138

with him, feeling slightly faint, but after a piece of potato and some meat, she felt better and realised that she had eaten nothing but a slice of fruit cake all day. Her colour returned and Alan smiled. Clare smiled back, tremulously. It was sinking in that he had done this for her and now that she felt better, it would be very pleasant to be even with Lizzie and to travel by road.

'Mother will be surprised,' she said, and brought in apple pie and custard, taking the skin off the bright yellow custard before serving Alan. 'I'll get a warm jacket and my hat,' she said.

'Aren't you having any pie?' he asked.

'It gives me heartburn,' said Clare. 'We can have a cup of tea at Mother's, so don't be all day over that.'

Once in the seat, the sidecar seemed bigger and she was surprised at the comfort and lack of draughts. Alan sat straight as he drove and Clare felt a trace of the old attraction he had once had for her. He was good-looking and very masculine and in a way reminded her of her father in old photographs. She shivered. Walter Darwen had been a real man who took what he wanted from life and from his wife. Clare put a hand over her flat stomach. If she was nice to Alan now, when nothing more could happen, he would expect her to give in to him after the baby was born.

She looked at the houses leading to the upper end of the Mall. The baby wasn't due until after Christmas and the summer promised to be good. They stopped by the steps leading up to the raised Mall from the road and she was helped out.

'I came the long way round,' said Alan. 'It's a good engine, and the man I bought her from had to let it go cheap as he is on short-time and needed to sell.'

'Are many on short-time?' Clare asked, with a twinge of anxiety.

'Not in our works. Just down the road a shed is closing. Being a big firm with a lot of orders, we should be all right for years, but some of the small factories and sheds are going to the wall.' Alan put a hand under her elbow to help

139

her over the rough stone where a step was loose, and for a moment, she leaned against his firm body to make her feel secure, then saw Emily at the window and waved to her to come out.

Alan walked to the door and Emily opened it before he could use the brass knocker. Jane followed, with Vikki wide-eyed and excited. 'What a family for contraptions you are, to be sure!' said Jane. She looked down at the sidecar. 'Did you really come in that, Clare?'

'There's plenty of room,' said Clare. 'It's the best make of motor-cycle combination that there is,' she added, with an air of superiority.

'Can I have a ride, Uncle Alan?' asked Vikki. Jane looked uneasy. 'Please Gran! Please Uncle Alan!' The stubborn set of Vikki's mouth boded ill for anyone refusing her and Alan was flattered.

'Let her come and you come too, Emily, to make sure she sits safely.' He laughed. 'Steady, young lady. We haven't started yet and we don't want accidents.'

Emily sank gingerly into the seat, with Vikki squeezed in beside her. 'Are you sure it's safe?' asked Jane.

'Safe as houses,' said Alan, putting on the huge goggles again. Clare led the way back to the house without another glance back. 'He brought me here in it, and he wouldn't unless it was safe,' she said.

'Yes, he does care for you,' said Jane quietly. 'He's pleased about the baby and he's the kind of man who will see that you never lack the essentials of life. Enjoy this time, Clare. It should make you feel blessed as nothing else in this world can do.' She saw the expression that told her that Clare would, as usual, do what she wanted and consider herself first. 'Come inside and see the garden. I'm becoming quite good at planting and clipping hedges. Dan comes once a week and we have a boy to cut the grass.'

'This house is too big for just you and Emily,' said Clare.

'There's Vikki, too, and George will be staying with us for a week or so when Janey goes up to Scotland to see Clive.' Jane brought out a cake tin and suggested that

Clare should have a cup of milky cocoa, instead of tea. 'I went off tea when I was carrying,' she said.

'I like it but I can't stand the smell of onions,' said Clare. 'I don't think I'm normal.'

Jane laughed. 'You sound normal to me. Some women have cravings for certain foods. With me it was lemons and with Janey it's turnips. Ethel wanted strawberries when there wasn't a berry left in the Island.' She paused, hoping that Clare wouldn't ask about Ethel as the poor woman had tried to take her own life and was very ill in the mental home.

'I like fruit but not pastry,' said Clare and found that she enjoyed talking about her pregnancy, and when the others came back, flushed and laughing, she was in a good mood.

'I want cocoa like Auntie Clare,' Vikki protested when she was given a glass of cold milk before going to bed.

'A cold drink is better for you. Just look at you! You are so hot and the milk will cool you down.' Jane was firm, sensing again that Vikki had a very strong will from both her parents, and must be kept in check.

'Well, I'll drink it if Uncle Alan will see me on my horse before I go to bed,' she said with a sweet smile so like Nellie at her most alluring that Emily shook her head in mock despair. Vikki pulled him along to the small room where she had her toys. The huge wooden rocking horse stood against the light from the evening window, its mane thick and bright over the painted dappled neck. Bright blue eyes stared for ever from the carved face and the flared nostrils gave an impression of speed and power even when the beast was still. Alan ran a hand over the cold shining flanks and smoothed the saddle ready for Vikki to sit on it. He settled her feet in the leather stirrups and patted the rump as if to make it run. Clare touched the real horsehair tail and the gilt trappings.

'It's like a fairground horse on a roundabout,' she said. The sweep of the rocker was lessened by two blocks of wood under it so that Vikki could take it only a limited way as she swung herself to and fro to gather momentum.

141

'Archie brought it here from the man who makes the fairground horses,' said Jane. 'I am afraid of it. In the dark it looks real and those eyes seem to hold something evil. We have the blocks there to control Vikki. She's too much like her father. She sees no danger and is as headstrong as both he and Nellie put together.' She sighed. 'Archie has promised to bring the man who made it to make permanent stops like the drag we used to have on the cart when it came down Hunny Hill, but until that happens, we put the blocks down as she will ride it whatever we say and there isn't a bolt on that door.'

Emily lifted the tired child down and took her to bed while Alan opened the bottle of wine and told Jane about the house. Clare tried to look pleased and sipped the sweet sherry with enjoyment, and Jane blessed Bert for his generosity over the house as she knew what it had cost him when he bought it.

'So it looks as if we are all in for a happy time,' said Jane, looking from one to the other. 'Clare and Lizzie expecting and well, thank the Lord, and both with good husbands. I like my new home and Emily is great on the piano even after only five lessons, and the others are well.' She stopped talking and went to open the front door.

'Mother?' Janey set down a basket of baby clothes and the sleeping figure of her son. 'I had a wire and I have to go much sooner than I expected. Clive is definitely joining the submarine service and I must see him before he goes on trials in the North Sea. He has a week's leave starting the day after tomorrow and I don't want to lose two days of that with him travelling.'

'Take George upstairs,' said Jane. 'It's all there waiting. Come in and have supper and get a good night before you go. Have you booked a seat on the train?'

'I sent a wire to Edward as he said he'd do that as soon as I knew, so I take the first boat across in the morning.'

Janey looked tired and sat down thankfully as soon as George was in bed. 'He's a lump,' she said ruefully. 'I hope he isn't too much for you, Mother.'

142

'Never that,' said Jane. Clare put on her gloves. 'Are you going now?' asked Jane in surprise.

'I'm tired, too,' said Clare, 'And Alan has had a very busy day.'

'I saw the sidecar,' said Janey. 'It's so useful to be able to drive. You'll have to learn, Clare.'

'I can't now,' said Clare. 'It would be bad for my nerves.'

'You sound like Lizzie,' said Janey and gave her a warm smile. 'I can't wait to see your babies. I think it's wonderful. I wish I was expecting, too.'

'You don't!' Clare regarded her with horror, and Alan looked serious. 'I'm quite sure that one baby will be all that I'll want,' she added.

'You wait. You'll want to fill the house with them once you start,' said Janey with a tender glance at her mother.

'We'd better go,' said Clare, and stood by the door until Alan was ready.

'Why don't you come down to the farm on Saturday?' asked Jane. 'Bring some food and a rug and we can have a picnic. Vikki is looking forward to it and Archie will fetch us now that you won't be here to drive us, Janey.'

Clare opened her mouth to refuse but Alan eagerly agreed. She shrugged. It filled the time spent with him and he could be quite pleasant when other people were there.

'Give my regards to Clive,' said Alan. 'Some day I want to look over one of those latest submarines. They say there is more engine than space for the crew.'

Jane went to the door with them while Emily and Janey set the table for supper. Upstairs were two sleeping children and under her roof were her two favourite children, now that Jack was dead and Sidney in America, but she was unhappy. She closed the door and went back to the warm and comfortable room and dismissed her miseries. Janey looked happy and on the piecrust-edged table in the hall was a letter from America. Enough to make her happy.

I'll read that later. It will be a treat when the house is quiet, thought Jane and concentrated on making supper and sending Janey away happy that George would be looked after well, and with many messages for Clive.

In the train to Cowes, Janey counted her pieces of luggage and sighed with relief that she would see her husband again so soon. She thought back to the night before and the kindness that had enfolded her as Emily made supper and Jane pressed her to have a drop of the wine to bring the roses back.

She understands how I feel about Clive. The porter came to pick up her luggage and take it to the ferry. Absentmindedly she tipped him and saw a boy standing by the barrier hoping to carry a bag and earn a copper. She handed her small bag to him and added the top-coat that was too warm to wear but might be needed in Scotland. He followed the porter and Janey saw how thin the back of his neck looked and how frayed the cuffs of his clean jacket. She gave him sixpence and he smiled but said nothing.

If that was my brother or if I thought that my child could come to that, it would break my heart, she decided, but knew that she could do nothing for the growing numbers of unemployed. On the boat, she bought a cup of coffee and ate a roll and butter as she had been too excited for breakfast. Another porter took her bags on a cart to the train and Janey smiled when she saw Edward's solemn face at the barrier.

'It was good of you to come, Edward. Have you found me a seat?'

He led her to a reserved seat in a very clean carriage and the porter stacked the bags efficiently, impressed that the Deputy Stationmaster had come in person to see the lady off. 'Take a taxi at the station in London as you have to change trains, but there will be a reserved seat on the one going North. The London Midland and Scottish are quite good,' he allowed, and grinned. 'Not as good as us, of course, but I sent word that you were coming and a friend will be there to see you have everything you need.'

'How is Alice?' she asked as she hung out of the window to say goodbye.

'Middling,' he replied and she saw the pain that he could never forget even when working on his beloved railway.

'Mother will be over next week. She said to tell you. They've settled in well and she might leave George with Emily while she visits Alice.'

'I'm glad,' he said. 'Sometimes, I wonder if my Alice will ever see the Island again. She always feels better when Mother comes over.'

Janey waved and put up the window as the trudge of the engines and the clouds of steam took over. Dark benches grimy with smoke and the smell of sulphur faded as she settled down to read a book and to gaze out at the flying landscape. I'm the lucky one, she thought. She felt different today. Yesterday she was a mother with an active and demanding little boy and worries over clean linen and fresh milk, but now, with every turn of the wheels lisping I'm coming, I'm coming, I'm coming, she was a woman going to meet her lover. She moistened her lips and tried to concentrate on her book but she couldn't make sense of the words.

London came and went and once again she was touched at the care that Edward, her brother, had shown as she was ushered into her seat with ceremony and given another magazine.

This train was an express and stopped only at major towns. She looked out at Birmingham and saw the grey houses with the grimy washing hanging in smoke-laden back yards. Old baths and bits of rope, battered chairs and thrown-out fireplaces littered many yards but in others a brave attempt to make tiny patches bloom with flowers showed against the gloom. Runner-beans clung to bamboo poles and roses climbed over a water butt, but soon the terraces disappeared and the fields stretched as far as she could see.

Janey dozed through the Midlands and rubbed a patch of window clear when the train entered Manchester. She stared out wide-eyed at the young men waiting idly by the track in case a passenger needed a taxi or someone to carry bags. From the city beyond came noise, and a heavy fog clung to the streets as if too depressed to lift. The sun was trying to come through and as the train went on further North, the city lay back under its pall as if spring and summer were not allowed to penetrate.

If it's like that on a fine day, how must it be in winter, she thought and had more sympathy with Clare who had hated being away from the Island. Surely babies needed fresh air and light, just as plants and animals did? Time and time again, she saw glimpses of poverty, and all that Clive had told her of conditions in the big Northern cities came back to her. She had never believed that people could starve in England, even though many went hungry and had the help of charity, but now she could see it was true and she could do nothing.

The hills lay to the east and the train went through tunnels and over viaducts, heralded by the steam hooter and whistle. At Glasgow station she climbed wearily from the carriage, feeling soiled and disheartened and very tired. A porter took her bags and she walked along to the barrier. She held the address of the hotel in her hand ready to tell the driver of the taxi and she wondered if she would have to wait alone for long.

A hand touched her arm and she turned. Clive lifted her clear of the ground and kissed her. 'I ran,' he said breathlessly. 'I heard the train coming and I was half a mile away. I ran up the station approach and here I am!'

'And here I am, my darling,' she whispered. 'It's so good to hold you again.'

The porter grinned. 'Home on leave, sir? I'll find you a taxi.'

Clive draped Janey's coat over one arm and took her hand in his. The spark of intensity between them smouldered and she glanced at his face as they sat together. It was older and there was a line between his brows that she had not seen before. He was quieter, like the men back from the war whom Jane had told them about, or like the men who watched the trains and waited patiently for something to happen.

'I love you, Janey,' he said as they locked the room in the hotel.

'And I love you, Lieutenant,' she said. Gently, she pushed him away. 'I need a good wash,' she insisted. 'I smell of trains.'

He laughed. 'I'll go down and order dinner while you change. We'll be first in the dining room and first out.'

Janey blushed. 'You be careful. They might think I'm your fancy woman.'

'And so you are.' He left her alone and she stripped and washed all over. Without knowing the past, she did as her mother had done when she was young and in love. She dabbed Attar of Roses over her breasts and in the soft creases of her thighs and felt her whole body soften ready for love.

Chapter 11

Nellie Morris stepped out of the dress and the bugle beads that encrusted the bodice clicked against the highly-polished floor. 'Thank heavens that's over. I'm putting on weight, Lucy, or that gown has shrunk.'

Lucy laughed. 'You know you haven't. You're as slim as ever and it's the fault of the dressmaker. I said the waist was too well-fitting at the last trying, but she only went by appearances and hasn't any idea what it must be like to sing in a tight dress.'

'Can you let it out?' Lucy bent to pick up the offending garment.

'A little, and maybe I could insert another strip of beads.' She took the dress to the brighter light that shone from a huge lamp by the bedside. 'Yes, I can do it if you don't want me for anything else tomorrow morning. It might take an hour or so.'

'Ready?' Monty put his head round the door. 'Not dressed?' He sounded impatient. 'C'mon, Nellie, get a move on. We'll be late. What's the use of me getting good seats if you can't be ready in time?'

'We have at least an hour,' said Nellie. 'They wanted an encore and I couldn't get away.'

He grunted, then grinned. 'Well, wear something that won't stop the show tonight,' he said. 'We're going to a fight, not to a personal appearance of Nellie Morris, the star of *Spangles and Butterflies*.' He couldn't hide the pride he felt.

'I'll be ready faster if you get out of here,' she replied, laughing. 'Take Lucy and mix me some orange juice and soda. I'll come through to drink it.' She ran to the shower cubicle and stripped off her underwear, and Lucy could hear her singing even when the door to the bedroom was shut.

148

'Well, Lucy? Orange for you, too?' Monty looked indulgent. 'You know what? You are good for my Nellie. She never drinks alcohol now, and together you are the perfect advertisement for the English schoolgirl complexion.' He poured out a small whiskey for himself and added ice to the tall frosted glasses he took from the ice-box in the corner. Lucy carried the jug of orange juice and five minutes later, a rather breathless Nellie burst into the room, dressed in a loose-fitting gown and matching coat of pale beige trimmed with bands of dark fur.

'This is the fight of a lifetime,' said Monty, rubbing his hands together.

'You haven't bet too heavily, have you, dear?' asked Nellie, without sounding the least bit concerned. After being married to Monty for long enough to know his nature, she knew that he was shrewd and hardly ever lost money on even the smallest bet.

'I hope not.' He chewed a dry biscuit and then put it down as if he found it unappetising. 'I am banking on Dempsey of course, but there are a lot of people yelling for George Carpentier. I don't think he'll last more than six rounds, if that.'

'Well, you know best,' said Nellie. 'Lucy and I might not wait to see it finish if there's any blood.'

'You can close your eyes, but you stay,' said Monty firmly. 'There's a party after the fight and we're invited. Everyone will be there, including two English dukes and some of the Boston families. They even said Hearst might be there, and that's one man I'd really like to see.'

Lucy looked away, trying to hide her own excitement. Perhaps tonight she would see Sidney. Nellie eyed her pink cheeks with speculation, and thought she knew what was going on under the sleek fair hair. Lucy had matured in the time spent with her and now dressed well and with taste. Her silk stockings and the crocodile shoes and handbag that Monty had given her for her birthday made the short pleated dress of deep rose pink look much more expensive than it was and Nellie began to wonder how long it would be before Lucy stopped looking for her

149

dream and actually saw the way that men looked at her.

'He might not be there,' Nellie murmured when Lucy came to offer her more orange.

'I'm used to it by now,' said Lucy, 'but one day, we'll be in the same place at the same time instead of missing each other by a whisker each time. It's just bad luck, Nellie, but he did say in his last letter that he was looking forward to meeting me again in New Jersey if we were there for the fight, or later when he was back in New York.'

'Does he like fighting?' Nellie wrinkled her nose. 'From what I hear, he isn't the type for violence.'

'He's like you, Nellie, famous and has to be seen at these places, even if it isn't to his taste. He was always so gentle, so kind.' Her face took on a dreamy expression.

'That was a long time ago, honey. You were children then and he has come a long way since the shop on Coppins Bridge and small puppet shows at the Chapel Hall.'

'It's funny but it doesn't seem so far away to me, Nellie. I often think of them all as my family, more than I do of my own mother.' She picked up her jacket and gave Nellie her lizard skin bag, then handed her a small mirror. 'A touch of powder on your eyebrow, but you'd better do it.'

'Come on, you couple of perfectionists,' said Monty. 'All the boys will be jealous of me tonight.' He put his silk top hat to one side and laughed. 'I can't believe it. I just can't believe that I am here, with you two, and going to the fight of a lifetime.'

Lucy followed the others slowly out to the waiting car and as usual became the perfect foil to the more exuberant woman who had taken New York by the ears and had travelled far and wide across the United States of America, being even more successful in the travelling shows, that played a week at a time, bringing a carnival of music and drama, art and everything from high-minded debates, to low comedy and cookery classes to the masses who otherwise could never see a show.

In the car, Nellie pushed a Lucky Strike cigarette into the end of an ebony holder studded with paste diamonds.

Monty looked disapproving although he was smoking a cigar. 'They don't like to see you smoking in the street here,' he reminded his wife. 'This isn't New York.'

Nellie waved a spiral of smoke towards the window and he shrugged. The huge advertisement on the side of a building, said, TO KEEP SLIM, NO ONE CAN DENY, REACH FOR A LUCKY STRIKE INSTEAD OF A SWEET. 'It's true, Monty. If I smoke, I don't need sweets, and it doesn't affect my voice.'

'The minute it does, you give up,' he said. 'But I suppose I have to let you have one vice.'

'Just one, Monty. I shall leave the others until I'm past all this.' She leaned back against the velvet cushions and when the car stopped at the door of the stadium, she stepped out with the confidence of her beauty and the fact that her face was well-known all over the East Coast and appeared in most of the fashionable magazines.

Monty put a hand under her arm and Lucy followed, like a lady-in-waiting. Curious eyes regarded them all and the expected murmuring began when Nellie was recognised, but the three went quickly inside to their seats by the ringside, among a glittering company of the rich and famous, the honest and the criminal brokers, smooth gangsters and social climbers, all dressed in well-cut evening dress, and the women in furs and silk and fine jewellery.

From the back, away from the arc lights that stabbed the smokey air and illuminated the square of canvas, roped and empty, the rumble of many voices came from the hundreds of people who sat or stood in the cheaper areas. Shouts of encouragement to the as-yet unseen fighters came from throats already lubricated by illicit liquor and the bookies were doing a lot of last-minute business.

A man walked up to the ring and climbed between the ropes. He was greeted with a ribald cheer and bent his head to hide his embarrassment as he checked the corners and the ropes and hastily slid back into obscurity. Next the referee came to talk to one of the promoters sitting by the corner where Jack Dempsey, idol of thousands of fight fans, would sit before the bell rang to begin the fight.

By the other corner sat the trainer, friends and promoter of 'Gorgeous' George Carpentier, hardly less famous and eager for the World Title. The atmosphere was good-humoured and Lucy wondered how men could be expected to stand up and punch each other just to entertain, but the excitement was infectious and her eyes shone as she looked about her, recognising faces of the famous and puzzling over faces that she was sure she must know.

One face seemed to force her attention. Lucy stared, trying to think where she had seen the man before this night. The smooth hair could belong to a thousand men, the sleek trace of black moustache could also, but the dark brown eyes that now seemed to burn as he watched her could only belong to the man on the *Mauretania*, who had given her the drink that had made her sleep and dream of terrible things. She looked away but knew that he was still watching her.

She turned slightly to look at the crowds on the other side of the ring and forgot him. Another face seemed to spring into being. Almost hovering in the smoke was the face she had come all the way across the Atlantic to see. The longish wavy hair and pale complexion, the deep blue eyes and mobile mouth was as it was in the pictures that he'd sent to his family on the Isle of Wight. Even the carelessly-tied cravat seemed familiar to the girl who had devoured every detail of every picture he had sent and had mingled them with her own childhood memories. The light and the colour not available in the flat pictures made him even more vital and she put a hand to her mouth to stop the involuntary cry that wanted to escape.

'What is it?' asked Nellie anxiously, seeing the sudden pallor. 'Is the smoke too much for you? Are you too hot? Take off your jacket, Lucy.'

'No, I'm fine,' said Lucy. She gulped. 'I've seen him,' she whispered. 'Look, Nellie. It's Sidney Darwen, over there.'

'Oh!' Nellie's cry lacked the joy that Lucy felt. 'I

suppose you had to meet somewhere,' she said, and nudged Monty. She whispered to him and he frowned. 'You can't leave your seat now, Lucy,' said Nellie, placing a firm restraining hand on her arm. 'They are coming in. Wait and I promise to let him know we are here.'

The first fighter sprang into the ring, his loose robe bright and making his wide shoulders even wider. He held his arms high in salute to the crowds and they went mad until he sat on the small seat in his corner. The next man repeated the show of confidence and power but Lucy didn't know which was which. She saw two men who shed their robes and stood before the referee naked to the waist, their bodies gleaming and supple, exuding power and masculinity, but she saw nothing to excite her there. A glance back into the darkness that hid all faces in the stadium now that the fight was about to start, told her that she couldn't see Sidney again until the lights went up. Her heart beat heavily. His face, pale and slightly effeminate, was the only one she wanted to see.

'Marvellous bodies,' murmured Nellie. 'No wonder all the girls go mad and faint when they see them in the street.'

'I wouldn't,' said Lucy. 'They look like common dockers to me.'

'They are real men,' said Nellie. She laughed, infected by the mood of the crowd who now cheered, now booed as the men slogged at each other, and the heavy shuffle of feet and hard breathing came clearly to them from the canvas. A bell rang and the fighters sank into the corners, ministered to by their seconds and trainers, while the crowd yelled advice and encouragement. The rank smell of sweat and the noise made Lucy feel limp but she sat and said nothing. Monty chewed the end of an unlit cigar and clenched his fists each time a body blow connected on the smooth torso of Gorgeous George Carpentier.

The bell rang again and Monty wiped his brow as if he had been in the ring with the men. He sat forward and Nellie watched him anxiously, when it looked as if Carpentier might win. Monty almost stood in his seat as the fight progressed. 'I must have been demented,' he muttered. 'I said that Dempsey would win before five rounds and they've done three already!' He loosened the tight collar and dress tie and Nellie tried to fan him with her handbag. 'I'm fine!' he said testily. 'It was that hooch. More like wood alcohol than whiskey. I'll be fine.' He sank into his seat as the men came out for the fourth round. Carpentier had blood on his face and Dempsey looked almost as tired, but they leaped forward as soon as the bell sounded and Monty wanted to die.

The first time I bet that much, he thought. He can't do it now! He wiped his brow again and his eyes, and heard a roar from the crowd. He looked up and could hardly believe what he saw. Dempsey stood in the middle of the ring with his arm held high by the referee and the fight was over.

Monty closed his eyes. He needed a drink badly, but it could wait. Dollar signs floated behind his closed lids as he calculated the odds he had bet.

'Are you ill?' Nellie bent over him anxiously, and Lucy forgot her dreams in the urgency of the moment. Monty was pale now and laughing hysterically. 'Monty!' said Nellie. 'Pull yourself together, and let's get out of here.'

'I'm fine, my girl. I'm fine and so are you. I've just made a hundred thousand dollars!'

A man in a long light overcoat came to them and handed Nellie a note. People made way for him as the messenger of one of the most powerful men in America, if not the world. 'Mr Hearst would like a reply now,' he said.

Nellie hid her excitement and eyed the man with a cool glance that hinted that he was intruding. 'We have been invited,' she said. 'Maybe we can meet Mr Hearst when we are there?'

'He is sending a car for you, Madam,' was the reply and Nellie inclined her head as if she must accept, reluctantly. Monty stood up and took Lucy by the arm. 'If you could follow me?' the man said.

Lucy held back, but the crowds milled round the base of the boxing ring and some even tried to climb up. Monty kept a firm grip on her arm and propelled her after the others to a side door. 'Take my card,' said Monty to one of the officials who appeared as if by magic to clear a way for those people in the Hearst party. 'Tell the hired car driver that we are going on. I'll settle with him later.'

The limousine was bigger and more luxurious than anything Lucy had seen and when she glanced at Monty, she had the impression that he had never been in such a motor before. Fresh flowers hung in silver vases by the windows and on a small table that came down from the padded leopard-skin upholstery, a set of decanters of finest crystal lodged firmly in velvet-lined niches. Their guide offered drinks and Monty accepted eagerly, savouring the fine Malt that could only have come from Scotland and refusing even Scottish water in case he lost any of the flavour. Nellie shook her head and refused for Lucy, too.

Everything was happening so fast. Lucy stared out of the window and wished she could enjoy the evening, but she could imagine Sidney being swept away even further in the crowd, and she had lost him again before they had exchanged a word or a touch.

'Cheer up,' whispered Nellie. 'He's almost sure to be at the party. There are over eight hundred invited guests and in a hotel that size there will be room for more.' She shrugged. 'Even the gate-crashers.'

'Sidney wouldn't do that!'

'I wasn't thinking of him,' said Nellie drily. 'Just be extra careful tonight, Lucy. The wolves will be out, ready to offer you the moon.'

Lucy relaxed and smiled, and Nellie gave a low chuckle. It was becoming a joke between them. Three men had tried to get to know Lucy on the pretence that they were from film studios and could make sure that she had a good career in Hollywood, and Lucy was almost as good now as Nellie, in the gentle art of the complete brush-off. 'There will be so many real stars there that nobody will even notice me,' said Lucy. 'Except Sidney. I hope he likes my dress.'

'I keep telling you, dear, that he will have changed a lot.

155

Look at you! Who would think that the quiet mouse who came with me on the *Mauretania* could be so cool? You have changed, too, Lucy, and you may find that you just don't get on as once you did back home.'

The car stopped outside the huge hotel and Lucy saw men with dark coats, and hats that came well down over their faces, watching each car as it came to the entrance. Invitation cards were checked and cold eyes swept over the occupants of the cars before any were invited to enter the foyer.

'They are Mr Hearst's men,' said the guide when Monty asked.

'But it isn't his party.' Monty stared at the small army of strong-arm men that were everywhere.

'Any party where Mr Hearst is, is his party,' said the man. He nodded to the doorkeeper and the swing doors were held back. Nellie walked slowly and proudly into the warmly-lit interior, looking like the rising star that had emerged since she came to America. Monty followed, jubilant and proud and Lucy close by him for courage, and trembling with anticipation.

'We might even meet him,' said Monty softly. 'It's one thing to be invited to the same party where he might put in an appearance, but to be escorted there as his guests . . . Wow!' Lucy laughed. Monty was fast adopting Americanisms but could never say them without sounding completely British, unlike Nellie who could imitate every accent she encountered and used some to great effect now.

'Yes, I hope we meet,' said Lucy, her eager gaze raking the faces in the crowd. Who was Mr Hearst? He wasn't of any interest to her. Where was Sidney Darwen?

Skilfully, Nellie was detached from them and led into a side room and Monty and Lucy were taken to meet a group of film producers. Monty settled down to talk shop and was happy, with another glass firmly in his hand and no one even thinking of Prohibition. Lucy sat still by a pillar and looked down. When Nellie came back, perhaps they could walk around to see if Sidney had come, but from her chair she could at least watch the main entrance

156

through which most of the guests were now pouring, later than the favoured few.

Four men paused at the door. From their rather Bohemian style of dress, she labelled them actors. She stared. They were laughing and one had his arm round the shoulder of the tallest. A waiter held a silver tray of drinks ready and three of the four helped themselves, but the other man shook his head and asked for fruit juice. Lucy rose slowly to her feet. The waiter who was bringing her own freshly-squeezed orange juice came over and the man by the door saw him offer a glass to the pretty girl by the pillar. There were several other glasses of juice on the tray and he stepped forward to help himself.

'Hello, Sidney,' said Lucy.

'I beg your pardon,' he began, thinking that she was another fan who had waited to catch him, then he stared, first in disbelief and then smiling broadly and with evident pleasure. 'It's Lucy. It's Lucy Dove, all the way from the Island!' Lucy nodded, unable to speak and her eyes shone with unshed tears of joy. 'Little Lucy, my other little sister.' He turned to the men, who looked on with obvious amusement and curiosity. 'Let me introduce you. This is Lucy Dove, who grew up in my home town and was the one who helped me whenever I needed anyone to dress my puppets.'

It wasn't the introduction she would have liked, but Lucy was too overjoyed to object. He bent to hug her and to kiss her cheek, and then the other, in the French manner of greeting that so many from the theatre and films had adopted.

Flushed, she tried to laugh as juice spilled on to the small table where she had put her glass when he approached. Her dress had touched it as he drew her close and one of the other men had rescued it before it fell over completely. 'It's wonderful to see you, Sidney,' she breathed. 'I've looked forward to this ever since we came over.'

'We've been unlucky,' he said kindly. 'First they changed my schedule just when I thought I could meet

157

you and then we seem to have been going round in circles and never meeting.'

He glanced at his companions. 'Are you in New Jersey for long?' Lucy shook her head. 'I have another week here, so could we meet tomorrow? I just have to hear all the news from home.' His face took on a tender look. 'Seeing you makes me realise how much I've missed them all. Are you free tomorrow? I haven't a matinée and we could have lunch and go to the park.' He took out a small notepad and scribbled an address. 'Any cab will take you there at one o'clock and we can talk.'

'Who's the lady? Mr Darwen, look this way if you please!' A man with a camera stooped to get a better picture of the couple as Sidney embraced her again. They turned to face him, startled as the camera flashed and made a study of two faces, close enough to seem cheek-to-cheek and very happy.

'They get everywhere,' said Sidney, no longer smiling. One of his companions grinned. 'I'll see you tomorrow, Lucy. Have you any pictures of the family? Bring them if you can and think up everything they are doing, wearing, how they seem now that my father is dead.' His smile was dazzling. 'I shall make you talk and talk and talk. It's so good to find you, Lucy.'

The reporter made a great play at adjusting the camera and as Sidney left with his friends, came over to Lucy. 'I thought I knew most of his friends,' he said in a conversational voice. 'You're new around here, Miss?'

'I'm with Nellie Morris and my Uncle Monty,' said Lucy in the tone she had used so often when asked about Nellie. 'Most of the time we are travelling or in New York, but Uncle Monty agreed to sign Mrs Morris for a show here so that he could watch the Dempsey fight.' She was getting used to reporters.

'You don't say,' said the man. 'And Mr Darwen? You and he seem . . . very good friends?'

'I've known him all my life,' said Lucy simply.

'You don't say. Well, who'd have thought it!' The man scribbled again. 'I couldn't help hearing,' he went on.

158

'He said "It's so good to find you, Lucy." Am I right?'

Lucy blushed. Those words had been singing in her brain. 'We haven't seen each other for so long. It's wonderful to meet again and we are having lunch tomorrow.'

'Oh, where would that be?' The dark eyes were now eager.

Lucy paused. Sidney wasn't as well-known as Nellie but perhaps he suffered as she did from too-persistent reporters. 'He didn't say, but he'll be in touch,' she said sweetly. 'Now, if you'll excuse me, I see Mr Morris looking as if he wants me over there.' She walked away but not before another photograph had been taken and she felt uneasy, hoping that the look of displeasure on Sidney's face wouldn't be there if he found that she had spoken to the reporter about him, even so briefly.

Nellie was with him and Monty looked pleased. 'Lucy, my girl, we have all been invited down to one of the Hearst estates for a whole week! Now – isn't that something?'

'But when do we leave?' Lucy felt cold. If it's tomorrow, I won't go, she thought desperately. I can't lose him now.

'The day after the final performance, at the weekend,' said Nellie. 'I need a break and we were booked for only two guest appearances on the way back to New York, and Monty can handle that.'

'Did you meet him?' asked Lucy, curious in spite of all that buzzed round in her mind. The legendary figure of the newspaper tycoon was illusive and he very seldom appeared in public at parties.

'No, he wasn't here but we met Miss Marion Davies and she invited us. An invitation from her is as good as one from him as she runs most of his life and is with him everywhere.' Nellie looked round as if to make sure that no other person could hear. The last time someone called Miss Davies the Hearst mistress, they had had a very nasty accident. 'They've been together for years,' she added meaningfully.

'I thought he was married,' Lucy said quietly.

159

'So he is but can't get divorced as she is a Catholic, and she is never mentioned,' murmured Nellie.

'Where is this place?' asked Lucy.

'Somewhere new again.' Nellie shrugged. 'It will be good to stay in a house and not a hotel. When we bought the house in New York, I thought we'd make it a home, but I've seen it only twice for more than a week at a time.'

'I don't want to sell just yet,' said Monty. 'Houses in that part of the city have gone up and will go up more.'

'I want to *live* there, not to sell it,' said Nellie. 'I hear that you met Sidney Darwen.' She hid any concern she felt. 'Monty saw you talking. Has he left?'

'He was with friends but we are to have lunch together tomorrow, if that's all right, Nellie. I'll mend your dress first and leave everything as you like it,' she added anxiously.

'Of course you must go! I work you to death and you have no need to think you're asking favours.' She smiled, still elated by her success and the thought of the money that her husband had won. 'I have put on a little weight, in spite of what you say,' Nellie admitted. 'You'd better have that suit I wore only once because it didn't fit.' She smiled a little sadly. 'I don't think you'll be in any danger from that quarter, so look as nice as you like.'

'I'll be safe with Sidney. He's so kind and he always did respect women.' She blushed. 'But he did kiss me when we met.'

'And when you parted, the kiss on both cheeks?' Nellie shrugged. 'No, you'll not be in any danger, Lucy, but please don't fool yourself. Don't expect heaven. It is often hell upside-down.' She shook off her sudden depression. Marriage with Jack Darwen had been like that, all passion and joy one minute, and jealous recrimination the next. She looked at her husband and her tone softened. 'Be good and happy, Lucy. There are men who really do make good husbands and some who can tear a woman in half.'

'I know. I think Sidney is the gentlest, nicest, most loving person I've ever met.' Lucy gave a deep sigh and

Monty took a long deep drink from his glass, after exchanging helpless glances with Nellie.

'Well, we can leave at any time now. You've been seen and photographed with Marion Davies, we've eaten enough food to last until next week and I've drunk far too much of this wonderful genuine Malt.' Monty stood up unsteadily. 'And if I'm to get myself into bed, although it's already tomorrow, I'd better have no more. I have the times we are expected next week and the address, and you have a show tomorrow, dear.'

'I'm so happy,' confessed Lucy. 'I've loved being with you, Nellie, and without you I would never have met Sidney again, but this evening is the best I've had in my whole life.'

'So long as you don't hold me responsible,' said Nellie with a wry smile. 'Promise me you won't make any snap decisions without telling me. I want you to be happy and yet I can't look after you for always.' She squeezed the girl's arm as they found the car sent to take them back to the hotel and wondered if Lucy was completely besotted or could be made to put down the rose-coloured spectacles.

Yellow cabs like the ones in New York were still busy taking people home after the fight and the first editions of newspapers were already on the streets. 'Stop for a paper,' Monty ordered the driver. 'I want the first pictures of the fight.'

He bought copies of every paper and handed them to Lucy to hold. 'Do you want me to sort them out?' she asked. He nodded, now half-asleep and obviously not able to read without his glasses, and when they went up to the suite, Lucy found the back pages with the sports news and put them neatly in a pile on the tray by the telephone, then opened the rest of the papers for the more interesting bits of gossip. To her delight, the photograph of her and Sidney had pride of place in one of the inner pages. She reached for her nail-scissors and cut round it carefully. She made a note of the name of the paper and made up her mind to buy extra copies later in the morning to send home to England. How thrilled they'd all be, she thought.

161

But this was morning and the edition might be sold out by the time she went for a late breakfast!

She slipped her coat on again and found some change. There had been a news-stand by the hotel so she wouldn't have to wander the streets at this hour. As she swung the revolving door, she saw the boy and called to him. She bought two more copies, almost the last he had as so many wanted news of the fight. She folded them and pushed at the door. A man stood on the other side, and he pushed too, but in the wrong direction as if to stop the door turning. Lucy saw the outline of the man and let the door turn at his will, knowing she would reach the foyer as quickly.

He followed her across the wide carpeted hall and she didn't look back, but she waited until a couple of middle-aged people stepped into the elevator before she joined them. To her relief, they were getting out at her level and she pretended not to see Frank Garsey as he watched the elevator ascend.

'Where have you been?' Nellie was shrill with anxiety. 'I know this isn't New York but it's dangerous at this hour.' She saw the fresh newspapers. 'I thought we had them all.'

'I'm sorry, Nellie. I only went out to the news-stand by the door. I wanted some for myself.' She showed Nellie the pictures and cut out the ones from the new copies. Nellie quickly looked through the other papers but there was one of her with Miss Davies and one with a group of actors, but none of Lucy. She gave a sigh of relief. Maybe it would end there. Girls threw themselves at handsome actors to have publicity, often enough to make other papers ignore the implication that the couple were more than friends.

She looked again under the square cut from each paper where Lucy's picture had been. Lucy was putting away the cuttings carefully in her handkerchief sachet, so Nellie was able to tear off the captions and crumple them all before Lucy turned round. Monty was sound asleep so she couldn't discuss anything with him until the morning, and she knew that she must be fresh for her performance.

'I'm sleeping in the other bed in here tonight, Lucy. Let me sleep until ten and then you can go to meet Sidney.' She undressed and removed her make-up with cold cream. 'Monty will snore like a pig all night and I need rest.' She put the crumpled papers under her pillow and put out her light. 'Ten o'clock and I'll have fruit juice and toast Melba,' she murmured.

Lucy tidied the newspapers. She had all she wanted and so did Monty and Nellie. On the floor she found a torn piece, crumpled up. She tossed it into the waste basket without a glance, and didn't see what had gone under her picture.

'A GIRL friend? Well, well, what will the faithful Ivor have to say about that? Watch this space and we'll bring you more news about America's new matinée star.'

Chapter 12

'My mother writes to me at least once a month,' said Sidney Darwen, 'but it isn't the same as having you talk to me.' His hand reached over the table to take Lucy's and she blushed. 'Go on, don't stop. I want to hear about everything. You were saying that Janey gets more pretty even after having a baby? And Clare, expecting?' He laughed with the kind of amusement a boy might feel when he's discovered something really funny about his sister. 'I'd never have believed it possible.'

'All women want to marry and have children, Sidney.' The first excitement was dying. Sidney had talked and asked questions about his family and about old buildings and places he remembered from childhood, as if hungry for every detail, but he said nothing of what he felt for Lucy.

'Do they?' He lapsed into silence. 'Some do, some don't and that goes for men, too.' His eyes were sad. 'Have you found someone to give you everything you want, Lucy?' His voice was low and he didn't look at her now but seemed lost in his own thoughts.

'I can do all the things a wife should do and I know that men find me attractive,' she said with a touch of defiance. Look at me! she wanted to say. Look at me and not through me at your childhood. I'm a woman and I'm in love with you!

They had eaten lunch and now sat under an awning in the coolest part of the park, drinking icecream soda and the hours slipped by. Sidney now smiled and turned his attention to Lucy. 'You must think I'm very rude,' he said. 'I haven't asked about you. How is your mother? Is she still working in the laundry? I heard that you had gone to live with Janey at the Lodge. I remember Maudie as being pretty. Has she married again?'

Lucy bit her lip. Gradually, she had come to know that her mother must have a man to keep her, for she no longer worked and yet still managed to dress fairly well and pay the rent. Rumours and talk that stopped when Lucy went into a room now made sense, but she couldn't think who on the island had enough money to keep her mother discreetly.

'I'm sorry,' said Sidney gently. 'I'm a fool to mention it, but if she's happy and well, we can't wish for anything different for her, can we?'

'Don't you think it matters that my mother is no better than she ought to be?'

He smiled at the old-fashioned euphemism. 'You sound like my mother,' he said. 'No, I think that we all must find happiness in our own ways. I expect you must distrust all men, Lucy.'

'Oh, no! I don't distrust you, Sidney. I've come all this way, longing to meet you again.'

'And here we are,' he said lightly.

'Did you see the picture of us taken last night?'

'No, I seldom read the papers,' he said, and his face was set in lines that she hadn't noticed.

'Here it is.' She unfolded one of the cuttings and handed it to him. He looked at it in silence and then gave a short laugh. 'Isn't it good?' she said eagerly.

'Very good. I wish my father could have seen it.'

'Your father?' Lucy smiled tenderly. 'Of course, you couldn't be at the funeral, could you? It must have made you very sad.'

'There were enough there without me. All his old friends and enemies, apart from the ones who died before he did, like dear old Sam Walmsley from the fruit warehouse and Aaron Sheath who supplied us with fish.'

'I think the whole town respected him and they had the old-fashioned hearse drawn by six black horses with black ostrich plumes. It was beautiful and your mother didn't shed a tear in the church.' Lucy laughed. 'There were many who did. Even my mother cried and there were two of the gypsies from Wootton there dressed in their best.'

'That makes sense.' His face relaxed. 'When we were children, the gypsies used to come to the house in the spring with pegs and things and my father sent for them if a horse was sick. That at least we had in common. I learned some Romany words from them.' He squeezed her hand. 'Lucy, my dear, you don't know how much this meeting has meant to me. It brings back so much and you've made me homesick.' He looked at his watch. 'I have to go. I expect you must, too, if Nellie has a performance this evening.'

Lucy gasped. 'Yes, I must go. When can I see you again?' He hesitated. 'We have to go to Florida at the end of the week, down to a house with a funny name owned by a friend of Mr Hearst's,' she went on. 'Nellie was invited last night by Miss Davies and we're all going.'

'*Vizcaya*?' Sidney sat back and stared at her. 'Everyone wants an invitation there. It means you are getting well-known and even famous.'

'But *you* are very well-known, Sidney. At least two men have taken our picture again today and I think that the man over there is the reporter who spoke to me last night after taking the picture with that terribly bright flash.'

'He spoke to you? Asked you questions about me?'

'He asked how long I'd known you and I told him the truth – that we'd known each other all our lives.'

Sidney smiled wickedly. 'They'll make a meal out of that, but I don't care if you don't.' He glanced towards the man who was gathering up his equipment and looking bored. 'I'll telephone the hotel and we can meet again before you leave.' He kissed her on the lips and held her close, just long enough for the man hastily to take another picture, then released her and picked up the light linen jacket that he had discarded in the heat of July.

'Take a cab from the rank over there,' he said. 'I must run.'

Lucy sat back in the cab and sighed with sheer delight. Her lips still trembled after his kiss and she felt happy enough to die. 'He loves me! He loves me!' she wanted to say to the taxi driver, but outwardly she was calm, and

166

turned her thoughts back to her duties. The dress she had altered would please Nellie she knew, and everything was ready for the evening show.

'Marion Davies has taken a box for this evening,' Nellie greeted her. 'I don't know who is in the party but of course the management has asked her backstage in the interval for some champagne.' Nellie was elated and didn't ask what had happened at lunch, and Lucy was glad to have her own private thoughts.

The evening went on as others had done, with the audience filling the theatre with warm appreciation and Nellie emerging in the interval with sparkling eyes after drinking champagne with Miss Davies and the others in her party. One of the group regarded Lucy with a puzzled air. 'Haven't I seen you some place?' he said. Lucy smiled. 'Not with Nellie Morris, but somewhere in a magazine? Do you sing, too?'

'My picture was in the paper last night, or rather, early this morning with Sidney Darwen. I had lunch with him today,' she added shyly.

'Is that so? I thought he didn't go for girls.' The pale blue eyes seemed to want to read her thoughts and Lucy was vaguely annoyed.

'Sidney is a gentleman,' she said. 'He doesn't run around with women but he's the nicest man I know.'

'He's a great success in magazines and on the stage, but he doesn't date the ladies,' the man went on. 'They all pine for him but he isn't the type.'

'Isn't that what I'm saying?' Lucy sensed an undercurrent of insult. 'He has so many women after him but he prefers my company. I've known him for years.'

'Is that so? Maybe Miss Davies got the wrong idea after all.' He went over and whispered to Marion Davies, who glanced towards Lucy and looked surprised. They talked for another minute and then she smiled and nodded. The man came back and touched Lucy on the arm. 'I'm sorry,' he said. 'Miss Davies says that if you like to include Mr Darwen in your party as he's your boyfriend, then why not ask him to go with you all on Sunday to *Vizcaya*?'

'I know he'll be pleased,' said Lucy, with engaging candour. 'He said he would like to be invited there and he really is getting quite well-known as an actor, isn't he?'

'That's right. They invite all the up and coming talent if they're straight. Trouble was that Miss Davies thought he was a pansy before today.'

He left her alone and Lucy tried to make sense of what he'd said. She'd heard the expression often when a man was mentioned and he was dismissed with a laugh. She frowned and decided to ask Nellie, but there wasn't time before the next change of costume.

'Nellie, I think you were even better this evening,' said Monty. 'That dress is a humdinger.'

'Thanks to Lucy. It really fits well and I could bend and stretch without having it rub my waist. No, thank you. I'm off sweets and chocolates for at least a month and if we're going South, then I must get in trim for the swimming pool. They say it's enormous and that everyone sits by it in the sun and we shall meet so many famous people. I'm so excited.'

'So am I. Miss Davies has invited Sidney too, and suggested that he might travel with us on the train.'

'What?' Monty almost shook the ash into his drink as he put down his cigar. 'That . . . man,' he said lamely, when he saw Nellie's warning glance.

'Were you going to say that pansy?' asked Lucy. 'What is a pansy? Apart from being a very lovely flower.'

Nellie glanced at Monty to tell him to keep quiet. 'A pansy is a man who doesn't go with women but goes with men instead, and if they sleep together, it's against the law and against society,' she said bluntly.

Lucy exploded into silvery laughter. 'Oh, you *are* funny. If men don't like women, what does it matter? There will always be one woman who'll love him and who he'll want. And men do sleep in the same room. They have to if there aren't enough rooms to go round. Clare and Lizzie used to share a room. Are they pansies?'

Monty coughed and went slightly puce. 'It isn't the same,' he said.

'It's a matter of sex,' said Nellie. 'Men who never have sex with women but who have sex with men are pansies, or queer is another expression you will hear.'

'How can they?' Lucy still found it amusing. 'I can't see how. Of course I know how people make babies. I've watched enough animals to know about it and girls have told me, but I can't see how men can *do* anything.'

'Forget it. Some day when I'm not tired and hungry and you have a little more imagination, I'll tell you about it. For the moment, something has convinced Miss Davies that Sidney Darwen is straight and we shall have his company on Sunday.' Nellie glanced at Monty and shrugged. 'At least we don't have to worry about Lucy if he's with her.'

'Do you think I should telephone the theatre and not wait for him to get in touch with me?' asked Lucy.

'It might be as well. He will have to make some arrangements, and he doesn't have much time to get someone to take his place in the revue.' Nellie tried to be fair and was beginning to like the idea of the handsome young man coming with them. He knew her background, and together they could all be natural and remind themselves of the old days. 'Ask the girl in the reception desk to get through for you.'

The girl looked impressed. 'Do you *really* know him, Miss Dove? I think he's wonderful and far more handsome then Valentino.'

'I come from the same town and we've known each other for years,' said Lucy.

'Are you the girl he's been waiting for? Nobody has ever been able to find out if he has a girl and when I saw him . . . it's five times now, in that love scene, it made my toes curl up and I wanted to cry. You are a very lucky girl.'

'Could you get through?' asked Lucy, worried in case he had left the theatre.

'Surely.' The girl plugged into the switchboard and got through to the theatre. 'Call for Mr Darwen from Miss Dove,' she droned. 'Yeah, I'll hold the line.'

She motioned to a telephone receiver on the desk and

Lucy picked it up. 'Who wants Mr Darwen?' said a male voice.

'Tell him it's Miss Dove . . . Lucy. He was to ring me but I have some news for him.'

'He's busy.' The voice was sulky. Behind him, Lucy could hear music and then another voice, and the line crackled as the telephone changed hands.

'Sidney Darwen here.'

'Oh, Sidney, I had to ring you,' she began.

'Why didn't you say? Ivor must have misunderstood. Obviously I want to talk to you!'

'I have a message for you,' she said, unable to hide her excitement, and told him about the invitation.

'Are you serious?' Sidney sounded stunned and then very excited. 'You *do* mean it! I've longed for this for simply ages and it might do a lot for my career. Most of the movie moguls go there and they have guests from Los Angeles and all over.'

'It was the picture in the paper that did it,' said Lucy. 'I was asked who I was by one of Miss Davies' party and it must have reminded her that you were popular in the theatre.'

'Clever little Lucy,' said Sidney. He paused and cleared his throat. 'Do I come alone?'

'Oh, no! You come with us. They said that you could make up our party as you would be with me. Isn't that nice? They thought I might be an odd one out with Nellie and Monty and no escort for me, I expect.'

'I see.'

'Sidney? Are you there?' she said and wondered if she had been cut off.

'I'm here. It's just so sudden and I have to think of certain arrangements.'

'That's why I rang. Nellie said you'd have to arrange for someone to cover for you in the theatre. You *can* come?' she asked anxiously.

'I'll ring you tomorrow, but yes, I shall come whatever happens.'

Lucy walked back to the suite, slowly. He had sounded

thrilled, but uneasy as if 'certain arrangements' might not be easy. Who had answered the telephone? Probably a dresser who wanted to get home and hated being called to fetch people. She shrugged. It was late and Nellie wanted to be in bed earlier than last night, but Lucy was restless. It would be wonderful to spend a whole week with Sidney in a wonderful place. Everything was really wonderful, wasn't it? I couldn't expect him to be more attentive, she thought. He kissed me and held me in his arms . . . just as he did those beautiful girls on the stage.

The melody from the latest popular song throbbed in her ears. It was the tune she had heard in the background when she was talking to Sidney and now it came from the hotel dance floor. '*Avalon, Avalon, where you go my heart goes with you* . . .' It was dreamy and smooth and sentimental, just right for dancing a slow and intimate foxtrot with the man she loved.

The phone rang. 'Who is that at this time of night?' Monty sounded annoyed although on other nights he might be out far later.

'Hello!' he barked into the phone. He listened for a minute. 'No, she isn't and I'll thank you not to disturb us again, whoever you are.' He hung up the receiver with such force that the instrument quivered on the stand. He glared at Lucy. 'Oh, there you are. I said you weren't here,' he admitted more calmly. 'I don't know who he is, but he rang before and I don't like the sound of him. Go dancing with him, at this hour, and alone? How do we know who he is and if he isn't one of those white slavers you hear about?'

'Hardly that, dear. Probably one of those nice boys we met in the lounge who obviously took a shine to Lucy.' Nellie yawned. 'But it's just as well to say no, Lucy. You shouldn't go alone to a dance floor even if it is in the same hotel as where you are staying. Did he say his name?'

'Garden . . . Gardel . . . Barcia. That's it. Sounded foreign.'

'Then it's a good thing you answered, Monty. That little

rat is staying here who was on the *Mauretania*. I don't think it's coincidence. His name is Garsey.'

'Well, I sent him off with a flea in his ear. He won't bother you again, Lucy.'

'He doesn't bother me. I just ignore him,' shrugged Lucy. 'With Sidney here, I shall not be troubled by men like him.'

'No, you won't be bothered in that way for the next week at least,' Monty agreed.

'Bed!' exclaimed Nellie. 'Tomorrow you must go shopping, Lucy. We shall need clothes for the trip and some smart outfits to wear by the pool.' Monty sighed and went into the main bedroom and closed the door. 'We can afford it now that Monty won all that money,' said Nellie. 'You have to look smart, too. Some people see everything and your clothes will be noticed; if you don't look smart, they'll think we are cheese-paring.'

'That will be lovely. Sidney always did care about clothes and he has such good taste.' Lucy's eyes shone and now that she was away from him, the old yearning took over. He was handsome and very sweet and he *did* feel something for her.

The week fled by in a mist of shopping and unpacking cardboard boxes lined with tissue paper, fitting dresses and choosing beach-clothes. Sidney called twice but seemed preoccupied, but Lucy was busy too and hardly noticed it. They would be together for a week, and what was that after all the months and years when she had only his picture to see?

On Sunday morning, they checked out of the hotel, loaded a taxi with their baggage and met Sidney at the railway station. By nightfall, they were rushing through the American countryside, asleep in their berths and ready for Florida.

The heat struck them as soon as they left the train and it was with relief that they reached the wide iron gates protecting *Vizcaya*, the home of Jim Deering, the close friend of Randolph Hearst and his entourage. Even Nellie gasped when she saw the white marble Venetian house set in huge, manicured gardens, looking like something out of a fairy tale.

Servants ran out to take luggage and to whisk them up to the suite of rooms reserved for them. The planning was faultless; Monty and Nellie had a double room, with its own bathroom. There was a sitting room, and two smaller bedrooms with connecting doors and optional bolts and another shower room for the two rooms.

Lucy ran to the sitting room window and saw the massive trees and green lawns, exotic flowers and the sparkle of a fountain. She turned and saw the expression on Sidney's face. 'It's unbelievable,' he said. His voice broke with emotion. 'You bring me luck, Lucy. Last night I had a call from a producer who will be here this week. He wants me to be auditioned for a very important rôle and I know it was because he'd seen my name on the guest-list here and knows I'm accepted by all these important people.'

Lucy crept closer and he put an arm round her. 'It's going to be wonderful,' she whispered. She kissed his cheek and he laid the side of his head on hers. She closed her eyes but he didn't kiss her and she drew away, disappointed.

'Ready to come down?' Nellie was laughing. 'I want to see everything. Dinner is at nine and until then we just ask if we want tea or drinks, or anything, and can amuse ourselves.' Lucy ran after her, curious to explore and they looked up at the black marble pillars and walked over the black marble floor of the main hall. A huge marble ship was set into one side of the house and on the other, away from the lawns and flowers was a sandy beach that looked exactly like one by the sea, but this bordered a vast swimming pool set half in and half out of the house. On the walls hung pictures and posters of Marion Davies in her latest movies. Her face was everywhere.

'She's very beautiful,' said Nellie. 'They say that

173

hundreds of men are in love with her but she remains faithful to Mr Hearst.'

Sidney looked about him. 'Is it any wonder? Men would sell their souls for this, and women their bodies.'

'I wouldn't,' said Lucy.

'No, not you, but you aren't like that, little Lucy.'

'I am a woman,' she said and blushed, but he was busy examining a statue that must have come from Italy and cost a fortune.

'I feel like a tourist and I shouldn't,' said Nellie. 'We are guests here.' She asked Monty to order tea and muffins and he snapped his fingers and gave the order to one of the many men who were ready to wait on them. Nellie subsided into a chaise longue by the pool under a huge sun umbrella and tea arrived in fragile china with perfectly prepared muffins, preserves and small iced cakes.

The waiter whisked away a bowl of roses that took up room on the small table and Nellie poured tea. Other people who had been guests on other occasions strolled by with towels over their arms, ready to swim, and some just sat and talked in the shade. It was hot and Lucy longed for the cool water, but was too shy to mention it. Would she have to change in her room and come down in the elevator in her swimming costume? Or were the doors over at the other side of the pool for the use of anyone for changing?

Sidney reclined on a rush mat, his long slim body relaxed and his face expressionless but incredibly good-looking. He reached for a muffin and bit into it, licking the ooze of butter from his fingers. Lucy watched him, fascinated, and realised that she was feeling a completely new sensation. It was one thing to sigh after a man and to wonder what it would be like to be kissed by him, and something much more to want him so badly, to long for his hands on her body, his kisses fierce and unrestrained and his body loving her.

'I'm going to swim,' she announced with sudden determination. 'I saw people coming out of that door over there and I think they changed in there. Do you mind if I fetch my swimming suit, Nellie?'

174

'Just be careful of the sun. It's very hot and the air is clear and you might get burned up,' said Monty. He lay back under the awning as if he had no intention of moving for hours, and Nellie had found a party of actors whom she had met before in New York and was engrossed with them. Sidney raised his head to look at the water and smiled.

'I'll come too. See you in the water.'

Lucy laughed. 'There are rubber mattresses and huge rubber animals,' she said. 'I've never seen anything like it.' She waited for him to walk with her to the suite and chatted like a child going on a treat, and when they were in the pool, she felt really happy. Sidney was like a boy again, playing with the huge toys and splashing anyone who came to push him off his favourite rubber horse. More people joined them and laughter filtered over to Nellie and Monty, drawing even more to watch.

They dived and swam and played a kind of water polo with no rules, and Lucy noticed how the women tried to swim close to the laughing man with the wide blue eyes, and to bump into him, quite by accident, of course. She also noticed with pleasure that he was pleasant to everyone and enjoyed the fun, but came back to her time and again as if he was happy to be with her.

'You're a good sport, Lucy,' he gasped, when she rose spluttering from a bad dive. He held her as they swam to the steps and then wiped the water from her eyes.

'Are you glad you came?' she asked.

'It's wonderful.' He kissed the tip of her nose. 'And you are the prettiest girl here.'

'Do you like this suit?'

He regarded her as he had done the statue in the garden, as if she was a work of art to be enjoyed for its beauty. 'I think it's very pretty, and very well-designed,' he said. 'You can wear it as you have such a slim body and nice shape.'

Her eyes felt hot with the chlorinated water but she no longer minded. He thought she was pretty.

'Better get dressed and dry or we shall be damp at

175

dinner,' he said. 'We can shower and wash our hair down here, I believe.'

Lucy found towels and shampoo and sweet scented talcum by the marble basins in the changing rooms and took her time washing away the smell of chlorine. Her hair dried quickly in the curling nimbus that was so easy to manage and she was pink and white like a cherub as she pulled on her stockings and linen dress and returned to normal.

Sidney had left and Nellie was ready to go up to change. 'He is going to meet us at dinner,' said Nellie when she saw Lucy looking about her. 'I think I was mistaken about Sidney. He's great fun and even made Monty laugh with a very funny story. Are you happy?' Nellie asked.

'So very happy.' And the expression on her face made Nellie turn away in case she said something to ruin it. 'You were going to tell me about . . . men, Nellie,' Lucy ventured on their way up to the suite.

'It doesn't matter now. If men are too good-looking, people say they are more like women and can only love women as sisters, and they fall in love with other men.'

'Sidney isn't like a woman! He has such broad shoulders and a very good figure.' She blushed, thinking of his male body with the thin swimming costume clinging to it.

'Forget it,' Nellie sighed. 'Just have a good time here and treasure it. We may never be invited again,' she added. 'If I broke a leg or lost my voice, none of these people would want us then. Take my advice – marry a good man who will look after you and care for you and take the rest like you would any luxury, in small quantities, knowing it might not last.'

'Sidney does care about me,' said Lucy and helped Nellie into the lowcut gown that had made Monty blench when he saw the bill.

At dinner, the guests sat along a wide table, with the hostess at the centre and the guests beside her in two directions, with the newest and most intimate of her friends close to the centre. Lucy was a little way down from Nellie and Sidney sat opposite, far enough away to make conversation difficult so she had to talk to her immediate neighbours. The man on her right looked forbidding and much older than most of the party. He ignored her until she put a hand over her wine glass and asked for fresh orange and no alcohol, then turned to her with interest.

'It does me good to see a pretty young thing like you refusing wine. This place is a sink of iniquity.' He glared round at the flushed and laughing faces. 'If I wasn't a good friend of Randolph, I'd have the FBI down on this place.'

'It's beautiful,' said Lucy, and smiled. Now she knew who he was like. Once, when she was quite small, her mother had taken her to a huge tent where a Hot Gospeller had thundered hell and damnation at a slightly bemused Island congregation.

'Keep your virtue and your morals, my dear. They are dearer to God than all of this.'

'I'll try,' she said. Sidney leaned forward and raised his voice.

'The lobster reminds me of home.'

'You know that young man?' The narrow lips clamped together.

'We came here together. I've known him since I was a child.'

'Is that so? It's Sidney Darwen, isn't it?' He stared across the table. 'He's good-looking,' he conceded, as if inspecting a prize bull. 'Nice profile and good voice. They like English voices and they come over well on film.'

'You mean the new talking pictures? Do you think they will take on?'

'I make them!' He was watching Sidney helping the lady on his left to relish and making her laugh. 'Is he married?'

'Not yet,' said Lucy.

'I like married men with respectable families to act for me, even if we don't tell the public, and my films don't corrupt the young.'

'Sidney is a wonderful person,' she said. 'I came all this way from England to be with him, and we are getting to know each other again.' Sidney smiled at her and eyed the

177

man at her side with guarded interest, knowing that he was a very powerful film producer with very narrow ideals.

'I want to meet him. Tell him to be in the pool-room at eleven tonight.' He turned his attention to the woman on his right, and Lucy made frantic signs to Sidney to meet her after dessert.

'He is very interested in you,' Lucy insisted when Sidney laughed in disbelief.

'I don't understand. I went for an audition and they refused to give me one. What did you tell him?'

'Nothing. How could I? I know so little about your work. I just told him how I came to know you and that we are very good friends.' She laughed. 'He was impressed to see that neither of us drank wine. He's dead against drinking.'

'Come with me, Lucy. That man scares me.'

'Of course.' She put her hand in his and they went into the pool-room, and she felt Sidney's fingers tighten on hers as they met the great man.

'Like to work for me, young man?' he asked bluntly. Sidney nodded, unable to speak. 'One condition. *Get married*.' The long black cheroot waved menacingly. 'Can't have my leading men labelled queer, and the press will do it, given the chance.'

'But I'm not even engaged.' Sidney looked desperate.'

'Ask her! This is as good a place as any and mighty good for publicity. She is your girl?'

Sidney shut his eyes for a minute and saw his future shining bright or dull with routine. He looked at Lucy and her eager eyes and wondered if it was possible. She was the sweetest girl he'd ever met and he did love her in many ways.

'Will you marry me, Lucy?' he asked.

Chapter 13

'Isn't it wonderful?' Jane Darwen spread the pictures over the embroidered tea-cloth and unfolded the letter for the umpteenth time. 'Lucy and our Sidney, engaged to be married – and you expecting again.'

'She'll be over the moon with happiness,' said Janey. 'We all know how she felt about him and now, they will be as happy as Clive and me.' She regarded her mother with curiosity. Jane had seldom been so happy even when she had the news that Clare and Lizzie were pregnant. 'Sidney always was special, wasn't he?' she asked without envy. 'We all loved him because he was different and much more affectionate than the other boys.' And Clive was wrong about him, she thought.

'Sit down, Janey. You've been on your feet for long enough, and you have extra weight to bear now. I've made tea but you can have coffee if you prefer.'

'No, I'm fine now and can eat or drink anything. I brought down my letter as well but the news is the same, only Lucy is more ecstatic. What it is to have a famous brother, or he will be soon, and I can't see Lucy ever coming back to the Lodge to work for us again!'

'I wonder if her mother knows?' asked Jane. 'I never go there, so could you leave a note for Maudie?'

'Didn't you hear? She's left Sea Street and lives out at the West Wight now. Bert took her to London on a day trip and they were seen by a party from the Chapel, so now everyone knows that she is his kept woman.'

'I'll tell Bert when he comes in,' said Jane. 'He wants me to see Annie this afternoon and he's calling for me in his motor. Annie isn't well and she keeps on asking me to go there.'

'Does she know about Maudie?'

'No. Annie thinks he goes with women but is blind to

what goes on under her nose. It's as well, and I'll not be the one to tell her.' She folded the letter again. 'This will give her something to talk about, and she won't like it. She always said that Lucy was too forward and should know her place more.'

She fetched her coat and hat, and Janey saw that she was very excited. 'I *am* happy,' said Jane. 'It's a great burden from my mind in more ways than one.' She heard the sound of the motor horn and hurried to the steps by the edge of the Mall. Janey need never know how many nights her mother lay awake dreading the last of the prophecies made by old Mother Lee, the gypsy, so many years ago. Everything had come true except for two things. Sidney would never marry she had said; but now he was to marry Lucy, so please God, the other terrible thing couldn't happen. Janey wouldn't be made a widow early. The spell, if that is what it was, is broken, she told herself. Holy Mary, thank you! Clive will come back to us again, safe and sound and raise his family.

'She's worse,' said Bert Cooper as soon as Jane was settled in the passenger seat. 'The doctor insisted that the nurse must stay and we have a day nurse now as well as the night nurse.'

'Is she in pain? Does she know how bad it is?' asked Jane soberly.

'She sleeps a lot, but that's the medicine,' explained Bert. 'At least this nurse has the knack of making her comfortable, not like the last one who lifted her like a bag of potatoes and dumped her on the pillows all anyhow. I got rid of her, sharpish. I can't have Annie treated like that.'

Jane glanced at the face beside her. It was a bit late for consideration now. It was a bit late for anything, including guilt, and there had been faults on both sides.

'I can stay for a few hours and I've brought some of her cream and some nice jelly,' she said. 'Has the doctor said anything?'

'It could be today or next week or next month. He warned me that with the morphia she might get spells of recovery and then have a crisis again. Some thrive on it for a while and she's having a big dose.'

'If it kills the pain it's good,' said Jane. 'The time isn't important if she dies with an easy mind.'

'As easy as Annie could ever be, Jane, but I do my best.'

'I know,' she said softly. 'You haven't been out to the West Wight for a week or so and I think that Annie knows that you do care about her.'

He went red. 'She's my wife when all's said and done, and I'm sorry for leading her a dance at times.'

'Don't be sorry now. You are doing your best, Bert. I have a bit of news that will make her take notice, if anything will. Our Sidney is engaged to be married.'

'Sidney?' He grinned. 'Wonders never cease.'

'He's marrying Lucy, Maudie's girl. Can you tell her, for I don't think they write to each other now.'

He glanced at her and shrugged. Everyone knew now about him and Maudie and in a way it was a relief. 'I'll tell her, but she'll be mad. She hated Lucy going off like that.'

'It was for the best,' said Jane. 'She was lucky to have the chance to go with Nellie and she has been fond of Sidney ever since they played together with the puppets.'

'How's Janey?'

'Fine, just fine. George is a handful now but she has plenty of help and Clive is due home next month after sea trials.'

'You aren't worried about him? I thought you had a dread of submarines.'

'Not now,' she said quietly. 'I wish he was in one of the big ships like Alex, Dr Barnes' boy, but in peacetime, I don't think he's in danger. Alex will be home at the same time and now he's over Millie's death it will be a wonderful reunion with them all together again. His cousin is in the navy as well, and they've been working in the same ship, so he will bring his wife to the Island for a visit, too.'

The house on the hill with the view of Pan Down and the scar of white chalk where it had been cut years ago was quiet and the curtains were half-drawn to keep out the sun. Jane wanted to fling them back and let in air and light but Annie had lived in shadows all her life and it was too late to alter things now.

'Annie?' she said gently, and bent to kiss the tightly-drawn skin on the yellow cheek. Annie stirred and opened her eyes. For a moment, the pin-point pupils focussed on Jane's face and then the eyelids drooped and she sank back into sleep.

'She's had her injection,' whispered the nurse. 'She'll be like that for a while and then have a wakeful period when she'll be able to talk.' She tidied the room quietly, and Jane smiled her approval, able to recognise calm efficiency and relieved that Dr Barnes ordered enough drugs to drown any pain, even if it shortened life. They wouldn't let a dog suffer, so why watch a human being thresh about in agony, she thought.

The second tiny gown was finished and the last frill sewn on the hem when Annie opened her eyes. Lizzie would be pleased to see how many garments her mother had made for her baby and there were the ones to make for Clare, now. Jane put aside the sewing and sat by the bed. She held the feeding cup to Annie's lips when she asked for a drink and helped the nurse to make her comfortable with more pillows.

'How long have you been here?' Annie asked. She shot a glance at the nurse, who smiled slightly, and left the room. 'That girl spies on me,' Annie told Jane. 'A fine thing if I can't go to sleep without her watching me. I think she's after my money.'

'She makes you comfortable,' Jane said mildly. 'Bert couldn't do that, could he?'

'He's been good and when I'm better, we shall go to see my aunt in Southampton. He promised.' Annie smiled. 'I feel better today and when I'm strong, I'll be up on the Mall to see what you've all been up to.'

'We bought new curtains for my bedroom and a lovely chair from Wadhams for the drawing room.'

'Nothing but the best for you Darwens,' said Annie with a return of her usual acidity. She tried to sit higher but was too weak. 'I expect that set you back a shilling or two.'

'You'll have to come and see, Annie.' Jane smiled. 'I have one bit of news that I've told to nobody.' Annie listened like a bird with its head on one side, a sad fledgling with no feathers and gaunt yellow skin. 'Sidney is going to be married.' Annie gasped and pushed at the bedclothes as if she wanted to get dressed and run to the shops and spread this choice morsel of gossip. 'He's marrying Lucy Dove,' Jane added, watching Annie for her reaction.

'Lucy Dove?' Annie tried to say more but sank back, exhausted. 'Lucy . . . Sea Street . . . There is a man there who keeps goats in his backyard,' she said. 'Her mother wasn't too fussy from what I heard. There's bad blood there, Jane. Don't you let it happen.' Her eyes were bright with excitement and the pupils were not so small as the drug wore off.

'They are very happy,' said Jane. 'Sidney thinks he will be in one of the new talking pictures and Lucy seems to have been a great success with Nellie and works hard.'

'Nellie Morris! That's another one. Who knows what they get up to over there?'

'It's only fair that Lucy stays with Nellie for the full year that she promised, so she and Sidney will be engaged for a few months before they marry.' Jane brushed away a tear. 'I shall have to imagine it all. I didn't see Janey married and now Sidney will be on the other side of the world.' She brightened. 'But if they are happy, and Janey is safe, what does it matter?'

'Janey? What's wrong with Janey?' Annie was getting restless. She picked at the sheets and moved under the light bedclothes. Her hand was almost transparent and the veins on the back stood out like blue cords.

'Nothing. Nothing at all,' said Jane in a soothing tone. 'Can I get you some of my nice jelly? Or a little snippet of bread and butter?'

'I fancy a boiled potato,' said Annie.

Jane hurried out to the kitchen where Bert was talking to

the nurse. 'Get a pan of water and boil a couple of potatoes,' she said. 'Don't cut them. Annie likes them whole, split down the middle with butter, making them nice and floury.'

'They'll boil quicker cut up,' said Bert.

'I know that but Annie must have it how she likes it,' said Jane. 'She's getting restless,' she told the nurse, who hurried back to the sick-room. Bert prodded the potatoes at intervals while they waited and Jane set a small tray with a small dish and a fresh napkin. 'Cover the pot and leave it,' she said. 'It will take another five minutes at least.' She looked towards the door. 'Can the nurse manage?'

'She likes to do it alone. Annie weighs no more than a breath of air and she can lift her easily. Stay here, Jane. I need you more than Annie does, now.'

He sat down heavily and put his face in his hands. 'I know how you feel,' said Jane gently. 'Is there anything I can do, or say, Bert? I know how it's been with you over the years but you've stayed together and made the best of a bad job.'

'And after this?' His face was distorted with something more than remorse. 'I've got myself into a proper mess, Jane. It should not have happened, but it did.' He got up and paced the room.

'Your shares? Something wrong with business?'

'If that was it, I would be a happy man! I've never done better and Annie never knew what we had half the time.' He came back and looked down at her. 'I need a friend now, Jane. If Walter was alive he'd have backed me but I need you and your . . . sanctity, if you like.'

'I'm no saint, Bert Cooper! If you are sorry, the good Lord won't hold things against you and you've done your best for her.'

He let his hands fall to his sides in a gesture of defeat. 'It's Maudie. We went to London for two days just before Annie was taken really bad, only six weeks ago.' He shook his head in disbelief. 'After all this time, Maudie says she's taken.'

'Maudie?' Jane looked as if she didn't know whether to

184

laugh or cry. 'It's too early, Bert. She might just be late.'

'She's sick,' he said, and gave her a hard look. 'It's happened to me, Jane. It could have happened to Walter, and what would you have done about that?'

If she had been slapped in the face, it would have had less impact. It was true. All the time that Walter had been enjoying Maudie in the stables, this could have been the result. 'Why now, Bert? Maudie knows how to prevent it. Did she do it on purpose?'

'Does it matter? It could have been my fault, but after years of Annie and no children, I began to think I couldn't give a woman a baby.' He grinned suddenly. 'At least that's one thing off my mind.'

'The potato!' Jane hurried to the pot and lifted the lid. The potato was beginning to split, showing the creamy, floury inside, just as Annie liked it. She lifted one carefully on to the dish, added a generous sliver of butter, put a silver spoon on the tray and carried it into the sick-room.

The nurse straightened her back. Annie lay flat on the bed with the sheet drawn up to her chin. The dull eyes were closed and there was no movement in the pulse under the sparse hair. Bert stood in the doorway and stared, then walked slowly over to the bed and kissed the cold cheeks. The nurse took the tray from Jane and tipped the potato into the pig-bin in the kitchen, then went back with a glass of whiskey which she offered to the bereaved husband, and left the room.

'She's gone, Jane.' A touch of almost superstitious awe made his voice tremble. 'Poor Annie.'

'At least she'll never know,' said Jane. 'Not in this life.'

Bert looked up at the ceiling but saw only the white moulding that had been repaired only last month to satisfy Annie when she spent long hours on her bed, gazing upwards. 'She's gone,' he repeated, as if to convince himself. 'Now what do I do?'

'I'll telephone the doctor . . . no, the nurse will do that and see to everything.' Jane packed away her sewing and picked up the newspaper cuttings and Sidney's letter. This time, she would not take over. She had washed Amy,

Archie's wife, after death and composed her limbs, but this was different. The nurse could do it with care and there were the living to consider.

'You'd best have something to eat, Bert. You'll be busy with the formalities and have no time later.' She found some cold meat and pickles in the larder and added the second boiled potato with butter, just as Annie liked it.

He ate everything she put before him and when the doctor arrived, he was ready to meet him. Jane now slipped away to her own home, where the windows were wide open and the sun shone on the carpet, even if it might fade the fabric.

It was a long walk back, but Jane needed time to think. 'I could have gone by train,' she said to herself, but that would have taken her back to the shop. She turned her steps towards Trafalgar Road and up to the Mall, then wondered if she should have called in at Shide to tell Clare the news, but went on home to Emily and Vikki and the house that was now her home.

Vikki was on the rocking horse and Emily sat by her, her crochet-hook busy on the huge border that Clare had said she wanted for a bedspread a long time ago. Emily looked up and saw Jane's drawn expression. She put down the work and said she'd make tea, while Jane offered Vikki a sweet if she'd come down from the horse and let her shut it away for the night.

'He's tired and you will make yourself sore if you stay on him for too long,' she said firmly. She locked the door, using the new key that Archie had fitted until permanent blocks could be made to lessen the impetus of the rocking.

'How was she?' asked Emily softly.

'Pick Gran a nice flower from the garden and put it in this vase,' said Jane. Vikki ran off and they were alone. 'She died just over an hour ago, and Bert is making all the arrangements. I made sure he had something to eat and came home. Oh, Emily, that house was never a home. I've been here for such a short time, but this is already ours, just as the shop was for so many years. Even death didn't make it more cold. I wanted to open the windows and not

186

to close everything to show mourning. Bert will be so glad when it's all over.'

'Who will see to the refreshments after the funeral?' asked Emily. 'Look, I'll go over on the bicycle tomorrow and ask if he wants help. I suppose there are relatives?'

Jane gave a tired smile. 'Only distant ones. Today, Annie said she was going to see her aunt in Southampton. She died at least fifteen years ago. Bert has cousins and there will be a few neighbours and councillors, but no real grief, and Annie would have begrudged every shilling spent on food.' She sighed. 'Isn't it odd that I've known her for so long and she thought of me as her best friend, when all she did was to find fault and make mischief?'

'Poor Uncle Bert,' said Emily. 'I like him even if he is a bit of a rogue.' She opened a biscuit tin. 'He ought to marry again.'

'Marry?' Jane smiled. 'Maybe he will. This may have happened at the right time.' Emily stared. 'No, I'm not matchmaking this time! That's been done.' She told Emily about Maudie. 'So she'll either have to get rid of the baby or brazen it out, and now Bert is free he ought to make an honest woman of her.'

'They can't get married yet, five minutes after the funeral!'

'They can wait for a few weeks and marry quietly, if that's what they plan. The baby won't show for a long time.'

'We'd better not tell anyone in case Bert has other plans. I heard from Nora that Maudie was boasting about the wonderful job her daughter has in America and how she might go out there.'

Jane laughed. 'Imagine Lucy's face if her mother turned up now, and pregnant! It's all talk and she probably uses that when Bert doesn't do as she wishes. He is very taken with her.' She unpacked her sewing. 'I'll press these tonight and let Lizzie have them tomorrow, then I'll start on Clare's baby clothes. She's knitting quite a lot now but I said I'd make the gowns of nun's veiling.' Jane sighed with delight. 'More and more babies. Janey has plenty if

187

it's a boy again, but I have put by a few pretty things in case it's a girl this time. Wouldn't you rather make something like that and put away that crochet? It's getting heavy and it must be boring to do the same pattern all the time.'

'I enjoy it, and I promised Clare that I'd do it for her.'

Jane said nothing, but wondered if Clare would appreciate all the work that had gone into the lace edging. By now, Clare might have forgotten it and would want the latest in coloured Indian bedspreads. Cheap and nasty, was Jane's view of them, but if something was new and no one else had one, Clare would want one – even if the colours were garish and ran in the wash.

When Lizzie came to collect the baby gowns, Clare arrived soon afterwards, saying she had heard the news. She looked at the work that her mother had done and made a mental note that Lizzie had been given five gowns and six binders.

'It was a happy release,' said Lizzie piously. 'Where is Uncle Bert having the funeral meal? They say that the new shop by the Victoria Memorial caters well. He could have it there. They are very smart now and have a fountain in the hall.'

'He'll have just a few friends back at the house,' said Jane drily. 'It isn't a dance he's planning. I'll do the ordering if that's what he wants and the girl who cleans the house isn't a fool. She can set it out on the day.'

Lizzie looked disappointed. 'I could help in the kitchen. I don't mind putting myself out for Uncle Bert.'

Clare smiled. 'He would want to know where it all went if there was anything left, Lizzie – and you couldn't have him blaming the girl, now could you?'

Lizzie flounced into the kitchen and brought back the cake that Jane had been saving for Mrs Barnes when she came to tea. Jane sighed. Lizzie had already cut it into generous slices and was busy filling her own mouth before offering it round. 'You've found your appetite again then, Lizzie?' she enquired politely.

'I have to keep up my strength, Mother. Harry says

I must have a snack little and often to stop heartburn.'

'Alan will call for me later, Mother. What shall I get for tea?' asked Clare. 'He can have it here to save us when we get home.'

'There's a bit of cold mutton and some runner beans,' said Emily. 'I shan't be going to the butcher again until Thursday, so if you want more, you'd better run down the road before they shut for dinner.'

'We can have the mutton now and fetch savoury ducks and green peas tonight,' said Clare.

Jane resigned herself to the company of Lizzie and Clare for the rest of the day and hoped that they wouldn't bicker. Lizzie had become used to the idea of being a mother-to-be and traded on her fragile condition, but Clare goaded her with the knowledge that when she first knew, Lizzie was very upset. Clare was well and had not even had as much sickness as Lizzie, but Jane had the uneasy feeling that she still hated the idea of babies and that Alan was no happier than he had been when they lived in the North.

'So – Sidney has been caught by that scheming little huzzy,' said Clare viciously. 'I thought he had enough sense not to get married.'

'There's many a slip 'twixt cup and lip,' smirked Lizzie. 'It might not last.'

'Oh, it will last once she's got her claws into him.' Clare was angry again, and Jane wondered how she would react when the news about Maudie leaked out. Emily raised her eyebrows and went to fetch Vikki for dinner. It only needed Janey to come now with George to make the family complete and to annoy Clare even more, as George was a heavy child and made Vikki cry when he took her toys.

Midday dinner went off well, with Lizzie eating enough for two, as she said each time she sat down for a meal. The fresh fruit and the plate of cheese soon disappeared but Jane took pleasure in feeding them all once again; when they sat in the garden afterwards drinking tea and relaxing, she was pleased that they were with her. Annie Cooper faded from her mind and her heart was full of

189

gratitude for health and good food and the fruitfulness of her family.

Janey came in later, leaving the motor car by the steps and holding George firmly by the hand when he wanted to swing on the rail that bordered the Mall. He let out a yell that Clare heard from the garden. She pursed her lips. 'I hope he isn't coming out here, disturbing us all,' she snapped, but when Janey came in she smiled as if pleased to see her.

'I promised him a ride on the horse, Mother. Can I go in with him?'

'The door is locked as Archie hasn't got the right blocks for it yet and I'm afraid that Vikki might move them.'

'I won't, Gran. I promise,' said Vikki. 'Come and watch me, Georgie. I can go fast.'

They ran into the house with Janey following slowly. Emily found the key and opened the door and Vikki climbed on the saddle with the pride of possession. George stared at the brightly painted face of the horse and backed away. He buried his face in Emily's skirt and refused to look again. Disappointed, Vikki made the horse go higher, as far as the blocks would let her but he still looked away.

'Wouldn't you like to ride?' asked Janey. 'I told you about it and you couldn't wait to get here.'

'No, Mummy, no! It's a bad horse.' As Emily went back out to the garden, Janey held him close. 'Hush, George. It isn't bad. It's made of wood and can't hurt you.' He struggled and screamed and she put him down. He ran away and into the hall and Janey saw the front door slightly open. She remembered the rails and the drop of six feet down to the road and ran after him, calling frantically. She caught him up as he tried to climb the rail and dragged him back to the house.

Clare walked past her into the kitchen. 'I'll make more tea,' she said. The shouts were quite unnerving and she had hoped for a quiet day when others would wait on her.

Janey took George into the garden and gave him a ball. 'The front door was open, Mother. George nearly climbed

190

the rail outside, so I've shut it now. I must have left it open when we came in.'

'Vikki didn't get out, too, did she?' Emily started to her feet. 'Is she still in that room?'

'She'll be all right,' said Lizzie. 'You do fuss over that child, Emily. When I have my baby, it will never be spoiled like these two, I'll see to that.'

Emily ignored her and went into the hall. Jane smiled. Emily was devoted to the little girl and would see that she came to no harm. Sure enough, five minutes later they came out together.

'George needs his rest,' said Janey. 'He gets bad-tempered when he's tired. Can I take him up to the cot, Mother?' She put him to bed in the room he used when Janey was away, and Lizzie made acid comments about people taking things for granted.

'You'll have a houseful when you have to look after all the babies,' she said. 'Harry and I will need a rest sometimes, too, and I expect Clare will want her turn.'

'Babies were never a bother to me,' said Jane, smiling. 'There's room for them all here.'

'There wasn't room for Alan and me when we had nowhere to live,' said Clare.

'We made a comfortable home for you from the first day you arrived, Clare, and you've done nothing but grumble about it ever since!' Clare stared at her, shocked to hear her quiet sister speak out for once, but Emily was flushed and went on, 'You are lucky to have a nice home of your own and a baby all of your own.' She pushed the crochet into a linen bag and took a piece of cake. 'As I made it, I might as well eat some while it's still there,' she said. 'You could at least ask if you can take what's in the larder. That was for Mrs Barnes and now I'll have to make another.'

'I don't think we'll stay for supper,' said Lizzie, her face scarlet. 'I know when I'm not wanted. If you aren't careful Emily, you'll end up as dry as Annie Cooper.'

'And as for a baby, you can have this one as soon as it's born,' said Clare. 'I never wanted one and I'll be glad to be rid of it!'

'Stop it!' Jane rose to her feet. 'I won't have that talk in my house. If you can't all get on, then it's better that you stay away until you are invited. I like to see you both, but you do treat this place as your own and I've earned a little consideration. Come to tea on Sunday and bring your husbands but don't expect it will become a regular thing again! I'll expect you about three, and we can talk over what to do on the day of the funeral.'

'Yes, Mother,' said Lizzie, and glared at Emily. Clare tossed her head and said nothing, but gathered her coat and bag ready to leave as soon as Alan called for her.

Jane sighed. They had so much and yet the twin sisters were never satisfied. She smiled at Emily who was looking very upset and suggested that she might like to take Vikki for a walk before her supper. 'Take her to see the horses in the big field down the road by the stream,' she said. 'There's stale bread in the crock if she wants to feed them and I'll have her supper ready when you come back.'

It left Lizzie and Clare alone and when Janey came down she sensed that the atmosphere was tense. She went to help her mother in the kitchen and started chatting. 'Clive is in the North Sea,' she said. 'They finish trials soon and will be brought off the ship by smaller boats as the submarines will go on to Scotland for re-painting. He may travel from Edinburgh or one of the Northern ports by rail and he hopes to be here in three weeks' time.' She looked relaxed and happy and Jane felt her own annoyance seeping away. 'He's better at writing now and I keep every word he sends, like you did, Mother. Sometimes I can't picture his face, though, and I have to look at the photographs. I find that with all the people I love, and yet I can picture faces of perfect strangers whom I've seen on trains, down to their last whisker or wart.' She laughed. 'He'll be home soon and I'll have to take a closer look.'

'I'm very happy for you Janey, and I wish that the others knew how lucky they are.' They talked about Sidney and Lucy and what they could send for wedding presents. 'I can't think what we could send that they can't get over there. They have far more than we do in the way

192

of luxuries. Everyone now has an ice-box, Sidney says. Can you imagine having your own cool place to keep milk from going sour and meat from rotting in this heat? Just like the old ice factory where we got ice for the fish, only smaller and in the kitchen.'

'I can't make anything for Lucy to wear. In the pictures she sent, she looks lovely and the clothes came from a very good dressmaker. Let's leave it until we know the date. I can't believe it even now.'

'I hope they marry soon, even if Lucy has to stay with Nellie for a while,' said Jane firmly. 'I don't believe in long engagements.' A wedding ring on the girl's finger would finally break the warning and she could forget Mrs Lee and the past for good.

The front door slammed and Vikki rushed in to tell them about the horses. 'One of them kicked his feet in the air higher than my horse,' she said.

'He kicks high enough, and he's here all the time,' said Emily. She sat Vikki at the kitchen table and laid her spoon and fork. 'I'll stay with her and put her to bed,' she promised. Jane nodded and took Janey in to her sisters, and Emily emerged only when they had left for their own homes.

As soon as they had waved goodbye to Janey and George, Emily made fresh tea and put the fish ready to fry for supper. 'I'll just pop up to see if Vikki is asleep and then I can close her door,' she said, but Jane heard her run down again quickly. 'She's not in her room!'

Jane called and there was no answer. They went into the garden and called again but the whole place was silent. Each room was searched. 'Do you think she could have slipped out when we were saying goodbye to Janey,' said Emily in a trembling voice.

'She wouldn't go out in her nightie.' Jane looked at the door to the playroom and put a hand to her mouth. 'Did you lock the door?'

Emily stared at the key in the lock. 'Yes, I locked it and Janey saw me do so. Vikki must have found the key and gone in alone.' Jane flung open the door and felt the room go round. She caught her breath and held on to the table for support, while Emily sank to the floor with a low cry and gathered the small, still form into her arms.

One of the blocks from the rockers lay askew, dragged from its place, and Jane knew just how high the child must have driven the horse, like the one in the field.

'She's breathing. Leave her here and cover her up,' said Emily. 'I'll go for the doctor.'

Vikki opened her eyes and looked puzzled. 'I don't like my horse any more,' she said. 'I wanted him to go faster and he tossed me.' Her face crumpled into tears. 'I hurt, Gran. My back hurts and I can't feel my legs.'

Chapter 14

'It will take time.' Dr Barnes sat on the new chair and leaned back as if his spine was stiff, too. 'Young bones have a habit of healing fast and I think she'll be able to walk again, but you must be patient, and above all, don't let anyone take the blame.'

'We should have watched her,' said Jane Darwen.

'You can't be there all the time or the child would never be independent,' he said. 'She's her father's child and from what I knew of Nellie, it adds up to a very potent mixture of self-will and energy. If it hadn't been for you, she would be a very unhappy girl with no roots.'

'Thank you for all you did,' said Jane. She twisted her handkerchief into a ball. 'What a week! I never want to see another like it. First Annie dying, and Bert telling me his news.' She glanced at the doctor, knowing that he had been told about Maudie Dove. 'Then, little Vikki lying there like a dead thing and unable to move her legs and lastly the funeral, with Bert trying to be sad but eager to get it over. Two people commented on that and I had to say that it was because he'd hated seeing her suffer, which he did, bless him,' she added. 'He did his best for her, but she wasn't easy and now he can settle down and enjoy the warmth he needed. Poor Annie, she was cold and bitter.'

He smiled. 'And how is Mrs Darwen? I thought when you came here you would have less to do, but as far as I can tell, you still take on other people's burdens. I can see I'll have to keep an eye on you when all the babies are born.'

'Oh, they will be a real blessing and no trouble at all. I'll be fine, Doctor Barnes. It will keep me young.'

'We're all getting older,' he said gently. 'I was talking to Archie only recently and he told me how he senses that time is passing by.'

'I know.' For a moment, her face clouded. 'Dear man that he is. He helps me in all sorts of ways but my home is here with Emily and to make a place for any of my children if they need me. And now there's Vikki. I have to be here and make sure that she is happy. Janey will leave George here when Clive comes back and I shall be busy.'

'Alex is coming back at the same time. He'll stay with us, but I'd be grateful if you'd include him when the family come here. He's fond of you all and it does him good. We have so little to offer in the way of young company and there are times when he looks sad.'

'He knows that he can come and go as one of my own, and with Clive home, they'll have a wonderful time.'

'I'm glad you are here,' said Dr Barnes. 'None of us likes passing the old shop now. The latest tenant is a draper, I hear, but no one stays for long. The ironmonger didn't get his stock settled before he left and the man who wanted to set up as you had done couldn't get Bert Cooper to agree.'

'A draper will be fine,' said Jane. 'I never go that way unless I'm with Janey in the car and then I look across the other way to the Ebenezer Chapel and up the lane to the Withy. It's gone in my mind and yet if I look over there, I expect to see Walter standing in the doorway.'

Emily brought in a tray with coffee cups and cream. She poured out coffee and handed a plate of thin almond biscuits to the doctor. 'You must send in your bill, Emily,' he said with a smile. 'I come to this house and get more benefit than I give.' He saw her questioning expression. 'The specialist found a bruised nerve and slight crack in the spine, but they will heal in time and if you can rub her back gently each day to keep the blood flow normal, he thinks that she can leave off the collar and brace in six weeks' time.'

'Thank you, Doctor.' Emily let out a long shuddering breath. 'She's a dear child,' she said and there were tears in her eyes. She picked up her own cup and went to sit on the bright chintz on the window-seat, where her crochet was kept under the fall of the cover.

'I shall keep on the girl now. We need someone to be here when Emily and I have to go out and we must make sure that we have a change,' said Jane with a meaning glance towards Emily.

'Very wise, and good for Vikki,' he answered firmly. 'In fact, my wife would like you both to come to tea on Thursday if it's convenient.'

Jane blushed with pleasure. After all these years, she still felt these invitations to be a privilege. It seemed strange to walk up to the house and not go in through the surgery door, as she had done so often when her children were young and she or they were ill. 'I shall enjoy that,' she said, and told him the news from America and all about the place where Lucy and Sidney were staying. 'It sounds like a palace, but I can't see how they enjoy their guests when they don't know half of them by name! It's almost like a hotel, but they have got to know a lot of people and Nellie is very excited about a tour that she has been asked to do.'

'When is the wedding?'

'Not yet, but they are making plans. The inauguration of the new President comes this year and that seems to take over everything, much more than our elections do.' Jane shrugged. 'I know nothing about politics, here or in America, but they've all voted for Warren Harding, so I expect he's a great man. Bert says that it's all rigged and that the gangsters rule America, but I can't believe that. I know there is a bad element there, what with the illegal sale of alcohol and drugs and those terrible murders we read about. They shouldn't be allowed to have guns if they can't control the people who use them.'

'It's not as bad as we think. The newspapers print only the things that will shock us and interest us.'

'Bert says that this Mr Hearst is so powerful that he stops things being printed if they could harm him. I can't believe that, can you?'

'I think that Bert is right. I think, too, that he should watch the American stock exchange. I hope you haven't any shares in American stocks?'

'No. I told him I wanted my money invested in safe British stocks and in property. I've also set up a small workshop for three dressmakers who were very willing but had no permanent workplace.' She glanced at Emily and smiled. 'Emily knows but the others don't. I'll see how it goes. It could be a nice nest-egg for her later. Even the girls who work there have no idea it's mine. When he likes, Bert can be like a closed oyster.'

'He came to see me about Maudie, as he told you.' Dr Barnes rubbed his ear as if puzzled. 'Apparently she isn't willing to be examined yet and he said that she'd be going away for a while but would come to see me when she returns.'

'Bert said he might sell the house,' said Jane. 'He wanted me to sort out Annie's things but I couldn't stomach it. I asked Lizzie and she went like a shot. She and Clare are getting rid of the clothes and Bert said they could have some of the trinkets, but he's kept back the fur and the necklace he bought her for the celebrations at the end of the war.' She wrinkled her nose in distaste. 'He brought them here for safe-keeping and some papers he didn't want turned over when they were sorting out. As for the rest, he didn't care what they did, so long as they got the drawers clear.'

Dr Barnes rose. 'I must go. I have a patient to see before my surgery. If you want a note to include with your letter, I'll be happy to write one, but I think it best to reassure her and to make light of the accident now we know that Vikki will not be a permanent invalid.'

'My letter?' Jane looked confused. 'Of course. I did write to Sidney and ask him to tell Nellie that there had been an accident, but I didn't go into details, so now I'll write to him again and tell him what you said.'

'Not to Nellie?'

'No. She has no claim on Vikki now and no interest in her. We agreed that it was for the best, and I think that Lucy has taken Vikki's place in many ways. Monty treats her as his own daughter and likes to forget that Nellie ever had a child.'

'So you don't think she'll rush over the Atlantic in a flurry of maternal feeling?'

Jane laughed. 'No, not Nellie.' It was a relief to laugh about it and to be objective, and when the doctor had gone, she felt lighter than she had felt since she saw Annie dead in that dimly-lit room.

'I really must go over to see Alice,' Jane said to Emily, later. 'The weather might get bad and the crossing rough, and I promised Edward that I'd go when he had to be in Salisbury.' She looked out a warm coat in case the wind was up in the Solent and packed her bag with fruit and fresh vegetables for Alice. Since she had discovered that Alice often ate the cakes that Jane took for her son Edward, she had stopped making them and a nurse now kept an eye on the diabetic woman and saw that she ate nothing sweet.

On the ferry, Jane thought of what Dr Barnes had said. 'Some of my old colleagues are on the brink of a cure, or at least a treatment for diabetes. I am in touch with them and they have already told patients to keep to a diet which helps. It's like the one I wrote out for Alice, but there are a lot of silly women who now follow it to keep slim and to lose weight quickly. They are not diabetic but they insist on "Banting".'

'Why call it that? I've heard of it of course, as they say that many of the smart set in London try to be as thin as rakes.'

'I once told you about the substance that Schafer isolated back in 1909, didn't I? Now, three men – Mcleod, Banting and Best have found a way to give it to humans to take up the excess sugar in their blood and replace the insulin not secreted by the body.'

Jane nodded, and felt proud that he talked to her about these things as if she was an equal. 'So Banting is one of those men?'

'Yes. It's sad that one of my colleagues who is also particularly interested in the disease is probably dying of it. He's rather worse than your daughter-in-law. I know Dr Lawrence well and if they can use it on him it will be a triumph, for he is a very fine doctor and has a good brain.'

If only I could take the news to Edward that Alice could have this new treatment, thought Jane wistfully. Edward seemed to be on the fringes of her life now that the couple lived in Southampton and he spent all his free time with his sick wife. He was so like Walter had been in his younger days, even if Edward did lack the forcefulness and virility of his father, and it did Jane good to see him.

The visit went off well, with Alice looking better after yet another spell in hospital, and Edward seeming rested because of it. She told them the news from America and left Alice with the bundle of magazines that Clare had finished with and Emily didn't want even for knitting patterns.

Alice listened eagerly, glad of anything to lessen her boredom and offered to make a vest for each of the babies when she felt well enough. Jane went back to the Island feeling more cheerful. If the cure came, Alice might even have to make clothes for her own baby. She walked up from the station deep in thought.

'You didn't stay long!' Archie looked at her affectionately. 'I was coming to meet the next train in case you were on it.'

'That was kind.' Her glance went past him to the door of the play-room.

'It's gone,' he said quietly. 'I saw it loaded on to the van and he took it back. He said he'd make it firm on a base that moves only to and fro and if we want it back we can have it.' She shook her head. 'I told him to sell it. Was that right?'

'Yes, I should never have given in to her but poor little Vikki did want a rocking horse and she doesn't have such a happy time as my children had, in spite of more toys and better treats.'

'She loves the farm,' he said. 'Jane, when are you going to see that you can't stay here for ever! The farm is waiting for you and for Vikki and Emily and I have time on my hands now that I've appointed a manager.'

'Some day,' she said, and kissed him tenderly. 'You're

the dearest of men and I love you but I have to stay until Vikki is better and the babies are born.'

'And after that? You'll wait until they walk, and then you'll wait until they are at school and by that time, I shall be in my grave!' He took her by the shoulders and shook her gently. 'I love you and I know we could be happy.'

'Would you give up all you have to come here?' she asked, and her smile was sad. He let her go. 'You would hate to live here, with a patch of garden and no animals.'

'I'd do it for you, Jane.'

'And give me that burden to bear? No, Archie, come when you need me, and I'll come to you, but I have to stay until my girls are settled with their families.' She touched his face with her hand, smoothing away the frown. 'Do you know that Walter never once said he loved me, not in so many words even when he was most loving?' She held him close and felt the safety and strength of Archie and the grief of not being able to take him to her bed. 'One day,' she said.

'One day,' he echoed. 'Or I'll kidnap you.'

'I've cleaned the room and put two chairs in place of the horse,' said Emily when she came into the room later. 'Vikki heard the men taking it and shed a few tears, but I told her that we'd go down to the farm with Uncle Archie and see the real horses as soon as the nasty cage is off her back.' Emily smiled. 'She can move her feet a little now and has more feeling in her thighs. I rub her legs as Dr Barnes taught me and she said just now that I tickled.' Her face glowed with delight and Archie wondered why Emily didn't marry. If she did, then Jane would have even less excuse for staying in the house on the Mall

'Nora said that she saw Maudie Dove on the boat yesterday, Mother, going to Portsmouth.'

'Oh yes? I ought to have a day shopping there soon,' said Jane.

'She wasn't going for a day trip,' said Emily. 'She had a suitcase with her and a bag and looked loaded down.'

Jane looked more interested. 'Was she alone?' Emily nodded. 'And going to stay?' They exchanged smiles.

201

'What are you two thinking?' said Archie.

'I was wondering if she is establishing residence, as they say, before the banns are called.'

'Three weeks?' Archie grinned. 'You don't think Bert really will marry her? There's no reason why he should now any more than when Annie was alive.'

'I think there is, but not a word to anyone. Bert is embarrassed enough as it is and I'm not going to be the one who can be accused of talking about it.'

'For two virtuous women, you are taking this very quietly,' he teased.

'No, I've come to the conclusion that there are worse sins than taking love and comfort and giving it. Bert never had much and neither did Maudie. Men, yes, but not love, as I know it. I think that Bert does love her now even if it didn't begin like that.'

She turned away. It must have been different with Walter. He took the girl and used her without really loving her. Jane clung to that belief. What Bert had said was true. This could have happened to Walter and brought shame on the whole family, so now, whatever she felt, she must not join in the whispers of condemnation.

'It's a bit soon,' said Archie. 'Is she far gone?'

'No, it won't show for weeks yet, but she might want to make sure of Bert before he has other ideas,' said Jane.

'If she *is* going to have a baby,' said Emily quietly. 'She knew that Annie might not live for more than a week, and she wouldn't want Bert looking around for a wife and leaving her to fend for herself.'

'Holy Mary! The things you come out with, Emily Darwen! She wouldn't do that, to be sure. Maudie hasn't the sense,' she added.

'Do we send Bert a present?' Archie laughed. 'It will be a nine days' wonder but it will pass and most people will forget about dates and times of mourning.'

'She shouldn't be carrying heavy cases so early on,' said Jane anxiously.

'She looked strong and very healthy, Mother. All that time working in the laundry made her have strong wrists

202

and she didn't even have that pinched look about her as Lizzie had,' said Emily. 'Maudie will be quite all right and will do very nicely over this.' She smiled, as if to herself.

'She refused to be examined by Dr Barnes,' Jane remembered, and they waited in a fever of curiosity for Maudie to return and for Bert to announce, rather defensively, that he missed Annie so much as a business partner as well as a wife, that he needed someone who understood him and who would be a help and comfort in his sorrow.

'I almost believed him,' said Clare when she heard. 'But why the rush when everyone knows that he and Maudie have a love-nest in Totland?'

Jane kept silent and after the wedding, when Bert and Maudie went over to Portsmouth to a small chapel and had only two witnesses and no fuss, she waited.

It was a time of waiting, she thought as she sat by Vikki and read to her one day in autumn when the trees were sending dry bright reminders that summer was over and it was time for harvest and storing up for the future. The leaves under the horse chestnut were crisp and light and Vikki had managed to walk through them, crunching and exclaiming at the sound. Her two walking sticks were hardly used now but Jane insisted that she must rest each afternoon.

Jane rocked in the comfortable chair by the fire while Vikki pulled at the woollen hair that Emily had replaced four times on the head of the favourite rag doll. Lizzie was very well and seemed happy, Clare was trying to ignore the fact that she was pregnant and did everything that the doctor advised her not to do, like reaching up to wash high window sills and picture rails, and carrying all her shopping before Alan had a chance to fetch it in the side car. Jane smiled. It seemed to suit Clare, who had never looked more blooming.

And Janey. It was early days yet with her but she had come back from seeing Clive off to Scotland with a wonderful glow of contentment and maturity, ready to take George back and get ready for her next baby.

'I can't tell you what this leave has meant to me, Mrs Darwen,' Alex Barnes had said when he left with Clive, but for another destination. 'You know, this is the only place where I think I belong. When I leave the Navy, I shall come back here and I might even open an hotel.'

'You aren't thinking of buying out of your commission, are you?' Janey had said.

'No, I'll stay on for a year or so, but I'm not a real sailor like Clive, or my cousin. If I had a wife and family, I'd leave the Navy as soon as possible. My cousin has two children, and Clive might have a big family. I have nobody who depends on me, but I can't see myself at sea in five years' time.'

'What do your parents say?'

'They agree with me. In fact, they suggested that I could take over the old Manor Farm that belonged to my mother's family if I need a hotel.' He sighed. 'It would need a partnership or a wife, and that is a blank space that can't be filled.'

'I won't say that time heals,' said Jane. 'It's more a smoothing out of grief but it does help, and you do have your cousins and their children. I hadn't met them before this leave. The boy must be six now and Vikki got on with him well. I like him – he's a gentle soul under that determined manner. He'll be a doctor,' she added, as if she really knew.

'And will you read my palm?' asked Alex, laughing.

'I don't hold with fortune-telling,' she said, and changed the subject abruptly, thankful that old Mrs Lee had no power to frighten her now.

When Bert visited, red in the face and alone, she poured out two glasses of sherry wine and refilled his glass as soon as he'd gulped down the first. 'Sit down and stop fiddling with your tie Bert,' she said crisply. 'Now what have you to say for yourself?' She smiled. 'How is the second Mrs Cooper? I half-expected you to bring her to visit.'

'Not until you say, Jane. I won't have you put to any trouble and if you can't see her here, then she'll have to stay away in the West Wight.'

'Bert! She is your wife. Whatever the reasons for marrying her, you've taken each other for better and for worse now, and Newport will have to get used to the idea. I don't want her here,' she said firmly. 'You know why and we have no need to play with words. The fact remains that you have married her and she is to have your child, so bring her here for afternoon tea on Sunday. If she can bear to come, then I can bear to have her here just long enough to make people know I support you.'

'You are a good friend,' he said with emotion. 'A lot will depend on women like you, Jane. All the old harpies in the town are watching and will follow your lead. Things have been said that opened my eyes to this, and I don't want to leave Newport for good.' He sipped his third glass and Jane waited. 'I don't know what to do,' he said, at last.

'There's something more?'

He nodded. 'Maudie now tells me that she isn't expecting.' He wiped his mouth with a large handkerchief, to hide his emotion. 'I wanted that child. I had no idea of the hunger I'd feel and it was a revelation. You might not understand. You had so many children easily, but I have never fathered even one.'

'I understand,' said Jane. 'Each one was different, but I wanted them all. Poor Bert. Poor Maudie.'

'Poor Maudie? Don't you see? She's tricked me!'

'You wanted her, Bert! You used her and had no thought for anything but your own needs until you finally knew that she was more to you than that. You were fond of her before you thought that she was in the family way. Nothing has changed, except that she is your wife and she is young enough to give you a child, if you have patience.'

She laughed. 'I've told nobody but Archie and Emily and the doctor knows what you told him. It went no further, so when the old biddies start counting the weeks and thinking you had to get married, they will be in for a shock and you can hold your head high, Bert. She'll need a firm hand, though, if you don't want her to rule you, but she could make you very happy.'

She watched him go, and thought how like Walter he

had become in the way he walked, as if the whole town belonged to him. He had a lightness in his step and a smile on his face and she chuckled when she pictured Maudie being made to face up to her marital obligations and respectability. Annie had seldom invited anyone to her house and so nobody would think it strange if Jane Darwen kept away now that another wife had taken over, but she braced herself for the unavoidable meeting on Sunday and decided to ask the girls and their husbands, Janey and Nora, and two young women who had once worked with Maudie and now had husbands and babies of their own.

'I shall have little time for chatting,' she told Emily. 'They can come and go and Bert at least will be pleased.'

'It will be quite a crowd,' said Emily. 'We'll have to put in the two big extra leaves in the table and have a side-table for the tea-tray. In fact, we might have to use two rooms. I'll make some fruit cake today and we can serve scones and jam and cream, but I don't see why we should give them high tea.'

'Clare will be cross,' Jane pointed out.

'Then she and Lizzie can bring their own ham and make sandwiches,' said Emily. 'They have enough energy for doing what they want, but never raise a finger here.'

But when Sunday came, the tables were well laid with four kinds of cake, sandwiches and thin bread and butter, scones and jam, enough to make even Lizzie smile. Jane shrugged when Janey asked how many she expected, over a hundred, and knew that she couldn't stint even if she tried, when people came to visit her.

Maudie looked pretty and well-dressed. Her shoes were polished and her lace petticoat, which showed briefly when she sat down, was spotless. Jane was impressed.

'She's come a long way from Sea Street,' murmured Janey as she passed Jane in the kitchen to fetch more hot water. 'Uncle Bert seems happy enough, too.'

'It's for the best,' said Jane, and sat with Maudie for a

few minutes when the men rose to inspect the garden and talk about the state of unemployment in industry.

'Bert says he wants to stay put,' said Maudie. 'I don't mind as long as we can have the house painted brighter and get rid of all that dull varnish.' She shrugged. 'He says I can do as I like about it, but I shall have to decide quickly as he wants a family.' She shot a glance at Jane, who continued to listen politely.

'That's only natural,' said Janey, smiling. 'It's a long time since you had Lucy, but you are still young enough to have more than one baby.'

Maudie made a face. 'I hate the idea, but they say it's easy the second time.' She laughed with a chilling lack of humour. 'I've always known when my bread was buttered on both sides and now, I should have jam on it.'

'You'll lack for nothing with Bert,' was all that Jane could say, and Maudie seemed to find the dignity of the older woman subduing. She picked up her bag and went to find Bert in the now blustery garden. He grinned, and went in to Jane. 'Goodbye, Bert,' said Jane. Her eyes twinkled. 'Keep her on a loose rein and she'll be fine, just fine.'

'Thank you for today. I shall walk her along the Mall very slowly so that all the net curtains have a chance to twitch and then we can settle down. We shan't come to tea again like this, but I'll be over to see you about the cottage roof and the sale of those bonds.' He lowered his voice. 'I'll leave those papers with you, if you don't object. I'd like to be sure of . . . things before I let her know too much. Annie never did understand business but Maudie might be curious. I'll wait and see what she gives me, before I let her know what I'm worth.'

'You're a hard man, Bert,' said Jane, shaking her head. 'But it makes sense. I kept the old bureau in the morning room. Lock it and keep the key. It was Walter's private place and I shall keep the habit of not knowing what is inside.'

He nodded as Maudie came up behind him and pulled

his sleeve. 'Ready?' he asked. 'I feel like a walk. We'll stroll up to the crossroads and back and pick up the car here.'

'It's cold out!' said Maudie.

'Do you good,' he said. 'Get your hat straight and put on your gloves. You are on parade, my dear.'

Chapter 15

'I'm sorry to drag you away from your beau,' said Nellie Morris. She looked at Lucy's woebegone face and then at Sidney Darwen. 'I know Sidney has to do more tests to see if he will be suitable for acting in a talking picture, while we have to be in Palm Beach for a three week engagement.'

'It isn't far,' said Sidney. 'I shall be in Hollywood after next week and I can come over to see you all.'

'You will telephone?' asked Lucy. Sidney nodded and bent to kiss her briefly on the lips. 'Promise?' she insisted.

'I promise. The tests might prove that I haven't the kind of voice they want. When talking pictures do appear, they'll need something that the public like better than the movies with subtitles. Some of the actresses are getting scared as they speak with such terrible accents.' He grinned. 'Who wants to hear a harsh Bronx accent when the lady is saying "I love you"?'

'They'll love you,' said Nellie. 'In any case, you have a contract signed for two films before they start the talkies. I wonder if they ever will have voices on the screen? It can't make films any better, in my opinion.'

'Yes, I have two contracts,' said Sidney in a tone filled with wonder. He hugged Lucy. 'It's your doing, you funny little girl. Do you know just what you have done for me?'

'You aren't married yet,' said Nellie. She fitted a cork-tipped cigarette into a long amber holder and lit it, drawing in the smoke and then regarding Sidney through the cloud as she exhaled. Her eyes were calculating. 'Make it soon or your sponsor might get impatient.'

'He knows that I have to stay with you for a while,' said Lucy. 'Sidney won't hear of me leaving you before the time I promised.' She looked up at him adoringly. He pressed her hand. 'You'd better get packed and then

209

we shall all have to leave this marvellous place.' Lucy
sighed. 'We can't say goodbye to Miss Davies. She left
yesterday for rehearsals for *Little Old New York* in Los
Angeles where the Hearst mansion is.'

'Maybe one day, we'll go there,' said Sidney. 'They say
it's even more wonderful than *Vizcaya*. What is it called?
The Monastery at Saint Simeon. It sounds wonderful but I
doubt if it's any more peaceful than this place has been.'

Lucy blushed. 'I was glad that we are engaged, Sidney.
Twice, men followed me to my room and thought I'd ask
them in. I showed them my ring and they laughed as if it
wasn't important. Some of the people here are not nice.'

'Well, it's Bradley's Beach Club for the next few weeks
Lucy, and we'll make sure they keep a room for you,
Sidney. I hope that Monty doesn't fancy being too long at
the tables. They say the casino is pretty hot.'

'He hasn't bet on anything since his big win,' said Lucy.

'I made him promise,' said Nellie. 'Not that he wants to
gamble now. He says it would be tempting fate after
winning all that money in one go.'

'I've never placed a bet of any sort,' said Lucy.

'It isn't much fun.' Nellie stubbed out her cigarette and
stood up. 'I'll leave you to say goodbye and I'll be in the
car in ten minutes.'

'Goodbye, darling,' said Sidney. He took Lucy in his
arms and held her close, then kissed her with closed lips
and gently put her away from him.

'Kiss me again,' she begged. 'Kiss me properly.' She
took his hand and laid it over her left breast. 'Feel my
heart beating. It beats just for you, my darling.'

'Lucy, we mustn't, not yet,' he said. She flung herself
into his arms, and he kissed her with greater warmth,
bending her over his arm as he did his film sweethearts.
'There, is that better?'

'A little.' She looked up at him shyly. 'I know girls who
do far more than that once they are engaged. Perhaps
when we are really alone again, in Palm Beach?'

'Yes, when we are in Palm Beach,' he said. 'You must
run now. Nellie will be waiting.'

210

Lucy giggled and went out to the car where Nellie sat, looking very much the well-known star, surrounded by an admiring group.

'Did you wonder what we were doing?' Lucy asked coyly.

'No!' said Nellie. 'Driver, you can leave now. My husband will join us at the station.'

'Some girls feel that they are almost married when they have said they'll marry someone and wear a ring.' Lucy glanced up at the beautiful, worldly face. Nellie smiled, faintly. 'I mean,' began Lucy.

'I know what you mean. They keep their man a little at bay but let him feel his way, so to speak! Don't worry, dear, you have nothing to fear from Sidney. I think he lacks a certain curiosity.'

'He *did* have a lot of sisters,' Lucy said in his defence.

'He's used to loving sisters,' Nellie agreed. 'Just take it slowly, dear. Let him make the pace.'

'That's the trouble.' Lucy was pink-faced and sulky. 'He never kisses me unless I make him, and he is always so correct. He is attentive and kind and very sweet but he isn't passionate. Do you think that will come when we are married? I want him so badly, Nellie. I could eat him.'

'Please don't. You'll scare him away for ever.' Nellie looked amused. 'His fans would kill you if he appeared even lightly chewed.' Lucy laughed too, but sat in silence for a while until they reached the station where Monty was waiting with tickets and the reserved compartment.

'Said goodbye?' he asked. Lucy nodded and went into the carriage. He raised his eyebrows at Nellie. 'Everything hunky-dory?'

'Lover isn't exactly a Tony Moreno,' she whispered.

'He's not the Latin type,' said Monty. 'The British take time to warm up.'

'And if he doesn't?' Nellie stepped into the carriage.

'There are others ready to step into his shoes,' said Monty. 'I use my eyes, and Lucy has it all in the right places.' He stopped as Lucy came to sit down by his side. 'You'll like Palm Beach,' he said. 'You can have your first

211

flutter at the casino. Not a lot and promise not to get into debt, but I'll give you a stake.'

'Thank you, Uncle Monty,' she said, but her eyes were filled with tears. 'How far is Palm Beach from Hollywood?'

'Not far but we'll all be busy for a while,' he said firmly. 'Enjoy yourself and make Nellie look nice and we'll all be happy.' He spoke impatiently. It was bad enough that Nellie hadn't completely forgotten her child and had shed tears over the news of Vikki's accident, but now he had two droopy women – or he would have if Lucy didn't do her work properly and Nellie was bad-tempered.

'We have the rest of the day to ourselves after we arrive, and start the show the day after tomorrow,' said Nellie. 'I need several things, Lucy, so you'll have to go shopping while I rest.' She sounded cross and Lucy knew better than to argue when Nellie was in a mood. She sank back in her seat and tried to close her eyes and close her mind to what was worrying her.

On the edge of the pool she had seen many couples who made no secret of the fact that they were more than good friends, even if the girl wore no ring of any kind. She had seen the looks exchanged, the caressing glances and even more caressing hands, the stolen kisses and the lingering embraces in dark corners or when the night made everything fragrant and romantic.

And Sidney? She set her lips. Sidney was cold and seemed to be almost repulsed by her kisses. She put a finger to her lips. They were warm and soft, trembling and eager for love whenever he was near, but he didn't notice how she longed to touch him, to hold him and have his body at one with hers. She expected the stars to explode when they kissed, but nothing happened, apart from leaving her feeling as if she had tasted a wonderful dish that was removed before more than a morsel had passed her lips.

It isn't my fault, she told herself. Many men admire me and I've been asked out with at least seven since I went to *Vizcaya*. I wish I'd gone now, she thought bitterly. At least I'd know what was wrong with me. Maybe when any man was with me alone for more than an hour, he'd be the same as Sidney.

She dozed and Nellie watched her, wishing that the girl was less vulnerable, less naive and less pretty.

A car was at the station to meet them and as soon as the luggage was checked and stowed away and Nellie had taken a cool shower, they ate a light meal and Lucy went to the nearest local shops for hairgrips, shampoo, a sponge and some white handkerchiefs.

'Hello there!' The voice was low and warm and Lucy looked up, startled. 'Remember me?'

'Yes! I mean no.' She turned away.

'I can't think why you avoid me,' said Frank Garsey. 'I hoped we could be friends.'

'I don't know you,' she said stiffly. She went to the next counter and asked for a special soap that Nellie preferred. It wasn't scented and had no harsh ingredients.

'I'm sorry,' said the girl at the counter. 'We don't stock that one.' She moved away.

'I think you'll find a bigger drug-store down the road,' said Frank Garsey helpfully. 'This is a two-bit place.'

He took her packages and asked the girl for a bag to hold them all and she gave him one with a smile. His hand under Lucy's elbow seemed caring and he guided her across the road at the junction as if she was a precious child. 'There,' he said when she saw the drug-store. 'I have to go now, but I hope to see you later.' Lucy walked into the store, aware that he was still there, watching her, but when she came out with the soap he had gone and she experienced a pang of disappointment.

Nellie was tired and was recovering from the rich food offered at *Vizcaya*. 'I'll have fruit juice and bed,' she announced. 'Monty, show Lucy the club and the dressing room and then have a meal somewhere. I don't want to see anyone until tomorrow.' She picked up the phone for room service. 'Just check that there are enough hangers. There never are,' she said. 'Monty, make sure the management knows what I want.'

Monty grinned as soon as they escaped. 'She's a bit

213

liverish and best left alone. Come on Lucy, I'll take you to the casino. We can eat there and you can see how the suckers lose money. No bets tonight. Just watch other people making fools of themselves, but first, we'd better see what Madam wants altered in the dressing room.'

The golden star on the pale blue dressing room door made Monty smile with pride. Lucy opened the door and inspected the wardrobe with a practised eye, and made notes of what was lacking. 'Nellie was right. There aren't enough clothes hangers and we need another table for the mending.' She opened another cupboard and found the ironing board and the heavy electric iron. 'Could you test it, Uncle Monty? The last one had fused before we tried it, and I have a lot to unpack and press.'

For two hours they were busy, sorting clothes and checking on the linen supplied. Monty spent half an hour trying to get someone to fix the arc of bright electric light bulbs around the pink-tinted mirror. 'I think that's it,' he said at last. 'I don't know what we shall do without you, Lucy.'

'You don't have to,' she began. 'Oh, Uncle Monty, I hate the thought of leaving you both. I can come back sometimes, can't I?'

He gave her a quick hug, 'We are your family, Lucy. If you ever need us, just come and we'll look after you.' He was serious and Lucy felt warmed and wanted as she never did with Sidney.

'Perhaps I'm not ready for marriage. Do you think I'm attractive enough?' she asked.

'If you weren't engaged, we'd be fighting off the wolves,' teased Monty. 'Sidney Darwen is a lucky cuss. I hope he knows just how lucky.' He watched her fold a gown with the ease of expertise and tuck pads of tissue paper into the puffed sleeves. 'Even if you didn't work for Nellie, you could be a dresser for any of the stars,' he said. 'You are also very pretty and I hope to God you aren't wasting yourself.'

'How can you say that? Sidney is very handsome and all the girls are crazy about him. I get quite jealous, sometimes. He smiles at them and they blush and try to

214

touch him.' She paused and looked pensive. 'He does treat them all the same,' she admitted. 'Men like him, too. You like him, don't you, Uncle Monty?'

'He's fun and very amusing, and he adds to any of our little parties,' he said.

'That's not what I mean.'

Monty looked uncomfortable. 'Come on, let's find a steak or something. I'm famished.' Lucy asked him again, and he picked up his wide-brimmed fur-felt hat and pulled it over one eye, almost hiding his expression. 'Well, he isn't what you'd call a lady's man and then he isn't what I'd call a man's man, either. He likes people, but I guess there are men who have a low libido, Lucy, and they can't do a thing about it.' He smiled. 'If anyone can make him spark, you will. He is very fond of you, Lucy.'

'Fond?' She slipped on her silky long cardigan that came almost to the hem of the short skirt. 'I want him to love me, not be fond of me as if I was a pet kitten.' Her mouth set and she tried not to look upset.

'You need some good red meat,' said Monty. 'A glass of wine too, tonight, to put some colour back in those cheeks.' He hailed a cab and they went to the Casino Restaurant. 'We can take our time as we have finished at the club and Nellie hates me wandering round the room while she's dozing.' He laughed. 'If people recognise me here, they'll think I'm having a gander at the artistes to see if Nellie would want to work here.'

'The stage looks very glamorous,' Lucy remarked.

'I refused a contract here,' he told her. 'Nellie has class and these girls have to take off most of their clothes. We can do without that rubbish.' He stubbed out his cigar and examined the menu. 'Most of the men who come here are straight from the tables in the casino and the rest are on their way there, so the food isn't expensive, for the more people who eat here boosts the casino.' He looked about him with a disparaging air. 'Nellie hasn't time to waste her talent on drunks and wastrels and worse.'

'Everyone looks very smart,' said Lucy. 'I think I'd like grilled salmon.'

'You always have grilled salmon!' She smiled. 'And a salad and potatoes?'

'No potatoes.' She laughed. 'You remember what I had the first time I ate in a restaurant on the *Mauretania*! Nellie was right. The salmon is usually good and not fattening.'

Four men in dark suits sauntered into the room, looking about them with bold, dark eyes. Monty turned his chair so that he could watch them and Lucy stared, fascinated. 'Now they might be worth watching,' said Monty. 'They are professional gamblers who go on a circuit round the casinos and usually make a killing.' He lowered his voice. 'Sometimes a killing in more ways than one.'

The men passed close to their table and Lucy shivered as she sensed their power and sheer animal magnetism. It was a sensation that she had experienced fleetingly when Frank Garsey had taken her arm to lead her across the busy interchange. It was less than attraction and more than a kind of stimulation; an awareness of their potential.

The girls on the stage were dancing, the tall ostrich feathers swaying on the diamanté headbands and the sequinned costumes glittering under the changing lights which filtered down through pastel to deep purple, pale pink and yellow to old rose and ochre, while the disciplined chorus thrust their legs high and fixed their smiles as if afraid to look tired.

'We could use that lighting system,' murmured Monty. 'I'll have a word with the management tomorrow. It's just what Nellie needs in that sentimental medley.' He grinned. 'And great if she feels off-colour.'

The four men had taken a table by the stage and sat with their backs to the band, watching the faces of the audience rather than the dancers. Monty turned away from them. 'I think if you're ready, we'll take a quick look in the casino and then go home.'

'Can't we see the rest of the cabaret? Nellie will be interested in some of the props.'

'Another time,' he said firmly, and walked between Lucy and the table where the four men sat. One of the

216

men eyed Lucy with cool speculation but she followed Monty and made no sign that she had noticed.

'You can have a few chips,' said Monty and gave her a handful of coloured discs. 'They aren't of much value so you can lose them all. Together, they add up to just ten dollars.'

'That's quite a lot!' Lucy looked uneasy. 'I hate to lose your money, and I know that Nellie would be cross if I gambled.'

'It's only a flutter and you needn't come here again if it bores you, but it's good to be seen at these places.' A man holding a flat rectangular flash-tray and a camera came closer and Lucy winced as the sharp light almost exploded in her face. 'See what I mean? They all know about you and Sidney and that you are with Nellie and me.' Monty laughed. 'It might be second-hand fame, but it's important. Be careful, Lucy, or they'll ask very awkward questions and tie you into knots.'

'What can they ask me?' She smiled as the reporter came closer, encouraged by her interest. 'Will you send me one of the pictures?' she asked.

'To be sure!' His voice was hearty and very warm. 'It's a pleasure to have a pretty face in our paper.'

'Is it one of the Hearst papers?' asked Monty.

'No.' The man looked cagey. 'We are an independent and fairly new, but our circulation is rising all the time.' He mentioned the name, and Monty tried to push past him. 'Come on, Mr Morris, give me a break, will you? You've been to *Vizcaya* and my readers want to know the truth about it.' He tried to look pious. 'It's their right to know and the Hearst papers hush up everything that goes on there.'

'I'm not interested, and if you print any lies saying that I gave you an interview, I'll sue the paper and report you to the Senate.'

'You, Miss Dove! You could give me the low-down. You must have seen the nightlife and the drinking and the snorting? Is Miss Davies in love with her new leading

217

man? Do the guests swim in the nude in that fabulous pool? Come on, give me *something*?'

'Come on, Lucy. Keep your mouth shut and never speak to that scum, do you hear? If anyone asks you, make sure you know what paper he represents first before you say a word.'

'But I can't tell him anything bad if that's what he wants.' She looked back and saw the man was following them. 'Everyone was very nice to me, or almost everyone,' she said.

'Well, that's the bit to keep under your hat,' growled Monty. 'Everything, and I mean *everything* was fine, do you hear? They can take a stray remark and twist it to sound as if you are a bad lot, so be very careful.'

They paused by the wide doorway leading into the casino hall where roulette was played. 'All those tables?' said Lucy, in wonder.

'The other rooms have blackjack and poker and pinball machines. We'll go there later. They are harmless fun and you can't lose or win much on them.'

'Blackjack?'

'No, I mean the pinballs. You'll enjoy them. Men like the ones we saw in the restaurant play blackjack for very high stakes, and it's no place for a lady.'

'When is the wedding?' The reporter was back again, so close by the table that Monty couldn't avoid him. He tossed a chip on to number seventeen and looked at Lucy with interest.

'Soon,' she said, and Monty smiled.

'How soon? Can I quote you on a date, or is it just a stunt to show the world what a good guy Sidney Darwen really is?'

'What do you mean?' Lucy clenched her hand on her pile of chips and sent them flying. Two landed on numbers just before the croupier called 'Rien ne va plus' and the wheel spun. The other chips were on the floor and the reporter bent to pick them up. Lucy bent down too and he whispered something she couldn't hear.

'I said, where does Ivor fit into your future plans?'

218

'Ivor?' She gathered the bright circles together and Monty almost shouted. 'What's the matter?' she asked.

The croupier pushed a pile of chips over to her. 'You won,' said Monty.

'But I didn't bet,' said Lucy.

'Two landed on numbers and won. Now pick up the winnings and give them to me and keep your first stake. That way, you lose only what you brought with you and keep the rest.' Lucy was excited. 'Now choose again,' said Monty, and a large man pushed aside the reporter and took his place.

Lucy didn't notice but was intent on the game. 'What was it on last time?'

'Six and eleven.'

'Eleven. That's Sidney's birthday! He's brought me luck.' She played twice more and won and then lost the whole of her first stake.

'That's it! Know when to stop, Lucy. Come on, it's late and Nellie will be sound asleep or wondering where we are.'

'One more go.' Lucy held out her hand.

'No, and we haven't time for the pin-ball tables.' Reluctantly, she followed him. 'One of the players had a notebook and took down everything that happened. He didn't play more than twice and won each time,' said Monty. 'Now, he leaves nothing to chance and makes a living out of gambling, but beginner's luck doesn't last, Lucy, and you have to be careful. Never throw down a chip without considering what you are doing. Lucky streaks do happen and you can follow them, but make it last and enjoy it. It should be fun and not serious.' He glanced at her over-bright eyes and wished they had gone to a movie.

'Who is Ivor?' she asked when they were drinking coffee in their suite. Monty choked on a biscuit. 'That reporter asked me something about him but it was when I won and I didn't hear.' She sipped her coffee. 'I've heard of him. He's a friend of Sidney's and he rang once or twice at *Vizcaya*. I spoke to him on the phone once and he sounded a bit grumpy.'

219

'I didn't know he was still in the picture. Sidney had a row with him and they parted. Ivor Sinclair was his manager at one time but never really did much for his career.' Monty tried to discover what Lucy had heard.

'So he's English? Sidney came out here with a friend, Herbie Walters who used to help with the puppets. What happened to him?'

'He got married and has a family. I believe that Sidney sees him from time to time but Ivor came on the scene and took over.' He set his jaw. 'What did he want? And he isn't British. His name is really Snitzler but German names got unfashionable, so he changed it.' He tried to sound nonchalant. 'Did Sidney ever say anything to you about him?'

'No, that's why I'm asking. It's funny that the reporter should know him and seem to think I must do so.'

'If you see that reporter again, don't get drawn into conversation about Sidney or Ivor Sinclair.' Monty broke a biscuit in half and dunked a piece in his coffee. 'You mustn't talk about Nellie or me, either,' he added hastily.

'What's wrong, Uncle Monty? I have a feeling that everyone knows something that I don't and it has to do with Sidney.' She frowned. 'You said they had a row? I can't imagine Sidney having a real row with anyone.' She smiled. 'He's so gentle and sweet and I know he'll look after me.'

'If that's enough, Lucy.' The brandy Monty was drinking with his coffee made him relax. 'I've said it before, my dear, some men aren't as . . . warm as others and you'll have to be patient.'

'I know. But he's the man I want to marry and I shall make him want me as much as I want him.'

'I'm awake!' said Nellie. 'I had a lovely deep sleep and feel much better.' She appeared in the doorway of the room. 'Before you undress, Lucy, would you mind fetching a bottle of spa water? Room service is off, but you can get it from the bar. I've drunk pints of fruit juice and water and I need some for the morning.'

Lucy went down and fetched it. She tapped on the half-open door of Nellie's room and heard voices, but nobody seemed to hear her gentle tap. She raised her hand again, then paused.

'That little heel means trouble,' said Monty. 'If the press have a whisper about it, then there's no smoke without fire.'

'But we don't really know,' said Nellie. 'Sidney seems keen enough now and he's shown no sign of meeting Sinclair.'

Monty gave a short laugh. 'When they are like that, they are worse than jealous wives, and some never let up.' He glanced towards the half-open door and put a finger to his lips. Lucy walked in, carrying the bottle and looking pale.

'Who means trouble, Uncle Monty? That reporter? Or is it this man I've never met, Ivor Sinclair.'

'Both,' said Nellie. She looked at Monty to make him keep quiet. 'Sidney's friend was no good for him and he is no longer Sidney's manager, but as he gets better and better acting parts, of course Ivor is jealous and wants what he thinks is his share. He would, as an agent, get ten per cent of all Sidney's earnings, and travel with him a lot as he did before.' Monty relaxed visibly, and behind Lucy's back gave a thumbs-up sign.

'I see,' said Lucy slowly. Her face cleared. 'He sounds nasty. I think I'll go to bed now.'

'Yes, there's no need to worry about him,' said Monty. 'He's gone and you will be married soon.'

'I suppose that Sidney needs a manager,' said Lucy. 'He hasn't mentioned it but I'm sure it is a good idea. Uncle Monty is your agent Nellie, and he sees to all the contracts and business and I doubt if Sidney is very good at that, either.'

'I can help him a lot,' said Monty hastily. 'Better to keep it in the family if we can. You don't want a strange man travelling with you all over the place, do you?'

'You are so good to me,' said Lucy and blew a kiss from the doorway.

'If it was that simple,' said Nellie when she had closed the door. 'It was fine in *Vizcaya* but Sidney's on his own

221

now, and Hollywood isn't as fussy as his Bible-punching Middle West sponsor. At least he has the two contracts in the bag.'

'At the moment, he's grateful and really as fond of Lucy as he could be of any woman,' said Monty. 'But he's very ambitious and when a man like that tastes the good life, he'll do anything to keep it.' Nellie sighed and yawned. 'We'll leave it until morning, but I think we should push the date of the wedding on before Ivor gets unpleasant. Don't forget,' he said with a bitter smile, 'hell hath no fury like a woman scorned, and that one is a bitch.'

Lucy sat on her bed and knew that she wouldn't be able to sleep. The casino had excited her in a way that she had never been before. She recalled being contemptuous of her mother when she placed bets on horses and lost her money and how Maudie had been so thrilled on the rare occasions when she won. Lucy filled a glass with orange squash and drank it. She examined her face in the mirror and grimaced. I hope I'm not like her she thought, and began to undress.

The house telephone that had been put in her room so that Nellie would not be disturbed, shrilled gently under the frilled cover that looked like a Dresden shepherdess. Lucy took the receiver. 'Miss Morris is asleep and mustn't be disturbed,' she said.

'Call for Miss Dove. I'll connect you, Miss.'

'Sidney! Where are you?' She laughed and could hardly speak. 'My darling, I've missed you so much.'

'I'm still in Hollywood but I wanted you to come over for half a day if you can. They want pictures of the two of us together for a couple of newspapers.' He sounded anxious. 'Do you think Nellie will let you come?'

'Not tomorrow,' she said. 'We have to get ready and she will need me there in the dressing room, but perhaps in two days' time, I could come.'

'That's marvellous, my darling.' His voice seemed to change. 'I've had dinner with my sponsor and he suggested it. He's here now,' he added. 'He'd like to speak to you.'

222

'Hello, Miss Dove,' said the formal gravelly voice. 'Sidney tells me that you are about to name the day and I suggest we do that in front of the reporters. It's as well to set the record straight or they cook up lies and it does no good to my pictures.'

'It can't be soon enough for me, Mr Gunnar, but I promised Miss Morris to stay with her for a year when I came here with them.'

'And it's very honest of you to stick to a bargain, but you can stay on even after you get married. Sidney will be very busy and have no time for a long honeymoon.'

'Does that mean he will be in Talkies?'

'I signed him up today and we'll let the press know when you come over.'

'That's wonderful!' Lucy heard the telephone change hands. 'Sidney? Isn't it wonderful?'

'I can't believe it. My voice was just what they wanted and the tests were all first class.'

'But why is Mr Gunnar in such a hurry to get us married? If you are to be so busy, I would have thought he'd have been unwilling to let you go. He's a dear under that crusty face. I really think he likes me.'

'He does like you,' said Sidney. 'Lucy, I do love you, but I . . . have things on my mind and you may find me very boring.' His voice broke. 'So many things happening, so many people pulling at me, and I never want you to be hurt.'

'What could hurt me now, Sidney? I love you and want you and I'll *make* Nellie let me come to you the day after tomorrow. Meet the noon train from here.'

She sank back on the bed, forgetting that she was still in her cami-knickers and stockings. He had said he loved her as if it pained him to admit it. He's so shy about marriage, she decided. She slipped out of her clothes and lay naked under the sheets, and smiled. 'I'll make you want me so much,' she murmured. She tried to see his face in the dark but when she drifted into a light sleep, she saw another face, dark and compelling and sensual. She turned away but he was still there, smiling, watching her and she woke shivering to find the bed-clothes on the floor. She pulled on a light kimono and peeped out through the gap in the curtains. The roads were deserted but the lights from the casino were reflected on the rooftops as they changed and changed and showed that some people were still at the tables.

On the dressing table were two gaming chips that had fallen to the bottom of her purse. 'I'll have to go back. I can't waste them,' she told herself.

Chapter 16

'That's enough!' The publicity man waved his clipboard and stood between Lucy and the cameras. 'Be nice, fellas, Miss Dove has been very patient.'

'Can we have a bit more leg? Over here, Miss.'

Lucy stood smiling but refused to pose in some of the ways the reporters suggested. She had been pictured sitting, standing, a little pensive and with Sidney, holding hands and gazing into each other's eyes. He had kissed her twice for the benefit of the cameras, and she wondered if they would have to have an audience whenever he kissed her, so that he would show some passion.

'That's fine,' Mr Gunnar smiled. 'I've ordered English tea and muffins and you can have them in private. Lucy my dear, you are a great asset to us all. The perfect picture of modesty – and the public will love you!'

'She is the star today,' agreed Sidney.

'She might even make the screen,' said his sponsor. 'I aim to try her for a test right soon but first you have a little matter of the wedding. The studio will fix all the details. Just turn up in eight weeks' time and we'll have it all ready for the world to see.'

'I thought that weddings were private affairs,' said Lucy.

'Not in Hollywood,' Mr Gunnar said firmly. 'We fix the dress and the attendants and the reception, and you can invite who you want apart from the press and gossip writers.'

Lucy frowned. 'Do you mind all the fuss, Sidney? I thought we'd be married and slip away somewhere quiet for a few days.'

'It's written into my contract that I can go away for only three days,' said Sidney. He looked apologetic. 'We'll take a longer holiday when the first picture is finished.'

They were left in the hotel room booked for them and where they had changed before the pictures were taken. A trolley of muffins and tea and small cream cakes waited with a large silver teapot and milk-jug. 'Have they finished with us?' Lucy asked.

'Yes. We can have tea, get changed and still have plenty of time for me to drive you to the train.' Sidney sighed with pleasure. 'I feel ten feet tall,' he confided.

Lucy put her arms round him. 'Because you love me? Because I love you?' He bent to kiss her tenderly. 'Oh, I do love you,' she whispered. 'Eight weeks and we'll be together for always.'

'You'll have to go back to Nellie at times,' he pointed out. 'And my studio wants me there from six in the morning to late at night for a while, so we shall have little time together.'

'So why not take time now?' Lucy breathed deeply. 'If you love me, then take me now, and let's not wait.' She threw down her jacket and kicked off her shoes. The bed on which they were sitting moved across the floor as she flung herself closer to her fiancé, and she fell across his lap. Her arms went round his neck and she pulled him down with his head on her breast. For a moment, he drew back, then kissed her. She saw that his eyes were shut and his kiss was more passionate than any he had previously given her. She clung to him and wished that he would caress her body but he held her close with an emotion that could have been passion or a kind of desperation.

'It isn't wicked,' she whispered. 'We are engaged and soon will be married.'

'No, Lucy. Not now.'

'You sweet old-fashioned man,' she said tenderly. 'I know you want me to wear white and be a virgin but we needn't go that far yet.' Her hand guided his to her breast under the thin pleated cotton of her blouse and he kissed her again, his face pale and his lips cold.

Lucy pulled away, ashamed. 'I'm sorry,' she said. 'I didn't know that you would disapprove so much. You must think I'm a very forward huzzy.'

226

'It isn't that.' Sidney paced the floor and she poured tea with trembling hands.

'Then what have I done wrong?' she asked in a small voice.

'Nothing. I don't deserve you, Lucy. I can never be everything you want.'

They stared at the door as it opened, slowly. A waiter stood with a silver dish of more muffins and behind him was Mr Gunnar. 'Thought I'd drop in for five minutes.'

'We haven't started tea yet,' said Sidney. He smiled as if very pleased to see the older man. 'Come and join us.' Lucy went into the bathroom and tidied her blouse and powdered her nose. She felt deflated and sad and vaguely resentful, but she smiled brightly and ate two muffins before saying that if she had to go, she must rush to catch her train.

'I have my car outside with a chauffeur. Let him take you. I want to talk to Sidney.'

Sidney made no sign of disagreeing and Lucy felt that neither of the men would miss her if she left. She shrugged and lifted her face for a last kiss and then went down to the car. Two reporters lingered in the foyer but she ignored them and smiled at the chauffeur. He drove off, quickly, and she hardly noticed the journey back to Nellie and Monty and the warmth of their affection.

'I didn't expect you back so soon,' said Nellie. 'You are a good girl. Monty and I have to go out to dinner this evening, so can you amuse yourself? Sidney should have come back with you.' She frowned.

'Mr Gunnar wanted him,' said Lucy. 'We've decided on a date eight weeks from now, and I shall come back here when you need me. Sidney will be very, very busy!' She tried to smile but her eyes were prickly with unshed tears.

'I wish we were staying in,' said Nellie. 'I can't ask you to come too, this time, but I hate to leave you alone.'

'I'm tired after all the reporters today. I shall go to bed early,' said Lucy.

'Then we shall creep in and not bother you if we're late,'

Monty announced. 'Nellie can do without you and let you have a good long sleep.'

'Shall I ask them to send up dinner for you?' fussed Nellie. Lucy shook her head. 'No, it isn't good to eat alone in a hotel room. André will look after you in the dining room.'

Lucy watched them leave and had a long hot bath before standing in front of her wardrobe and wondering what to wear. I've been so busy looking after Nellie that I need to go through my own clothes, she thought, and brought out an armful of garments that she rarely wore. That was the suit I wore when I met Sidney again. That was the dress I wore at *Vizcaya* and haven't worn since. She picked up a slim shift of pale silk and her expression softened. She pulled it over her head and let it slide over the artificial silk slip. 'The very first dress that Nellie gave me, on board the *Mauretania*,' she murmured. It fitted even better now and she decided to wear it to dinner. She found the bead-trimmed jacket that went with it and felt comforted. No present had given her more pleasure and with it, she had felt real care and love for the first time since she left Janey and the Darwen family.

The restaurant was half-empty and André had been told to look after her. He led her to a small table under a potted palm with a good view of the other tables and the piano, where a talented black singer would later take his place. Lucy took the menu and smiled. Grilled salmon? No, tonight, she would do none of the usual things.

She ordered clam soup and veal in a cream sauce, and a bottle of spa water. Some of the early diners were leaving to go to the casino and more guests from the hotel came down. Lucy looked up as the waiter brought her soup and saw who was standing by the next table. She lowered her glance and concentrated on eating, but knew that Frank Garsey was sitting only a few feet away from her. She had to look up at last and he smiled. In spite of her caution, she found herself smiling at him and was glad to see at least one familiar face.

The waiter listened to him and looked her way, then

brought a scribbled note on the back of the menu to her. She took a deep breath. He wanted to join her for the rest of the meal, and there seemed no reason why he should sit over there when at least she could have someone to talk to. She nodded and the waiter laid a place for him at her table. He sat with his back to the room, hiding her from the view of the other diners and making a tiny oasis of privacy under the potted palms. 'No wine?' he said. He called a waiter and slipped some money into his hand.

'I drink mostly water,' she said and watched the waiter pour a sparkling liquid from a bottle from which the lable had been removed. 'Champagne?' she asked after the first sip. It was not as dry as some wines she had been given at receptions and on board the ship and she was thirsty after the rather salty clams.

'Lemonade,' said Frank Garsey with a grin. 'You must have known I was coming tonight.'

'I didn't know where you were staying,' she said.

'You are wearing the dress that you wore on the boat coming over.' He smiled and she blushed as he took in every detail of the flimsy fabric, the half-concealed curve of her breasts and the way her arms emerged, slender and smooth from the ruched shoulders. 'It's a lovely dress,' he went on, 'but not as lovely as you.'

The waiter saved her blushes and they sat in silence while he served the veal, but Lucy felt her throat restricted and hot as she tried to eat. She drank more wine and then water, refusing the champagne and feeling suddenly afraid.

Frank Garsey became serious, talking about people in the restaurant, places he had seen and knew she would like to visit, making her laugh at anecdotes that he could tell against himself and yet not make himself seem ridiculous. Long after the cheese had been waved aside and Lucy had eaten a water ice with fresh raspberries, they sat and talked, and Lucy wondered how she had ever distrusted this amusing and flattering man who didn't try to hold her hand across the table but wanted only to please her.

'I must go now,' she said at last. 'Nellie will be back and might want me.'

'Surely not,' he said smoothly. 'It's so early and nobody goes to bed at this hour. Don't you find the place hot? We can walk a little and come back for a nightcap.' He smiled. 'You must take pity on me, Lucy. I sleep badly and I shall be so lonely when you leave me.'

Lucy put on her jacket and picked up her purse. She looked inside for her handkerchief and the two gaming chips fell out. Hastily she reached for them but Frank Garsey was faster. 'They were left from the other night when I went with Uncle Monty,' she said.

'I didn't know you gambled,' he said, in mock horror.

'I don't. I've been there once, that's all.'

'You ought to cash them in,' he said. 'We'll walk as far as the casino and you can either put them on a number or cash them.' She followed him slowly, half-hoping that Nellie would appear and rescue her but aware of rising excitement.

'I feel lucky.' Frank tossed a coin in the air as they walked along the brightly-lit avenue and saw the sea glinting between the trees as if sprinkled with silver. 'There,' he said. 'It came up heads which means I have to place a bet or two. You will bring me luck and let me stake you for a modest amount.'

'No, I have some money,' said Lucy firmly. 'I shall do as Uncle Monty taught me. Use a certain amount and not go over that amount if I lose.'

'Very moral and very boring,' chuckled Frank. 'Where's the fun in that?'

'I enjoyed it and I think he's right,' said Lucy, walking more slowly.

'I agree.' He sighed. 'I can understand how the love of a good woman can turn a man away from sin.' She laughed. 'There have been a lot of rumours about many of the stars and yet one picture of a face like yours can dispel every evil or unworthy suspicion.'

'What do you mean?' She tore away from him as they entered the hall of the casino. 'Are you making some kind of sneering remark about Sidney?'

'No, not me, but many do,' he said calmly. 'I'm only

jealous. I bought a couple of papers and it breaks my heart to think you look at him that way and not at me.'

She stared at him, and he wasn't laughing. 'You can't be. You can't be jealous of Sidney?' He nodded and took her arm again, leading her into the bright lights. 'I want to go back,' she announced

'He will have you for the rest of his life,' he said softly. 'Give me one evening, Lucy. Just one and I'll fade away if you say so and never trouble you again.'

Somehow, she found herself sitting by the table where she had been with Monty and her hand was filled with discs of various colours. She put them in a pile and pushed them to one side. The two that she had with her almost seemed to burn a hole in her hand. 'Eleven,' she whispered. 'Sidney, bring me luck with your number and make it safe.'

She waited until all the bets had been placed and then put one disc on eleven. Frank Garsey reached for her hand as if excited, as he watched his three piles of chips on rouge sixteen, eighteen and blanc six. Lucy didn't even try to get away and found a current of awareness that was pleasant and dangerous between them.

Frank laughed as his chips were raked in and Lucy was given her winnings. She put them all in her bag and smiled at him. 'Use your own. I do very nicely with my own,' she said. She pushed away the chips he had bought for her and he took them with a shrug.

'I had hoped to put you in my debt,' he said, and she knew that he was not joking, although he laughed.

'I've had enough,' she insisted. 'Champagne gives me a headache.'

'It wasn't dry enough,' said Frank. 'I thought that ladies liked it sweet but I agree that it wasn't so good.' Lucy made way for a couple who wanted to watch the wheel spin and made for the kiosk to cash in her chips. She was surprised at the amount of money she was given and gasped when she saw that the innocent pieces of colour that Frank cashed, the ones he had wanted her to use, were worth five hundred dollars.

She glanced at his expressionless face, the smooth skin and well-tonsured hair and the mouth that promised every sensual pleasure at which she could only guess. He took her hand casually, and tucked it under his arm in a way that should have meant nothing but made her heart beat faster. His fingers smoothed her palm and made tracings over her wrist as his other hand came across and captured hers, and she was breathless.

They walked back to the hotel and she knew that it was late. The restaurant was in darkness and the small coffee shop held just one customer and a tired waiter. 'I'd like some coffee,' said Lucy.

'We could have some in your room.'

'No, room service is over. I had to fetch something for Nellie one night from the bar.' She walked to the counter of the coffee shop. 'I'll have black coffee,' she said. Frank Garsey nodded and sat with her at a banquette inside the door. 'Has Miss Morris come in?' she asked the waiter.

'Over an hour ago, Miss. They ordered breakfast for nine-thirty, and went to bed.'

'You'll have to go in very quietly,' said Frank.

'I am in the next room along the corridor,' said Lucy. 'In the last hotel, I had to go through their suite to my room but this time, I'm on my own.' She bit her lip, aware that he might notice what she had said.

'Have you finished?' he asked. She nodded. 'But you have a headache and nothing to cure it?'

'The coffee was good, and I think I shall be able to sleep.' She smiled. 'It's been such a good evening, Frank. I've enjoyed it so much.'

'And now, I have to give you up to Sidney Darwen?'

'Of course. We are to be married.' Her voice trembled. 'I love him and he loves me.'

'I'll see you to your room,' he said. 'But I haven't quite finished my coffee.' He brought a tiny pill-box of chased silver from his pocket. 'I suffer from catarrh,' he said and took a pinch of white powder which he sniffed from the dip of his thumb as men take snuff. 'Have some? It will clear your headache.'

232

He took a pinch and placed it on Lucy's hand, and laughed softly. 'What is it?' she asked.

'Sniff it all in one go and then breathe deeply,' he said. 'It's wonderful.'

Lucy did just as he suggested. She felt as if she might choke and then her head began to reel. Frank Garsey pulled her from the seat and walked with her to the elevator. Lucy felt as if she was walking on a cloud of feathers and the walls dissolved as they went into her room. Frank Garsey locked the door and laid her gently on the bed.

He kissed her on the lips and her limp hands hung over the edges of the bed. In dreams, she had found herself hovering over her body on the bed and now it was a dream again. His hands smoothed her hair and throat and he kissed her ears and closed eyes. She knew that he smelled good and her arms came up to hold him close. His kisses probed her mind and made all other kisses seem like the touch of innocent flower petals as his hands began to undress her with relentless and gentle purpose.

Colours throbbed through the room and her skin was cool and taut under his hand. Her breasts felt wonderful as if made for a god to fondle and she moved to let him take away the last of her clothes. If she opened her eyes, she felt dizzy, but with them closed, she imagined that Sidney was with her, doing all that she had hoped he would do, with such expertise that she was a rag doll with no resistance.

'That is good?' he whispered, but she was unable to speak. Small sounds that were half-moaning came from her as he pressed his body close and down and entered her with one swift movement that was pain and then a great release of warmth and pleasure and explosive satisfaction. Her body arched and sank and her fingernails tore tramlines in the smooth skin of his back, drawing blood.

At last, he sank back and lay by her side, his hand over her breast. Lucy began to cry slowly and with shuddering breath. Her head felt terrible and she was wet. She tried to sit up but nearly fell off the bed and she wanted to be sick. Her teeth began to chatter and he covered her with a sheet.

233

'Listen to me,' he said in a hard whisper. 'You wanted me! You wanted me and I was the first! You will have to come to me, Lucy. I want you. Do you hear? I want you for always, and you haven't a hope in hell of living with that queer.' He picked up his clothes and watched her as he dressed. He smiled, almost fearfully. 'I was the first and there'll be hell to pay if it gets out.'

'Don't leave me,' she whispered. 'Please come back.'

He felt his body harden again but kept away from her. 'Listen, I have to go but I shall come back, Lucy my darling. You must never tell anyone about tonight until we can be together for always. Promise me?'

'I promise,' she said, then sat up and held her head. 'But I promised to marry Sidney. I'll have to tell him.'

'No! You must never tell him.' He laughed. 'Not yet. In time, he will want other amusements and we can enjoy each other as we did tonight.' He bent to kiss her and she clung to him. 'He already has a lover, and it's as well that you know.'

'He never looks at another woman!' Lucy pushed the damp hair from her face. 'You're lying because of . . . this.'

'Can he rouse you as I did tonight? Believe me, my dear, I shall have no need of coke the next time. You are dynamite.'

'Where are you going?'

'I have a date with a party in Hollywood tomorrow. I shall drive there now and think of you. Forget me if you can and make believe that he really does love you, at least until you are married. I can wait now.'

He left softly and she didn't hear the elevator. Lucy clung to the walls on her way to the bathroom and sank into a cool bath. She took off the bottom sheet from her bed and washed away the stains before putting it by the open window to dry. It was hot and she knew she could put it rumpled on the bed ready for changing the next morning when the maid came. She was tired and drained and her head hurt so much that her eyes seemed to bulge outwards.

234

Her dreams were strange and filled with violent colour and vortices of swirling rain and wind and faces of evil beasts. When she woke to hear Nellie calling and tapping on the wall, she had to blink and shake herself to know where she was.

'You look terrible!' Nellie exclaimed.

Lucy dabbed the end of her nose which had started to run. 'I think I have a cold,' she croaked.

'Then back to your room, Miss! I can't have a cold now we're opening. I can manage as you set up the dressing room so well with Monty. Get some aspirin from the maid, and Monty will come in later to see how you are.'

'I'll be fine later,' said Lucy and went back to convince the maid that she had spilled water on the bed and tried to dry it. By nine o'clock she was sitting up in a clean bed and having scrambled eggs. Her nose was sore and still runny but she felt better. The coffee almost burned her throat but she needed to feel it go down, harsh and unsweetened, and to savour the crisp toast. When Nellie left for rehearsal, she got up and dressed and ironed all the clothes that needed it, both in Nellie's room and her own. The dress she had worn last night she put out for cleaning and knew that she would have to mend the neckline where Frank had torn it.

The telephone rang and she started back as if it might bite her. 'Lucy? I wanted to say I love you. I wanted to make you know how much I love you, and that in one way I'm sorry about last night but in another, I wouldn't change the smallest moment.' It was the same soft seductive voice and she knew it had the same effect on her. 'Are you there?' he said, as she didn't answer.

'I'm here, and I think I hate you,' she said clearly, and put down the phone.

It rang again and she picked it up, listlessly. If he kept on ringing, she would have to tell Nellie that Frank Garsey was annoying her. I can't see him again, she thought as she said her name.

'Lucy?'

'Sidney?' The relief was enormous. He sounded so normal, so English and so brotherly.

'Have you seen the papers? They gave us a big spread in all the Hearst papers and in some of the independents, and the photographs are very good.' He went on to tell her what other people had said and how impressed Mr Gunnar had been with the film rushes.

'I thought you had rung to say how much you loved me,' she said at last. 'How much you want us to be together for always. How you don't love anyone as much as you love me.' Tears streamed down her face and she tried to stop from sobbing.

'Lucy? Of course I love you. You know I do.'

'And you don't have a lover? You promise me you'll never look at another woman?'

'Lucy! I don't have to promise that. You know we are going to be married and I do love you. I have never looked at another woman. I must have been waiting for you.'

In her mind, Lucy heard Monty, or was it Nellie, telling her that a pansy was also called a queer?

'And what of other men, Sidney?' She heard a gasp. 'You must tell me, Sidney. I can't believe it's possible, but they say that you love other men.'

'I am going to marry you, Lucy. You mustn't believe the lies you will hear. People are jealous of my success and make up stories. I'll be with you as soon as I can and we'll show the world that we are only meant for each other.' Lucy put down the receiver. He had quoted that phrase when rehearsing his test pieces before the film trials. I'd have more passion from him if I acted with him, she realised, and felt as if someone had died.

'Are you better?' Monty came and sat on the chair by the open window. 'I left Nellie rehearsing with her new man. He sings well and is tall enough to make a good foil for her when they dance.'

'Do you trust her to be with other men?'

'Nellie?' he laughed. 'She has a way with them that they can't resist but I trust her. We've been through a lot together and we know every mood.' He glanced at her sad face. 'We also love each other, even if we do sound off at times. Sometimes, a real spat can make it even better for some people. Nellie is like that and I go along although I prefer a calmer life.'

'Like Sidney. He never argues.' Lucy swung her legs as she sat on the bed and Monty thought how like a child she looked in the short linen frock and sheer pink stockings. 'Sidney never argues, is sweet and gentle and says he loves me when I remind him to say it. Sidney doesn't really care for kissing and hardly ever touches me except when there are people to watch.' Her depression grew.

'Come on, Lucy! Snap out of it. You sound as if you're coming up from a snort.'

'What do you mean?' She turned sharply and he felt uneasy.

'You know. You must have heard about cocaine? They used it at *Vizcaya*, but not a word to the papers, mind. It makes people feel bright for a while then terribly depressed if they aren't used to it. After that, it becomes a habit that's difficult to shake off and it can destroy a lot of things.'

'What is it like?' Lucy asked, but she knew and she felt sore and used in body and spirit.

'White powder that is sniffed up the nose to give a lift. It's a terrible habit and one that you must never try, Lucy. People do things that they would never do without it and it clouds the judgment.'

'It sounds horrid,' she said viciously.

'Did you have a good meal last night?' he asked.

'Yes. I met Frank Garsey in the restaurant and he came and sat with me.' They'll find out if I don't tell them, she thought. 'He offered me some champagne and it gave me a headache. We went to the casino to cash in those chips I had left. He tried to make me use a lot of his but I won and had no need to. I made quite a lot of money, Monty. I did give back the ten dollars you staked for me, didn't I?'

He nodded. 'Did you stay long?' He glanced round the immaculate room. 'Did he bring you back safely?'

She smiled. 'Here I am, safe and sound and feeling

better. I don't think I'm going to have a cold after all, so I can go with Nellie this afternoon.'

'Are you seeing him again? He's a bad lot, Lucy. He gambles and trades in all sorts of shady deals and is a menace with women.'

'At least he notices them,' she said bitterly. 'But you needn't worry, Uncle Monty. 'He's going away and I shan't see him again.'

'Well, that's a relief. Now, Nellie has been on the telephone to Mr Gunnar and he's agreed to let her choose your wedding dress. The ones they select for films are not your style, or so she thinks.' He laughed. 'I imagine she has it all mapped out to fit in with what *she* will wear. It will be good publicity for everyone concerned.'

'But not for me. I shall just have lots of rude men pushing cameras at me all day.'

'You are a celebrity now, Lucy. Look at the papers.' He opened one and showed her the headline: RISING STAR SIDNEY DARWEN IS TO MARRY THE GIRL NEXT DOOR. There was a whole article about how she had come across the Atlantic to join him as they couldn't bear to be apart for any longer: '*Lucy, the girl who every right-minded man wants is young and fresh and makes even the hardest of newsmen wish they had a daughter like her.*'

'Who told them all that?' she asked, forgetting her depression.

'The studio mostly. Sidney filled in for them and Nellie told them about your work with her. That's in another paper, but we'll save all the cuttings for you to send home.'

'I'm not a star. Who would want to read about me?'

'You and Sidney will capture the hearts of America,' he said, and she guessed that this also was a quote from one of the slushier articles. Monty tried to read her face. 'Gunnar and his crowd sell films because they are without sex and crime and all the bad things that his church forbids. That's why he wants to see you two married, and America will view you as the perfect couple, in films to which they can take their daughters and grandmothers without embarrassment.'

'I am not an actress,' she protested.

'You could be if Gunnar has his way.' Monty laughed. 'You have a lot more intelligence than most of the women in films. They say that Marion Davies is a star because Hearst arranged it and finances her. Money talks.'

'I have no money and Sidney will need all of his for a while.'

'There are always men who will back a pretty woman,' he said.

'Like Frank Garsey?' She laughed as if it was funny.

'Yes, he's typical, I'd say.' Monty lit a cigar and saw none of the pain that showed for a moment in her eyes.

'So he wouldn't do it out of love?'

'Unlikely. He might fall heavily for someone, but I doubt it. You don't take sweets to a sweet shop, and he is rumoured to back a very elegant little cat-house in Chicago.'

Lucy felt sick. 'I need some air,' she said. 'I still have a headache after that sweet champagne so I'll go for a walk before lunch. Is there anything you want in the drug-store?'

Monty shook his head and went to the door. 'If there's anything worrying you, or if you want to call off the wedding, don't be afraid to say, Lucy. We can weather that storm if that's what you want, and you could be happier without him.'

'You mean Sidney?' she smiled. 'I think I know how he feels. I must make up my mind that I shall never be first in his heart.'

'No, his work will come first,' he said. 'I'm glad you know.'

'His work and other things,' she said softly, when Monty had gone. She looked again at the note she had received just before Monty came in. It wasn't signed and just said that Sidney was staying with his lover Ivor Sinclair at a certain motel. 'Goodbye, Sidney,' she said and tore up the letter into four pieces before tossing it into the waste-basket.

She pulled on a pretty hat trimmed with cornflowers

and poppies and carried a long thin cardigan of pale pink that matched the dress. The foyer was busy and nobody saw her leave. Lucy walked across to the boulevard and strolled by the sea, breathing in the warm, humid air and hearing nothing. Couples sat side by side or with arms round waists, and a boy kissed his girl as they walked to the icecream stand. It was a dream again with her watching everything and yet having no part in it. It would be like this if I died, she thought. It would be quiet and interesting, with no pain.

Someone stared and she knew that he recognised her picture. A pile of fresh newspapers showed her and Sidney kissing, and another photograph had them sitting hand in hand, looking shy.

Lucy turned away as the man spoke to his wife and pointed. Others noticed her and she hurriedly retreated from the avid faces and the sudden burst of voices. The intersection was to the right and she walked quickly towards it, her intention to escape into the big department store nearby and be lost in the crowds. Would it be like this after she was married? Excitement in public and Sidney showing how much he loved his innocent young wife?

She looked at the lights that blinked even in the day and saw the shop she needed, then stepped out to cross the road.

Lucy heard a scream and a sudden racing noise that exploded inside her head. There was pain and she didn't feel at peace, she thought as she lost consciousness.

Chapter 17

'At least Sidney wasn't with her when it happened.' Emily handed back the letter and made her mother sit down while she made a cup of tea.

Jane Darwen was shaking as if suffering from a great shock. 'She might die and Sidney will not marry,' she repeated numbly.

'You keep on saying that, Mother. I hope she gets better, but if she doesn't, Sidney will have plenty more girls after him.' Emily added sugar to her cup. 'Lucy is young and healthy and they say that she might respond to treatment even if she can't walk.' She spoke without any sense of conviction. Who would be able to walk, or to live even an abnormal life after such terrible head injuries?

'It's over six weeks now,' said Jane. 'How they could let those photographers in to take her picture lying there like a dead thing makes me ashamed of the human race.'

'She looks very peaceful and so young,' Emily mused. She read one of the accounts in a paper that Nellie had sent them, rather than feeling that she must write a lengthy explanatory letter. Sidney had written too, a long sad letter saying that as soon as Lucy regained consciousness, he would marry her and make sure she had everything possible to bring her back to health. 'The paper says that Sidney wept when he heard the news but is bearing up well with the help of his sponsor, Mr Gunnar and his manager, Mr Ivor Sinclair. It's good that he has friends round him, Mother. We can't do anything to help and Lucy may get better.'

'I pray every night for her,' said Jane. She felt the urge to say a rosary, but she had no beads after years of chapel life. The family had no idea that she had gone to the Catholic church on the other side of the Island to burn candles for the girl.

241

'We must try to forget them. Vikki needs us still and so do the girls. You'll have three babies to love after Christmas, Mother, and there'll be no time for sadness.'

'Four, as you can't say that George is more than a baby,' said Jane. She folded the papers and put them away in a drawer. 'Sidney wrote to Maudie and she sent a card, I believe, but if she isn't concerned I hope that Lucy never knows. I've asked Sidney to send her flowers from us instead of sending us silly Christmas presents.'

Emily smiled. The latest had been two paintings that Jane had taken round the entire house in an effort to find a suitable spot for them. Eventually, she had given up and hung them in the hall in the darkest place.

Mrs Barnes had admired them with a wicked smile, and Jane had led her past them quickly. 'The dark hall cuts down the colour at least,' Jane had said. 'But they don't fit in and it's no use me saying I like them.'

'They are very fashionable,' remarked the doctor's wife. 'Maxfield Parrish is famous in America. All that violet and rose and castles in the clouds are quite pretty. His *Daybreak* has sold a million copies.'

'Janey had a painting from Sidney, too. She likes it but I wouldn't give it house room. It's rude! Imagine having it on the wall when the minister called? *Nude Descending a Staircase* indeed!'

'I share your view but Alex has one by Duchamp, too. He keeps it in his room.'

'When is he coming home?' Jane looked anxious. 'I worry over those boys.'

'He hasn't told many people but he is leaving the Navy next year. His eyesight isn't as good as it should be for some work in the Navy and his heart has never been in it since he and Clive went to different branches of the Service.' Mrs Barnes smiled. 'We never sold the old house and it's in good repair. After a course at college, he will set up a restaurant there. I hope he finds a nice girl to help him.'

'I wish that Clive would leave, too.'

'He's as keen as Alex's cousin and they both say that the

sea is their career for as long as they are wanted.' Mrs Barnes frowned. 'With two children and another on the way, Geoffrey has a lot of responsibilities. Clive has too, now that Janey is expecting again. I wonder if they know how lucky they are?'

Jane's thoughts were interrupted by Emily speaking. 'Flowers would be a good idea,' her daughter agreed. 'I'm sure that people in that kind of coma can sometimes smell nice things. They say that patients who have recovered have heard a lot of what goes on around them and yet couldn't talk and say what they wanted.'

'I'll write and so can you,' said Jane. 'If Sidney reads the letters to Lucy, she might know that we love her.'

'I doubt if the others will write. Janey does every week but Clare and Lizzie have no feelings for the poor girl. They are completely tied up with their own affairs.'

'Clare was cross that she couldn't get into the side-car to come to tea,' said Jane, smiling. 'It seemed funny to have to carry the cakes there and travel in that contraption to their house. I shan't do it often as Clare expects too much.'

'She's due in February and Lizzie in March with Janey after that.' Emily put down her crochet. 'I shall make another jacket for Lizzie now. You were right. This edge is getting very heavy and I need a change.'

'Why not make a soft lace collar for that new print dress of yours, Emily? You never make anything for yourself.'

'I don't wear lace, Mother. It doesn't suit me.'

'You'll never find a husband if you dress in brown all the time.' Jane tried to sound as if it was a joke, but wished that Emily would marry.'

'I'll never marry. I shall care for Vikki and you and in time, I might help Alex for a change or look after Clare's baby, but I shall never marry.'

'Alex will need help,' agreed Jane.

'I'm not setting my cap at him, Mother. He's already far too fond of Janey to look at another woman and we wouldn't get on in that way.'

'He's like a brother to you all,' said Jane, and Emily only smiled. They sat by a small fire in the morning room and Jane added coal to the bright flames. Emily regarded her with worried eyes. A fire in the house had been important for as long as she could recall and they both missed the vast black range that was lit day and night at the shop on Coppins Bridge. The new gas-fire and cooker in the kitchen produced food as good as the range and the cooker wasn't temperamental, but the 'Yorkist' range and open fire that Jane had recently ordered would be more like the old one, but far more attractive. With its surround of dark red tiles, far less effort would be needed to keep it clean.

But Jane had gazed into fires with that same faraway look so often that Emily knew that she was really worried. 'We can't do anything, Mother. I think that Lucy will die and that Sidney will have to find another girl,' Emily said quietly. 'We must face it and let him live his own life.'

'It's not only him.' Jane made an impatient gesture and ash fell out on to the hearth. 'I worry about you all and most of all about Clive.'

Emily laughed. 'He'll be home just after Christmas and again when Janey has the baby in May. They've cleared the North Sea of mines, or very nearly, and we are at Peace. The biggest show that the Navy will put on now will be for Cowes Week and goodwill tours. Clive loves it and Janey might be allowed to join him later if he gets sent to somewhere really wonderful, like Singapore.'

'I know.' Jane stopped poking the fire. 'I'll see Alice next week, make sure all the baby clothes are ready before Christmas as we'll be busy, and write to Sidney.' She straightened her back and dismissed the superstitious fear from her mind, but the weeks went on and the weather set badly with rain and sleet as winter came, and the old shop looked as if it could do with a new coat of paint.

The draper who now rented it, as Bert wouldn't sell in case it became the property of someone trading in the same way as the Darwens had done, against Jane's wishes, was not doing very well and the whole frontage showed neglect. Jane avoided the place and felt guilty that it should look as it did, but Bert said she was being sentimental about bricks and mortar, and she should wait until the draper gave up before ordering redecoration.

'They are never prompt with the rent and you let them have it for far less than the market value,' he insisted when Jane objected.

'These are hard times for some, Bert,' Jane said. 'A lick of paint will do no harm and I shall ask Mr Amey to do it after Christmas.' He shrugged and smiled, and Jane was amused to see how tolerant and mild he had become since his second marriage. 'You look like the cat with the cream,' she teased. '*Some* people have money and make even more!'

'I do all right,' he admitted. 'But it isn't just that. This time, Maudie *is* expecting and has been to the doctor to make sure.'

'I'm glad! Oh, Bert, you've no idea what it's like to hold the first child in your arms.' Her face glowed. 'I never thought that Maudie would knuckle down to running a home as she has done now.' She sighed happily. 'And now this. I must buy something for the baby. Emily can go down to the draper and buy material and wool. We've bought all we need for our babies and this will help a little.'

'Maudie wasn't pleased at first but she's come round to it now. Hearing about young Lucy must have made her think, and you'll be pleased to know that she has written and asked to be kept informed.'

'Everyone having babies,' snorted Clare when she came with Janey in the car. 'I'm sick of people talking about baby clothes and what happens when they are born.'

'Well, you are healthy enough, Clare,' said Emily, 'and you have a lovely home for the baby.' Clare smiled. She had nagged Alan to paper the walls in the kitchen and the sitting room that was to be the nursery, and he was busy painting banister rails white and laying new deep-blue staircarpet with brass stair-rods. The crimson flocked wallpaper in the living room gave an impression of warmth and comfort as it did in the house on the Mall, from which Clare had copied it. It hid the chill of the marriage and Clare's discontent.

'I almost wish that Christmas was over,' said Jane. 'We seem to be waiting and waiting and nothing happens. The babies will come as the days lengthen and Lucy is still in a coma.' She hardly glanced at the newspaper cuttings from America now. It sickened her to see what a circus they made of tragedy, and pictures of Sidney in a flowing black tie and dark suit as if he was in mourning did nothing to cheer her. At least she is alive and if she recovers they will marry, Jane told herself.

Clive came home and filled the house with laughter. Janey saw him off on the second of January in a biting wind and grey seas, and then brought George over for an afternoon. 'I hate to think of that ship under all those waves,' she said. 'Play something cheerful, Emily.' Janey roamed the house and Jane let her be. It was best to let her think and to weep in private if that's what she needed to do, but it was a gloomy day. Then a pipe in the kitchen leaked, making a heavy dripping sound into the bowl put to catch it and Jane knew that the frost had got into it the week before.

'I'd better get home,' Janey said at last. It was dark at four o'clock in the afternoon and very cold.

'I'll come and sleep the night,' said Emily. Jane nodded. It was the first time that Emily had offered but she sensed the need and urged Janey to agree. The motor started smoothly and Emily sat with a sleepy George on her lap as they drove down through the High Street and over Coppins Bridge under the railway line and up the hill to Staplers.

The girl opened the door to them and took George to have his supper, and the two sisters played cards until it was time for bed.

Janey pressed her tight abdomen as she woke in the morning and felt the child move within her. She smiled until she was really awake and remembered that Clive had gone and was probably joining his submarine now, ferried from the frigate that had taken the relief crew from Portsmouth. She turned over and went back to sleep. Emily left her to rest while she made breakfast and told the girl what to do for the day. Rain lashed the windows and Emily made sure the house was warm. Her mother was all alone back in the house on the Mall and she wondered if her duty was with her, but the maid would be there by now and Jane was never afraid of solitude.

'I'll stay if you want me,' said Emily, later. Janey seemed restless and was looking pale.

'I am glad you are here, Em. I didn't think I'd feel so depressed about Clive going back. I suppose it was the sight of that grey ship on the grey water and the waves breaking over the pier. I think I've got a cold, too,' she said.

'Then go back to bed and I'll see to things down here.' Emily settled down in the living room and asked Daisy to take a message to Mrs Darwen when she did the shopping. The rain eased and the girl took her bicycle and the message and came back with the groceries. Janey looked flushed and Emily began to wonder if she had the 'flu, but said nothing until she could see how her sister was after another long sleep.

The evening news came crackling over the wireless set that Clive had bought just before he left and Emily listened, still fascinated by the voices from the air. Storms had swept the East Coast and two fishing boats had been sunk by huge waves. Emily bit the thread and smoothed out the linen table napkin before taking fresh thread and continuing the neat drawn-thread work round the edge.

'Mines that may have been on the seabed since the war have been sighted and are loose, floating in the shipping lanes,' she heard. 'Mine-sweepers are on their way to clear them again just when it was thought they would not be needed and some had been put in dry dock.'

Emily listened at the foot of the stairs but the door to the bedroom was shut and the house lay quiet. She hesitated before the wireless set. Clive had said they must keep it on for short periods only as the accumulator battery had to be recharged frequently and the two spares had not arrived. She switched it off and sat before it, consumed by a deep anxiety. Clive would be back in that horrible grey slug of a boat now, and safe under the waves. She made coffee and took it up to the bedroom. Janey was still flushed and restless and George was grizzling.

'I think you should see Dr Barnes,' said Emily. Janey shook her head and gratefully drank the coffee. 'I shall send Daisy, or I suppose I could use the telephone.' Janey managed a smile. Emily hated anything new and the telephone held all her worst fears.

'I'll telephone,' said Janey. 'I don't feel too good, it's true. Clive and I went out to the West Wight and got cold. It was dry and bright but the wind was bitter. Dr Barnes might be able to give me something for this headache.'

She rang through the doctor's house and Alex answered it. 'I thought you had gone back ages ago,' she said.

'I was told to stay here and report to Portsmouth each day as my ship is waiting for spares and we can't sail.' He sounded anxious when Janey said that she wasn't well, and told her he'd pass the message on to his father.

Janey went back to bed feeling limp and with a heavy head. Emily brought her up barley water and beef tea and looked after George. She sent another message home to say that she would stay until Janey was better.

From time to time Emily switched on the news but nothing more was said about mines. The battery was low and she could hear very little, so she left it silent.

'I can't do anything that you haven't done, Emily,' said Dr Barnes later. 'Telephone Alex if you want anything and give her this mixture if she gets too hot. I think it's just a heavy cold but keep her warm.' He sat by the fire, drinking freshly-made tea and sighed. If only Alex had fallen in love with Emily, he might be looking forward to his first grandchild now, instead of looking after other men's families. The room was bright and clean and Emily was accomplished at so many things in her quiet way.

'He should wait until tomorrow. Janey is away from everyone and I'll keep her there until she's over the worst and can't spread it,' said Emily firmly. 'We don't need anything just now.'

By the next morning, Janey was looking better but refused food. 'I could drink a well dry though,' she said. 'How about Alex coming over to play cards with us tomorrow?'

'Not until you are downstairs,' disagreed Emily. She saw the loose hair and pretty face and the feminine curves of the taut breasts under the thin robe and thought that Alex would have more peace of mind away from Janey just now.

A pale sun made a square on the wall in an apologetic burst of mild energy and Janey brushed her hair and made up her own bedroom fire. She sat in the big armchair that Clive had bought for her to use after the baby was born and listened to the sounds of the house, with little curiosity, as if suspended in time.

The front doorbell rang and Daisy hurried to answer it. Emily's voice came loud and vehement. 'No, Daisy, give it to me!' Janey went to the door of the room and listened. It was unusual for Emily to raise her voice to anyone.

'But it says it's for the missus!' said Daisy. 'It must be important. I hates them buff envelopes.'

'I'll take it!' Emily snatched the envelope and Janey saw her rip it open. Emily put a hand to her mouth and glanced up the stairs. The two sisters stared at each other and Janey had no need to be told what the telegram contained. She reached out for the banister rail and felt dizzy.

'Clive?' she whispered.

'Stay there!' Emily rushed up the stairs, just too late, and Janey fell heavily, knocked Emily over and then they were in a heap on the hall floor.

'Janey?' Emily pulled herself up and stood, trembling with shock. She lifted the woman's head and rested it on her lap, the words of the wire still in her mind. '*We regret . . . etc*,' which meant that a stray mine, wallowing on the surface of the water, had touched the naval launch transferring the crew to the submarine and one of the protruding tentacles had snapped, causing the boat and mine to explode.

'Don't just stand there, Daisy. If you can't use the

telephone, run for Dr Barnes and say we'll need an ambulance.'

She sat on the floor and felt for a pulse. Janey stirred and opened her eyes. 'Clive?' she whispered.

'The boat hit a mine,' said Emily. She couldn't think of any way to lessen the horror of it. 'All of them were killed.'

In an hour, Janey was tucked up between white sheets in the Infirmary at Ryde. A tall nursing Sister stood by the bed, her square linen cap a shadow against the light and her stiff cuffs gleaming. Two doctors murmured on the other side of the wooden screen and outside, Jane and Emily sat in the draughty corridor and waited.

The door swung open and Dr Barnes came out. He held Jane by the hand in a way that was not wholly professional. 'My dear,' he said. 'Janey will be fine. Emily broke her fall considerably so no bones are broken, but,' he looked back as if he wished that the impersonal Sister could have done this, 'I'm afraid she might lose the baby.'

'Holy Mary, is there no end to this?' said Jane, and Dr Barnes noticed for the first time that there was grey in the rich dark hair.

'We can find no heartbeat and that recent infection may have deprived the baby of resistance. Shock, of course, can cause this to happen. Sister said that Janey received a telegram?'

'Clive was on the launch that hit a mine,' said Emily flatly. 'I was going to read it and break the news to her gently, but she heard the boy at the front door and Daisy wanted to take it up to her at once.' She turned away, her face sad but without other emotion, and sat quietly while the others talked.

'You ought to go home, Mrs Darwen,' said the Sister much later. Jane stared at her as if she hadn't heard. 'There must be others who need you.' Jane blinked. It had happened, and the fact that old Mrs Lee was right came as no great surprise, however much she had fought it over the past year.

'You'll let us know?' she asked.

'In the morning, or later today. It's morning now.'

250

Alex came to drive them home. George was already installed in his room on the Mall with Daisy to look after him. 'I locked the house and turned off the water,' he said. 'I assume that Janey will come to you before she goes back home?'

'Yes. You've been very good, Alex. 'Jane squeezed his hand. 'You are like one of my own.' He hugged her and left, and Emily silently made cocoa and handed Jane the biscuit jar. Jane rocked to and fro and wished she could weep but they both sat dry-eyed through the dawn and into the new day.

'Clare is coming today, Mother. They don't know yet. Shall I send a card and put her off?'

'Sweet Mary! She's coming to dinner and there isn't time to let her know. Alan has the day off and is bringing her in a car a friend lent him.' Jane brushed away the biscuit crumbs from her skirt and cleared the tray. 'It will have to be mutton stew and we'd better put it on now.' She peeled onions but even that didn't make her cry, and Emily arranged the triangles of bread and butter neatly round the edge of the rich bread and butter pudding as if she was entering a contest and had to be precise.

The kitchen smelled homely and Jane was soothed but she dreaded having to tell Clare and Lizzie who were both expecting babies that Janey had lost hers, an hour or so after Alex had taken Jane home.

'Mutton stew?' Alan Dewar sniffed and rubbed his hands together. 'We came early,' he said. Emily glanced at the clock and saw that it was only eleven o'clock.

'Dinner won't be ready yet,' she said and looked at her mother.

'Well, aren't you going to make a cup of tea?' asked Clare. She wandered round the room, picking up magazines and papers and putting them down again in an irritating way. 'More pictures of the rich and famous?' she said with a short laugh. 'They are the lucky ones. Some of the men at Cowes are on short-time and we never know what's going to happen next.'

'You are lucky, too, Clare.' Emily was white-faced. 'Sit

down and listen!' She told them the news and Alan blew his nose hastily. He looked at Clare, who tossed her head and picked at the glove she held on her lap.

'She should have waited before she started another baby,' was all his wife had to say.

Emily went into the kitchen and busied herself with vegetables, and Jane fetched George to see Alan who was fond of him. Outwardly, they were a family, eating together and even laughing at the things that George did and said, but Jane felt as if she was losing control of her life and that others were being swept along on an irresistible tide. We must be cheerful for George, she thought and was grateful when Alan offered to take him out during the next weekend he had off.

'When ours is born, I know you'll do the same for us,' he said, which spoiled his offer as if he'd made a down-payment on goodwill.

'Janey is the one to need help,' said Jane firmly. 'She'll be ill for some time and I don't want you making unkind remarks, Clare.'

'And what about me? My time is nearly due and the doctor says it could be earlier than I thought. I shall be ill, too, but I haven't heard you offer to have me here to look after me properly.'

'You are well and healthy and so is Lizzie. Janey had an accident due to shock and the fall and you have only yourselves to please and you never did neglect number one!' Emily cleared away the dishes and disappeared once more into the kitchen.

Clare followed her. 'And when mine is born, you don't want to have it here? Is that it? Janey always was your favourite sister and you don't care about me.'

'I shall love your baby, Clare. I love George but if you have a girl, I shall love that even more.'

Clare looked taken aback. 'I'm sorry, Em. I get worked up with *him* around night after night.' She laughed without real humour. 'If it's a girl, I shall call it Emily after you. No, Emma. That's more genteel.'

'I'd like that,' said Emily, and tipped away the washing-up water. 'You have everything ready, Clare?' Her sister nodded. 'The midwife is very good, and Dr Barnes will make sure that everything is all right.'

'I know.' Clare walked about the kitchen and even took a tea towel and helped dry the dishes. 'It's afterwards I dread. I can't bear the idea of feeding a baby . . . you know. I want to have it bottle-fed from the beginning but the midwife was very rude when I mentioned it.'

'You may want to feed it when it comes,' said Emily comfortingly. 'Janey enjoys it and Mother said she fed all of us.'

'I'm no cow!' Clare flung down the cloth and took the tea-tray into the sitting room where Alan was playing bears with George.

'Alan will like being a father,' said Emily when she returned.

'I shan't let him have much to do with it. He'd spoil it and I can't bear spoiled children.' Clare seemed to cheer up. 'If you help me with the child when it comes, I shall be glad, Em. I really am not a natural mother.' She laughed. 'You know how they say that a baby looks like anything that frightened the mother? Well, I hate it so much that I'm sure it will be ugly and have something wrong with it.'

'You are mad, Clare!' Emily drew away and went out to hand round the cups. She thought of Ethel, Clare's oldest friend who was still a patient in the mental hospital, and prayed that Clare wouldn't follow her after the baby was born.

Alex came later with flowers for Jane and left them with Alan to take to the hospital the next day when he returned the borrowed car to Ryde. 'I'll take some more in when she is better,' said Alex. 'When can I see her?'

'Not in hospital,' said Jane firmly. 'I don't want her to feel that she is an invalid for longer than necessary. The sooner she can come home and look after George, the sooner she will come to terms with what has happened and begin to look ahead. Lying in bed with too much time to think never did anyone any good.'

'But she is ill and needs sympathy,' he protested.

'She's had a dead baby and no other bodily damage,' said Jane. 'She is heartbroken and very low in spirits and yet not really ill. She will be home in a week after they've dried up her milk and made sure she is all right inside.'

'That's too soon. *I'm* going to stay in bed for three weeks,' interrupted Clare. 'The midwife says that all her patients lie in to have a good rest.'

'She can go to bed here and get up when she feels like it. I found that I was better on the move and my legs didn't ache as much if I walked round the room and did simple jobs.' Jane sent Alan for meat pies as he and Clare showed no sign of going home before supper and Alex stayed, too. He talked of Clive as if he was still alive and even made them laugh a little.

'You are a tonic,' said Jane when he was leaving. 'Say all those things to Janey when she comes home. It will do her more good than saying how sorry you are and sitting with a long face.'

'I wasn't going to say much,' he began.

'You will be good for her. You will see her for a few days before your ship sails; she'll need a broad shoulder and bit of humour, and you knew Clive so well.'

'I'm very fond of her,' he said awkwardly.

'I know,' she replied. 'Go away for a while after you've seen her and let her sort out her life, Alex. She may want you, she may not. Time will tell.'

'I'll wait,' he said.

Jane shut the door on the darkness and shivered. Archie had said the same words and yet she'd never had the courage to agree to marry him. But Janey was young and needed a man to love her as Clive had done. I am getting old, thought Jane – but why do I send for Archie whenever I am in trouble? She smiled sadly. Clive not dead for more than a day or so and she was matchmaking for his widow. Annie Cooper would have had something to say about it all, if she wasn't turning in her grave over the coloured curtains that Maudie had put up and the white paint everywhere in her dark old house.

'We can look after her here, Mother. Don't leave her

there to get low,' said Emily. 'It will do her good to have George chattering and a normal house being run.'

Jane thought of the quiet hospital and the smell of antiseptics and nodded, and Dr Barnes arranged the ambulance to bring her to the house on the Mall two days later.

'Mummy!' George rushed to see her and flung himself on the bed. 'See what I have.' Emily smiled and left them together. Janey would have little time to herself whenever he was awake and she must still sleep and regain her strength.

By the end of the week, Janey could talk about Clive without weeping, although his body had not been recovered from the sea. When Alex left for Gibraltar, she clung to his hand and then watched him leave the house, her face thinner and more mature and very beautiful.

'He'll be back,' said Jane cheerfully. 'Did he tell you about the hotel?'

'A little,' said Janey. 'He doesn't know enough yet and will have to learn hotel management and find himself a good cook and housekeeper.'

'I might have to lend him Emily,' Jane joked.

'Emily?' Janey blushed and looked confused. 'I suppose so,' she said. 'Yes, I couldn't go, could I?' Jane watched her daughter each day and saw that she took greater care of George and played with him more. She had to take in all her clothes as they were too loose and she no longer talked of Clive in a sad way.

'How will you feel when you go home?' asked Jane.

'I don't know. I feel as if he has gone back to his ship and will walk in for his next leave at any moment.'

Jane swallowed hard. 'That's how I felt about your father when he was away. It never leaves you but dulls with time. Does it worry you that he hasn't been found?'

'No, it makes it easier. Does that surprise you?' Jane nodded. 'He would rather be there. He loved the sea and I couldn't bear to follow his coffin and see it sunk into the clay. Now, I can look across the water and think he's there, somewhere, and I loved him so much that I'll never

255

really lose him.' She picked up one small scuffed shoe. 'I would have liked a girl to make a family.' She burst into tears and sobbed for an hour and Jane found her first relief in tears, too. They were tears that embraced Lucy and Sidney, Clive and the dead baby girl and all her friends who had gone. Walter seemed far away and when the doorbell rang, she was tidy again and not at all surprised to see Archie.

'Jane, my dear,' he said and gathered her into his arms. For a moment, she closed her eyes and let the luxury of his manhood comfort her, then drew away as she had done so many times. 'I came as fast as I could, but we have a new calf and it was difficult.'

She smiled. It put everything into perspective. 'I'm glad you could spare the time now,' she said.

Chapter 18

Emily heard the telephone ring and smiled. Her mother was getting used to it now and Archie rang each day to talk to her if he couldn't spare the time to visit.

'How is he?' Emily asked.

'Fine. He is thinking of raising turkeys now, bless the man. He knows I like birds and he thought I would enjoy seeing the young ones next week.' Jane looked more relaxed than she had done for weeks. 'Now Janey is better and taking up golf with Mrs Barnes, we have more time to ourselves.'

'Go today just for the trip, Mother. Next week, you may have Clare and the baby on your hands. It's due now and Clare hinted that she would like to come to you and not stay in her own home.' Emily shrugged. 'She says it is more convenient here with the wash-basin in the spare room and the lavatory next door.'

'She has it all worked out,' said Jane drily, 'but the midwife has taken all the linen and rubber sheets there to be ready and Alan has made a very nice cot for the baby.'

'We have a cot that George used when he was small,' said Emily. 'Clare hasn't forgotten that.' She laughed. 'It's going to be quite a pantomime when those two have their babies.'

'I'll walk to Shide and take the train after I've seen Clare,' said Jane. 'I can come back past the shop to Janey and she can drive me home later.'

'I shall take George up to the stream by the recreation ground. He wants to take a net and look for sticklebacks but we may be too early in the year. He'll get wet even if we never see a fish, but I'll make sure he's well wrapped up. He grows so fast and takes up so much of Janey's time that it's good to give her a rest and let her do something completely different,' said Emily.

Jane put on a thick coat and pulled her hat well down to keep her ears warm. Her good strong brogue shoes would do on the farm as boots felt heavy now that there was a little warmth in the sun, and Archie had made his yards mud-free over the last year.

'I didn't expect you!' Archie hugged her and kissed her on the lips.

'I'll go back if I'm unwelcome,' she said, laughing.

'Never that. Come and see what we have done.' He went ahead with the enthusiasm of a boy and Jane followed slowly, noticing the well-painted picket gate and the general air of prosperity. The large turkey-shed was still reeking of new wood and pitch and the windows were wide open to let it dry out.

'It's clean enough for a family,' Jane said admiringly.

'I want no disease here, you see, and in about three years I shall have the best breed of turkeys in the south of England. Next week, the first chicks come and I must have the oil-stoves ready to heat the enclosure over there where they will live for a week or so until they get acclimatised.'

'It's a long-term plan,' said Jane thoughtfully.

'That's the worst, or the best of farming,' he said simply. 'There's no end to it. It goes on as life goes on, Jane, and I can't sit here, biting my nails in the hope that you will give up your house and come to me.'

'One day,' she began, then smiled sadly as she saw his disbelief. 'We both have things to do,' she added quietly. 'I must see the girls safely delivered and Janey happy again. Now that Vikki is a big girl, she spends a lot of time with George and has asked if she can stay at the Lodge for a few weeks.' She laughed. 'I think she is afraid that Clare and Lizzie will want her to feed the babies when they come. She loves George and I can't let her be made a little slave to those two, so Janey will have her there for a while. She can come and go on the way from school and not feel left out, and now that her legs are strong, the walking will be good for her.'

'You sound as if you are clearing decks for action,' said

258

Archie. He grinned. 'Clare was always one for having what she wanted. Leave them all and bring Emily here. We will hide you until it is all over.'

'I'll not shirk my duty, Archie, any more than you ever did.' She picked up a handful of straw and smelled it. 'I miss the horses but I'm glad you had them. I miss a lot but the gaps get filled.' The memory of so much hung between them.

'Come inside,' he said. She hesitated. 'There are no ghosts now, if that's what puts you off marrying me, Jane.' The farmhouse door no longer stuck at the top and let in a draught at the bottom. The main room was covered with linoleum and had a good carpet square in the middle and rugs by the fire. Jane glanced at the wall where the tiny room had been in which Rose, Archie's tuberculous daughter had died. The wall was smooth and covered with pretty floral wallpaper. 'I had it blocked off,' he said. 'The main bedroom downstairs that we used to be near Rose is now a store, and I sleep upstairs again.'

'I'll come more often now that Vikki is with Janey.' Jane walked out into the yard and sniffed the air. 'It smells better than it did in the old days,' she admitted.

'I've got rid of the pigs except for one to use up the swill and give me a bit of ham once a year. The cows went before the last frost and I have a couple of calves ready for market and then that's all. From now on, it's poultry – and flowers for Emily if she wants to go on making bouquets and decorating weddings.'

'It sounds grand, just grand,' said Jane softly.

'It could be better,' he said and kissed her so tenderly that she almost said she'd come to marry him. A distant train whistle brought her to her senses, and she fixed the pin in her hat and buttoned up her coat.

'I said I'd be at the station for Janey to pick me up on her way back from the golf-links,' she said.

'Take some eggs,' Archie offered. 'If that's all I can give you.'

'You give me more than that, you dear man,' she said, and reached up to kiss him. 'I'll be down with George to see the chicks.'

Janey was waiting in the motor car and opened the door as Jane hurried down the station approach. 'How was he?' she asked.

'The same sweet man as always, and so excited about having a turkey farm now. Would you believe how different it all is?'

'He wants to impress you, mother.' Janey laughed. 'He thinks that you'll marry the turkeys even if you don't want him. Why don't you, Mother?' Her tone was brittle.

'I might, one day,' said Jane. 'Do you really think I should?' she asked cautiously.

'I think that you should do as you like, just as you did when you gave up the shop. You are lucky – you have not got just me and George, but all the others with their babies. For me, married life stopped when Clive died and I shall never have another baby to call mine.'

'You've been so brave,' said Jane. 'I don't talk about it but I admire you more than I can say and I've never loved you more.' She glanced at the pale face beside her. 'You have so much love round you, Janey. Everyone loves you.'

'I know.' Her expression softened. 'That kind of love.' She parked the car by the steps of the Mall but made no attempt to open her door. 'Am I wicked, Mother? In the night, I cry out for Clive and want him near me. I want him to make love to me, fill me with another child and it's not just in my mind.'

'I know about that, too,' said Jane softly. 'Your father was away for two years and before that we couldn't . . . Dr Barnes knew that I mustn't carry another child, so we couldn't.'

'Was it as bad as that?' Janey looked horrified. 'Oh, what must you think of me? Clive has been gone for such a short time and I'm saying all this to you.'

'Walter came back, that's the difference, Janey. You need love as I did and in time, you will marry again. You must. You can't go through life without it. Just let the tide take you and find its own time.' She thought of the letters that Janey had every few days from Alex which she read eagerly. It wasn't in her mind, yet, and wouldn't be spoken for a while, but it would come.

'I can't think of that, Mother. It would be disloyal.'

'George will need a father,' said Jane firmly. 'He's a very lively and sometimes very naughty boy and by the time he goes to school will need a firm hand and a touch of the slipper on his little bottom if I'm not mistaken! By the way, Clare wasn't in when I called today.'

'I won't come in, Mother. George and Vikki will want supper and Daisy has the evening off.' She leaned across to open Jane's door and kissed her on the cheek. 'Thank you, Jane Darwen,' she said softly. 'You make life so much easier to bear.'

Jane walked with misty eyes up to the front door. She found it open and Emily waiting for her. 'Is something wrong?' Emily glanced towards the stairs, and Jane tore off her gloves and scarf and took the pin from her hat. 'What is it?' She put her coat on the hall-stand. It couldn't be Vikki, who was with Janey, and yet there were voices from an upper room.

'It's Clare.' Emily was red in the face. 'She walked all the way here and sat on the settee refusing to leave.'

'She knows she can come here,' said Jane, surprised.

'Having labour pains?'

'Dear Mary! How far on is she? I must telephone Janey to take her home.'

'It's too late, Mother. She saw to that. She walked here having pains every fifteen minutes and knew enough from the time when you had babies that she had time to get here safely but probably not time to go home again.'

'Is Dr Barnes here?' Emily nodded. 'Does the midwife know?'

'Clare sent a message that she would be having the baby here. Oh yes, they are all here, you can be sure of that!'

Jane sat down on the chair in the hall. 'We'll have to put up with it, Emily. In one way it's easier than having to go there every five minutes. We can always send her home for the nurse to deal with after a few days.'

'Don't go up yet. The midwife said she'd call if they

need anything. Alan has brought all the sheets and rubber and the baby clothes, so it looks as if they planned this together. Come on – we need a cup of tea with something in it!'

'I should go up,' her mother demurred.

'Remember the strong black tea we used to have from the pot on the hob that was always on the simmer? It isn't the same out of a silver teapot.' Emily led her to the kitchen where the new range glowed and the old brown teapot was on the hot-plate. 'I made it after she came. We're going to need a lot of this,' said Emily. She poured the dark, fragrant liquid into thick cups and added a good dose of whiskey. Jane stirred in the brown sugar and sipped.

'Glory be!' she whispered. 'You were right, Em. It's wonderful.'

A clattering of feet made Jane put aside her cup and go to the door. The kettles behind her sang and Emily put them further over the range, the gas-stove neglected and cold.

'We've boiled the string and the instruments and I've put on plenty of hot water,' said Emily. 'Do you want it now?' The midwife nodded and took the big enamel bowl in a thick towel. 'Do you need us?'

'No, Miss Darwen, you stay with your mother. I'll let you know when it's all over, so try not to worry too much.'

'We'll try,' said Jane and sat down to her second cup.

'I expect Dr Barnes would like some,' said Emily. She giggled. 'I think I'm getting tipsy, Mother, but we must try not to worry, the midwife said!'

'I'll get the small bath for the first bathing,' said Jane.

'It's done. I cleaned it and put it in Vikki's room and lit the fire,' said Emily. 'The old cot is in there, too, and it's been well aired.'

'You have been very good to her,' said Jane, suddenly knowing that Emily was very excited and it wasn't all Irish tea.

'I'm going to love this child,' said Emily. 'Clare won't, so I must.'

262

'Sure, she'll be different once she holds it.' Jane listened. Screams came from upstairs and the front door-knocker thundered at the same time.

'She times it well, doesn't she?' said Emily drily. 'That will be Alan back again.'

'I'll pour him some tea,' said Jane. Emily brought him into the kitchen. 'No, you can't go up,' said Jane firmly. 'They have enough people getting in the way up there and husbands shouldn't go near a woman in labour. Have some tea. I think Emily put a drop of something in it. Drink it up and thank your stars you have a very healthy wife.'

They sat and waited, warmed by the tea and the bright fire. Emily went to see that all was ready in Vikki's room and came back. 'I saw Dr Barnes. It is nearly there. I'll put these towels to soak in the scullery. The waters went half an hour ago and she's pushing well.'

'I ought to see her,' began Alan. Jane put a hand on his arm and he sank back in his chair, thankfully. 'I'm not good at times like this.'

'Men aren't,' said Jane. 'Best out of the way until it's all over.' She smiled and wished that she liked him better. 'You'll be able to have her home soon as the nurse will be coming in every day, and my girl can do the shopping during the week.'

'Clare said she wanted to stay here for three weeks,' he said.

'Then Clare can think again! Her place is in her own home with you and the baby. She'll go home within the week if the doctor says she is fit.'

'She doesn't know much about babies,' he protested.

'And she won't learn here with someone to do everything for her,' said Emily. 'If she was ill, it would be different, but Clare is stronger than most and she *does* know about babies. We were a large family and she had to help with the little ones, and there were always babies about the place, belonging to neighbours.'

A cry that seemed to split the air came from the newly-delivered baby. 'One of them's all right,' said Jane wrily, but her eyes sparkled and she couldn't hide her impatience to see the baby, but they waited until the midwife put her head round the door. 'It's a girl,' she said. 'A very bonny child and they are both fine.'

'May I go up?' asked Alan.

'Just for five minutes and then your wife must sleep. She was telling me she had to walk all this way when she was having pains.' The nurse looked reproachful.

'Nobody knew she was coming!' said Jane. 'It was all ready for her in her own home.'

'But you said, last week, Mr Dewar . . .' The nurse fled and Alan followed her, red and very annoyed.

'So they did plan it,' said Emily. She sighed. 'We might have known. Now, I wonder if I can see the baby?'

The crying had stopped and the midwife was filling the small bath when Emily went in. Clare had smiled at her and then at Alan, with more tenderness than she had shown anyone for a long, long time. He held her hand and bent to kiss her and Jane looked on, hoping that this would soften the hard woman that Clare had become.

'I'm sorry, Mother,' Clare said.

'If you felt you needed to come, then you had to come,' Jane answered simply. 'Now you have something all your own, yours and Alan's and this is a very precious time.'

She said no more and didn't refer to her annoyance over Clare's devious ways, but bent to smooth the dark brown hair back from her daughter's brow with an emotion she had almost forgotten. She was once my baby; Lizzie and Clare, the twins, and now married and starting their own families. Jane smiled. 'I think they've nearly finished bathing the baby. I'll send Alan in with her.'

Clare picked at the dead, split fingernail that had been crushed when she was a child. 'Is she all right? Has she any blemishes, like this?'

'That was not a family thing, Clare. You couldn't pass that on to any child,' Jane said firmly. 'I've only had a glimpse of her but she looked lovely.'

She crept out of the room when Alan came in with the baby. The tiny face was all that was showing among the

264

warm folds of the shawl and Clare touched the baby on the cheek gently. Jane sighed with relief, and the fear that Clare would reject the child faded. 'Is the baby all right?' she asked Dr Barnes who was washing his hands and getting his bag ready to leave.

'She's a lovely child. Healthy and with all the good looks of your family.' He laughed. 'You fey Irish would say she had the look about her as if she had been here before. Let's hope that Lizzie is as fortunate.'

The midwife left and Clare was sleeping. Jane sent Alan home and told him there was no need for him to take any time off work as he had so many willing hands to care for his wife. He had the grace to blush and to say he was sorry for imposing on her good nature, and Jane nodded without her usual warmth. Emily sat by the cot and when nobody was looking, took the baby and held it, rocking the chair and relishing the baby-smell and the snuffling attempts to reach her breast.

'Emma,' she whispered. 'I can't show you a lot of love in front of your mother, but I'll be here when you need me as if you were my own.' She put the child back in the cot and turned down the light. Her crochet was nearly finished and there was only a few weeks' work to be done before she could give it to Clare. Emily began on a corner. Clare doesn't want it, she thought. The heavy intricate lace was pale in the firelight and very beautiful. She put it away in its bag and took out some knitting. I'll save it for Emma, she decided. She shall have it when she grows up and gets married. I shall leave it unfinished, wrapped in black tissue paper to keep it white and complete it when Clare has forgotten I ever started it.

Alan drove to Cowes to tell Lizzie the news and Lizzie put a hand to her side as if she had pains, too, but it was another month before Lizzie emerged from labour, startled at the force of birth and vowing that she was far too delicate to have any more children. She looked down at baby Henry who was small and had inherited none of the Darwen features. Fondly, Lizzie told everyone that he was the image of his uncle Sidney, the famous film star. 'He'll be like him, I can see it now,' she said proudly. 'He won't be a nasty rough boy.' She wiped away the dribbles and put on another clean frilly bib and tried not to be disappointed that he wasn't a girl.

Bert brought gifts and was able to be really interested in the babies as he would soon be a father. Neighbours and friends paid court to Clare as she sat up in the pretty bedroom on the Mall, surrounded by care and attention but rapidly losing her first joy and relief. Alan took her home after two weeks, more because she wanted to get on her feet to see Lizzie at Cowes than because she wanted to go home, and the house on the Mall was peaceful again.

'I miss Vikki,' said Jane, 'but we must get out more, Emily. If we stay here, we have people coming in all the time and Clare is hinting that she needs a rest. I can't think why. She had a good lying-in and the baby gives no trouble.'

'Emma is beautiful,' said Emily. 'I'll have her here any time Clare wants me to, but I dare not suggest it or I shall never see her.' She sighed. 'I know my sister. She's a dog in the manger, and even Alan isn't allowed too much contact with the baby. She'd rather leave it with the girl who cleans for her than with the child's own father. Do you wonder he goes to Cowes with Harry and has joined the working men's club?'

'That doesn't please Clare. She likes to think she's a cut above that, but she's married to a man who works with his hands, and so do his friends.' Jane tidied the small cot and put it away. George was too big for it and it could wait for the next. 'We'll call in on Lizzie and go over to Southampton next week,' she said. 'Dr Barnes has heard the good news that he can give Alice's doctor insulin for her. This should save her life, as it's saved the life of his friend, Dr Lawrence, who had given up all hope and went abroad to die.'

'The men on the quay say we shall have a bad storm, Mother. Let's wait until the sea is calmer.' Emily looked up from her knitting. 'We could go away for a few days and see the Exhibition in London.' Her eyes sparkled.

'Lizzie wants a gramophone record of *Sonny Boy* and I could get one there. It's a pity that Henry is so plain but Lizzie thinks he's beautiful, so why should I worry? To them he will be 'Sonny Boy' and she'll weep each time she hears it played.'

Janey came to collect them, insisting that they must stay for the day and be waited on for a change.

'Primroses,' Jane exclaimed as soon as she saw the shallow bowl packed with the sweet yellow flowers.

'There are plenty more behind the house,' said Janey. 'Vikki picked some big bunches and we put yours in a cool place.' Janey bent to smell them and smiled. 'It comes round every year, just like when we picked them behind the Priory as children. I thought we'd drive down to see Lizzie and then you needn't bother to go by train. It's too windy for Vikki and George to play outside and Vikki has a piano lesson so they must wait in for Miss Davies. George wants to play, too, but he will have to wait. Ready?'

They drove to Cowes and along the front beyond the Royal Yacht Squadron and the range of brass cannon pointing out to sea, ready to fire salutes to passing ships and visiting royalty. The sea was vicious and grey and small boats moored in the haven of the river-mouth were swamped. Janey looked pale but Jane said nothing. It had been Janey's suggestion to come here. She looked out beyond the spray to the line where sea met sky and were the same colour, then turned back.

'It's over, Mother,' she said. 'I saw the primroses and remembered when you were ill and we brought them to you. You recovered and so will I.'

They had tea in a café close to the shore and went home as the evening darkened. Winds howled over the river and Janey put on the headlights. 'I thought the floating bridge would sink.'

'Take us home and then get back in the warm,' said Jane. They went down Snooks Hill and Janey braked sharply. Water streamed across the road from a gap in the parapet overlooking the river. The wall of a house hung and dropped as they looked on in horror and people gathered to take the huddled woman who lived there to neighbours.

'It's all going, Jane.' Bert Cooper appeared, holding on to his hat and wading ankle-deep in water to reach them. He seemed not to notice. 'The shop is crumbling and the one next to it. It's forced a way through the cellars of the Sheaths' house and they say the whole row will have to be rebuilt. Pity you hadn't sold and we wouldn't have the trouble,' he added.

Jane watched the water and the broken wall. She saw that the present occupants of the shop had never changed the wallpaper in the top bedroom which was visible now where the bricks had gone. How undignified, she thought. A bed, exposed with a chamber pot under it and a dressing gown on the brass rail.

'Get home,' said Bert gruffly. 'It's all over, Jane. I'll see to it now.'

Chapter 19

Emily come out of the kitchen wiping her hands on her apron. 'You're soaking, Mother!' she said. Jane sat heavily in the armchair near the fire and Janey stood warming her hands.

'I'll have to go, Mother,' said Janey. She glanced at the face that had smiled at her and given her comfort so many times and now seemed made of stone. 'Are you all right?' she asked. 'I can telephone the house and ask the girl to stay.'

Jane managed the glimmer of a smile. 'No, you go, Janey. Emily is here and all I want is a cup of tea.'

'Let me take your coat.' Emily unbuttoned the front and slipped it from Jane's shoulders. 'What ever has happened? Did the car have a puncture? Has there been an accident?' She looked in alarm at the two pale-faced women.

'I think I'll have a cup with you.' Janey now found that she was trembling. She sat on the ladderback chair and began to cry, softly. Emily ran to the kitchen and blessed the fact that hot water was there, ready to boil as it had done when they lived over the shop on the Bridge.

'Here you are.' The tea was hot and strong and laced with spirit and Janey closed her eyes as the steam found her face and she held the cup between both hands.

'The shop's gone,' said Jane. 'I never knew how much I disliked that wallpaper up in Sidney's room.'

Emily looked anxious, but Janey gave her a warning glance. 'The Bridge collapsed and some of the shops have gone,' Janey told her gently. 'One side of our house went and left the other wall exposed.' She giggled with a hint of hysteria. 'It was as if someone came into the bathroom when I was undressed. It was our room and private and not for everyone to gawp at.'

'Not our room,' said Emily firmly. 'Come on, drink your tea, Janey. The shop hasn't been ours for ages and this is our home now.'

'It was still ours,' said Jane quietly. 'I knew I could never sell it but I'm glad it's gone now. So much happened there from long before you were born and I couldn't sell the good times just to forget the bad.' She drank up her tea and held out her cup for more. 'Walter brought me there as a bride and we worked hard to make it pay and to give you enough as you came, so soon after.'

'When I was little, I couldn't imagine living anywhere but over the shop,' said Emily. 'Father was good to us then and I shall never forget that, never, even if he . . . changed.'

Jane nodded, unable to voice her own memories, suddenly sharp in her mind as if they might soon be swept away in the flood that destroyed the shop. A procession of faces would trouble her dreams for nights to come, of Walter with his uniform hat slightly to one side and that bold look in his eyes, saying, 'Well, what about it? I've a shop and business back on the Island and I need a wife. Are you coming with me?'

He had never said he loved her, even when he was most loving, and his healthy ardour had found a happy echo in her until she was told not to bear any more children.

She would remember Bert Cooper and his acid wife Annie when she hated them. She smiled to herself. How that man had changed for the better and was now her trusted partner as if he wanted to pay back a secret debt. So many had gone. Aaron would have been heartbroken to see his house go down on the tide and Ethel, lost in her own world of madness and grief would never know what had happened.

'We went to help the people out,' said Janey. 'There were two young babies in the end house and they were cold and wet. Mrs Attril took them in. Lend me some shoes, Em, and bring Mother her slippers; our feet are wet.'

'Bert was there,' said Jane. 'He's a good man, so he is.

270

He sowed enough wild oats in his time but he's a good friend to us.'

Emily went into the hall and telephoned the Lodge. 'The girl is glad to stay the night as it's really wild and she has a long walk,' she said when she came back. 'You'll sleep here, Janey. I'll get something to eat and we can sit and talk.'

'I ought to go,' said Janey, but was glad to be told what to do. She felt a sense of loss that was deeper than anything since Clive had died, but this time it was shared.

The room was warm and the rosy light from the standard lamp shone on the thick crimson flocked wallpaper and the gleaming polished furniture. Jane relaxed, listening to the others talking. Emily was pink-cheeked and more animated than she had been for a long time, and Janey capped each tale with another memory.

It's like a wake, thought Jane. It's a healthy laying to rest as they do in Ireland. We can talk about it all and laugh and cry over the past. Did all that happen? Did I say that, feel that, make them do that? she wondered.

'When Queen Victoria died, Clare wanted to dress in black and sulked for a week because you gave her only a black armband and some black crêpe for her hat.'

'And Lizzie used to go home with as much free fish as she could carry. Do you think she sold it to her neighbours?' Janey giggled.

'Edward will be sorry,' said Jane more soberly.

'Nothing can make Edward sad since Alice was given those injections. She's a new woman and even takes an interest in the house. It's a wonderful thing, medicine,' said Emily. 'Dr Barnes had said that he could do no more for her and she would have died soon without this insulin.' She glanced at her sister who was blushing. 'I expect Alex told you all about that, Janey.'

'He's coming home soon,' said Janey. 'He and Clive used to come to the shop making any excuse and Clare thought they came to see her.'

'And now, Clive is dead and Alex still comes to see you, Janey.'

271

'Yes,' she said softly, and shut her eyes as she leaned back in her chair.

'This is nice,' said Emily with a sigh of contentment. 'I love this house and my piano and having you here. It's more peaceful without Lizzie and Clare and now that Vikki lives with you, Janey, Mother has time to do what she wants to do for the very first time in her life.'

She picked up her knitting. 'What happened to the crochet?' asked Janey.

'I put it aside. It was heavy and I might save it for later. Just now, I have enough to do knitting for the children, and I must make something nice for Maudie's baby.'

'Bring the children here for a day and take a trip to Portsmouth and see the shops,' said Jane. 'I want a few things and some material for a blouse that Mrs Barnes told me they have in the colour I like in that big new store. You needn't tell the others. I can cope with Lizzie and George but not Emma at the same time.' Jane was feeling better and the ghosts were fading. Even Amy, the wife of Archie at the farm at Wootton, was a grey shadow now with their one little Rose. She drank more tea and laid the table for supper. Dear Archie. Her heart saddened whenever she thought of him and yet she wasn't sure that she could ever answer the question in his eyes that was there when he saw her.

'Oh – I've seen the man who comes each year with onions,' remembered Emily when they were eating thick soup and fresh bread.

'Not at this time of year?' enquired Jane.

'He looked quite smart and was here with his daughter. They want her to go into the hotel business and as he doesn't approve of her living in a big city he asked the owners of the big hotel in Ventnor if they'd take her. André had been there for years with onions and had the family to stay at his farm in Brittany, so they are old friends.'

Jane laughed. 'I remember Annie Cooper's face when she caught him in the back room drinking wine with me when your father was away at the war. She labelled me a

272

scarlet woman and she would have spread it all over Newport if Aaron hadn't stopped her. André is a dear man, so he is, and I must write to his daughter and say that she can come here in her free time.'

'Now, don't take on too much again, Mother,' Janey warned.

'Would you have me neglect old friends when I can do a kindness?' Jane retorted with some of the spirit of the young Jane who had run the shop and the business for two long years with Walter away fighting the Boers. 'I remember so many kindnesses and other things,' she added. 'I have so much to treasure.' She fingered the brooch that Sidney had sent her when he landed in America. 'I must write to Sidney,' she said to herself. Emily bit her lip and said nothing, but Janey saw that tears were not far away.

'Have you heard anything?' asked Janey. 'Anything since those awful newspaper cuttings that Nellie sent?'

Jane shook her head but Emily took a deep breath and brought an envelope from her pocket. 'I wasn't going to tell you until tomorrow after you'd got over one shock,' she said. 'Nellie wrote to me. Lucy died without waking up and they had a grand funeral.' She wiped her eyes. 'It seems wrong. All those people who went didn't love her. They climbed over the other graves with cameras in their hands to get pictures of Sidney and his party. They didn't care about Lucy; not the Lucy we knew, who was sweet and kind and so innocent.' She was weeping now, softly and without sobbing. 'Sidney looked very handsome and sad.'

Janey took the newspaper photographs of the crowds, the masses of flowers and the men in dark suits and hats who stood waiting, and then gathered, bareheaded, at the graveside.

A headline told them that Mr Sidney Darwen was heartbroken and swore that he would never forget his dead fiancée and would never marry. Janey pursed her lips. She recalled her father's harsh voice calling Sidney a pansy and she remembered Clive hinting the same. It was as well, she

273

thought. Poor little Lucy would have died a thousand times if the two had married.

Jane stared into her cup. The tealeaves clung to the white china and she put it down and pushed the cup and saucer away firmly. 'So it really is over, thank God,' she whispered.

'You aren't glad that she died, are you, mother?' Emily sounded shocked.

'Not that. I shall weep for her and hold her dear that she loved my Sidney, but it's all come true.'

'What has? You didn't know any more than we did that Lucy would die.' Janey gave a shaky laugh. 'I know you are a bit fey at times, Mother, but I wouldn't say you had second sight.' She shrugged. 'I don't know, it could be so. You always knew if any of us was in trouble long before we told you.'

'Do you remember old Mrs Lee who was the mother of the tribe at Wootton?'

'She sold pegs and flowers and you gave her old clothes and specky fruit. The boys were wild and Sidney used to sneak off to play with them down at the river fields. He rode those piebalds with no saddles.'

'He never did!' Jane was indignant. 'Holy Mary, what a thing to do! The young monkey, I'll . . . .'

'He's in America now so you can't take the hairbrush to his seat, Mother,' said Emily mildly. 'Yes, I remember them. Mrs Lee came to the shop quite often and when Father wasn't there, she used to come into the back room and drink tea with you.'

Jane glanced towards the door as if Walter might still come in and find her with someone he didn't want in his house. 'She read my cup and told me marvellous and terrible things,' she said. Janey smiled indulgently. 'You can smile, my girl, but so did I at first until she told me that I'd forgotten to put the skein of green thread into Walter's hussif when he went to the war. I found it later and he had to borrow.'

'She was a witch,' said Emily uneasily. 'Her eyes looked through me and never at me.'

274

'She was a good woman,' said Jane. 'I respected her and she was kind.' She thought it best not to dwell on the knowledge that Mrs Lee had saved her life by giving her crude birth-control pessaries of herbs and cocoa butter, and she blocked off the memory of the huge grey pill that had nearly killed her but really saved her life when it brought on a miscarriage.

'Some of the boys came to Father's funeral,' said Emily. 'He liked them, too.'

'What else did she tell you, Mother?' Janey laughed. 'They usually say there are tall dark men and a few enemies and that you'll travel over water. Not hard to predict as we live on an island,' she added drily.

'She told me enough to keep me awake at night,' said Jane.

Janey stared. 'She told you about Clive?'

Jane nodded. 'She told me about all of you but I thought when Sidney was engaged that it was over and nothing bad could happen. Mrs Lee had said that he would never marry and I prayed that she was wrong to say that you would be widowed and Emily would remain with me.'

Emily raised her head. 'I knew I would never marry when Arnold died.' She served the stewed apple and custard. 'Did she tell you about Edward and Clare and Lizzie?'

'She did.'

'And was it true?' Jane nodded. 'And what about you, Mother? If you say it's all over, you must know what she had in store for you.'

Jane looked surprised. 'Me? I never thought to ask her. She said I'd never want, and isn't that enough for any woman?'

'No, it isn't enough,' said Janey.

'For you it isn't, but after seven children and the hard times, it's enough for me,' said Jane simply. 'I have you both, and the little ones, praise be. I have health and energy enough to enjoy it all. I shall make sure that Clare and Lizzie don't put upon Emily and me and I can enjoy the babies when I want them and not when they cry all night!'

'We'll be awash with tea,' said Janey when Emily brought in a fresh pot.

'We have all night,' said Emily. 'With Clare and Lizzie and the babies we shall have less time just being together like this.'

'And if you marry Archie, things will never be quite the same,' said Janey. 'The telephone is ringing. You go, Mother, it's bound to be him.'

Jane sat by the table and picked up the receiver. 'I heard about the Bridge and the shop.' Archie sounded anxious. 'They have told you, Jane?'

'I saw it when Janey was bringing me home.'

'Did it upset you very much?' he asked with such tenderness that she wanted to reach out to touch him.

'No. It woke a lot of memories and set them to rest. Lucy has died and the shop is gone and I feel a certain relief.'

'You are really free?' There was a note of hope in his voice and Jane steadied her own voice before replying.

'Free to look forward again, Archie, and to have many more years loving my family and my dear friends.'

'And is that all?' She put out a hand as if to stop him fading away as the other ghosts had done. 'Marry me, Jane. Come to live on the farm and let me look after you.'

'No, my dear. I'm past all that now. I love you better then any man I've met since Walter, but you need the farm and I need people.' She laughed softly. 'If you can stand a long, long courtship it will make us both young and I shall come to stay at the farm from time to time.'

'Soon? Come at Whitsun and stay for a week or so.'

'Whenever you say, my dear, but I'll have to bring Emily, too.'

'I don't care if you bring the whole lot of them so long as I can look at you across the table and love what I see.'

'You'll come to dinner on Sunday? Bring the rabbit you promised George. I got Mr Amy to make a nice hutch for it.'

'I'm investing in more sheds for the birds and thinking of ducks if we can make a deep pond along by the orchard.' He talked for another five minutes and Jane listened, smiling. The dear man, she thought. He's wrapped up in his beasts and fruit and flowers and he doesn't really need me. It's a dream that would shatter if we came to bed and underwear and petty quarrels, and I'd be embarrassed.

'Goodnight, Archie,' she said when he paused for breath. 'The girls are waiting for their cocoa and we are all tired. Come early on Sunday and we can walk a little way before dinner, and everyone can wonder what we intend to do. . .'

'He's well and worried about the shop,' said Jane when she came back in briefly. 'And you can take that look off your face, Janey. I was married once to the man I shall love to my dying day, and I'll not marry again just to stop the net curtains from twitching! You can tell George that his rabbit will be here on Sunday.'